I want more

Roland DeCarra

I want more

Roland DeCarra

Acorn Independent Press

Roland DeCarra was born in Epsom, Surrey, England.
After leaving school he worked as a draughtsman for various
engineering establishments, Government agencies and the
Metropolitan Police.

He currently lives in Dorking, Surrey, England.

This is his second published book.

*In memory of Heidi, taken from me suddenly
13 July 2018, aged 9.*

Contents

Acknowledgements

I would like to say a very big thank-you to everyone at Acorn Independent Press, London, for all their help in realising my dreams. And also to the following for all their support in their own individual ways:

Traudl von Scheidegger for keeping me sane with her dreams and visions of a better World, Emma Tilley, Debbie Coombes (aka Party Popper), Albina Francis, Esmeralda Doll, Zee Nix, Alice Walker, Ella Alexandra Rodriquez, Francis Lizarraga, Melanie Romain, Matt Deubert at *HolmPC* for his computer wizardry, Ben Morris at *All About Horsham* magazine for giving me my first review, Erica Ridgeway, Shameera Maheswaren, Cindy Smith, Avree Chanel, Lula Pinkk, Candy Calypso, Petra HisMoon II, Kiki Kuss, Jenna Mayo, Kandy Perez, Nancy Harry, Catherina Stone-Mill, Ica Vaskone, Elizabeth HortonHailey Gencosmanoglu, Tina Lavazza, Ruby Vega, Kimberly Hayle, Stephany Brown, Jennifer Smith, Nichole McGrath, Cheryll Gill, Andrea Hutchins, Summer Love, Lisa Noble, Kaitlyn Klutch, Inga Carlson, Aja Sandoval, Rhonda Jorgensen, Becky Wallace, Candice Fletcher, Todd Johnson, Victoria Rivers, Kelly Tziouveli, Ioana Mihai, Angel Ang, Lynda Zappa, Brenda Kipler, Brandi Cockroft, Autumn Carmichael, Lyliane Jacky

ACKNOWLEDGEMENTS

Thozet Patonnier, Jamie Hector, Spunk Girl, Bella Demayer, Leonie von Riefenstahl, Barbara von Wallenstein, Lily von Tease DuBois, Barbie Hoffman, Erika Molfese, Veronika Hagen, Gianna Kollmorgen, Karina West, Liv Schneider, Alexis von Kuntz, Katerina Knijnenburg, Sebastian Bromide, Alexandra Nuvolari, Soppy Tart, Marsha Dyer, Clari Bi, Marley Aldridge, Wet Isobel, Brisa Sousa, Amber Sheffield, Christine Josephine, Emily Smith, Candy Sunshine, Grace Cruz, Clarisse Sexe, Beth Sosa, Eva Tits, Sofia Buffer, Queen Sexy, Tamara Lauren, Sasha Hotbabe, Jennifer Hope, Encarna Grx, Amy Carter, Pandora Schiattarella, Mayra Reeves, Sonya Erikson, Shauna Monge, Cheeky Bitch, Hannah Prentice, Rebecca Sex, Christina Guerrero, Mary Owens, Clarissa Pornstar, Annmarie Hicks, Stella Carini, Marie Cunni, Horny Love, Kate Banks, Beverly Edwards, Sarah DeAngelis, Larissa Touch, Lovely Mia, Santa Rodriguez, Maria Lopez, Jeune Sexy, Lucy Potter, Chastity Jesseman, Lisa La Nympho, Selena Gomez, Mia Sia, Alexis Ferrari, Vero Libertine, Lucie Hum, Cami Fucks, Dusti Astwood, Marisex, Julie Gros-Seins, Imeldark, Natalia Sexx, Fern Howe-Shepherd, Sasha Kixxx, Shantel Peterson, Lucretia Wildflower, Paige LaWhore, Georgette Moon, Abbi Clark, Alice Naughty, Peaches Campbell,

Also to Depositphotos.com for the usage of the front cover image.

1

Fucking Amanda

Amanda's vagina parts easily as I insert my tongue into it with all the tenderness and love only another woman can give and she loves me. I suck on her lips and her clitoris, stimulating and tweaking it around in a circular motion and I am totally overboard for her as I drink her honey.

We roll around on the living-room floor, located at the rear of our flat, it opening out via a pair of glass sliding patio-doors onto the small enclosed back garden. I have no inhibitions as well you know as we snog and touch each others breasts and vaginas and laugh at our mutual excitement of being 2-beautiful naked women fucking.

We 69 and drink each others fluid as I cum first into her mouth and then she into mine and we both swallow and love. Her discharge tastes so sweet and I can't get enough of it as she cums again onto my tongue and I lose my mind and self-control as I then also start to shudder and spit myself into her face for the second time. We spin around and lick at each others faces, cleaning them free of our muck.

We stand and caress each others flesh, she squeezing and licking my tits and pulling at my belly-rings with her teeth as I tongue and nibble at her perfect firm round breasts. Amanda then attempts to insert her whole right-hand into her punani, it taking a while to manoeuvre her body into the right position to succeed but eventually she manages to get most of it in there, making her whole body shake and wobble like jelly as she does so, especially her beautiful legs.

"

I drop to my knees and simultaneously lick at her fisting, using Amanda's fanny-batter to masturbate both my vagina and rectum with both my hands.

I remove her hand from her box and lick it clean of her goo as I jerk and cum once again down my long legs and onto the carpet with a small gush. Amanda leans down to me and we kiss lips to lips like lovers and we are both so happy that we giggle like 2-naughty schoolgirls.

I cannot believe how much I love her, everything about her - her life, her personality, her pretty face, her accent, her hair, breasts, vagina, legs, bum - everything. I am the luckiest girl in the World and I wouldn't swap my life right now for all the tea in China.

We recover ourselves into the garden, it bathed in the hot afternoon sun. In fact it is so fucking hot I feel like I'm about to melt! I lay down on the large wooden patio table and spread my legs as wide as they will go until it starts to hurt my hips. At once Amanda goes down on me and fucks me with her tongue and playfully bites at my lips, the sensation making my whole body shake spasmodically. I cum into her mouth within a matter of only 20-seconds or so, it is sheer bliss and I jump into the air at my orgasm. Her tongue is quickly replaced by 3-fingers of her right-hand, her left manipulating my firm tits roughly. I moan loudly as I have 4-fingers in me now and her thumb on my clitoris and then her whole hand in my tight honey-hole and I can't take any more. I flail about violently on the hard table, bruising my elbows and shoulders and banging the back of my head as I do so. Still Amanda enters me deeper until I almost pass-out with the sensation of being just one person, our bodies joined together at my vagina.

Amanda senses my distress and releases me from our entanglement with a stupid hollow plopping-sound that reduces both of us to fits of laughter. I grab her sodden hand and suck my own juice from each of her fingers one by one and then we French-kiss and hold each other once more, our beautifully smooth skin so soft to touch that we fall in love with each other all over again, the gorgeous sensation of touching another naked human being.

We lay intertwined and talk and kiss and touch more. We talk about life and where our relationship is going and the conversation starts to get a bit heavy and I somehow sense in which direction it is heading:

"Do you think you'll ever marry? I know you're against it but do you think you ever will?" She quizzes me.

"I can't really say. Who knows what the future holds?"

"What if I were to ask you? To marry me I mean." She suddenly says, sending a massive chill shooting up my entire body, causing me to shudder.

"I haven't really thought about it. Do you really want to?"

"Of course I do, I wouldn't be asking otherwise would I ?"

"No, I guess not."

"Well then Sarah? Will you marry me?" She says, looking at me with her gorgeous doleful eyes and I just can't resist her, I want her so much that it's painful and makes me start to cry like a big soppy girl.

"Yes. Yes I will marry you." I blubber back to her

"I love you Sarah." She starts to say but her words come out completely broken as she's crying as hard as I am now and we kiss passionately as we touch each others breasts and wet vaginas. And why the fuck shouldn't we get married, we are the perfect match for each other and that's all there is to it.

I get up and go and raid our special toy-draw in the bedroom, picking out our Doc Johnson 12-inch white double-ended bendy dildo. I don't really like those smooth dildo's as they just slide in and out of my body far too easily. I don't get much satisfaction from them really, I much prefer the feeling of a more realistic one as they're, well, more realistic!

We position ourselves on the patio decking facing each other, our legs spread wide apart. I insert one end of the fake cock into myself and shuffle my body forwards until the other end kisses Amanda's lips. She comes to meet me and the dildo slides into her easily and we moan in unison at our double-fuck. We hold hands as both ends of the phallus is now completely within ourselves and our vaginas meet and I cum at the sensation of our lips touching and the firmness of the cock inside me. We both moan loudly at our tribbing as Amanda cums herself over my hole and the feeling of her wetness is out of this World as we fuck each other harder like crazy and in perfect beautiful synthesis.

We snog and play with each others breasts as we grind-away, heat and sweat pouring out of our skins as we love. I orgasm, scream and cum once more, adding more fuel to our fire and I can't control myself. I shake erratically as Amanda touches my minge and I cry in ecstasy as I roll about on the hard wood surface like a lunatic.

She pulls out of me with a squelching sound and I emit a sigh of relief as my fanny is by now red and somewhat sore, as is hers. I crash in total exhaustion but I'm not finished yet as my girl - my fiancée! - rolls me over onto my front. With my perfect bum in the air Amanda uses the dildo on me again, pushing its lubed length into my bumhole in one fluid motion. I feel my internal organs and muscles shift to make way as my lover fucks me and I lose my mind and my body to her. I moan like a girl as she anals me - it's just like having a poo in reverse! - as then I cum once more as I feel her mouth biting and kissing my bum-cheeks and her fingers playing with my labia.

My brain goes into overload and I can't take any more fuck but I do, I want to stay in this position in time and for her to fuck me forever - I want nothing more.

We swap around as now it's her turn. I spread her bum-cheeks apart as wide as they will go, her rectal-passage opening-up accordingly in all its glory. She begins twerking her bum in my face as I twirl my tongue around the ring of her hole, sensing her scat. It disgusts me a little but I don't stop the analingus. I gob a stringy spit at it and using 2-fingers immediately push them into her anus, feeling her sphincter tighten in protest at my action. She lets out a deep sigh and arches her back as I wank her passage slowly but firmly. I use my other hand on her bum-cheeks, slapping them until they redden, then squeezing my erect nipples and then turning to my minge as I rub away at my clit until I cum myself and scream a breathless scream of nothing.

We both lay exhausted on the decking and kiss and stroke each others others faces and breasts. We giggle like new lovers do as we chat and laugh and love at having found each other in this crazy World.

"I want to give myself to you." I whisper in her ear.

"Take me Sarah, do what ever you want to me." She pleads back with love.

I roll her over onto her back and fondle her tits with one hand and spread her beautiful legs apart with the other. I gaze into the chasm of her hole and fall in love with its glistening reflection and she sighs as I touch her virginal lips and clit. I look at her beautiful tight body as I squat-down on my haunches over her pussy. I pant heavily as I push my internal muscles beyond straining-point as I know I have something left inside me. I touch her breasts again, this time to steady myself as I tighten and I can feel it moving. I struggle to push but I win it over as I shit on Amanda's cunt, my whole body heaving as my waste falls from me and onto her.

"Oh Sarah please." She begs to me but I don't reply. There are no words needed between us as she accepts me completely, every part of me, including my crap.

Repositioning myself between her legs I take hold of my excreta with my right-hand and push it into her vagina, it squishing between my fingers as I force the muck into her hole.

We have travelled beyond the point of being disgusting as I wank my shit in and out of her twat. We love each other on a plain higher than normal love, a level that connects us together stronger than the mere physical or emotional ever could or will. She orgasms and cums, breaking the inner-seal of detritus filling her pie. It splits and leaks her juice of love as I continue to wank her slit with the brown and I see her eyes light-up with fire as I push us both over the edge of acceptability.

We hit the shower together to clean-up and wash off all the crap - literally! I caress Amanda's smooth, gorgeous skin as the water cascades down her beautiful face, her neck, breasts and her body to her shaved vagina, her thighs, legs and to her feet. We embrace and kiss under the power and heat of the shower as it sprays its cleansing water down upon us both and I am in Heaven. We finger each others holes as we kiss and clean away the remains of our sex.

After drying-off each others bodies and hair we head back outside into the burning sun. The blinding heat scorches our naked skin as we both sit ourselves down on the bench-seat on the patio decking. We kiss and snog as we chat and drink wine - white and German - under the afternoon glare and we are so in love that I cannot express my feelings for her in mere words. We talk about our future together and how we're going to rule the whole fucking World with our undefeatable lesbian passion and we French-kiss as we fondle each others breasts and drink our wine.

I leave her to go and fetch our latest sex-toy from the bedroom. On my return I have to fill it up and charge it with its special "milk" in the kitchen otherwise the game will literally be an anti-climax. I fit it onto myself and wander back out into the garden with Amanda hysterically laughing out loud at the admittedly rather silly vision of me standing before her with my giant *Futanari* cock protruding from my tall, slim, perfect female body. It's ridiculously long at just over half a metre and thick too, being some 7-centimetres in diameter - it is comically funny!

I sit back down next to my love amid tears of laughter as Amanda grabs hold of the end of my shaft and begins licking at my giant cock. It's so fucking hilarious that there is no way that either of us can take this seriously. Our pleasure is pure imaginary as she starts to wank my fake willy up and down. I wish and dream that it was my real cock and that I was a bisexual transgender, the amount of fun I could have with a real cock this size along with my beautiful looks and figure would be amazing - I would be unstoppable, I would be both a King and a Queen at one and the same time!

My lover continues to wank and suck me as I play with her tits and pussy. We giggle at the stupidity of our scenario as Amanda rises to her feet and stands before me, still playing with my giant phallus. She masturbates my cock to a frenzy and so I release its pressure, squirting her entire body with my fake cum. It shoots everywhere, even over her head and down the garden for several metres, and fills her face and tits and vagina with its white glue - it having a similar consistency of wallpaper paste, not that I've ever done any wallpapering that is!

It's a good job the bloody neighbours can't see us, although they can probably hear all our laughter and screams of ecstasy as we fill the surrounding hot air with both emotions. I don't actually give a flying-fuck about them anyway. I am guided by my female Libertine attitude towards life and those around me. I am an extrovert on the outside but an introvert on the inside - that is the ongoing confusion to my life.

We gather ourselves together once more as Amanda wipes-away the mess from her eyes and face and I remove my cock and hold and kiss her with all my female love. I hand over the giant penis to her and lay back on the wooden bench, spreading my legs apart as wide as they will go with my feet high in the air, exposing the wonder of my cunt to her. She stares at my perfect body with a wry expression across her pretty face - she knows me well enough now to guess what I want and need. Amanda places the massive knob of the phallus against my lips and I sigh deeply at its touch, she standing at its opposing end smiling at me wickedly.

"Come on. Fuck me my love." I demand of her.

"Do you want it all my lover?" She says with a voice that oozes pure sex.

"Just give it to me. Come on, fuck it."

"I don't know whether it's going to go in?" She questions.

"I don't care. Just push it in. You know what I want." I beg back.

She does as she's told and gives the big fat cock a shove from behind and I feel my pelvis crack as she almost splits my vagina in two with the enormous girth of the tool. The thick residue of its fake cum eases entry only slightly as Amanda gives it another quick shove and my internal muscles tear as I accept her cock into me, the pain being a mixture of Heaven and Hell but I want them both. My love can only go in about 10-centimetres due to its thickness as it hits my cervix and I cry in pain as it reaches my limit but I want more, I want the entire length of the cock within me, all 50-centimetres of it filling my body with its enormity.

Amanda fucks me slowly, she can't go any faster as it is so fucking tight and slippery, and I scream a hollow scream at the blinding sun as it beats down on our lesbian lust. I touch my beautiful firm breasts as they heave up and down at my punishment, they are so perfect in every way that I fall in love with them a little bit more every time I fuck.

I literally can't take any more and I beg my love to stop. She obliges at once and pulls the massive dick out me with a strange and funny sucking sound and a plop. My pussy is absolutely red raw with the abuse and I need to cool it down quickly before it catches fire! I pour the last remainder of the wine from the bottle over my fanny and the relief is so ecstatic that I moan loudly.

"Do you want me to give you oral pleasure?" Amanda asks me breathlessly.

"Oh yes babe. Lick my cunt. Lick my cunt and make me cum. You can do it." I plead back to her.

She drops down on her haunches before me and gives me oral, her soft tongue on my sore vagina easing my hurt. I squeeze and pinch my nipples as Amanda my love licks and sucks my hole and in no time I cum at her my special sweet mucus. She drinks me and I scream out loud to all the stupid fucking neighbours at my joy and fuck.

She climbs on top of my body and we French-kiss my cum between our mouths and tongues. We are beyond love and sex and fucking, we are more than that. We are more than 2-beautiful young women exploring each others bodies, we are Queens beyond Queens, flying with pure freedom above the Earth and sky and into space where nothing and no-one can touch us for a thousand years and a day.

* * *

I've been looking forward to tonight for absolutely yonks. I'm taking Amanda off to see one of my favourite bands of the moment, the Yeah Yeah Yeahs from New York, who are playing a gig at the Dome in Brighton, East Sussex. I've seen them once before at the Hammersmith Apollo in London ages ago long before I ever met Amanda and I was hooked straight away. They are totally awesome live.

Amanda's not too keen on them though as Michael Buble is more up her street - yuk! I've played her all their albums but she's still not convinced, I guess some people just don't appreciate good music when they hear it?

Anyway, I've managed to drag her along tonight and I just know that she will have a good time, and if she doesn't, at least I will, guaranteed.

I'm wearing a black strappy jumpsuit tonight from New Look that really shows off my figure, especially my long toned legs. My underwear is in red lace from Victoria's Secret whilst on my feet I have a pair of black suede ankle-boots from Miu Miu. My hair is as is, tied-up with a black satin bow. For my make-up I've gone for a more vamp-look featuring lots of black eye-shadow, black eye-liner and black lipstick as I want to fit-in with the mood of tonight's act. I know I'm not twenty any more but I can still carry it off. Being tall, slim and gorgeous is something that I have always had in my favour.

Amanda hasn't quite got the hang of the theme of the event and is wearing a green sleeveless top from AliExpress, a pair of grey stone-wash jeans from Gap, green suede platform court shoes from Spylovebuy. com and not much else, apart from lace knickers from Ann Summers. She's not wearing a bra tonight as she doesn't want to - it's her choice after all - and as she's not as big as I am in the chest-department she can get away with it easier than me. If I went bra-less tonight I'd probably end up with 2-real black eyes with all the dancing and jumping around I intent doing! Her perfume tonight is *Kenzo Flower* by Kenzo.

The gig doesn't start until 8.30pm so we leave in good time, it's really not that far from where we live anyway. We leave the flat empty as we no longer have Mum's old cat Suzie with us any more. She had to be put-down - again by Amanda my love - just before Xmas as her poor little kidneys had failed and it was unfair to let her suffer in pain like that. Like Lacey, she also lived to a grand old age so I guess I must be doing something right? Obviously it was incredibly sad to see her go as it brought back all the horrible memories of Lacey's death, but it had to be done, it was the kindest thing to do. I do miss having a cat around the flat though. I would dearly love to get another moggie but the heartache of when they go is more than I can take. Amanda would like to get a dog but I'm not that keen on them, I much prefer cats. I've had a bit of a phobia about dogs since I was a kid - when I was about 10-years old I guess - when I was out shopping with Mum and my sister Kate one day in an old-fashioned store - I seem to think it was Woolworth's (remember them?) in Epsom in Surrey - and a little dog got one of its paws trapped on one of their old wooden-slatted escalators. It's pity- full howl of pain and terror still haunts me even to this day, it was terrible.

I want to drive tonight so we take my car. We wizz down the A24 to Worthing - not sparing the horses obviously! - and do a left when we hit the town instead of going the arse-end way to Brighton along the A27. This route is so much nicer along the coastal A259 and is usually a lot less crowded - famous last words! Through Shoreham, Lancing and Hove and then into Brighton itself we park in the Regency Square underground car-park, located opposite the burnt-out remains of the old West Pier. It's well-expensive in this car-park but it's totally gated and secure so I don't mind paying through the nose to keep my pride and joy safe. I'm not leaving my baby - the car that is! - anywhere else. If anyone pranged it I would go mental!

We walk along the seafront hand-in-hand without a care in our beautiful free vainglorious manner, minding our own business. Suddenly we're accosted by a young guy in his mid-20's begging for money as he sits on his lazy arse slumped-up against the old turquoise-painted railings:

"Spare any change girls?" He fires at us. Surprisingly he's got an English accent and isn't a bloody Slav immigrant, as true to form they've even infiltrated this far South now as well as everywhere else.

"Get a bloody job." I spit back at him as we continue to walk on by. I turn to kick him in the bollocks when he calls me a: "Arrogant lesbian bitch" but Amanda pulls me away. What a fucking waster!

It's such a beautiful evening and the sea is as flat as a pancake as it shimmers its silver reflection in the setting sun. We cross over the road by the Palace Pier and head past the Brighton Pavilion. I've never really been a big fan of this building, I guess its a bit too Indian-looking for my liking, although Amanda thinks its "lovely" - typical!

The Dome is situated just around the corner from here on Church Street and outside the venue there are already crowds of people everywhere - the pavement and the road both a sea of humans.

Eventually we all filter our way in, and with my usual forward thinking I pre-ordered our tickets online to save any hassle, we then make our way into the main concert hall. Unusually there's no support band on tonight for whatever reason, just the main act. Dead on time it's lead-singer Karen O that leads the rest of the band on stage and the crowd go wild in a cacophony of noise when they all emerge from the wings. She looks absolutely beautiful with her short, cropped blonde hair and is dressed entirely in black - I knew I had made the right choice in clothes! Everyone cheers as they burst into song, playing *Zero,* one of my absolute favourites of theirs and I become lost and engulfed in their beautiful powerful music. Her voice is so hypnotic that it swallows my very soul and I am completely lost to her.

The evening thunders on as she guides me, Amanda and the collective audience through their back-catalogue of beautiful songs - *Bang, Down Boy, Kiss Kiss, Rich, Date with the Night, Black Tongue, Maps, Gold Lion, Cheated Hearts, Heads will Roll, Runaway, Hysteric, Sacrilege, Mosquito, Under the Earth, Slave, Despair* - and by the finale, I think I've actually got Amanda hooked - to some degree at least!

After 3-encores the show is over and I'm absolutely knackered. All the dancing, singing along, holding and kissing Amanda, the noise, the power and the motion, has left me psychically and emotionally drained.

We emerge back outside into the darkness of Brighton town and the streets are actually busier now in late-evening than they were earlier. We stroll back to the car-park with our arms around each others waists and not a care in the World. We look at each other and laugh as we stare at the pseudo-sophisticated snobs coming out of The Grand Hotel, they in turn looking at us - the hoi-polloi - with their arrogant attitudes and turned-up noses. Who the fuck do they think they are? Middle-class twats! The only people they're fooling are themselves.

Back in the car we race back home to Slinfold Village, taking the scenic country roads home via Henfield rather than the way we came or going all the way up the A23 to Crawley and then cutting across town. We're home in only 25-minutes flat as the traffic is light and my right-foot is heavy.

***

Once back indoors we strip each other naked and fuck. I lick Amanda's vagina and she shakes violently as she cums into my mouth and screams with pleasure as I lap-down her female acid. I wank her with 2-fingers and she flails as I continue to swallow her juice. She fucks me on all-fours with our giant 16-inch dildo from Bondara. I feel it squirming inside me, forcing my internal muscles apart as she slides it in and out of my hole and I cum. My love squirts out and down my legs and I catch it with one hand and lick it and swallow myself.

On my back Amanda uses her knee to pound against my box, jerking it against my wetness and I start to pant heavily. Within a minute I cum again and my head explodes in an array of both colour and noise and I fuck. I reach for the bottle of vodka and snort a single inhale of the nasty liquid up my nose for a laugh. It stings me like fuck, making me reel backwards in shock and pain but this is me - this is what I am and what I do.

I love Amanda so much that I want to kill her so no-one else can take her away from me and have her. I push her onto her back and place both my hands around her beautiful throat and tighten my grip. A sudden wave of evil power takes command of my will as she starts to cough and asphyxiate but I carry on. Terror enters her eyes as I begin to knee at her smooth wet pussy and she cums on me her internal love. I let her go when her orgasm subsides and kiss and tongue her mouth with passion. I give her one last jerk to her sore vagina and she moans: "Fucking Hell" at me for the pain I have just inflicted upon her body but I don't care – she is mine. She is mine to love and fuck as I love and fuck myself.

You may think that I'm unstable in my actions but have a look deep down inside yourself and you will find that you're the same basic animal as I.

It's been such a wonderful night that I don't want it to end, although I know that it surely will. Why can't every day be like this?

***

For the past 10-years I've been paying a little money each month - £50 actually - into a high-interest savings account with an investment company called Surrey County Savings. I started doing this as some kind-of small security venture for my future;

no-one really knows what's around the corner do they? So I thought it was a good idea. Anyway, the upshot is that those 10-years are now at an end and I want my money out, including all the interest of course! At the end of the day I should get somewhere in the region of £7,000. I know it might not sound much to some people but it's lot to me.

My initial phone-call to the investment company's head office - which for some bizarre reason isn't in Surrey at all but in bloody Yorkshire of all places! - doesn't go well. Not only has the company changed hands but they've also changed my account number without informing me and changed my actual account itself into an online one - what the fuck! I holler down the phone to the woman on the other end of the line, demanding: "What the Hell is going on?"

She informs me that I have to set-up an online account with them to access my own money and then I can withdraw it in full - unbelievable! What the fuck is this country coming to? She then explains to me how to set up a new account on my computer and gives me my new superseded account number before I hang-up on her in disgust. How fucking dare they change my fucking account and not ask me for permission or even tell me that they had done it? Outrageous!

I click my computer on and follow the instructions on their company website, entering my new account number into the specified box. It doesn't work. It won't accept my new number. Cancelling it, I then enter my old account number into the same slot just to see if that might work. Does it? What do you fucking think? Immediately I'm straight back on the phone to their head office once again, only this time though I get through to someone else, another woman, and have to re-explain my situation yet again. This one then informs me that to sort the problem out I will have to physically go into one of their branch offices and show them proof of who I am, and that way they can verify both myself and my new account number. Is this for fucking real? Why does every fucking thing have to be so fucking complicated? And guess where my nearest branch is located? South fucking London that's where! Almost 25-bloody-miles away - fucking typical! It looks like I've got no alternative, I'll have to get my arse in gear over there if I want to sort this problem out. The woman on the phone said I need to take 3-forms of identification with me and so I dig out my passport, driving licence and one of my utility bills - one for the electric - and then hit the road.

Today I'm wearing a white v-neck t-shirt from AliExpress that really shows off my wonderful cleavage to the max, a black mini-skirt from New Look, and a pair of white suede open-toe ankle-boots from Polyvore. My underwear is in sexy red lace from Ultimo. My perfume is *Luxe* by Avon. My make-up is classic but sharp, done in my own unique way, and I look as gorgeous as always!

This being a Saturday, Amanda is having a lay-in as she's not on duty at the vets practice until later this afternoon. I go into the bedroom and kiss her cheek as I sit on the edge of our bed and touch her right-breast as I do so. Its firm and beautiful - as is she! - and I love her with all my heart. I leave her a quick note to say where I'm going and then I'm out the door, the journey up to South London I'm expecting to take the best part of an hour or so to get there - fucking Hell! I could really do without this crap, especially on a bloody Saturday.

I guessed right of course, the traffic on the A24 to Dorking, then the A25 and up Pebble Hill is one thing, but the amount of cars on the A217 heading North to South London is just taking the piss, it's a bloody joke!

An hour and fifteen minutes later I eventually find myself on the end of a small queue for the multi-story car-park and I have to wind my way up to the bloody 5th-level in order to find a space, and then it costs me the best part of 5-quid just for the minimum of 2-poxy hours parking for fucks sake! Matters only get worse when I head for the lift to go down, there being a big yellow *"OUT OF ORDER"* sign stuck on its double doors! This obviously now means I'm forced to use the stairs and walk down to ground-level, which I can assure you isn't very charming at all as it's clearly been used as a toilet by either bloody tramps or the local scum. The smell of piss is horrendous and I have to be careful where I'm treading as it's pretty much everywhere. Someone has even had a shit on the landing floor on the next level down - fuckers! Not only that, I also have to dodge the odd syringe here and there as bloody junkies have obviously also been using the stairwell to shoot-up their evil crap. What is wrong with these fucking people?

Once at ground-level I head off to the High Street to try and find the shop I'm looking for, although I'm almost immediately accosted by some dirty fucking Slav bitch selling small bunches of flowers, undoubtedly stolen off some poor bastards grave. I hiss at her to: "Fuck off" but the stinking Romanian has no idea what I'm saying and just turns away to annoy someone else - scum.

I quickly find the right place after only a short walk. Heading into the building I find the shop is completely deserted apart from the 2-women stationed at the main counter, one of those having a *"PLEASE USE THE OTHER COUNTER"* sign in her little window. The other available counter is occupied by a woman of about 30-ish, reasonably okay-looking, with a big round baby-bump that look like its about to explode at any second! I explain to her my situation - that's the third bloody time today and counting! - and hand-over my 3-forms of identification as requested by the woman on the phone earlier at their head office. My predicament is met by silence, long stares, whispering between the 2-women and frantic pressing of keys on the pregnant one's computer.

"I'm afraid we can't accept your passport Miss Knowles." She amazingly informs me.

"Why? What's wrong with it?" I stab back at her quickly.

"There's nothing wrong with it. It's company policy that we can't accept passports as proof of identification."

"What! You're joke me? I can fly to any country in the World on that passport but you can't accept it as I.D. That's crazy!"

"I'm sorry but it's company policy. Your other I.D."s are okay but we do need to see 3-different forms for confirmation purposes."

"That's ridiculous! I've never heard anything so bloody stupid! What sort of company is this?"

"If you could go and get another form of identification then we may be able to process your details."

"Yeah well, it's not as simple as that. As you can see from my address I don't live around here. I live a good 25-miles away so that's a 50-mile round trip you know?"

"I'm sorry, but we can't do anything without proper I.D."

"This is bullshit, you're just wasting my fucking time." I scream at her as by now I'm completely fucking mad and I'm starting to totally lose it.

In the end I realise I'm going nowhere with this silly cow and causing a scene is only going to make things worse for myself and I reluctantly have to bale out. All I want is MY money.

"I'll be back later with some more I.D." I tell her. What a fucking performance!

Back in the car-park I decide to avoid using the stairs and the wee and the turd and the needles and instead walk up the car ramps up to each floor level. If anyone fucking complains I'll bloody kill them. I tear out of the car-park with screaming tyres and head South for home back along the same route as before, the traffic now though at mid-day being considerably heavier.

Almost an hour-and-a-half later I'm back through my front door and I'm so fucking mad I can barely control my anger. What a stupid fucking company? I've never heard the like! I wish I'd never gotten involved with them in the first bloody place. I have a quick slug of vodka straight from the bottle to try and steady my mind as I then go and get one of my bank statements from my mini-safe that I keep hidden-away in our bedroom.

Amanda my love isn't here by now of course, she having left for work a short while ago. I grab my latest statement from the safe as well as my birth certificate, my thinking being that some sort-of extra back-up would probably be necessary knowing how bloody useless these bunch of tossers have turned out to be.

I have a quick pee and then head out the door once again, to join yet even more traffic and all the idiots on the road.

Unbelievably - no, not really! - it takes me an hour-and-45-minutes to get back to South London again, the amount of fucking cars on the road at this time of day is by now a fucking nightmare and it's a pleasant relief to finally come to a stop in a space in the multi-story car-park. This time I thankfully find a vacant space on the 2nd-floor level, so at least that's one good thing - but only just!

Back in the Surrey County Saving shop, once again I'm faced with the same 2-females serving as before, the pregnant one I spoke to earlier and the other, a young brown-faced one with some sort-of scarf wrapped around her head. The one with child is busy tied-up serving another customer - some old guy in his 70's who looks like death - and so the Asian asks if she can help me? I decline her offer with a "No" gesture shake of my head and then look away. I don't want to be served by one of them, I want to be served by one of us.

The old guy pisses-off after only a couple of minutes or so, turning to look right at me and stare at my body as he does so - dirty old git! I walk up to the pregnant woman's window and hand her both my bank statement and birth certificate along with - once again - my driving licence and utility bill as before. She waddles-off to get them photocopied so she can fax them off to their head office - for verification and their records I guess? - and then waddles back. I accidentally look over at the Paki and she smiles back at me a big beaming smile of perfectly white Asian teeth. I get a sudden urge to smash them all out with a hammer and then strangle her with her stupid fucking scarf but in reality I just look away. The pregnant one opens up her side-door and comes out into the main part of the shop to hand me back my documents. She is absolutely huge and looks like she's ready to drop her load at any moment - poor cow! She tells me that my details will take 3 to 4-days to clear, so I should be able to transfer my money from my online account into my bank account by the end of this coming week. I'm not counting my chickens on that one!

I make my way home as quickly as I dare and it's just gone 4pm when I finally put my key in the front door. The whole of my free Saturday has been ruined by all this bullshit, but unfortunately I'm too worn-out to either care or even be angry. Instead I have a quick vodka, strip naked in the bedroom and have a nice long soothing shower and try to wash-away my wasted day. I don't bother to re-dress afterwards, so I just put on my white pure-silk robe from LilySilk over my beautiful soft smooth body. I fix myself a light dinner of sausages and pasta in tomato sauce along with a glass of German white or 6.

It's 9.45pm before Amanda comes home to me. She showers and I softly pat her naked body dry of any moisture and we fuck. She flicks her tongue in and out of my vagina and I tell her to: "cunt me". We scissor one another hard and we both cum our love over each other and the sensation of her wet lips on mine sends me into orbit and I orgasm myself stupid and scream like a whore bitch.

***

It's 6pm the following Friday. I'm on my lap-top logging-in to my account with Surrey County Savings. I've given them plenty of time to sort my verification documents out so here goes with trying to access my account. I key-in my new account number, along with my password, and hit the enter button.

Now, you know my life and how it runs don't you? What do you think happens next? Yep, you've got it. My password is NOT accepted!

I sit there transfixed to the screen before me as I desperately try not to believe what my eyes are telling me. This is a fucking joke right? I am beyond words.

I leave my desk and hit the vodka bottle, taking several large gulps of the nasty liquid as I gaze at nothing like the lost girl I am out the living-room window. I'm not angry. I'm not upset. I am way beyond any of that shit. I take another large slug and then get straight on the phone to their head office yet again - Fucking Hell!

I get through to some sweet girl by the name of Sarah Swan in their Customer Complaints Department who has the loveliest Yorkshire accent there surely is. Once again I have to explain myself and all the fucking crap I've had to endure recently with her stupid bloody company etc. etc. etc. When I ask her if she's had anyone else with a similar problem she quietly informs me that they've been inundated with complaints left, right and centre! Hardly bloody surprising really is it? She guides me through resetting my password - yet another set of over-complicated questions, 99% of which are pure bullshit - and I'm supposedly good to go.

Finally, my fucking password is accepted and I'm through to the next stage where I can at long-last transfer my money into my back account. Unbelievably I have to complete another set of online questions and then I'm done - my transaction is complete! What a fucking performance!

Why do these fucking companies have to make these things more complicated than is necessary? What goes through their feeble minds when they're setting-up this crap? Do they make it fucking difficult on purpose?

At the end of the day I receive the grand total of £6,720. Not quite the 7-grand I was hoping to get, this being largely due to the poor interest rate over the last few years. Even so, it's better than a poke in the eye with a sharp stick so I can't really complain!

***

I have to wait until the following bloody Thursday for my money to clear in the bank. Even so, with everything seemingly settled, I'm not letting all this rigmarole go unpunished.

I'm back on my computer, sitting on the sofa writing a letter of complaint to those stupid fucking idiots at the savings company. Amanda questions me as to why I'm even bothering? The thing is though, there's a principle here that needs to be addressed. Not accepting my passport as proof if identification is just plain bloody crazy for one thing, let alone all the other bollocks I've had to go through.

As I type-away my love comes up behind me and places her arms around my shoulders and kisses my left-cheek. I kiss her left-arm as I continue to compose my letter and she touches one of my breasts, the right one. My breathing immediately becomes heavier as she plays with my chests and I feel my nipple become erect at her touch. We giggle and feel and kiss and I am so in love with her and I want more.

She walks around to my side of the sofa and almost literally jumps on me, sending my lap-top falling to the floor with a soft thud, thankfully undamaged. We kiss and grope each other like we're both possessed and I feel her hand between my legs fingering my vagina through my clothes.

We strip each other naked and get pissed on vodka and gin and sex as we fuck like rabbits on the sofa and I love her.

2
Oxford Street

Amanda and I are going on a little trip today up to London, to Oxford Street to be precise, as she's never been there in all the time she's been here in England. I personally haven't been up to town for nearly 8-years myself now either. I use to go up there virtually every Saturday in my late-teens and early-20's, starting out early in the morning on the Tube, not only for Oxford Street but also to the Kings Road in Chelsea and Kensington Market as well. Sadly both places now are either decimated or long-gone. I would shop all morning for clothes, shoes and the latest records. Nowadays I just couldn't be bothered, it's too much hassle. Oxford Street itself just isn't the same as it was back then, exasperated once again by the massive influx of immigrants ruining everything.

It being a blisteringly-hot day - it's Monday and we've both taken the day off work - and so I'm dressing light, plus the fact that neither of us are "on" at the moment, in fact we're both pretty-much on similar times, which is great for us in many ways. Today I'm wearing a white cotton mini-dress from Shanghai Trends which is fairly tight and shows-off my curves beautifully. I leave it open to the max of course, revealing my gorgeous curves and more than ample breasts. On my feet I've got a lovely pair of white Clarks Raffi Scent strap-sandals as I don't want sweaty feet or blisters as no doubt we'll be doing a lot of walking around. My underwear consists of a white bra and thong, both from Figleaves, making me feel and look super-sexy, even though I know that already. I've kept my make-up light as well, nothing fancy, apart from my eye-shadow which

I've done in a medium-grey fading-out to a lighter shade that looks quite striking.

All the crap I need for the day - cash, debit card, keys and other stuff - I've contained within a white and gold clutch-bag from Missguided. My perfume today is *Luxe* by Avon.

Amanda is similarly dressed, in fact we look more like sisters than lovers - engaged lovers that is! - how amazing does that feel? She's wearing a white mini-bodycon dress from ASOS that is also quite tight, and underwear in red from Ultimo that I bought her for Christmas. Her shoes are a pair of white flats from SimplyBe, while her perfume is her usual *Kenzo Flower* by Kenzo that makes her smell fantastic and really turns me on - not that I need much encouragement! Her make-up is also close to my own but without the dramatic eye-shadow effect. She doesn't have a clutch-bag like mine and so is using a large shoulder-bag made of some tan-coloured canvas-type material. It does looks pretty cool though. Both of us have near-identical hair styles, tied-up in a pony-tail, although my hair is slightly longer.

We're taking the Tube up to London as Amanda has never been on the Underground either, so that means driving to Morden in South London, the last station on the Northern Line - not far from where I was born and grew up - as that's the nearest Tube station to us from here, a distance of about 30-miles away.

Seeing as it was my idea to go up to town in the first place, I offer to drive. I've still got the very same white Fiesta ST that I've had for some while now, and although I love it, I have been thinking of trading it in for something with a bit more power, something a bit different. I can afford it so what the Hell, we'll just have to wait and see what happens?

Even though it's gone 9am - it's actually 9.20am - the bloody traffic heading towards South London is heavy, but moving at it's own steady pace. We make our way up the A217, passing the outskirts of Banstead and Epsom and onto the Mad-Mile, a really quick piece of straight road 1-mile long - obviously! - that everyone races along regardless of the speed limit, hence the nomenclature. At the far-end before the roundabout some arsehole in a Transit van cuts right in front of me and I have to take evasive action, swerving to the left to avoid crashing into him - fucker! He continues to block me, preventing me from overtaking him like a fucking idiot, and it's not until we get to the next duel-carriageway section of road that I'm able to burn him off. As we speed past him I notice that he's some old cunt in his 60's and not a young guy as I first thought. Amanda gives him the finger as we pass but he takes no notice, which is just typical of these arrogant old shits on the road. People like him need shooting.

Further on we brush by Sutton and Cheam and do a left-turn at the shit-hole that is Rose Hill, the scummy place that it is. As far as I'm aware it's also the home where "He" resides - "He" being the nasty, evil bastard that used to call himself my "Father". That's if he's still alive that is? And, knowing him and also my appalling luck, he probably still is, lording it up with that fucking Thai bitch that he married after divorcing Mum - poor old Mum - and all her fucking family that he had shipped over to England to sponge-off the State, just like most of the other scum in this area.

I cut through the arse-end of Morden High Street to the car-park as it's quicker this way. There are several spaces available up the far end and so we park easily, although the parking bays themselves are stupidly tight. The cost of parking here for the whole day has gone up considerably since the last time I was here - £5 for the whole day - but we don't have much of a choice but to pay up.

It's a short brisk walk to the station which is located back the way we drove in and over the main road. Anyone can see that we're now in the clutches of London as there are bloody foreigners everywhere, especially bloody Paki's and Wogs. I remember back to when I was a little girl, Morden seemed a much more cleaner friendlier place, not the multicultural stinking shit-hole that it's become now.

The station itself hasn't changed much, it still looks old and dirty just has it always has done. There used to be a hole in the wall, over to the right, that was once the pay-booth but that is now long-gone, replaced by confusing sole-less ticket machines that tie the both of us in knots. One of the station staff comes over to help us - a blonde girl with brown eyes and a pretty face and in her mid-20's and I fall in love with her instantly. Just like the parking ticket, the tube ticket prices have also escalated through the roof.

We then make out way though the automated gate barriers and down the Victorian stairs to the lines of rail-tracks, there being only one train ready waiting on the platform, this one bound for the Bank Line, which means we will have to change trains at Kennington in order to get to Tottenham Court Road Station.

Fortunately there are not that many people around us at this time of the morning, having missed the early morning rush-hour - a couple in their late-20's with their 2-kids, a businessman in a dark suit with his obligatory briefcase, a black girl in her early-20's and 2-guys of a similar age who continuously keep eyeing us up and down but judging by the shape of their heads I'm pretty certain that they're a couple of Slavs. They're both quickly put off the scent and have their notions of chatting us up extinguished as I take hold of Amanda's hand and we turn to face one another and stare into each others eyes with love. I move closer to her and give her a light kiss to her lips and she reaches out to me and holds my waist. The platform becomes suspended in time as we kiss, only to be reawakened by the hissing-noise of the carriage doors opening up to us at last.

We board and sit next to each other in "our" carriage - I say "our" as everyone seems to have moved away from us for some strange reason - weirdo's! The doors hiss shut and almost immediately the train jerks forwards as we make our way up the track towards the dark tunnel entrance. Amanda looks at me with some trepidation as we enter into the blackness but I assure her that everything is okay as I hold her hand to allay her fears as the rush of air swishes past the carriage windows as we jostle-along up the tunnel with the metal wheels screaming on the metal tracks.

We're joined in our carriage at the following stop by another girl - in her late-20's with a sweat face, pink lipstick, blonde hair (not real!) with a plated pony-tail and wearing a big pink woolly jumper. I can't take my eyes off of her and fall desperately in love yet again. I just can't help myself!

We stop at every station along this line of track; all the Tooting's, the Clapham's and all the others, picking-up and dropping-off all manner of human traffic from seemingly every nation under the sun. In fact by the time we get to Stockwell and the junction with the Victoria Line our carriage is heaving, with everyone squashed-in like proverbial sardines! Amanda and I still get plenty of looks of course, not only because we're still holding hands, but also as we both look so similarly gorgeous. She squeezes my hand for reassurance and I tell her I love her and we kiss. I look back to see the blonde honey opposite sitting there smiling at our action and I want her to join us in a 3-way kiss but it's never going to happen.

Finally we reach Kennington where we have to change trains, requiring us to take a quick dash across the station, sandwiched between the throngs of our fellow passengers. The awaiting train on the opposing platform is pretty much full already with all the seats taken, meaning we're forced to stand for the rest of the duration, which fortunately only takes us some 20-minutes or so.

At Tottenham Court Road we first have to take some steps and then 2-sets of escalators to get back up to station level and then another flight of steps up to reach ground level. We emerge out of the station into the blinding sunlight and the thick heat of Oxford Street and the whole area is absolutely heaving, with all manner of people everywhere, all jostling and darting about like they're all on drugs - a lot of them probably are!

It really is like the bloody League of Nations up here, with bloody foreigners everywhere. The ethnic claustrophobia that is London. The level of immigration makes my heart break, at least every other person is non-white or non-Aryan. I'm not talking about the true Europeans - the Germans, French, Spanish, Italians, Scandinavians and others, the ones I mean are the so-called Eastern Europeans - the Slavs - or White-Paki's as I call them. They're the ones that are putting the strain on my country - jobs, services, housing, the NHS, schools, roads, and the nation in general. There's no telling what the rest of them are, just a stinking multitude of cultures all mixed in together, all attacking one another for space and bragging rights. The amount of blacks swarming around us makes me nervous to say the least - one nigger is one too many as far as I'm concerned, always bleating-on about how misrepresented they are in society, trying to turn my country into theirs and turning our icons black. Before we know it they'll be turning Jesus black!

Mixed in with all this lot are the Jews, I can easily spot them a mile off with their funny curly hair, strange black clothing, big hats, big noses and pale faces. They too always harp-on about how hard done-by they always are and how the World has always dealt them a bad hand by persecuting them throughout the ages, but I've never seen one single Yid on the dole or homeless and begging on the street for money, they always seem to have a secret stash of cash hidden away somewhere to fall back on. Funny that?

What isn't funny is the fact that because of all this change, we're rapidly running-out of living-space for our own people, that's the real travesty in this country.

We make our way down the right-hand side of Oxford Street, passing the Tottenham Pub and then what was once the massive Virgin Megastore, several serial-scroungers and yet more bloody immigrants handing out crappy flyers that nobody wants or takes.

We pass shops selling tacky souvenirs of London, numerous coffee bars and eateries, expensive clothes shops, the excellent 100 Club that I've frequented at least half a dozen times in the past in my younger days to see various bands - and always on my own. I try to find the really good newsagent that was on a corner - an amazing place that sold magazines and newspapers from all around the World, titles that I'd never heard of before - but that seems to have disappeared also, along with most of the shops that I remember from back then. All this change makes me feel really old.

Finally we reach one of my favourite stores of my youth - the HMV Megastore - and we amble around all 3-floors hand in hand, looking at everything and nothing much in particular. In fact, neither of us actually buy anything as if there's something we want in terms of CD's or DVD's we usually get them from Amazon as they're cheaper and easier. I know that's not the point as far as the survival of the High Street shop in concerned, but that's the way things are now so what can you do? It is nice however to nose-around a shop like this, especially the World Cinema section as you never know what you might find, something interesting and something different maybe? In our case though, we both come away with nothing.

We continue to stroll down the road, the surrounding crowd checking-out my élan as we take-in a few posh clothes shops but, once again, we come away empty-handed. Just before the crossroads with Regent Street we cross over the road and head up Argyll Street, past the London Palladium on our left and then across Great Marlborough Street and into Liberties department store. We take a photo of each other on our phones at the entrance door, with Amanda taking another of the stores mock-Tudor facade to send back home to her Mum in Australia as they don't have anything that looks like this place over there. We wander around the stores various departments, looking at stuff way too expensive for either of us to afford, although the quality of the items are all top-notch it has to be said.

From there we amble around the corner to Carnaby Street, once THE place to be seen during the swinging-60's and the Punk-era of the 70's. Now though this too is a shadow of its former self, the shops here today are too over the top and expensive for the average person and are a bit of a sick joke.

We enter a few but we don't linger, in fact we spend no more that half an hour in the Street in total and that includes taking a couple of photos of each other under the famous Carnaby Street sign.

We double-back along Argyll Street again, turning right to go back up the other side of Oxford Street. By now it's lunch-time so we stop and buy ourselves a couple of fresh hand-made sandwiches from a Deli, Amanda paying. We stand around watching the World go by as we munch-away on our food which is super-tasty and slides down lovely into our rumbling empty stomachs. I spot a gorgeous girl walking along, a real honey in her late-20's with a perfect figure, perfect face, perfect hair, perfect clothes, perfect shoes, perfect everything. She's perfect in every way except for one thing - she's hand-in-hand with a fucking nigger! What is wrong with these women? What is she trying to prove? Who is she trying to fool? She is disgusting and makes me sick and I have to look away.

With our food eaten we continue our walk up Oxford Street - forever hand-in-hand - and I suddenly become confused. There used to be a fantastic shoe shop along here somewhere years ago called Shelley's, on the corner, but no matter how hard we search that too seems to have disappeared in time. I just can't believe that that has gone as well, the number of shoes that I'd bought there over the years must be well into double figures? Time moves on I guess but is it for the better?

At the other end of Oxford Street there's not much else to be found and nothing lights our fire at all. We decide to cross back over the road, taking our lives in our hands as the traffic is tighter than a ducks arse - not that I've ever studied a ducks arse! - even though the road is only open to buses and taxis. We take our chance and thread our way between two cabs, the driver of one of them giving us a parp on his horn as we do so - cheeky sod!

We head into the Tottenham Pub for a drink or 6, all this bloody walking and not buying anything has left us worn-out and a bit cheesed-off. At least we have our love for each other and we laugh and smirk together at knowing it. I order our usual tipples - a pint of lager for myself and a gin and tonic for Amanda - and we sit ourselves down on our pert bums at the one and only vacant table, virtually right underneath the multicoloured glass skylight. The pub is pretty rammed, mainly with suited business-types, and it's not too long - about 2-seconds actually! - when we start getting eyeballed and subjected to the usual crap from a couple of guys - actually both quite nice looking it has to be said. We quickly and easily dispatch them when we lean forward and kiss each other full-on the lips, with Amanda mouthing at them: "Not interested" and telling them to: "Piss Off", making them look away somewhat dumbstruck and disgusted.

A couple of girls on another table stare at us with equal shock and horror, even more so when I blow them a kiss - Mary's! Amanda and I chat about life and our future together and other stuff as we hold hands and kiss again.

With our drinks finished we head back out into the haze of Oxford Street, crossing back over the road once again and heading down Charing Cross Road to check-out Foyles bookshop, another of my haunts from the past. Its an amazing place, spread out over several floors - six I think? - and is jambed from floor to ceiling with books on every subject you care to think of. Looking around inside it somehow seems a lot more organized than I remember, everything seems tidier and neater and square? I wonder if age is catching up with me? I hope time doesn't do the same, well, not yet anyway. We make our way up to the art section where I find the most beautiful book ever on Jackson Pollock - my favourite artist of all time. I simply have to have it, even though the cost is a bit steep at nearly £50. Amanda begs me to buy it as a special treat to myself, so fuck it, that's what I do.

With our trip done and dusted we decide to make our way back to the station and head for home, passing Centre Point Tower on our right as we walk on. The Tube is even more rammed-full of bodies than it was earlier as we head towards the Northern Line for our return journey. We stand amongst the crowds of people on the platform with our arms wrapped around each others waists with not a fucking care about who objects. And why the fuck should we? What we are and what we do is nobody else's business so fuck off!

When the next train duly arrives there is absolutely no room whatsoever in the carriage so we're both forced to stand squished together into this tin can on wheels between all the sweaty stinking passengers. We have to change trains once again at Kennington and the throng thins out enough so we can at last grab a seat each, much to our relief. At Stockwell yet more passengers piss-off, leaving us and 4 other commuters on board. By the time we get to Tooting Bec there are only the 3 of us left and I lean across and kiss Amanda softly on her left-cheek as we hold hands with love and chat about inconsequential stuff. We tell each other of our deep love and I'm so overcome with my pure love for her that I almost choke my words. At Colliers Wood Station our last passenger deserts us - an old guy of about 60 with a funny walk - leaving us alone at last. Out the corner of my eye I spot a middle-aged woman in the next carriage peering at us every now and then through the door windows at the end of the train, no-doubt probably inquisitive as to what we're doing and what we are? The train jerks its way back up to speed and I turn and tell Amanda once again that: "I love you with all my heart and soul." We kiss and I tongue her mouth and touch her breasts with my right-hand and she responds with heavy panting and small moans of pleasure. I look over to the woman in the next carriage as she stares at us in horror and it turns me on even more knowing that she's watching us making-out as I snog and grope my girlfriend. Amanda reaches out to me and plays with my breasts also and I love it and we tongue each other harder.

Suddenly our surroundings turn from the pure darkness of the tunnel into blazing light, making us both start, as we exit the underground and emerge into the daylight of

Morden Station. We laugh at the split-second transformation as we continue to kiss and touch each other. As the train grinds to a halt, we collect ourselves together and make for the sliding-doors, as hand-in-hand we step out onto the platform, followed a little way behind by the spy in the cab who still continues to stare at us but says nothing. What can she say? What can she do?

We wiggle our way up the old steps to ground-level, pass through the electronic barriers and then out into the bustling High Street with its buses, taxis and general traffic clogging the road, not to mention the stifling heat that takes our breath away. We make our way back the short distance to the car-park where we're soon reunited with my little white ST.

***

I grab Amanda's hand and gently swing her around to face me. I hold her tenderly and kiss her lips and she mine. There is no-one else around us and I wouldn't give a shit even if there was. Up against the passenger-side of my car I touch her breasts and they heave madly at my caress. She touches mine also and we love. I reach down and work my hand up her dress until I discover the softness of her knickers and the joys within. She pants loudly as I finger her vagina and she jumps at me, wrapping her beautiful legs around my body. I manage to bypass her underwear and insert 2-fingers into her pussy, enjoying her wetness as I wank her in a cyclic-motion. She grips me tightly as I finger-fuck her and she moans ever louder until I bring her to her crescendo and she shakes and screams and cums at me, pissing over me her sweet juice of love. She falls from Heaven into my arms and we kiss as I realise her back down onto the ground and we are so in love with each other that we have become one singular person and no-longer individual.

Amanda opens the passenger-side door of my car and begs me to get in. She positions me so I'm sitting sideways on the bucket-seat with my gorgeous long tanned and toned legs dangling over its side. Amanda squats down in front of me like a servant kneeling for her Queen, opening my legs for her as I shuffle my bum forwards. I quickly guess as to her intentions as she discards my underwear, throwing them onto the rear-seat of my car. She moves-in closer to me and I feel my labia swelling in anticipation of her mouth and then the pure sensation of her tongue on my vagina. All my breath escapes me in one long exhale as my excitement rockets me into orbit. My whole body shudders uncontrollably as she licks me and I die as I cum into her mouth. She eats me totally and it's all too much, my brain becomes starved of oxygen and overloaded on love as at the same time I cum once more into her face. She climbs on top of me and we kiss softy, the taste of my own cum on our mouths adding to the moment.

Suddenly a car drives past us but we don't care, we kiss once more as we untangle ourselves from our position. We laugh at ourselves at what we are and have become - two gorgeous lesbian lovers with all the power and freedom to do anything we fucking-well want to and no bastard is going to destroy that.

Famous last words!

***

We try to straighten ourselves up the best we can and then head off, with Amanda taking-over the reigns of the driving, and then heading back home to West Sussex.

I guide Amanda as we drive back home a different way, turning left out of the car-park and along the A24 London Road. Just before the bridge we pass the enormous Baitulfutuh Mosque, the largest one in Western Europe, although when I was a kid it was in fact just a milk distribution depot! I remember once, I tell Amanda, a few years back when I was visiting Mum one week-day, I drove past this very same spot and the amount of cars that were parked-up on the kerb and grassed central-reservation was unbelievable. There were fucking swarms of dirty, bearded, robed Muslim shit everywhere. The worse thing though was the amount of Police assisting all the rag-heads in parking wherever they fucking liked - amazing! If I had wanted to park there I would have been told to fuck off! It just goes to show doesn't it? - you can never trust a copper.

We head back through Lower Morden, passing what was once a really good video shop on our left that is now a fucking Bulgarian mini-market - fucking typical! - and then Garth Road where I had my very first job working for an engineering company, then by St. Anthony's Hospital on the right, though the outskirts of Sutton, the massive Sainsbury's on the left that many moons ago used to be just a field with horses running around care-free, and the Queen Vic crossroads where I had many a near-miss in my car back in my early years of driving. We divert off the main road and turn right as I want to show Amanda the old "Family" home, presumably still owned by the Paki's who bought it when Mum died. We park-up outside the house and I can't help noticing just how small it looks, and dirty too, with the front garden overgrown with weeds and looking in a right state. Mum would have hated to see it looking like this, she must be turning in her grave. What a fucking mess, just like the rest of my old home town.

Back on the A24 we then pass Nonsuch Park on the left, once the site of one of Queen Elizabeth 1st finest palaces where now not even a trace remains. The tales I could tell you of what I used to get up to in that park when I was in my teens could quite easily fill another book all on their own!

We then cut through Ewell Village, featuring Bourne Hall, the tiny jail, and the towns many pubs.

The next town is Epsom, a bit of an old-fashioned place with a clock-tower at its centre which features the occasional market at its feet. The shopping here is a bit hit and miss but it's okay really I guess. Once past Epsom Hospital, the next town we come to is Ashtead, way smaller than Epsom with fewer shops and piss-poor parking. The country opens-up on the other side of town and the houses become larger, not the sort of houses for your average worker, more like snobs-corner.

The A24 is clearer now so Amanda puts her foot down as we head over the M25 and do a left and make for Dorking. We soon pass by Box Hill on our left and then on to Dorking itself, a town similar to Epsom in a way but with much more charm. We don't need to go through the actual town itself though so instead we bypass around the roundabout with the giant silver chicken mounted at its centre and carry-on up and along the A24. At Beare Green we then turn off onto the A29 and after about 9-miles or so we're back in our sleepy little village of Slinfold.

It's been a long, tiring day and now we're back home I feel a bit disappointed at our trip to London. Nothing was as I remembered it. Why can't things just stay the same? I guess it was my fault really for trying to recapture the past. And that's just what it is - in the past. The past is dead and gone and I should have left it there. Amanda enjoyed herself though so I suppose that's one good thing. If she's happy then so am I.

***

Even though it's been such a long day both Amanda and I still have enough energy for love. We always have enough for that! We take a quick shower together in cool water to wash-away the day's grime from our trip up to London. It gets bloody everywhere, even up our noses!

After drying each other off we make our way hand-in-hand to the rear of our flat. I slide the patio doors open that lead out onto our small back garden and the oppressive heat hits my naked flesh like fire, sending a shiver down my spine.

I jump a little when I feel Amanda's hand touch my bum and I turn myself to face her, kissing her pert mouth. She runs her fingers over my vagina and my breath skips a beat and I kiss her harder. We tongue each other as we finger each others clits and we are both wild on love for one another.

I through some cushions out onto the hard stone slabs of the patio and we both sink down onto them and I lick Amanda's hole, swallowing her wet love. She moans and groans at my action, again regardless as to whether our stupid neighbours can hear us or not, it doesn't really matter, they are nothing to us and we don't fucking care anyway.

I fuck her roughly with my middle-finger on one hand as I squeeze and squash her clit with the thumb on the other. Her breathing becomes increasingly erratic until I finally have her totally and she spits her love at me, it splashing itself over my beautiful tits. I lick at her sore, redden orifice and make her cry tears of passion for me.

On all fours I feel the pressure of the dildo on my anus, it's our Pearl Shine 8-inch one from Lovehoney. After some initial resistance it slides in easily and Amanda fucks me steadily but surely. Several minutes later I suddenly feel another at my vagina, it being Amanda's own Private Dick dildo from Bondara as she inserts it into me, it going in easier than the first. She pumps-away at me alternately and then as one and I scream as it feels like both ends of the 2-plastic cocks are actually meeting together inside my body and I love it.

Before long I can take no more and I lose control of myself and spasticate and I shout and scream as I cum as the lower-half of my body implodes. Amanda doesn't stop pummelling me even though my brain has vacated my head and continues to fuck me. I lay there motionless for almost 5-minutes as she fucks- away and I feel like I've had all the stuffing knocked out of me!

We lay side-by-side on the cushions under the beaming afternoon sunlight and I am the luckiest girl on Planet Earth. I simply could not be happier than I am right now here with my love.

***

"Shit on me."

"Oh Sarah no, not this again. You know I don't really like doing that."

"I want you to. Shit on my tits. Come on."

"I don't know if I can."

"Of course you can, you're a modern girl."

"No, that's not what I mean. I don't think I have anything inside me."

"Try. Squat over me."

I lay face-up on the hard patio surface and watch Amanda position herself over me and begin to strain. She moans as she pushes hard and before long I see it, her beautiful scat in all it's brown glory, poking out of her tight Australian arse.

The first pellet plops out onto my breasts and I touch it, rolling it around with my fingers. A much larger piece then makes its way towards me, looking like a deformed brown cock and I want to suck it but that's not the idea. Amanda uses her hands to part her bum-cheeks and out it falls, down onto my chests and I grab it and rub the poo into myself, playing with her dirt. It feels warm and sticky as I squash her turd into my skin, rubbing the smelly mess over my gorgeous firm tits.

Amanda stands and spins around to face me before sitting back down on my pelvis. She helps me rub her scat all over me and it feels so sexy and we laugh. She really does like doing this, it's just that sometimes her mind says "no" when her heart says "yes."

She stands above me again and this time pisses on my tits and I love her so much that I feel like crying. She wanders off momentarily, returning with the garden hose and squirting me with a jet of cold water on full-power, blowing away her waste and soaking me entirely over my hot naked body. I open my legs as wide as they will go and lay back and stretch out my arms. It's an open invitation that Amanda accepts freely, shooting the hose right at my wanting vagina. The sensation is amazing and I love it and cum within seconds as the water crashes against my vulva and penetrates right up inside my hole, filling it completely and I fuck it.

3

Las Vegas

The South Terminal at Gatwick Airport is so bloody crowded that it's actually made the air I'm struggling to breathe so thin that I'm starting to feel a little bit feint. I grip Amanda's hand tighter for some sort-of reassurance as we wait amongst the throng of our fellow humans. Our Virgin Atlantic flight to Las Vegas departs at 11.20am, and it being a non-stop 10-hour journey, means we're scheduled to land at McCarran International Airport at 5.30pm US time, so they inform us.

I have to say that I'm not that great at flying, in fact I'm not that great at heights per se, so this is going to be a bit of a mission for me. I'm pretty sure that with Amanda by my side though and a few stiff vodkas down my neck I'll be able to make it to the end!

I'm wearing a white cotton sleeveless blouse today from H&M - open low of course! - a pair of grey stone-wash slim-fit jeans from La Redoute, and on my feet a pair of white suede open-toe ankle-boots from Polyvore that are to die for. My underwear is from Ultimo in sexy red and black. My jacket is from Very, also in white. My hair and make-up are done to my usual impeccable standard, and if you don't know what my style is by now then you should have been paying more attention! My perfume is *Luxe* by Avon.

Amanda is wearing a black Reisse Paige shirt from ASOS that really highlights her lovely blonde hair and gorgeous features, light blue super-tight jeans from Gap, and yellow suede wedge court-shoes from Polyvore. Her underwear is in sexy white from Victoria's Secret, knickers only though as she's not wearing a bra. She's wearing my black poncho by Peter Hahn which also really suits her, along with a smattering of the same perfume as I have on today.

The time eventually comes for us to board our plane. We've been waiting here for over 2-hours now already since we checked-in this morning and I'm both tired and bored at the monotony of doing nothing. Still hand-in-hand, we make our way along the entrance tunnel to our awaiting plane, a Jumbo, one of those big fat ones with the bulge on the top, not that I can see it from here I can't.

A girl from the airline greats us at the entrance to the plane. She's absolutely beautiful and has the most perfect face I've ever seen except in my own reflection. Her green eyes sparkle at me when she says: "Good morning" and my stomach gives a momentary grumble at the sound of her beautiful sweet voice. Her teeth are unreal - maybe they are! - and are equally as perfect as the rest of her. She's actually a little bit lovely! My mind goes into overdrive as I try to imagine her naked before me, all smooth and hot and willing to explore my love. I want to kiss her cherry lips and her pert young breasts and to taste the delights of her pussy on my tongue but in a split-second she's gone and I'm forced to walk-on to try and find my allocated seat. I never see her again for the rest of our whole trip or the rest of my life. She has disappeared into my memory just like all my previous loves, although the thought of her sitting on my face with her lapping at my vagina haunts my mind for several hours to come.

Amanda and I find our places easily enough, over to the right-hand side of the plane by one of the windows, although I don't particularly want to look out of it when we're going up or especially when we're zooming along miles up in the sky, that always freaks me out!

We're soon underway and the whole plane begins to rumble as we taxi forwards. We accelerate hard and fast along the runway and before long I feel the awful sensation of being lifted off the ground as we become airborne. I squeeze Amanda's hand hard as we're propelled into the blue horizon and I start to feel sick. She leans over to me and kisses my cheek and I smile a false smile of thanks back at her. I take a big gulp from Amanda's water bottle as we start to level off and I feel the pressure on my belly start to ease off. With the worst bit over I order a large vodka for myself and a gin and tonic for my love from one of the stewardesses - as I've already said, not the sweet honey that stole my heart earlier - but another young thing in her early-20's with a hardbody and as pretty as Hell.

Amanda and I chat about our life and our future together for the next couple of hours or so, the main topic obviously being the actual reason for making this trip to the US - to get married in Vegas! How crazy and romantic is that? In fact this trip is going to be our wedding and honeymoon all rolled into one.

I really do hope that it's the right move? It certainly feels right for the both of us so that's exactly what we're going to do, come what may.

Neither of us have actually told our respective families or friends either, we just booked the flights and hotel - I paid for everything out of the sale of Mum's house money - and so here we are, on our way! I know it was a tad impulsive but it's what we both want so what the fuck? It makes no difference to me if people love it or hate it, it's completely immaterial as far as I'm concerned.

The effects of the anticipation, the early start, the boring wait at Gatwick, the plane and now the vodka, all start to catch up with me and I doze off for several hours into a beautiful sleep. I dream of fucking Amanda and both the Virgin stewardesses in a 4-way orgy of love and then another where I shoot that stupid bitch at work that I hate in the back of her head and other such delights.

***

"Hey, sleepy head. Time to wake up." Amanda whispers to me as she shakes me by the arm.

"You've been out for hours. Are you OK?"

"Yeah, I think so. How long have I been asleep?"

"Just over 5-hours. You were dreaming and making some very strange noises. People were staring."

"Bollocks to them." I say, sniggering.

"What were you dreaming about? Me I hope?"

"Of course." I say to her as we lean towards one another and kiss.

It's still an hour or so later before we actually come in to land at McCarran International. The journey of over 5,000-miles wasn't so bad after all, seeing as I slept through the best part of it anyway!

Like Gatwick, McCarran is equally packed full of people, all jostling about like headless chickens. I look around at them all and come to realise to myself how much I despise and hate the human race, each and every single one of them.

We grab our luggage from the conveyor and make our way to the check-out desk and yet another bloody queue. We wait in line and in turn with all the other humans and we chat and laugh together and touch and kiss like lovers.

Once through the typical stringent American checking-out rigmarole, we make our way out of the terminal and step into the stifling Las Vegas heat that hits us in the face like a hammer. It's so bloody hot I can barely breathe!

They're a strange bloody lot the Americans, they all seem to think that God is on their side and that he will save them from destruction. How long is it going to take them to realise that there is no God and that nothing is going save them? Why are they always so complacent?

We have to get ourselves a Taxi to the hotel and we find a whole swarm of them lined-up waiting for punters outside the terminal. We grab the lead one, driven by some horrid swarthy foreigner, possibly a Middle-Eastern immigrant judging by the looks of him, with his rancid clothes, tombstone teeth and his typical arrogant manner. I shove the name of our hotel under his wet hairy nose and after we've loaded our own bags - once again typical of these women-hating bastards - off we zoom. The radio in the cab - which in itself is in surprisingly good condition - blasts out its shitty Arabic music, all wails and sitars and all that crap. Amanda laughs at him, the awful music and the situation we find ourselves in but I don't find any of it funny, in fact I just want to shoot this pig in the back of his head right here and now, just for being alive. It's also a good job the cab has air-con as the sweaty tosser stinks to high-heaven.

The journey to the hotel is relatively uneventful, the traffic being quite heavy but flowing steadily, and we arrive at our destination at the North-end of the main Strip in not a moment too soon.

The Stratosphere Hotel is absolutely mind-blowing, it really is out of this World, something that you could only find here in Vegas. It has nearly 2,500-rooms spread over 24-floors. There's also a crazy observation tower at one side with its incredible revolving "Top of the World" restaurant that reaches up over a thousand-feet into the Las Vegas sky. In fact the hotel boasts no less than 6- restaurants with one of them - McCalls Heartland Grill - that quickly becomes our favourite place to eat for the duration of our stay. Naturally the hotel also features its own casino - it wouldn't be Vegas otherwise would it? - featuring its beautiful purple ceiling, gambling tables and money-swallowing machines. You could only find all this here in Vegas.

Amanda pays the Arab his stinking money - we even have to unload our own bags once again! - before we make our way into the hotel itself. Inside is even more incredible and we both "Wow" at the breathtaking sight before us. There is nothing in England (or presumably in even Australia?) that comes anywhere close to this as we're both struck dumb by its magnificence.

We're greeted at the reception desk by one of the reception staff, a girl of about my age, pretty, but with way too much make-up slapped all over her face in typical Vegas style. After exchanging the usual fake pleasantries and signing-in, I grab the room entry swipe-card from her pretty American fingers and follow along behind our hotel porter up to our room. We eventually make it to our door after a short hike and our room is completely lovely, decorated in a classic modern style. Being a Premier room it's a cut-above some of the others in the building and of course has air-conditioning as standard - absolutely essential out here in the desert - along with a flat-screen TV that has a million-channels to choose from.

No sooner as the porter pisses-off we race about the suite like 2-hungry schoolgirls, looking at everything like it's candy in a sweetshop. But it is at one of the windows that I come to a silent stop, the vista before my gorgeous blue eyes overlooking Sunset Strip becomes a moment in time that I will always remember for the rest of my days on this feeble Earth. Everything really is awesome, just as the Yanks are forever saying.

We both stand there looking at the view together, gazing out in amazement with our arms wrapped around each other and we kiss tenderly on the lips. My day is not complete without her and we fall onto the massive king-sized bed and run our hands over each others bodies as we tongue one another with love.

We don't do much for the rest of the evening as we're both so incredibly knackered. We shower together as always and then have a wander around the hotel and casino downstairs. We decide to have dinner in the crazy revolving restaurant, so we both tart ourselves up to the max. I'm wearing a white bandeau bandage dress from Lipsy. My underwear is in sexy white lace from Figleaves and my shoes are a pair of white suede open-toe ankle-boots from Polyvore. My perfume is *Luxe* by Avon. I've done my make-up to look super-sharp featuring coal-black eye-shadow and pale-pink lipstick.

Amanda is dressed similarly in a super-tight white knee-length bodycon dress also from Lipsy and a similar pair of white shoes to mine although hers are from ASOS. She's not wearing any underwear at all while her perfume is the same as mine once again. Her hair is also up in a ponytail similarly to how I always have mine and she looks and smells absolutely gorgeous.

We both tuck-in to our beautiful food - we've both ordered identically once again! - fillet steak with red wine in a wild mushroom sauce that is all to die for. It's all cooked absolutely perfectly, mine being rare and Amanda's medium-rare, and the steaks are both tasty and juicy, just as we are! I will say one thing about the Americans, they certainly know how to cook a steak!

Later, back in our room, we both go straight to bed to sleep. Not even attempting sex as today has been so bloody knackering. We both feel like we've been awake for days on end.

***

Neither of us get up until 10.15am the following morning, except for a pee on my part. Our wedding at the little chapel down-town is pre-booked for tomorrow so today is pretty-much a free day, albeit with some small preparations still to do of course, like going to the County Courthouse to get our same-sex marriage licence that I pre-paid for online weeks ago for the grand total of only $60 - result! - and then sorting out our matching dresses and other stuff.

One major issue is to find ourselves a witness, but we've both decided we're just going to be brave and pick someone at random from the crowd for that - crazy!

We're going to have to go to the chapel today as well, just to make sure that everything is okay, the last thing either of us wants is any more hassle - yesterday was bad enough on its own! - although that could have been worse to be fair.

We stand naked before one another and I am so in love with the image of the 2-beautiful women we are that I can't help but smirk to myself as to how fucking lucky I am. Amanda looks gorgeous, her body is so tight and I just have to have her, I have to make her mine forever. We embrace and kiss and tongue and play with each others vaginas with our fingers. I cum first and I feel the heat from my juice run down my thigh turning me on even more. She takes a little longer so I use my mouth on her pussy, inserting my tongue in and out of it until she shakes in a rhythmic shudder and I taste her honey, drinking down her elixir in my total devotion to her being.

I'm on my back on the floor, laying on one of the floor-rugs with my legs open as wide as they will go and with Amanda's right-hand completely inserted into my pussy, fist-fucking me with carnal love. I almost lose consciousness at the motion of her pushing and sucking her paw in and out of my body. I cry out in pain but order her to continue to love and hurt me until I spasticate myself orgasmically with flailing arms and legs and my juice squirting out under pressure everywhere.

We shower together using all our love for each other, dry one another, do each others hair, make-up and dress each other - we are as one.

Today I'm wearing a white halter-neck top from Boohoo and a short white pencil-skirt from Forever 21 that altogether makes me look really hot. On my feet I'm wearing a pair of tan-coloured ankle-boots from AliExpress, whilst my underwear is in sexy white lace from Lovehoney - the bra being a strapless one. My perfume is *Poison* by Christian Dior.

Amanda is wearing a green v-neck short-sleeved jumper from M&S, white high-rise super-skinny jeans from Boohoo that really show off her gorgeous legs and lovely pert bum, and a similar pair of boots to mine except her's are from New Look. Her perfume is *Kenzo Flower* by Kenzo. Once again she's not wearing any underwear.

We order room-service for breakfast and it is typically American; massive pancakes smothered in thick maple syrup that are so filling that we're unable to eat more that 2-each - they sent us 10 in total! It's hardy bloody surprising the Yanks are so fat if that's the way they eat!

We catch a cab outside the hotel to the chapel - not a foreigner this time but a big fat American guy at the wheel munching away on a doughnut the size of a house! The chapel itself is situated just a short ride away up the Strip, a building way smaller that it looked on the Internet, more like a glorified shed really, but pretty I guess and quite quaint looking. Inside it's actually really sweat, all decked-out with bunting and sheer drapes in white and all that kind of stuff.

The minister, a cheerful round woman in her mid-50's, greets us in true American style and seems genuinely really nice, if a little gushy. She shows us the ropes for tomorrows ceremony - to be held at 9pm in the evening - and doesn't seem at all bothered at marrying 2-women - Oh the joys of Vegas!

We're only in there for about 30-minutes or so chatting away and then we catch another cab as we're going to hire a car for the rest of our stay in Nevada. The cab driver looks like the very same stinking Arab as our first one yesterday but he isn't, it's just that they all look and smell the bloody same.

At the Hertz rental place we decide that we both want to hire something typically American for our stay, preferably a convertible, and certainly something that goes, not some horrid namby-pamby re-badged Eurobox piece of crap. In the end we settle for the most beautiful Ford Mustang GT Convertible in pure white. It is so gorgeous and it suits the image of both of Amanda and myself down to a tea, with our white outfits, blonde hair and our natural beauty.

Amanda doesn't want to drive the car - it being left-hand drive - so I take charge of our gorgeous beast. It costs me an arm and a leg to hire it for the duration whilst in the States but who gives a shit - we're only getting married once so we go for it!

We roar out of the lot onto the freeway with a small screech from the cars tyres and off we go, this is what being in America is all about - freedom. Heading out of town we cruise along without a care in the World, 2-free young women in love with each other.

After several miles Amanda spots a sign for a rifle-range. Neither of us have ever fired a gun before in our lives so we decide to have a laugh and take the plunge. The cost is $90 each for firing an automatic pistol and so we both plumb for that option - what the Hell! The instructor is a big guy in his 50's who seems very expert in what he's doing but he's also a bit too touchy-feely for my liking as he keeps putting his hands around my waist as I take aim at the targets on the horizon, trying to manoeuvre my body into the right position. Amanda laughs at his attention but I don't like it, it just makes me nervous and gives me the creeps and spoils my aim. Obviously we have to wear protective glasses and ear defenders for safety, and after briefing us on how to use the weapon correctly I step-up to the plate first. The gun is way heavier than I expected and I find it difficult to aim straight, not helped by the instructor and his mitts, but the real shock comes when I pull the trigger as the noise and the recoil from the shot almost knocks me off my feet and I stumble backwards - Wow! It is one of the most amazing experiences I've ever had and I could do this all day long - I love it! I can't believe how easy it is and the feeling of power is incredible. I fire off all fifteen shots - admittedly only hitting the target once! - but I don't care, the feeling is fantastic.

I hand the empty weapon over to the instructor who then reloads it before Amanda has her turn. To my amazement, and typically, it quickly transpires that she turns out to be a bit of an ace shot, hitting all but 2 of the targets! The instructor is equally taken-aback, not only by her shooting skills, but also when she and I celebrate with a hug and kiss each other with full-on exuberance and passion - get over it man! Her being such a good shot is also a bit worrying, I'll have to watch out for her in the future on that score!

On the way back to the hotel we stop off at one of those typical American diners - one of those big square silver ones straight out of the 1950's - for a burger and Coke each. It's full-on waitress service in here and one of them quickly appears on roller-skates at my car door to take our order. She's really good looking - and young - in fact even better looking than Amanda and with a beautiful pert round bum that I find near impossible to resist. I would just love to stick my fingers and tongue her.

Once again the food portions are massive. The burgers also come with fries - that's chips to you and me! - as well as a side-salad and the drinks. Everything tastes fantastic, so much better that the ones back home in England.

With our lunch consumed we return to the hotel and fuck like crazy. I pretend that I'm the pretty waitress girl from earlier as I position myself on the floor with my arse up in the air for all the World to see. Amanda uses her fingers to lube me and it feels so fucking good that I almost cum at once as she makes my quim twitch like mad. Following a short amount of finger-pummelling, my love gently pushes her small delicate hand into my anus and I collapse inwardly at the joy, pleasure and the discomfort.

I moan loudly as she fist-fucks me and I start to pant rhythmically at my pleasure and pain and I love her so as it stings and hurts my bum.

We 69 with me on top and we lick and tongue at each others vaginas. Amanda is the first to orgasm and I drink her as she spits into my mouth. I feel myself about to explode and I piss my juice over her face and tits and she laughs with me as I finger my hole into her mouth and she sucks it clean.

***

This evening we're both going out onto the Strip to do a bit of nocturnal sightseeing; this should be an event all in itself! We've both dressed similarly once again. I'm wearing a pale-yellow mini bodycon dress from Boohoo that is super-tight, underwear in white lace from Victoria's Secret and yellow suede platform court-shoes from Primark. My perfume is *Poison* by Christian Dior. I'm not carrying a bag of any kind tonight as Amanda is taking her's.

My love is also similarly dressed as I say, although her dress is in a sharper yellow than mine and from Very. Her underwear is also in white lace but from Agent Provocateur. She's also wearing yellow patent heals from AliExpress. Her perfume is *Kenzo Flower* by Kenzo once again. Her clutch-bag is a small chrome metal one from Vintage Styler that I bought for her, just for being my girlfriend and lover.

You would not believe the amount of people there are out and about along Vegas Strip, it's heaving so much that we can barely move. We first find ourselves in a gigantic casino with slot-machines, roulette tables and all that stuff as far as the eye can see, there is no beginning or end of it! We head for the one-arm bandits first, a sure-fire way of losing our money, and true to form that's exactly what we both do - over $100 between us down the drain with no wins at all! Neither of us are great gamblers anyway so things like the roulette and poker tables are non-starters so we soon decide to leave and try somewhere else.

Back out on the street there's a bunch of car-nuts in their low-riders, custom cars and hot-rods cruising up and down posing and doing burn-outs and stuff, so we decide to join the crowd and watch their antics from the side-walk for a bit.

We then stroll past massive fountains spraying giant plumes of water into the evening sky and then even a replica of the Eiffel Tower - what a crazy town this is! We venture into one of the numerous malls, illuminated by neon lights everywhere. The heat is so overwhelming that we have to get ourselves a couple of bottles of water to rehydrate ourselves. As we drink and wander around we laugh at a mime-artist dressed as some kind-of Frenchman, doing his thing entertaining our fellow late-night shoppers.

Further along there's a strange band playing outside yet another casino, bashing-out cover versions of 1980's hits, They're actually quite good and everyone sings and dances along to them including Amanda and I as we hold each other arm-in-arm. There's another group further on down doing circus-type tricks such as fire-eating and sword-swallowing as such like. Next we stumble upon about half-a-dozen or so over-the-top transvestites - or transgenders or whatever they are? - larking about amongst themselves in their own unique camp way, outside one of those anything-goes nightclubs. They're dressed in all sorts of weird outfits in crazy garish colours, just like the characters from that film *Priscilla Queen of the Desert,* and when they spot us they start taking the piss out of us, not in a serious way, but in a friendly humorous joking manner. Some of them even appear to have real breasts by the looks of them, or implants at least! When they hear our English and Australian accents the banter suddenly gets a bit wilder so Amanda and I start to bitch back at them, calling them things like "scrubbers" and "old queens", all in good humour though. We mention to them that we're getting married tomorrow - although that should really read today as the time is now 1.15am! - as suddenly a crazy thought flashes across our minds; why not invite all the trans-girls to be our bridesmaids and witnesses at our wedding - yes really - and why the Hell not, it will be a riot that's for sure!

When we ask them they all accept in unison and without question, in fact their exuberance is as over-the-top as their image, hugging and kissing us like the big girls they are - weird!

After exchanging details with them Amanda and I then decide to head back to the Stratosphere, making our way through the throngs of strange and wonderful people. It's the craziest place on Earth, like one giant theme park that goes on for 24-hours a day, no-one ever seems to sleep!

It's been a really great day and a strange fun night, with tomorrow promising to be even more of the same. Bring it on!

***

Neither of us rise out of bed until gone 11am that same morning. I lay there staring at Amanda's beautiful face and body and count my lucky stars that I've found someone so perfect to spend the rest of my life with. Subconsciously I also wonder to myself how long our partnership will last before I fuck things up yet again? All good things must end I know but hopefully not just yet.

After a late-breakfast - or "Brunch" as the Yanks call it - we shower and dress together, but we don't have sex though as we're trying to save ourselves for tonight.

We venture back out once again in the Mustang. Today I'm wearing a pale-lilac v-neck sleeveless top from Polyvore, a white 1950's-style high-waist pencil-skirt from Unique Vintage, and my pair of white suede open-toe ankle-boots, also from Polyvore. My underwear is in white and pink from Figleaves. My perfume is *Mademoiselle* by Coco Chanel.

Amanda is wearing a lime-coloured open-shoulder crop-top (without a bra once again) from New Look, a pair of white shorts from Island Company that really shows-off her legs to the max, and a pair of white sports shoes from Cotton Traders that are really cool. Her thong is also in white and from HerRoom, whilst her perfume is *Kenzo Flower* by Kenzo.

The Vegas traffic is reasonably light as we burble-along the main Strip, heading South East towards our destination for the day - the Grand Canyon - a distance of approximately 275-miles. After stopping for petrol - or "Gasoline" as the Americans call it - at the next station / mini-market and to pick-up some snacks for our journey, the car quickly eats-up the miles before us. We while-away the next 4-hours of driving by laughing and joking and pissing about as we kiss and hold hands and touch each other intimately as we motor along without a care.

Out of Vegas we take the I-93 past Henderson and Boulder City and on to Kingman. We soak-up the most amazing stunning scenery around us - albeit fairly barren and also terrifyingly lonely - as we motor on. Our fellow road-users are pretty sporadic, with the occasional enormous truck driven by their equally enormous drivers. On the I-40 we head to Seligman and then on to Ash Fork, and from there we catch the I-64 past Kiabab Lake and then eventually to the Grand Canyon National Park itself, over 250-miles of red rock, gauged out centuries-ago by the Colorado River.

The parking lot here at Mather Point is a little tight as we've obviously arrived by what is now mid-afternoon, but luckily we eventually find a vacant space. I almost pass-out at the sheer size and splendour of the giant Canyon laid-out in front of my unworthy eyes, it's actually quite difficult to comprehend the scale of it all, it is the most awesome breathtaking spectacle that I've ever seen in all my days. Both Amanda and I are simply blown-away by the magnitude of the Canyon and we just stand there awe-struck at the vista before us, an overwhelming vision of unparalleled natural beauty with its different shades and layers of rock reflecting their power in the afternoon sun.

After a couple of hours just chilling-out at the Canyon being 2-lovers together, we decide to head back to Vegas, to get ourselves ready for the main reason for coming out to the States in the first place - to get married - bloody Hell!

Our return journey is soaked-away by time, and we arrive back in town at the end of our trip a little tired but definitely not out. We eat a light dinner in the hotel itself in the grill, neither of us having much of an appetite due to nerves I guess? Back in our room after we get ourselves ready for our nuptials. Even though it's considered bad-luck to see your intended before the wedding, this is a different situation for both of us due to the route that we've paved for ourselves and so we just get on with it. And anyway, what could possibly go wrong?

As far as our wedding outfits are concerned, we pre-hired a couple of matching dresses months ago from a specialist shop here in town and have had them delivered to our hotel room this morning, ready and waiting for us upon our return trip earlier to the Canyon. They're both in white, very short in length and both with low-cut tops with a v-shaped split front and back. The material is made from some kind-of crinkly cotton that has very small folds all the way down it from top to bottom. I had to order my one one-size larger than Amanda's due to me being taller and curvier. Our shoes are a matching pair of white suede platform court-shoes from ASOS that we brought with us from England.

Neither of us are wearing any underwear as we're both clear, plus the fact that both dresses arn't see-through and are nice and figure-hugging tight and supportive so there's no real need to. I doubt if we're going to be out and about in them for very long tonight anyway.

We do each others hair and make-up - both really full-on that accentuates our features. This is going to be a one-off event so we both want to look our best obviously. My perfume tonight is *Poison* by Christian Dior whilst Amanda's is her usual *Kenzo Flower* by Kenzo. She smells good enough to eat and that's exactly what I intend to do to her later!

The funny transgender girls are due to pick us up at 8.30pm and take us to the Chapel. All of them are going to be our witnesses even though we only really need the one person. They're also going to provide us with the veils and posies which is a lovely gesture on their part, although I hope they're not too crappy-looking, I really don't know what to expect?

We make our way down to the hotel lobby to be greeted by the "girls" who are already here waiting for us with whistles, much clapping, kissing and general over-the-top camp performances from each and every one of them. The items they've gifted us are perfect - beautiful white posses of delicate flowers (real ones) and veils made from sheer English net patterned with gorgeous butterflies and topped with a garland of white leaves. They simply could not be more perfect and we both thank them from the bottom of our hearts with hugs and kisses and tears all around.

Our ride to the chapel is equally crazy, a big clunky old white Pontiac Station- Wagon straight out of the 1970's, all decked-out with ribbons and a pink sprayed-on message saying: "JUST MARRIED", and a pair of pink boots and pink tin-cans tied to the rear bumper! Everyone passing stops and stares at the commotion as we all pile into the old banger but not one of us gives a flying-fuck as to what they may be thinking - it's got nothing to fucking do with any of them.

As we head through town a bottle of Champagne is suddenly produced from nowhere and is quickly dispatched between all of us, instantly making the mood in the crazy car even more crazy as we all laugh and act stupid - this is really turning out weird!

We're soon at the little chapel and in we all go. Amanda and I stand face-to-face and hand-in-hand as the female minister reads us our vows and we repeat them with all our love and devotion to one another. The chapel is bedecked with flowers and drapes and looks so beautiful, just like a little Christmas grotto, and the setting could not be any better if we tried.

I look at my love and see her beauty. I am so happy that tears of joy begin to form in the corner of my eyes and I fall in love with her all over again. We exchange rings, our tokens of our everlasting love, and then we are one as the minister declares us married. We are entwined in body, mind and soul for now and for evermore, until death do us part. We reveal each others beaming faces as we remove our veils and then kiss passionately with the TV-girls crying tears of joy as much as we are. Confetti of paper and rice fill the happy air as we all kiss and hug each other like the mad things we are.

We are complete now, 2-young lovers about to embark on a journey to the rest of our lives. We all hug and kiss the minister and then Amanda and I sign our lives-away in the Chapel register, as witnessed by all the TV's. Both of us have decided to keeps our respective surnames, a condition we both agreed on ages ago.

And then it is all over and we are away, tearing up the road in the old heap of a car with more flowing Champagne, tears of joy and laughter.

So this is it then is it? I've finally gone and done it, even though I always said I would never would. I am now a married woman. So where do I go from here?

The trans-girls take us for a surprise stop-off at a strip-club in town - this is Sin City after all! Inside the dark interior of the club it's packed full of all the weird and wonderful of Las Vegas - transvestites, transgenders, gays, lesbians, bisexuals, vampires, zombies, smack-heads, goths, punks, skinheads, rockers, freaks, lost souls, dirty old men, dirty old women, whores, junkies, and the dead. No-one stares at us at all and why should they, we're all different but we're all the same. We grab a table to ourselves over to the right of the club, facing the live band who are emitting a slow, beautiful, melodic, dreamy music, the sound capturing the images of the surrounding crowd perfectly and holding them within its grasp.

Amanda and I get pissed as farts along with the girls, so much so that we can hardly stand up! Time passes on and hours later the evening and the night starts to drag - if you pardon the pun! - and I want to go home. Not back to the crazy hotel but back to England - MY England.

We decide to make a break for freedom when we get a chance and so we leave, stepping back out into the humid Nevada night-air and catching a cab back to the Stratosphere.

In our room we're both so completely fucked that neither of us has the energy to screw around, even though we both really want to. It's been such a long and emotional day. I stand and strip naked in front of Amanda as she lays semi-comatose on the bed. She is so beautiful as am I, and I run my hands and fingers over my tight body. I touch my breasts and squeeze my nipples hard but all that Champagne had dulled the pleasure and the pain I was trying to induce on myself. I insert 2-fingers of one hand into my vagina and one from the other hand into my bum-hole and wank myself as I stand there watching my love - my wife - as she watches me back. Her dress rides up as she spreads her legs for me, revealing the wet pinkness of her minge and my heart skips a beat. She gives me the finger, beckoning me to take her right now and lean forward and bury my tongue into her vulva, making her writhe and moan as she ejaculates her love into my mouth as I eat her. I rub my firm breasts into the wetness of her pussy and then suck on them, biting my nipples as I do so. She moans even louder as I insert 2-fingers into her sweet hole, making it squelch. She almost faints as I gob on her and push all my fingers of my right-hand into her twat and she implodes on me.

I have to give her a dry-slap to the face to keep her going, making stars dance before her eyes.

I remove my hand from her and then her clothes. She is like a beautiful rag-doll and I have her completely under my control.

We 69 each other and I cum in seconds from the sensation of her tongue in my hole, squirting my goo in her face. I scream as I eat her pie and I am so knackered. Spinning around I sit up on my knees and use my right one to knee at her vagina firmly, fucking her with it. She swears at me, calling me: "Fucker", "Bastard", "Cunt", "Fucking Bitch" and other such dirt as she knows that it turns me on even more.

I lean over her gorgeous Australian body and push 2-fingers down my throat and within a matter of moments my guts start to heave and I sick myself a horrid wet mess of Champagne and shit over Amanda's pert breasts. It truly is quite disgusting but she laughs and starts to rub the puke into her mounds in a swirling motion, making me laugh also.

We pull each others hair as we snog amongst the puke and cum on the duvet. We smack and bite each others bum-cheeks until they're both red-raw and then there is no more - we are gone - wasted - and we drift off to sleep.

***

The following day is spent in a haze. We try to clean up the mess from last night the best we can before the hotel cleaners descend on the room, it's not really fair to expect them to deal with all this shit, not this time anyway.

We just chill-out for the rest of the day as our hangovers seem to linger on forever. We hang around the hotel for most of the afternoon and then hit a couple of casino's, again without any luck - unsurprisingly! Neither of us have even bothered to dress to kill either, just t-shirts and trainers - simple and light.

Our honeymoon lasts for the next 6-days before we then have to catch our long-haul flight back to England and the return to the shit that is work.

Our adventures over the remainder of our honeymoon takes-in trips to Madame Tussauds where we take photos of each other on our phones and rip the piss out of the waxwork dummies, an exhibition of Titanic artefacts, the massive Caesars

Palace - completely crazy! - and 3-more goes at the rifle-range, even having a go at shooting a machine-gun which was fantastic! I would have loved to take it home with me, I could use it on that bunch of idiots I work with!

We meet up with the trans-girls once again and get pissed and act stupid. We swap Email addresses with them and promise to keep in touch but none of us ever do.

We also take a long trip out to Tooele County in the Mustang to see the Salt Flats at Bonneville, taking the Jetty Road right into the heart of the Flats itself, the scene of many Land Speed Records and disasters. We're both awestruck by the sheer size of the place and its natural beauty - it's as flat as a witch's tit! The arc of this scary and wondrous planet actually bends before us in the distance, 40-square-miles of compacted salt. Although you wouldn't want to put any of it on your chips, I bent down and rubbed my fingers on the surface and then tasted it - it was bloody disgusting!

We have plenty of fun with the Mustang on our various journeys - I might even consider getting one back in England, although the fuel consumption is a bit much and it is a bit big really for our roads.

* * *

I know one of us is supposed to carry the other over the threshold when we go through the front door to our flat - tradition and all that crap! - but we don't bother with any of that, we just want to get indoors and close the World out behind us.

After another long flight back to England and another long day, we're both so bloody tired that we don't even bother to unpack until the following day. It is from this moment on we live like any other newly-weds on the eve of our lives together.

A cloud of dread hangs over me like I'm stuck in some sort-of entrapment. So this is it then is it, married life? Where do I go from here?

One thing is certain though, I'm not going to be like other women who let themselves go as soon as they get married.

Although I'm in my mid-30's now, I still look gorgeous and I intend to stay looking that way for as long as I can bloody-well stretch it out.

You might very well laugh at me and my actions, but the only reason your laughing is because you don't understand. The point is, I am beyond reproach. I am so far removed from your World that mine defies description, even when it comes down to left or right, up or down, and even right and wrong.

In fact, the lines between what is right and wrong in my life have become such a blur that they have meshed together to form what is now the very ethos of what my life has become to be.

***

Since we've been back from Las Vegas, both Amanda and I have poured ourselves into the preparations for our wedding reception party. We both felt we had to do something for family and friends seeing as we didn't invite anyone to the actual wedding itself.

We're holding it at our local village pub, The Red Lyon, in their marquee out the back in their garden. Hopefully it should be quite a turnout as Amanda has loads of friends and many work colleagues who are all coming, as well as her parents and sister who are flying over from Australia especially.

As you all know, my circle of friends is very limited and that's through my own choice, I didn't even invite my own sister Kate or her dickhead boyfriend Mick. I very much doubt they would have turned up anyway so that's no loss as far as I'm concerned. I want to keep them and my real private life strictly apart.

The only people coming from my side are Rachael and her husband Gary. You might think that it's a bit strange and even sad that I've only invited them and no-one else but that is my want, and my want is the way I like it.

***

I stand before my love and we exchange a cheeky smile. She goes to say something but I stop her with a finger to her lips. I remove her clothes slowly, item by item, until she is completely bare. I rub my breasts and nipples against hers and she is so beautiful that I have to choke-back tears of happiness that are welling-up in my eyes. I lay her down on the soft white duvet on our bed and I kneel beside her and bend down to kiss her lips. I move to her pert left-breast and lick and tongue at her nipple and it reacts to my touch and wetness, making it proud.

Moving down to the foot of the bed I open her legs and glimpse her vagina, so sweet and perfect. I push her legs apart forcefully, beyond their limit, making one of her hip-joints emit a small popping-sound as I do so. Amanda stretches-out her slim tight body as she arches her back and grabs hold of the headboard of the bed tightly with both-hands. I start at her feet - her beautiful feet - sucking her toes alternately and then kissing her souls. I kiss and bite gently at her ankles and calves and then move up to her knees, licking them.

As I make my journey up her legs to her thighs she starts to moan louder and I sense her breathing becoming disjointed. I gaze at her beautiful vulva as it starts to swell under her excitement as I begin to move nearer to it. I kiss her softly either side of it with all my love and she can contain herself no more and cums amid screams and convulsions of her gorgeous body. I sit there staring at her hole as it pulsates its goo in all its glory until I too cannot wait any longer and lick her, making her orgasm wildly as my tongue flicks at her bean. I use my fingers to pull her lips apart, revealing her internal blackness. I try to bury my whole face in her vagina and it feels so glorious that I never want to emerge from its empowering heat.

I lap-away at her until neither of us can take any more and we collapse together prone in each others arms. I never ever thought I could love someone as much as I love Amanda, she is my life and I never want to lose her - she is mine unto death.

We have a nice piping-hot bath together with lots of bubbles, laughter, kissing, touching and fingering. She bites my bum but we don't have any more time for more sex, Amanda's parents Ray and Irene and her little sister Debbie are over here in England for our belated wedding reception and they're due here at the flat for my first meeting with them at lunchtime. The time now is 10.35am.

We pat and rub each other dry with more kissing and fondling and then ready ourselves for our visitors. Today I'm wearing a pale-yellow v-neck cardigan from AliExpress that really shows-off my cleavage, a pair of pale-blue stone-wash jeans from Boohoo and my pair of tan-coloured ankle-boots, also from AliExpress. I'm not wearing any underwear because I don't want to. My perfume is *Mademoiselle* by Coco Chanel. My hair and make-up are done as per usual featuring a very light shade of pink for my lipstick.

Amanda is wearing a lovely lime-green knee-length sleeveless bodycon dress from Wanelo and a pair of tan-suede platform court-shoes from Polyvore. She also isn't wearing any underwear and she looks so beautiful. Her perfume is identical to mine and it is so intoxicating it makes me want to fuck.

We prepare lunch for the 5 of us - cold chicken, pasta, salad, pickles and a large baked potato each - whilst a couple of bottles of white wine chill in the fridge, one German and one Australian.

We both open the front door to our guests - it's 12.55pm - and there are big Australian hugs with a few tears thrown in for good measure all around as we introduce ourselves. I can certainly see where Amanda gets her looks from as her Mum is lovely. And so to is her little sister, I could definitely take her to Heaven!

After some initial banter we all sit down to lunch with Amanda my love and I serve, naturally, as is my want.

They all seem really nice enough but the air is thick for some reason and the conversation soon becomes somewhat strained. Amanda's Father is an archetypal Aussie bloke - tall, thick-set, tanned, and with a grisly face and a blunt manner that I quickly have to put a stop to when he suddenly comes out with:

"So you're a dike as well then are you." He questions me abruptly.

"No, I'm bisexual actually, not that it's got anything to do with you." I stab back at him.

"And just what does that mean?"

"It means I like cock as well as pussy." I say, immediately wiping the know-it-all grin off his stupid face.

"I don't take kindly to being spoken to like that young lady."

"I'll say whatever I like in my own house and if you don't like it you can fuck-off back down-under." I fire back at him.

Amanda interjects our verbal battle and comes and stands by my side. I put my arm around her waist and she responds the same.

"Listen Dad, whether you agree with it or not, Sarah and I are married now and we both love other." She tells him bluntly.

"Love? There's nothing normal about what you're doing and don't I know it. It's not natural, and it's not Australian. Come on you two." He says, gesticulating to both Amanda's Mum and sister to leave.

"We're going back to the hotel, and the sooner we're back in Australia the better. We shouldn't have come to this pissing little Country in the first place."

"Dad please, there's no need for that. Don't forget that both your parents were from England." Amanda snipes at him.

"Yeah, and now I can see why they bloody left. Come on girls, we're outta here."

The 3 of them leave in silence and Amanda slams the front door behind them. We look at each other and both simultaneously burst out laughing.

We hug and kiss and touch each others breasts and caress each other between the legs. We strip each other naked and love and kiss and lick and suck at each others bodies and we orgasm and cum and scream and orgasm and cum.

***

It's the day after the meeting Amanda's parents debacle and we're all meeting up once again for lunch - our second attempt! - at the Crowne Plaza Hotel near Gatwick Airport. It's a lovely place, all very modern and clean and chic but the meeting itself turns out to be another disaster, with Amanda's Father being as pig-headed as they come. Just what is his fucking problem?

Both Amanda and I look absolutely gorgeous - especially me! I'm wearing a little black mini bodycon dress from The Xclusiv Boutique that I barely squeeze into, in fact my tits are more out than in! My underwear is in sexy red lace from Victoria's Secret that makes me feel really horny. On my feet I'm wearing a pair of black suede open-toe platform court-shoes from Polyvore. I've done my make-up a bit on the "trashy" side, featuring coal-black eyeshadow and tons of blusher. I don't care, I know I look fantastic and if other people don't like it then they can fuck themselves.

Amanda - my love and wife - is wearing a pale-blue mini-dress from Poshmark that is super-tight and really shows-off her tight figure. She's also wearing my old pair of Lola platform court-shoes and they really suit her. Her underwear is in white lace from Figleaves and her perfume is as mine - *Luxe* by Avon. Neither of us are wearing tights or stockings as we both have great legs - toned and tanned.

The meeting with Amanda's parents and sister once again ends in complete chaos, with her arrogant pig of a Father saying that we both look like: "A pair of dyke whores." He's right of course, we do, so what?

I really wish that our first face-to-face meetings had gone better. I don't want to fall-out with Amanda's parents but if her Father wants to be an ignorant old tosser then that's his bloody problem, not mine, and after only half-an-hour our ridiculous meeting ends with a fanfare of trumpets and a loud clashing of symbols as we decide to depart and head off home.

Back at our flat Amanda and I shower together and pat each other dry with soft touches of care and love. I lay her down on the bed and push her legs apart as far as they will go and then start flicking my tongue in and out of her vagina. She touches her breasts and squashes them together in wild screams of ecstasy as she orgasms and spits her cum into my face and I love her and drink her juice as I lap-away at her hole.

***

The band that Amanda and I have booked for tonight burst into a cover version of the classic Blondie hit *Denis*. Their singer is a young girl in her early-20's, quite pretty with mousy-brown hair and a nice tight firm body that I'd love to see naked and kiss all over. Her best feature though is her incredible voice, she's absolutely amazing, and kicks-out song after song with power and precision. She really turns me on and her beautiful voice has made me hot for attention.

The evening is in full swing and is already half over. We've had one set from the band earlier along with the buffet, followed by the "Thank-you" speeches from both Amanda and myself. Surprisingly, both Amanda's parents and sister have stayed-on in England and didn't leave as her obnoxious Father had said they would. Apparently they're staying over here for 10-days in total before flying off to Paris for a couple of days and before taking the long trip back home down-under.

I'm dancing centre-stage with Rachael, my old work-friend from that crappy company I last worked for, when she suddenly gives me some fantastic news:

"Have you heard about Joan?" She asks me.

"No, why? What's that old bitch been up to now?" I question her back.

"She's dead. Heart attack."

"You're joking?" I say in amazement.

"No, straight up"

"How come she had a heart attack, she never did any fucking work!" I joke back as we both laugh at her demise and carry-on shaking our things. It's 9.15pm by now and I'm as pissed as a fart and I desperately need to go and get some air or I'm going to pass-out in front of everyone and I don't want that. How embarrassing would that be?

Out in the car-park the atmosphere is cooler, mild and still. I breathe-in the night air to try and sober myself up a bit as I wander around by myself between all the parked cars.

"Are you alright Sarah?" Says Gary, Rachael's husband, who's also out here wandering around for some reason, maybe the same as me, as he suddenly appears from nowhere.

"Yeah, I'm okay. I think I've had too much to drink." I reply.

"Nothing new there then!"

"Hey cheeky!" I smirk back at him.

"I haven't congratulated you on your wedding yet have I?"

"I don't know, haven't you?" I return.

He grabs hold of my waist and pulls me close to him and I sense his strong arms - the arms of a man - and I'd forgotten how powerful and beautiful they they can be after only ever being with another woman for the past year or so. He kisses me on the lips, full-on, and I respond to him with passion as I feel him pressurise against my body. I can't control myself as we kiss and tongue and caress each other up against the side of someone's van. I pull up my dress - the white cotton mini-dress from Shanghai Trends - and wrap my legs around his body as I simultaneously tear at my knickers, a pair of super-sexy Ultimo ones in black lace, as is my bra.

I sense the touch and the heat from his cock on my lips and it feels so beautiful to have a real cock against me and then inside me once again compared to a stupid piece of rubber or plastic, even more so as obviously he's bareback. I open my thighs to him and my internal muscles part willingly to accept his meat into me and I love him as much as he loves me right now. He fondles my breasts and bum as I hold him tight while he bangs-away at me. We French-kiss with lots of moaning and groaning and I pant uncontrollably as he cums and shoots his white muck up and into my love and I sense it connect with me internally. I cum with him and I remember now how much I love cock as I almost pass-out with the sensation of his fuck as he continues to pump-away at me even though he has now spent his load.

We release each other and we laugh nervously at what has just happened. Of course we know that it was wrong - we are both married after all. We both wanted it and there it is, it's not an excuse, it's a straight fact.

We tidy ourselves up the best we can as we try to take control of our emotions before we head back inside to the party. I take the lead and go to re-enter the marquee first, followed by Gary a minute or two later, as I sheepishly attempt not to look guilty in front of everyone - fat chance! A couple of Amanda's work colleagues - both guys and fellow vets - are lurking outside the entrance having a fag. One of them - in his late-20's and quite cute - asks me if: "I'm alright" but I don't answer him and just throw them both a sideways smirk as I pass and go back to the party.

It's just my fucking luck that it's Rachael that's the first person to approach me once I'm back inside the marquee, quizzing me with:

"Have you seen Gary on your travels Sarah?" Bloody typical isn't it, of all the sodding people to bump into it had to be her!

"No, no, I haven't. Maybe he's gone outside for a fag." I reply sheepishly.

"But he doesn't smoke, you know that." She fires straight back at me and I can immediately feel my face turning to stone with embarrassment.

I abandon the situation there and then and head off to the loo in the pub to collect my thoughts and to try to flush myself out if possible. It's all to no avail once again as the toilet is just as crowded as the bar with every cubicle taken.

Why did I let him inside me? I want to scream at myself for being such a stupid bitch but instead I have to put on a false facade of happiness for my collective audience.

I venture back into the throng of the bar in the pub where immediately I come face to face with Amanda - my love - my life-partner, looking as gorgeous as ever. She's wearing a similar dress to mine but her's is from Revolveclothing, her underwear is in sexy red from Victoria's Secret and her shoes being my pair of tan-suede platform open-toe court-shoes from Polyvore.

"There you are! Where have you been? Are you OK?" She shoots at me in her ever cheerful Aussie manner.

"Yeah, I'm fine. You know me? I just needed some space." I say like the bloody lair I am.

"You don't look OK, in fact you look like you've been up to no good."

"What do you mean?"

"Drinking! That's what I mean. What do you think I was talking about silly?"

"Yeah, you're right, as per usual. You caught me."

She comes to me and kisses me full-on. I bloody hope she can't smell Gary on me or even the smell of sex that is still oozing from every pore of my body. Why do I do these fucking things? Why can't I live a normal peaceful life?

The rest of the evening passes reasonably okay considering the fact that I feel both disgusted and ashamed of myself. How many more times must I wrestle with my conscience? Somehow I manage to totally avoid both Rachael and Gary for the remainder of the soiree, I don't think I could look either of them in the face ever again.

What have I gone and fucking done this time? This is going to be a can of worms, I just know it and one day it's going to explode right in my face, I can just see it coming.

***

I hit the shower - alone - as soon as we get through our front door, douching myself as thoroughly as I can. If Amanda doesn't detect that something's up then she must be bloody blind that's for sure? But she doesn't quiz me, she just carries-on with her simple life seemingly without a bloody care in the World. I wonder how she would cope if she were me?

I clean myself out the best I can, squirting the shower head up inside myself and then scrubbing my skin as hard as I dare until I'm red-raw. It's futile - I still feel dirty.

We kiss as we prepare ourselves for bed. I want to go straight to sleep tonight and I tell my love in the nicest and most gentle way I can that I don't feel like sex tonight as my excessive drinking has made me feel ill. She seems okay with my lame excuse and we just kiss and cuddle ourselves to sleep.

How could I let her go down on me knowing that I've just had sex with a guy? It wouldn't be fair and none of it is. Life isn't fair. I'm not fair. I feel like punching myself in the face but I know that wouldn't do any good, I'd still be a stupid bitch at the end of the day.

***

That night I dream a horror nightmare. I am the guilty. It's medieval England and I kneel on stage-right before the baying crowd. I am naked and bound with my hands tied behind my back as the giant masked man pokes me with his sharp pointed stick, pushing me to confess my sin. On stage-left stands the masked executioner, poised to kill at any second. At his feet lay 6 giant tuna fish, all black and shiny-wet. They are beautiful. They are perfection.

I am stabbed in the back but I remain silent and the executioner chops at the first fish, slicing-off the top of its head, exposing its brain. He rips the organ from the animal still alive and I cry tears of terror. There is blood and Hell and all the remaining 5 scream at me for mercy but I don't give in until every poor fish is dead.

It's all my fault and I cry myself to a restless sleep.

4

Free at Last

It's 1.30 in the afternoon - it's Saturday - and Amanda and I have just finished lunch. We both had chicken with fusilli pasta in a spicy tomato sauce with jalapeño peppers and it was lovely. We're just having a chill-out day together, seeing as the other-half has a day off work. We don't actually have anything planned, we're just going to take it as it comes, although we might go into Horsham this afternoon to do a bit of shopping, followed by some love, maybe a film on DVD later along with a nice bottle of wine, followed by more sex.

The door-bell rings and my love goes to answer it as I place both our plates and utensils in the sink, I'll wash them up later as it's not worth filling the sink up just for that small amount of items.

"Sarah honey." Amanda shouts-out to me from the hallway.

"Yeah, what is it?" I answer back.

"It's the Police, they want to speak to you."

"Bloody Hell, what the fuck do they want now?" I say to myself as I head to the front door to find a single officer - a female - standing there with my love on the doorstep.

"Miss Sarah Knowles?" The cop questions me.

"Yes, what is it?" What's happened?"

"May I come in please?"

"I guess so. What's all this about?" I quiz her as I show her in with Amanda shutting the door behind her as I then lead them both into the living room.

"I'm sorry Miss Knowles but I have some bad news for you regarding your Father, John Knowles, is that right?"

"Yes. Why, what's happened?"

"I'm sorry to have to tell you that your Father passed-away during the night. He was discovered deceased in bed this morning by his wife, Mrs. Nuanjan Knowles."

"Oh, I see." I say back to her, obviously a little stunned by the news but at the same time I'm actually quite calm.

"I understand that she's not your natural Mother?" She says, yet more stupid bloody questions.

"That's right, my Mum died last year. She had a heart-attack in the garden." I reply with a sorrowful tone, albeit somewhat fake for whatever reason, although I guess that's just me being me?

"I'm sorry to hear that Miss Knowles." Says the copper, who I think is somewhere in her late-20's at a guess with short brown hair and carrying far too much weight on her thighs and arse. She does have nice boobs though!

"I don't make any apologies for not being overcome with emotion. My so-called "Father" and I hadn't spoken for quite a few years. We didn't exactly have a very good relationship." I inform her.

"Oh right, I see. Well, you have the to right to know what's happened of course. Unfortunately I don't have any other details to give you at present, so I'll leave you to it then." She says bluntly as she turns and starts heading for the door, saying: "Goodbye" to my love as she does so.

"OK then. I'll see you out."

"If there's any more information forthcoming, I'm sure someone will be in touch. I'm sorry to be the bearer of bad news, he was your Father after all." She quips as she leaves.

I slam the door behind her a little harder that I expect, making the whole flat shudder. Bloody sarcastic cow. What the fuck does she know about the old bastard and the way he treated me? He took advantage of me when I was young and vulnerable by tormenting me at every opportunity. And now that he's gone, I've lost my chance at sweet revenge and any hope of patricide.

"Sarah, I'm really sorry about your Dad."

"Amanda don't. I've explained to you my so-called relationship with that old bastard and I'm glad he's gone. I just fucking hope that he died a long lingering painful death in agony that's all, fucking old cunt, he deserved nothing less.

She stands before me in silence, looking a little shocked at my statement. I suddenly feel a strange wave of light pressure reaching out to me, and it feels like I'm being lifted up in the air by a giant cloud of peace, like a burden has been taken from me. Is it actually possible that old shit really is dead? He has to be, yes? This had better not be another one of those sick jokes that the Spirit World has been plaguing me with all my fucking life? If it is then that really is the absolute end of my existence on this fucking rock. I really won't be able to take any more pain and humiliation.

My mind scrambles to retain any sense of rational thinking and starts leaping about inside my skull like a demented rubber-ball. Amanda and I kiss and we hold each other in our arms and her touch is so comforting that I let out a deep-filled sigh - not one of sorrow but of relief, relief that that old bastard is no longer walking on this Earth any more. I don't have anything other than contempt for him. He rejected me, not ever showing me any affection or loving kindness. Probably - to my mind - because I wasn't born male.

I only ever really remember him attempting to try and connect with me just the one time, and that was when his parents Bert and Daisy, both died in quick succession. He came and stood before me with a blank expression across his horrible face. What was he looking for - sympathy? He received nothing from me of course, just a cold icy silence. What did he expect me to do? We had no connection whatsoever. If he expected me to say sorry he was mistaken. Of course I was a little sorry that my estranged paternal Grandparents had died, but I certainly wasn't sorry for him. Love has to go both ways and now I had underlined my stand in his time of need. That's the way it was between us - as cold as ice.

I go and shower - alone once again - to desperately try to wash-away my thoughts. It's no use of course, the events of the past are indelibly etched into my brain and cannot be removed - that fucking bastard will be inside my head for ever more until the very day I die. Fucking old cunt.

He tried to destroy me and I'm still paying the price for it even now he's dead. I know that I've inherited his tortured depressive genes, they're buried deep within me, in my blood and in my soul and there is no escape from them and my life is forever fucked because of it.

***

It's a good hour later before I emerge from the shower, dry my hair and change clothes - nothing special, just jeans and a t-shirt and nothing else. For some reason I look around me and I jump out of my skin when I see a shadow of a man behind me, reflected in the mirror. Who is it? Who can it be? What does he want? Is he going to take me to Heaven of lead me straight to Hell? It is the dead shadow of "Him", the ghost of my past omnipresent in my future.

"Are you okay?" Amanda asks me softly, putting one arm around my waist and pulling me close to her.

"Yeah, I'm okay. It's just that, even though the "Old Man" was a bastard to me and Mum and Kate, he was still biologically my Father. I'm not sure if I'm feeling a sense of loss or what it is? I just can't believe that he's finally gone from my life."

"What do you want to do? Do you want to go out somewhere, for a drive maybe?"

"No, lets crack-open the Champagne. Talking about him will only open a can of worms of horrendous memories so fuck him, lets celebrate his death - the old shit. I'm free at last."

"Are you sure? Don't you want to take it easy a bit?"

"What the Hell for? Amanda he's gone and that's all there is to it. Come on, don't be such a party-pooper, lets get pissed and fool around."

***

I sleep really well that night. It was one of those super-deep sleeps like being in a coma. It wasn't without its problems though. I dreamt of being an old lady in my 80's, stuck in some hospital for whatever reason, sitting on the edge of a trolley in a corridor wearing nothing but a white gown. I was served a potion of death by a Slav nurse but I refused to accept it, knocking the small plastic cup out of the bitch's hand and onto the floor. She screams something at me and I tell her to: "Fuck-off back to Poland" and then the dream is no more - Fucking Hell!

***

The time is now 7.20am and I'm staring out the living-room window of our flat at nothing in particular as I munch-away on a bowl of cornflakes. I need something

to sharpen myself up for later so after finishing my breakfast I have a couple of slugs of gin and then of vodka straight from the bottle, just to give myself a little spike.

There is absolutely no way, or point, that I'm going to dress up for the so-called "meeting" this morning. It's now several weeks later, and last week I received a rather snotty letter from the "Old Man's" solicitor stating that I am required to attend the reading of his Will at their chambers in South London at 10.30 am today. I guess I'll have to go, even though I obviously don't bloody want to, as I just know this is all going to be a complete waste of a days leave from work. It would have been better spent shopping or making love with Amanda - or preferably both! My sister Kate has also been summoned to go, so I'm picking her up at her place on the way there.

By the way, the "Old Man's" funeral was actually held last week, Tuesday I think? And, as you can probably guess from my attitude, I had no intention of going, and I didn't. Kate did attend though, which I also think you've probably worked out for yourself. It was her choice of course, as it was mine not to go. Why the Hell should I have gone after all the fucking shit he put me through over the years? Attending this stupid meeting is going to be bad enough let alone having gone to that farce. Mind you though, I would have loved to have watched him burn in the oven, even though he was already dead. That would have given me some satisfaction at least.

As I say, I'm not tarting myself up for the old fucker, even though he won't be there of course, so I'm just wearing my pale-yellow v-neck cardigan from AliExpress, pale-blue stonewash jeans from Boohoo and my tan-coloured ankle-boots from AliExpress. My underwear is in white lace from Victoria's Secret. My hair and make-up are as per usual - done to perfection - while my perfume today is *Poison* by Christian Dior. Also I'm carrying a beautiful little silver-pearl clutch-bag from Catherine Mee. I don't need anything else.

I arrive at Kate's place on time, but, typical of her, she's not ready, and so I have to wait a good 20-minutes for her to stop faffing-around trying to get my little niece Abigail her breakfast. Quite why her lazy bastard boyfriend Mick can't do it I will never know? He just sits there on his fat arse in his dressing-gown watching crap on the TV with a mug of tea in one hand and a fag in the other. When I begrudgingly say: "Hello" to him all I receive in reply is a grunt - just like the big fat pig he is. You may be wondering why the big slob isn't working? Well, surprisingly he's lost his job - yet again! How many times is that now in the short space of time that I've known him, it must be half-a-dozen at least?

The solicitors chambers is a gloomy old place, it looks like its stuck somewhere in the 1950's with its horrible brown overtones and stacks of paper and files everywhere. Even the computers are straight out of the Arc! Both Kate and I are ushered into the solicitors little office where we're immediately confronted with frozen stares from the "Old Man's" ugly Thai widow - whatever her fucking name is? - along with her evil-looking sons and her equally ugly daughter, all from her previous marriage in Thailand that she brought over to England when she married the old bastard. I don't know why she didn't bring the rest of bloody Thailand over with her as well and have done with it, just like all the other stinking foreigners bloody do?

We both sit ourselves down on the individual wooden chairs in front of the solicitor, a funny-looking old bloke in his 60's with a bald head and little round- framed glasses, as he then starts rattling-on about some sort-of legal crap regarding the Will before telling everyone who gets a cut of what.

The old Thai bitch is - no surprise! - handed the keys to his house along with 50% of his savings. Her horrible offspring - who through the voice of the solicitor the "Old Man" laughingly calls them his "sons" and "daughter"! - are given a lump sum of £15,000 each.

The old guy then turns to Kate and myself and reads on and I can just hear the sound of the "Old Man's" voice emitting from the pages of his Will. It's just like he's actually here in the room with us, his nasty tone whispering into my ears and freaking me out:

"To my dearest daughter Kate Knowles, I leave her the sum of £2,000." Says the solicitor.

"Big fucking deal." I blurt out before everyone. What a fucking insult? It being just typical of the bombastic attitude of that old fucker to give his real daughter 13-grand less than his fake imported one!

Little did I realise though that the best was yet to come - yours truly's startling offering:

"To my other daughter Sarah Knowles, I leave her nothing except the memories of the past."

"What? Are you taking the fucking piss? What do you mean "The memories of the past". What the fuck is that supposed to mean?" I holler at the old bugger as I jump out of my seat to face him.

"Miss Knowles, I have been instructed by your late Father to read his Will, nothing more. I am not privy to the "why's" and "wherefores" of his wishes or their meanings."

"You're having a fucking laugh? What's the fucking point of me being here if he hasn't left me anything?" I scream.

"Miss Knowles, I'm sorry if you're upset by this testament but what is written in your late Father's Will is bound by law and is non-contestable. There is nothing I can do about it. I'm sorry."

"Well, you can fuck the law if that's the way it's going to be, I'm off." I shout at him.

With that, I exit the office and run out of the building, steaming with rage that that old cunt has got to me yet again - even from beyond death. I pace up and down the pavement outside, totally out of my skull - I am mortified. Why does everything have to be a fucking wind-up? Why can't things be straightforward for once in my life? And where the Hell has Kate got to? I notice she hasn't followed me out here. That's just typical of her - Daddies favourite little girl.

I get back in my car and exit the solicitors car-park and piss-off home. She can find her own way back. Bloody spoilt bitch.

***

I don't know how the Hell I made it back to the flat, my mind and vision are a blur of hate and destruction. I want to kill everyone in the World - including Amanda and myself. I will slash out throats so we can die together and drown in the pool of our own blood.

Fortunately Amanda's still at work so she's not here to see me smash myself to pieces. Poor Amanda, what will happen to her when she finds out the truth? What will happen to me when she finds out the truth? I hope and pray to my own personal God that she doesn't.

I guzzle-down virtually a whole bottle of German white straight from the bottle. I am so fucking mad that I actually let myself be taken up the garden-path by something connected with "Him". How could I have been so foolish to have been hood-winked yet again after all these years? Then again, what the Hell was I expecting? That old shit was a born lair and swindler and is still cheating me even now. There was never an atom of remorse, regret or compassion within him even in life let alone death. Not once in all the years did I ever hear him say "sorry" to anyone, not once, not even to Mum when he cheated on her. Spineless bastard.

I haven't been feeling well for a while now and today's stupidity has just made things worse. I sick myself down the toilet and then wash my mouth out with neat Bombay Sapphire gin and gulp-down several slugs of that as well. I follow the gin with my special dear old friend, my ever-faithful vodka, courtesy of Vladivar. The next time I puke I don't even make it to the toilet, razzing all over the living-room sofa and down my chest like a drunken lush.

Why why why am I being persecuted like this? Have I really been so bad in my life that it warrants all this shit?

***

Amanda arrives home at 2.30pm and tries to comfort me but it's fruitless, I've been humiliated beyond comprehension. She kisses me and touches my breasts but I don't want that, I want to be left alone to die in the corner in peace and sorrow for being born me.

The sound of my own voice and thoughts echo in my head. I don't know who I am or what I want. I feel the need to say something but I don't know what. I just don't know what to do. I want to stand up and sit down at the same time but equally I don't want either. My head feels like its spinning around on my shoulders and I can't stop it - no-one can. It's not my fault I come from a broken home. Being "Fatherless" (even when the old bastard was still alive) has given me power, power far greater than the love from any parent. It has given me independence, one of my favourite words.

And so my nightmare life continues. I don't care if you think my troubles are nothing compared to other people's - that's not the point. If you don't like reading the diary of my life, my thoughts, my failings and my failures then you can fuck-off. You can all kiss my pretty arse.

I am nowhere.

I am lost.

***

Two-days ago I received a text message from Kate. Apparently the "Old Man's" solicitor has contacted her - why her and not me? - regarding some personal items of his that the "Old Man's" horrible yellow wife doesn't want, some stuff that she says we can have - isn't that sweet of her! Not that I want any patrimony, I just want to be left in peace as I say.

Anyway, the upshot is that if we want whatever the items are, we have to go around to the "Old Man's" house first thing this morning - Saturday - with the solicitor due to meet us there to discuss what we can take. Great, I can't wait, bring it on!

I'm up at 7am as both Kate and I have to meet the solicitor at 9am. I have toast for breakfast but no tea as I don't want to be having to take a leak at the "Old Man's" crappy house and be forced to use his toilet. That would be way too degrading. Forward thinking is the key.

Once again, I'm not getting all dressed up just to venture into his shit-hole, so I'm keeping my clothes nice and simple. I'm wearing a black v-neck t-shirt from ASOS, pale-blue stonewash jeans from Boohoo and my black suede open-toe platform court-shoes from Polyvore that kill my feet a bit but look super-cool. My underwear is in sexy black lace from Figleaves and my perfume is *Luxe* by Avon. I've done my make-up with everything a couple of shades darker than usual today as that's the way I'm feeling - dark and moody. I just know in my frozen heart that this is not going to go well, not if the Will reading episode was anything to go by anyway.

I arrive at the "Old Man's" house in Hackbridge, Surrey, at 8.50am only to find that both Kate and the solicitor are already here. Not only that, but it turns out that he actually picked her up from her place this morning! Nice, so where's my free fucking lift then? Is there something going on here that I don't know about?

I say a half-hearted: "Morning" to them both and then begrudgingly follow them into the spiders web. Inside the house it's dark and gloomy but the first sensation that hits me is the smell - the horrible stale stench of old people.

The "Old Man's" widow leads us all into the living-room. When I say "living" I only mean that very loosely as the room is old and brown and in a desperate need of redecorating. There's more life on the Moon than there is in here!

The solicitor shows Kate and myself an old brown leather trunk with metal corners that I do somehow vaguely remember from my childhood way back when, positioned on the crappy antique wooden sofa – if you can call it a sofa that is!

According to the yellow Thai widow, all the contents in the trunk are ours to keep if we want it - whoopy-fucking-do!

I open the box to reveal what looks like a load of old junk and both Kate and I start to pick our way through it's contents - tons of old photos from the "Old Man's" time in Germany when he was in the Army, some old school books that belonged to the both Kate and myself, love letters from when he was courting Mum - what the Hell she saw in him in the first place I'll never know? Love is blind as they say, whoever "they" are? There's also loads of knick-knacks and other small ornaments and stuff from years ago when we were all once a "family", and also an old cardboard box sealed with wide brown sticky-tape. It's this item though that catches my eye, as when I remove it from the trunk I quickly notice that it has my name scrawled on its lid in the "Old Man's" handwriting, sending a shiver down my spine like ice. Removing the tape and opening the box I'm horrified by what I see before me - old school photos of me with my face cut out, an old t-shirt of mine from my late-teens that he'd stolen from me, some of my early pieces of jewellery that at the time I had blamed Kate for their disappearance, a couple of girly magazines from when I was in my teens, some old 45-rpm records and some cassettes from the same era and a silver party-dress that I had completely forgotten about from when I was about 4-years old.

Next I discover more - and worryingly worse - an old training-bra of mine from when I was only about 12-years old or so and developing from a girl into a young-woman and also a pair of my old soiled and stained knickers from around the same time - disgusting.

And then there is the real shocker, a black cloth parcel tied at the top with a small piece of string. When I untie it and peer inside, its contents send me reeling backwards in horror. There inside, staring up at me glares the eyeless sockets of a cats severed head, mummified in time. I scream and drop the parcel, quickly realising that the head once belonged to my old cat Blackie, who went missing one day when I was a kid of only about 7-years old or so, nearly 30-years ago now.

Kate grabs the parcel off the floor and takes a look herself, she also emitting a small scream when she too sees the vile object within. Once again that old fucker has nailed me from beyond the grave. I just know this shit is going to go on forever. He will haunt me until my dying day. I will never be truly free.

All this beggars the obvious question - why? What was the point of all this? To teach me some kind-of lesson? What had I ever done to him? Why steal off your own child? What a horrible thing to do. And why kill and decapitate my old cat, what a bastard. There was no need for that, to take the life of an innocent defenceless animal - fucking cunt.

I tell Kate and Mr. Solicitor that I'm leaving. There is nothing for me here and even if there was, I wouldn't want it. I slam the front-door as I leave and race back home into

Amanda's arms, my love. I shower and try to wash the stench of "Him" and his memory away but yet again I am beaten, the smell is infused in my nostrils for the coming days and weeks - possibly forever. Fucking bastard.

***

I suddenly jolt myself awake that night, in fact it's 3am the following morning.

"Hey, are you okay?" Amanda asks me softly, putting one hand on my shoulder as she does so.

"Yeah, I'm okay. I just had the most horrendous dream. I had a car accident and I woke-up in Hospital and both my hands were missing. They had been cut-off in the accident. It was all so real."

"Oh my God, that's horrible. Come on, come here, everything is going to be okay, I promise." She comforts me.

We both snuggle back down together under the warmth of the duvet and hold one another arm-in-arm and kiss. Her reassurance comforts me and it's not long before I drift-away into another deep sleep and another dream, a dream of death to the enemies of my Country and my race with me as some sort-of commander all dressed in black with a whip in hand overlording my ultimate power and will over their useless existences. I watch with joy as I commit their souls to the fire and laugh as they are transformed into smoke and ashes.

***

It's a couple of days later and I've come back down to Planet Earth now with a little more perspective. I still cannot believe that I'm now finally free of "Him",

I feel as though I've just been reborn. His ghost that has hung over me like a vampire has been exorcised. My entire body has been refreshed and I feel so immensely alive that I find it impossible to put into words. All the hate that has existed between us for years has now been extinguished for good. I will never again have to see that old fuckers face staring at me like death or ever hear his bloody condescending voice berating me. It is all over for good.

I honestly never thought he would ever die. Now that he has finally gone he can belittle me no more. On the last day of my existence, I still shall not forgive that bastard for the foul way he treated me. Freedom has been my aspiration since the day I was born and now I have it all.

When poor old Mum died I shed not one single tear. There was none to give. Now though, with the death of the one that appears on my birth certificate as my "Father", I can cry all I want to, cry at being free, cry at being who and what I am. And, as ever, I can do whatever I fucking want.

5

Crash 6

Today I'm wearing a white sleeveless crinkle-effect dress from Polyvore. It was well-expensive but I don't really give a shit about that, I look even more gorgeous than ever before and I feel like the Goddess I know I am. My underwear is from Victoria's Secret in white lace, whilst my shoes are my favourite old pair of blue Lola platform court-shoes that I know are getting-on a bit now and have seen plenty of action but they're still in great condition, and besides, they look super-cool. I'm only taking a clutch-bag with me on my little trip, my silver Greta Deco Shell one from Vintage Styler that is ultra-stylish.

My hair is done in its usual imitable style, as is my make-up, which today features dark-grey eye-shadow, pale-pink lipstick and plenty of blusher - but not too over-the-top - that really accentuates my sharp cheekbones. My perfume is *Kenzo Flower* by Kenzo that I pinched off Amanda this morning - sorry lover!

Once again I'm off to Chichester for the day, which seems to have become a bit of a regular haunt of mine for whatever reason? I'm going there alone as Amanda is working all day today - poor cow! I didn't book the day off work either as I didn't want to use-up any more of my allocated holiday time. They don't give away much - if anything at all really! - so I just take. It's way too nice a day to waste at shitty work anyway, so I phoned-in sick this morning, telling my section supervisor Paula that I had a "personal issue" to deal with - which I haven't obviously! - so they can get stuffed as per fucking usual. I honestly can't believe that they fall for my lies every fucking time!

By the time I've tarted myself up it's just gone 10am as I head out of the village and turn left onto the A29 and head South. There's not too much traffic to speak of, a small number of boring nondescript cars and a few lorries and not much else, so I put my right-foot down hard along the arrow-straight section of road that leads to Billingshurst, tramping-on. The fun I've had with this car is amazing, especially during my little trip to the Lakes a while back. It never ceases to put a smile on my beautiful face.

From there I head to Pulborough, another one of those once medium-sized English towns that has quickly become decimated by a succession of stupid Governments and Councils with their incessant building programs, mainly to cater for the increasing influx if immigrants no doubt. In the town itself I do a sharp-right and then left around the 2-ridiculous mini-roundabouts and then onwards to Bury.

I ignore the stupid speed-limit signs, there's no fucking way that I'm going to do 30mph through this section and so I up my speed to 50 and then 60 just because I can - I don't have time to slow down. Driving, for me, is not just a means of getting from A to B, it's more than that as you well know. It's pure pleasure, the power and the freedom it gives me, being at one with the machine. It is everything - I am a DRIVER. The only thing I don't like though around this area is driving at night, especially around here out in the sticks on these narrow unlit roads that are always seemingly covered in mud and horse-shit. It's like playing Russian Roulette with the other drivers - I hate it.

At the summit of Bury Hill I say: "Hello" to Mum's spirit as I quickly admire the breathtaking view overlooking Amberley to my left. I still miss her terribly, even though she was so bloody annoying sometimes!

Eventually I reach the junction with the A27 and I immediately notice the increase in the volume of traffic. I turn right at the roundabout and head West for Chichester along this fast stretch of road. I feel fantastic as I blast the car along without a care in the World, the power of the engine turning me onto myself and I laugh as I touch 85.

I quickly notice some bastard coming up behind me really fast in a dark grey or black BMW estate - really tanking-on - so I indicate and go to move over into the left-hand lane to let it by me. There's no way I can keep up or even beat the power of that thing so I don't even bother to try.

Suddenly I hear a horrible loud crashing-sound behind me and I feel the rear of my car being pushed around to the right. I try to correct the motion with opposite-lock on the steering but it's no use. I break hard but I spin sideways and then pure terror overwhelms me as I see the shape of a tall grey metal signpost as I head straight for it sideways and I scream. I hear the sickening sound of metal to metal and then metal to bone as I come to a shuddering halt, followed by a sudden moment in time when everything becomes frozen as the car stops with a jolt.

I think my car is on fire but it isn't, it's just the discharge from the airbag in front of me and I immediately begin to feel cold and sick. My brain can't comprehend what has just happened and I just sit there completely numbed by the whole situation. I try to pull myself together but I'm in a daze, I don't know where I am or what I'm doing and I seem to be floating about inside the car somehow - well, at least I think I am?

When I look to my right I notice that the drivers-side door is completely smashed and has been caved-in, so much so in fact that I'm pinned right up against it, although I also notice that the steering-wheel isn't in front of me and that I've somehow been shunted left into the centre of the car, even though I'm still sitting strapped in my seat.

It's when I look down that I see the real horror, my right-hand is facing the wrong way and my arm is severely twisted and oozing a steady stream of thick red blood. And yet I feel no pain, not psychical or emotional - I feel nothing except confusion. I am suspended in time. Am I dead? Is this Heaven?

It is said that your life flashes before you in situations like this and it's true, it does. Time becomes compressed. Every minute becomes a second and my brain overloads with information as it desperately tries to analyse what has happened. I then see flames suddenly shoot out from under the bonnet and start to lick over the cracked windscreen, turning the broken glass black. They are the flickering flames of impending death.

For several minutes I just sit there wondering if I should try to get out of the car or just sit there and let myself die? I have no fear. I long for death. Do I really want to continue living or shall I just end it all here and now? It's my life and I'll die if I want to. The future almost certainly means more pain whereas what will happen if I just let it all go right now? Maybe I'll get some peace at last if I die? Is there something on the other side of life? Is there a Heaven or some kind-of spiritual existence waiting out there for me, I just don't know? I don't know what to do? Please don't let it end like this. Please help me.

"PLEASE HELP ME" I cry out to the guy I suddenly see to the right of me at my mangled car door as he frantically tries to pull it open but fails.

I cannot comprehend what it is I'm seeing. Is it real? Am I dreaming? I sense that there's someone to my left and I turn my head to face a fellow human. There is some old guy there of about 50 with slicked-back hair and a soft voice right next to me but I can't understand what he's saying, everything is muffled. He starts to pull at my seatbelt but it won't come unclipped and I see him put his hand on my arm - my left one - but I'm unable to detect his touch.

Suddenly he's gone and is instantly replaced by someone else, another guy, wearing a black uniform and talking silent words to me. I just stare at him in bewilderment. There is not a single sound in the whole World. What is going on? He leans forward to me and I think he's about to kiss me but no, he touches my neck and then I feel the rigid plastic of the neck-brace as he clips it in place.

I then sense the breaking of glass around me, I know the windscreen was already smashed as I noticed that when I came to a halt, as is the glass in the drivers-door as that has shattered its splintered remains all over my dress and my legs - my beautiful gorgeous legs. I feel a horrible sense of smothering as something is placed over my face - it's an oxygen-mask but I don't know that. I shout at my Guardian Angel:

"WHAT DO YOU WANT OF ME ?" as suddenly the whole sky is lit-up and I'm surrounded by a brilliant burst of sunlight that burns my eyes. I guess this must be Heaven or have I actually ended up in Hell just as everyone predicted, even myself?

It's neither of course, as the emergency crew lift-off the severed roof of my precious car. I then feel lots of tugging and pulling at my body and a strange sensation like I'm bleeding inside. What the fuck are they doing to me? Are they dissecting me or raping me or what?

"PLEASE DON'T CUT OFF MY BEAUTIFUL LEGS. PLEASE NO. LEAVE ME ALONE" I scream at them.

I'm lifted up in the air by what seems like the giant hand of God but I know that can't be true - there is no fucking God. I'm then brought back down to Earth again and I hear voices and sirens and then nothing as the Sun is switched-off before my very eyes.

***

The first thing I remember is opening my eyes and seeing the white of the ceiling above me and then sensing some horrible smell, like some crappy detergent or cleaning fluid or something like that.

I look to the right and then the left of me and can only see beige-coloured walls. A stream of sunlight blinds me when I look down towards my feet as I then notice the thick bandage covering my lower right-arm. The lower half of my body - my belly area - also feels strange, like I've been kicked in the stomach or something, and I try to think to myself what the Hell has happened to me this time?

I manage to manoeuvre myself up one-handed to try and regain some sort-of better orientation of my surroundings and I'm guessing I must be in Hospital. My powers of observation never cease to amaze me!

At that moment the door to the left of me opens and in-walks Amanda with a horrible worried look across her face - it's also obvious that she's been crying - and a short, fat Asian guy in a white coat who I brilliantly deduce is a Doctor.

"Oh Sarah you're awake, I thought I'd lost you my darling." Amanda says tearfully as she lunges at me and wraps her arms around my neck and we kiss full-on, albeit lightly due to my condition.

"Hello Miss Knowles, I am Doctor Patel, how are you feeling?"

"OK I guess? What's happened to me? Where am I?" I question him.

"You're in St. Richard's Hospital in Chichester. You were unconscious when they brought you in. You are lucky to be alive. You have suffered a nasty car accident but it could have been worse. You have broken your right-arm quite badly. We had to operate and insert a plate along the bone to secure it. It is only small so there should not be much scaring." He cheerfully informs me.

"How long before I can get out of here?" I ask.

"I want to keep you in for at least 2-more nights and then you can go home. Unfortunately I also have some bad news for you both."

"Why? What is it? Is there something else wrong? Don't tell me I'm crippled, anything but that." I say with dread in my voice and concern written all over my face, just as Amanda has. As I say this I know I'm talking crap, I can move my legs and toes just fine. I don't even know why I said it?

"No, it is nothing like that I can assure you. Unfortunately you have lost your baby in the accident. You had suffered a miscarriage when they brought you into Hospital. I'm very sorry."

"WHAT DO YOU FUCKING MEAN "BABY" ?" Shouts Amanda at the Doctor.

"BABY! I'M NOT PREGNANT!" I also jab back at him.

"You did not know? You where pregnant Miss Knowles. I estimate about 6 to 8-weeks." He tells me.

I instantly feel all the blood drain from my face as questions and accusations fly about in the air around me. I become detached from it all as the true realisation of my predicament hits home - that it's Gary's baby - Rachael's husband - on the night of the wedding party - out in the car-park - up against the side of the van.

So that's why my periods have gone awol. That's why I've been feeling like shit. That's why I've got this ache in my body. I've really fucking fucked things up this time. Fucking Hell what have I done, I just don't fucking believe it?

"But you can't have been pregnant, it's not possible?" Exclaims Amanda - my partner, my lover, my friend and saviour. My wife.

I sit there like the total and complete bitch that I am, covering my eyes with the hand from my one good arm. Amanda reads my face and my reaction as then all Hell breaks loose about me.

"SARAH NO. THIS CAN'T BE HAPPENING. WHAT HAVE YOU DONE?" She screams at me and I deserve it. I deserve it more and more with each passing second.

"I'm sorry. I really am. I didn't mean for it to happen, it just did." I whine pathetically.

"You stupid fucking bitch. You've fucking ruined everything. What the fuck is wrong with you?" She tears into me.

"I don't know? What do you want me to say?" I whine again.

"Who was it? Come on, tell me. Who's the Father?"

"It was Gary, Rachael's husband." I bleat back at her like a sheep.

"Rachael's husband! I don't believe it! But she's pregnant herself. She's only got a couple of months to go before gives birth! How the fuck could you? You've fucking ruined everything. How long has this been going on?"

"It's not like that. It was just the once. I'm sorry Amanda, I really am."

Without another word Amanda turns on her heals and runs out the door in tears and in total devastation, leaving me sitting here like the complete arsehole that I am. The Paki Doctor makes his excuses and also leaves and I sit there and sob my lonely tears of regret to myself.

I've really gone and done it now. I really have dropped myself in the shit. I just knew all this would come tumbling down about me. And all for a quick poke, and with someone I don't even really like that much. How the Hell am I going to fix this one?

I know Amanda will never forgive me so what can I do about it? I've destroyed the one person who loves me and believes in me and I'm ashamed of myself even though I'm not. So where do I go from here?

I know I'm cold. My life is cold. All my relationships are cold, on the inside anyway. That is my life.

Why am I so fucking stupid?

***

I didn't get much sleep last night, if hardly at all. The cracks in my psyche are even wider now than they were before. This is the jigsaw-puzzle that is my life, at the end of each and every episode there is always one piece missing. There's a knock at the door and in-walks some foreigner - another Asian - another Paki - a woman - who I guess has come to check-up on me as I notice she has a white Doctor's coat on and a clip-board in hand. She starts fannying-around with my notes and heads towards my bedside cabinet and then suddenly makes a beeline for my watch - my old Russian one that was a birthday present from Mum. I stop her in her tracks as I suddenly turn and snap at her:

"If you lay one-finger on my watch I'll fucking kill you."

"Sorry, sorry, sorry." She bleats back at me, just like they all bloody do. Fucking bitch.

She looks at me like I'm dirt and I stare the fucker out and I want to kill her right here and now. She turns and pisses-off out of my room to leave me alone to contemplate the awful bloody mess I've landed myself in. I lay there thinking about Amanda and how I've hurt her so badly. It's not my fault I'm so hard-hearted, it's just the way I've evolved over the years.

I don't care if you think I'm artificial or deceitful or even a little bit mental, it's meaningless as far as I'm concerned. The path I'm following is my own and no-one else's. I know I'm shallow but I have my ideals. I make my own decisions and ultimately depend on no-one.

I don't know which loss has hurt me more, Amanda or the car? My beautiful car was part of me and I was part of it. We shared the same DNA. If your not a real driver then you will never understand. It was more than just a car, it was an extension of myself, my very being, my soul, my freedom. And now it's been totally destroyed by some bastard.

My tormented mind wanders back in time to memories of the "Old Man" again - I don't know why, I just can't control it. I remember my very first car accident - I've had 6 now, and not all them were my fault - when I hit someone, some old guy driving some old piece of crap, up the arse at a roundabout on the A3 in South London. The damage was only minor to both cars, one of his tail-lights and one of my headlights, so there was no real harm done. When I got to my parents house - I'd actually left home by then and was just visiting - Mum was naturally very concerned if I was alright, as Mum's are and do. But the "Old Man"?

He didn't even get out of his armchair. He wasn't in the least bit interested.

Do you see what I had to put up with? Is it any wonder I'm a damaged soul? What if I had had a nasty accident and been killed, would he have got off his arse then? Don't bet on it - bastard.

So what about this latest crash? Was that just misfortune or fate or whatever? Or maybe my Guardian Angel is actually trying to kill me? And the baby? My baby? Was it fate that I got pregnant? Was it fate that I lost it? I just don't fucking know any more.

* * *

Kate's picking me up from the Hospital any minute now, and for once in his life that lazy git Mick has actually got off his arse and is looking after baby Abigail, now there's a first! I had a quick chat with the consultant this morning and he's okay to release me and let me go home. I really can't wait to get out of here, the claustrophobia is driving me insane.

I really must try and stay off the drink for a while also, it'll only make things worse. Even though I've had a brain-scan and other tests and everything has checked out okay, I still don't feel particularly great - I guess it must be some form of shock or concussion. Either way, the Doctors have given me the all-clear to leave.

Amazingly Kate's actually on time - wonders will never cease! - and has also brought me a change of clothes from my place as the gorgeous white dress I was wearing at the time of the crash was splattered with my very own special red juice and was ruined.

The conversation between us in the car on the journey back to mine is strained to say the least, we really don't have anything to say to one another, and when I do try to initiate a conversation between us it's like getting blood out of a stone.

We've never really had much in common from day-one anyway - only our parents - and since I hooked-up with Amanda the communication has gotten even colder.

It's 11.20am by the time I get back home, home to an empty flat as Amanda has obviously moved all her stuff out already and is staying with one of her vet colleagues. And who can blame her? I've treated her appallingly and I should be ashamed of myself. But do know what? I'm not.

Kate has to get back home straight away and so we say our "Goodbyes" and go our separate ways. I close the front-door behind her and breathe a sigh of relief, relief in the fact that I'm actually still in the land of the living. To be honest, I'm lucky not to have been more seriously injured. I guess my willpower has chosen life? I've really dodged a bullet on this one. Having said that though, broken bones can be screwed back together, broken minds can't. My life has been torn to pieces.

Why does it always take a bloody disaster to put everything into perspective? I never once thought I was pregnant. Can you really imagine me with a sprog, an unmarried mother at my age? My life would never have been the same again. Bang would go my freedom for a start. Even the very idea of having a kid leaves me cold as I have absolutely no maternal instincts at all. There is no bloody way I'm ever having a kid and that's all there is to it. I guess I would have had a go at maintaining my filial duty to the child if it had survived, although I'm not sure what the result would have been? One can never know these things until you try them. At least I know that I'm fertile and I have the power to produce life, but so what?

And my freedom? I've lost that for the time being anyway with the loss of my beautiful car - my poor little Fiesta. Having my car taken away from me is too much. Losing her feels just a bad as when Lacey died. A part of me has died also. I will kill the bastard that took it from me. I am heartbroken beyond description.

In a cruel twist of fate, the very next day after returning home, I decided to take a short plod around the corner to the small local village shop to get a newspaper. Now, what type of car do you reckon was parked outside the pub opposite the shop? Yeah, that's right - a white Fiesta ST, exactly identical as mine, even the very same year. That really is taking the piss. Talk about rubbing salt into the wound.

***

Several weeks have past by now since my accident and nothing and everything has changed. Obviously I'm not working at the moment, as I've been signed-off sick for the next 6-weeks, although I still have to go back to the Hospital for physio to my arm twice a week for the next 2-months. What a pain in the arse that is going to be.

My head is a bit more back to normal now. I had real trouble trying to concentrate on anything at first, even doing my shoelaces up was a struggle at times, I'd actually forgotten how to do it! I was also doing other weird things like pouring hot water over my cornflakes in the morning instead of into my mug of tea! I was a complete mental and emotional wreck.

I'm not so bad now though fortunately, although I know I'm not the same person that I was before the accident - I know, I can sense the change in me. When things like that happen it gives you a sense of your own mortality. I do actually believe that I'm even more alienated from the World and everyone than I was before.

The past few weeks have been a bloody nightmare, not only with the crash but the pregnancy as well, and then having to deal with the aftermath. I now realise my mind must be way-stronger than I ever imagined as I honestly don't know how I've coped with it all? Having said that it was me that got myself into this situation in the first place by allowing myself to get knocked-up from some cheap liaison, so I only have myself to blame - once again. I guess it's just not in my nature to remain faithful? When I'm with another woman this sort of thing can't happen of course, but I really need a man in my life as well so I'll have to take better precautions in the future when I'm fucking a guy - or guys!

Once again though I find myself withdrawing into myself. I've decided that I'm going to cut myself off from the World even more severely than I did before the crash - back before I hooked-up with Amanda - back to the state I was in after Lacey's death. I'm going to destroy myself and everyone around me. No prisoners will be taken.

***

I received the payout cheque for the car today from my insurance company. After much wrangling and a couple of stiff letters to them - they don't do Emails for some strange reason? - they've finally sent the money through. Even though the car was valued at £7,500, wouldn't you just know it, I only got £6,500 from them - bastards!

It also turns out that the driver of the car that hit me was another woman - bloody bitch. Not only that, but she was also found to be on drugs - and I'm not talking about Paracetamol's here, I mean REAL drugs, the hard stuff, the Class A shit. She also had her 2-young kids in the back of the car at the time as well - how fucking stupid is that? I know that I've done a lot of crazy things myself in the past but that really is stupid. Fucking junkie bitch.

And so here we are. I guess the next logical thing for me to do is to try and get myself another car?

6

Orange

I really have to get my arse in gear and get myself another car, I miss my little Fiesta ST so much you wouldn't believe. No-one will ever understand how much losing her has hurt me. I'm also so glad I didn't see her all smashed-up and broken though, that would have been too much to take. It would have been like having my heart ripped out.

Having said all that, I've actually decided not to go for another one. Although she was great fun and was reasonably quick, I want something a bit faster this time around, something that looks the part and suits my image and personality even more than she did, something a bit different.

It's taken me hours to trawl through the internet looking for a car that fits the bill. There's plenty on here that come close to what I'm after - Honda Civic Type R, Subaru Impreza WRS, Mitsubishi Evo, Nissan Skyline and all that stuff, but I don't really like Japanese cars that much. I'm certainly not interested in a BMW either, I'm not driving around in Black-Man's-Wheels! I've always found French cars a bit weird so they're also out. I can't afford a Porsche or anything flash like that so there's no point in going down that road either. I have to find something with a bit of poke to it as well as I don't see why I should drive around in a piece of crap just because of someone else's incompetence - the stupid junkie bitch that hit me I mean.

In the end I try a dedicated nationwide auto search engine site that someone at work suggested. There are literally thousands of cars for sale on here, both private and trade sales, so I must be able to find something amongst that lot?

Eventually I stumble upon a crazy-looking beast in bright orange that when I think about it, was right under my nose all along, having seen a couple of them locally tearing around town. The car is the logical next step-up from my poor old Fiesta, it being a Ford Focus ST-2 Turbo. One of the cars advertised that I really fancy though is bloody miles from me in Nottingham, which is a good 3-hours drive away from here. Or at least it would have been if I had a car to get there! There are plenty of similar cars on this site but none that are equal to this one, they've either got too much mileage on the clock or are too expensive. This one though is perfect, it's even been chipped and remapped - whatever that means? - to over 300-horsepower and I just can't resist it. I have to have it. I want it.

I ring the dealer straight away and make an appointment with the guy there - Dave - to go and have a look at the car first thing tomorrow morning. I guess I'll have to get the bloody train there, and that's going to be a laugh in itself - not!

***

The following morning I'm up at the crack of dawn both in anticipation of getting another car - possibly anyway, I really hope that it's not a dog? - plus of course I have to catch an early train, and that means getting a cab to the station. I just know I've got an extremely long day ahead of me - oh well!

As the weather report is for a bright and reasonably warm sunny day, I'm dressing quite light. I'm wearing my pale-yellow v-neck cardigan - with the sleeves scrunched up - from AliExpress, a pair of white denim jeans from H&M that really show-off the curves of my hips and my bum, not to mention my long slender legs, and a pair of grey suede ankle-boots from Ophelia that look gorgeous on me - no surprise there then! My underwear is in red lace from Figleaves and is super-sexy and turns me on all by itself just because I know I have it on underneath. My clutch-bag is a classy white leather one from Swankyswans that is typical of my style and contains only my essentials - mobile phone, £300 in cash, debit cards, house keys, driving licence, the previous car insurance certificate for my poor old Fiesta ST, a packet of mints, a small packet of wipes, a compact, lipstick, and a few other odds and ends.

The cab to the station was fairly painless. The driver was a big fat bloke with multiple chins who couldn't keep his eyes off of looking at my tits and on the road - typical! The cost of the cab fare was one thing but I can't believe the extortionate bloody price of the train ticket when I only ask for a single to Nottingham - 80-bloody-quid! It probably would have been cheaper to get the fat cabbie to drive all the bloody way there!

My carriage is thankfully reasonably free from hoards of other passengers, this cheering me up no-end as I don't like being hemmed-in by crowds of strangers all brushing themselves up against my person and spreading their germs about.

Once underway we tear-along unhindered. It's been absolutely years since I've been anywhere by overground train, in fact when I try to remember I think I was actually still at school so that must be nearly 20-years ago now! It's almost as long as the last time I visited Nottingham, and that must be over 25-years ago when as a "Family" we all went up there to visit the "Old Man's" parents who had moved there when I was really young. In all I think I only ever met them about half-a-dozen times in my life anyway, I can't even remember what they looked like. Funny things arn't they, families, memories, and all that old shit?

I watch my England wizz by my window like a movie on fast-forward. What a beautiful country it is. And it still is of course, despite the efforts of the Politicians and the Left as they continue to fuck it up the arse and letting it rot without a care. I dream the rest of my journey away as the train-wheels clip-away to themselves and it's actually quite a nice experience being hurried-along the tracks without having to be on the constant lookout for idiots trying to crash into me.

After a journey of nearly 4-bloody-hours the train finally pulls-in to Nottingham Station. I have to say that I've actually quite enjoyed my trip, so much so that I really must do something like this again in the near future. I catch a cab to the dealers place - this time the driver being a stinking Paki, and he really does bloody stink! - a distance of only about 20-minutes or so away.

The selection of cars at the dealership is really impressive, all mainly top-end stuff - Mercedes, Jaguars, Porsche, Aston Martin's and such. Parked virtually in the middle of the pack though I soon spot my prey - actually it's difficult not to miss it! - and it's both crazy-looking and beautiful at the same time. Dave - the owner of the garage - greets me with a big: "Hello" in his local Northern accent. I see him quickly eye me up and down and hear his wicked thoughts ricocheting around inside his skull as he tries to take in the vision of my stunning beauty. I suppose he must be in his late-50's, a bit rugged around the edges and definitely not my type, although he seems nice enough.

"Hi, I'm Sarah. I've come to see the orange ST. We spoke yesterday." I say smiling.

"Yeah, sure, right." He stumbles his words as he tries to comprehend what his eyes are telling his brain. I can even see his Adams-apple moving up and down as he gulps - poor sod! I don't think he's seen anyone quite like me?

We have some idle chitchat about cars and stuff and I tell him about my accident with the poor old Fiesta and how my arm was damaged - although thankfully that's now pretty-much on the mend - as he shows me around the car. It's surprising how big it actually is - low, wide and mean - and very orange! When he fires-up the engine it bursts into life with a deep, throaty roar from the twin-exhausts and I think I'm in love with it already - it sounds as amazing as it looks. Inside is just the same, even the front Ricaro bucket-seats and the rear seats are partially orange!

He says I can take the car out for a test-drive - on my own - and instructs me to keep turning-left around the block as that will bring me right back to square-one again in a full-circle. He sticks one of his trade-plates to the inside of the windscreen for insurance purposes, shuts the passenger door and lets me go - so here we go then! I manoeuvre the 6-speed gearbox into first and pull-out and away from the forecourt. I give the gas-pedal a stab and the car screams off down the road like something demented, it's so bloody quick that I literally have to hang on to her to keep her steady - fucking wow! I take it relatively easy for the rest of the test as I traverse the unknown roads around and back to the dealer, although I do give it a few blasts of right-foot now and then - it would be rude not to! The massive grin I have across my face when I pull-up back on the forecourt just about says it all really - I want!

I try to talk shop with owner Dave back in his office about the car as I work my way through the car's paperwork, looking for signs of past trouble and old bills and stuff, but surprisingly all he seems to want to know is personal stuff about me - like if I'm married? Any kids? Boyfriend? My job? Interests?

I wonder what his reaction would be if I told him that one of my pleasures was sticking my tongue into another woman's vagina? He'd probably have a heart-attack right there and then - poor old bugger!

With the car's details and my body both fully checked-out, we strike-up a deal - after a bit of friendly haggling of course! - and shake on the sale. She is mine - bloody Hell!

After a bit more friendly banter and yet more breast-gorping, we shake hands once more and I prepare myself for the long drive home in a strange car. I ring my insurance company quickly to give them the details of my new acquisition and pay them the increased difference on my debit-card. Surprisingly it's not that much more than the Fiesta, only £150 - result! We say our "Goodbyes" and "Thank you's" and Dave wishes me: "A safe journey back home Sarah". I bet that's not all he bloody wishes!

I head-off and make my way first to the petrol station up the road to gas-up and get myself something light for lunch also. I fill the tank to the brim, swipe a spicy chicken wrap thing and a

Coke off the shelf in the shop, pay the smelly Butt-Butt-Ding-Ding manning the counter in cash - I don't trust those bastards with my card - and then hit the road.

After traversing around town for a while - and getting lost twice! - I soon find my way out and onto the A52 and then the A1 and head home South, giving the car some beans as I do so. The miles are eaten-up quickly, as is the time, as I roar along - what a weapon of a car this is?

I didn't tell my insurance company that the car had been modified you understand, they would either have thrown the book at me or put the bloody phone down if I had! I always seem to have to bend the rules in order to survive. I wonder if other people have to do the same thing? Do you, or are you all too innocent and straight?

The colour of the car seems to be attracting lots of attention from my fellow motorists as I cruse-along at a steady 80mph, from the guys who look at her and then notice your gorgeous narrator driving it, and also the women who stare at both of us with green-eyes of jealousy, burning like daggers. Although I'm minding my own business doing said speed in the middle-lane of the motorway, I soon notice a woman and her female friend in what I think is a crappy blue Vauxhall Zafira people-carrier thing, hurtling-up behind me in my rear-view mirror. I can't bloody believe this, not this shit again, as my mind flashes back to the time of the accident - Crash 6 that is. I put my foot down a bit harder and the car increases to 90 but the silly cow behind me still closes up even more. I decide to play her at her own game and let her come alongside me in the fast lane. She takes the bait and drives along by my side and I notice that the 2-women inside the Vauxhall are not as young as I suspected they were, but are a couple of old-bags in their 50's, yacking-away at ten-to-the-dozen. Once they're completely alongside I plant my right-foot down hard on the accelerator and the car growls deeply as it takes-off like a bloody rocket. I leave the shitty Vauxhall for dead in a couple of seconds and as I glance down at the speedo I see that I'm already doing 135 and its still accelerating hard with a whining howl from the turbocharger. Just how fast can this bloody thing go?

I keep pushing-on as I want to test my nerve as much as test the car, the needle now just over 150. I back-off quickly as the traffic ahead starts to loom nearer and nearer, plus of course I don't want to get nicked by the fucking traffic cops or even blow the car up on our very first day together!

I hit the M25 soon enough and then turn left and head for the Queen Elizabeth 11 bridge at Dartford. The traffic is quite slow when I get there so I decide to have my lunch and a drink as I creep-along at the snails-pace of 30mph. I've never really liked going over this bridge, I always get this horrible feeling that its about to collapse and I will plunge to my death below - weird!

Down the other side of the bridge the traffic clears as it fans-out and I can put my foot down once more, keeping it steady between 80 and 90.

***

I sail-along nicely as there are no-more hold-ups and so it's not long before I reach my exit at Junction-9 at Leatherhead, the drive having taken me nearly 3-hours already. On the A24 I pass through Dorking and head further South, travelling through Beare Green, Kingsfold and Warnham where I head for Horsham, as I need to stop-off at the supermarket to a bit of food shopping.

I park-up in their car-park with no problem, that is until I spot the dreaded Slav car-washers eye-balling both me and the car, waiting to pounce as soon as I extract myself from my seat. I wave them off with a single shake of my hand and head, I don't even want to look at them let alone converse - bloody scum.

I grab one of the smaller shallow trolleys from the rack - I can't stand the bigger deeper ones, even when I've got a lot of stuff to get - and make my way to the automatic entrance doors. I only make it about half-way though when my path is suddenly blocked by another shopper coming in the opposite direction - a black, the enemy of my race - with repulsive skin the colour of the darkest night sky, massive rubber-lips and pasta hair. I'm certainly not going to get out of the way for the likes of one of them and seemingly neither is he as our respective trolleys crash into each other head-on. He glares at me with his horrible dead black eyes, obviously expecting me to move out of his way. There's no fucking chance - BOY.

"Well? Out of my way." I say to the "Jig" in a curt tone.

"Why should I move? What don't you move?" He comes back.

"You know why. And don't try appealing to my better nature because I haven't got one." I retort, as I stand my ground. And I really do mean MY ground. This stupid stalemate continues for a good 30-seconds or so until he eventually - obviously - has to back-down, and so moves out of my fucking way. Fucking Zulu. At least my skin isn't the same colour as my shit. Black cunt.

Once inside the store I pass by a line of smokers all queueing up to get their fix from their dirty fags. I look at them with disgust, fucking stinking junkies polluting my air. It's fucking typical isn't it? They put the bloody fag-counter right at the front of the shop but if someone elderly and infirm needs a prescription they have to hike all the way to the back of the supermarket to get it! Why is everything back to front?

I strut my stuff in my usual way as I collect things into my trolley - a small box of sushi, the latest copy of *Skin Deep* magazine, a bag of *Pink Lady* apples, a small broccoli, a beautiful piece of fillet-steak, tampons, condoms, 2-boxes of Paracetamol, bangers, a couple of ready-meal curries - one chicken phall and the other a chicken vindaloo - both with pilau rice, a 2-pint carton of milk, several tins of soup, a jar of mango chutney, a loaf of bread, a bottle of vodka (Vladiva of course), 3-bottles of lager (San Miguel), a bottle of gin (Bombay Sapphire), cornflakes (Frosties), frozen fishcakes, burgers, a jar of picked shallots, and some peach-scented bubble-bath.

As I do all this I have to traverse all the other shoppers getting their individual items as well. The vast majority of them all appear to be in a World of their own, probably just as I am I suppose? It's just like being out on the road in here, trying to avoid the idiots who can't fucking drive, as occasionally one of them swipes into me with their trolley without looking where their bloody going. The worst lot are the coffin-dodgers, the nearly-dead's, the silly old buggers who wander around half fucking blind procrastinating for half-an-hour over each and every item and not looking where they're going. I can spot them a bloody mile-off, with their signature brown shoes, their universal old-fashioned coats - even in the height of Summer! - and their trademark "snow on the roof" grey hair. And it always seems to be the old woman that takes the lead all the time, closely followed by their dithering old husbands, all desperately trying in vein to steer their trolleys in the right direction - without much success obviously!

As I unload all my bits and pieces onto the conveyor-belt at the checkout, I suddenly realise that the old girl on the till is one that I've encountered a few times before, yet another stupid old cow that doesn't bloody listen to a fucking word I say. She's completely forgotten my cashback money the last 2-times I've had her, so this time I'm really on my guard. Even though it's been a long and tiring day, I'm not going to allow any slip-ups.

Amazingly, I find myself stuck behind more old duffers in front of me in the queue, arguing between themselves as to which items they should put in which bag! Here we go again, 10-minutes to do my shopping and half-an-hour to pay for it!

The old-bag on the till says a begrudging "Hello" to me as I step-up to the plate but I don't reply. I bag-up my items as she scans them all through, loading everything into 2-carrier bags. I ask her firmly but politely for £50 cashback and she acknowledges me with a small nod. But do I receive my money - do I fuck?

"Where's my money?" I fire at her as she hands me just my till receipt.

"Oh sorry, did you want cashback?" The gormless old bitch replies.

"Yes, £50 I said."

"Oh sorry love. There's an ATM machine outside." She then informs me feebly.

"You're fucking unbelievable. This is the third time in a row now you've done this to me." I curse at her as I also curse at myself for not spotting her before I started loading my stuff onto the conveyor in the first place - damn it!

She sits there looking at me with an empty expression across her face that I just want to punch - senile old cow. There's no point in continuing with the stand-off of course so I turn and leave and head outside to the ATM, carrying both bags with my left-arm as the weight of all my shopping would be too much for my injured right-arm to take, which is still not 100% fit.

As I exit the store, there are a couple of charity scroungers outside, shaking their bloody collection-tins at me for money - to no avail on my part! Heading back to the car after collecting my money I notice another couple of old-fogies trying to park their little car in a small space between 2-others. The silly old git driving is revving the guts out of his poor car as its engine screams its head off and the clutch whines-away in mercy of its abuse. The old tosser shouldn't be on the bloody road in the first place, he must be 120-years old if he's a day! He can't even turn his head let alone see where he's going! It's so excruciating to watch I just have to walk away in disbelief.

I pass a mother and her screaming kid as she tries to settle it down in its pushchair after removing it from the rear-mounted baby-seat of her 4x4. When I look closer though, I notice the kid isn't a baby at all but a sick-looking retarded flid, dribbling and spluttering and wailing its fucking head-off to itself, trapped in its own deformed and distorted World. I can't bare to look at its ugliness and I just want to kill it, to smother its horrible screaming face until I put it out of its misery in the ultimate act of euthanasia. It is one of the worst fucking noises in the World. I hate it.

Back at my new car I unload my bags into the tailgate and think about the girl with the cripple. She looks younger than me - probably in her late-20's - and her life is in ruins already. How does she cope having to deal with that waste of human life all fucking day, every day? She's lumbered with that burden on society for the rest of its days. There is no-way on Earth that I could do what she's doing and I genuinely feel sorry for her. But then again, if you want and have kids then you have to expect the occasional reject - that's life. She should have got ridden of it when she had the chance.

I count my lucky-stars for being the way I am - young, beautiful, intelligent, free and childless.

I fire the car up and head out of the car-park and home. I pass the girl with the handicapped kid and she turns and looks at me and my orange bomber as I burble past her, both of us wondering what the other is thinking? I also pass the old-codgers car and notice that it's parked completely skew-whiff in it's space. What can you do?

* * *

It's only a 15-minute drive back to my flat - even less now in my new baby! - so it's not long before I'm home after this bloody really long and eventful day, it now being almost 6pm, and I could really murder a drink.

When I round the corner of my road though I find that some bastard has parked in my fucking parking space, not only that but when I get nearer to the big white box-van, I notice the thing has fucking Bulgarian number-plates on it! I just don't fucking believe it, are these cunts following me around the fucking country or what? My heart sinks and I almost cry. This cannot fucking be happening?

I don't block them in as I know this will cause even more problems and I don't want to have to deal with them in any shape or form. These scum are worse than animals and would rape and kill me at the drop of a hat. Even if I put a brick through their windscreen they would still know that it was me that did it as my car would be back in its rightful spot the following day, so they'll easily be able to get me - even they're not THAT bloody stupid? Also, there's no point in ringing the useless bloody Police either, they won't do anything about them, they'll only be accused of being racist and so they don't bother and just ignore them. The fucking Government just lets this scum into the country and let them do whatever they fucking like. They even dish-out passports to all and sundry and then brand them as British - madness! Am I the only person with eyes in this fucking country? We have become the laughing-stock of the whole World. It's just like everything else, nothing is ever sorted out properly, it's all bodged. There's no decisive action done by anyone, with successive Governments being no better than the one before.

The Slavs don't want to give anything to us, all they want is to take, like the fucking parasites they are. I have no answer, apart from gassing them all and unfortunately that's not going to happen, not in my lifetime or the next. I'm so Far-Right that sometimes I think I've fallen off the edge! I can't keep moving further South to avoid them either as before long I will end up in the bloody sea!

Just what has happened to my beautiful England, my country and love?

***

I'm determined not to let those fucking Slav bastards ruin my day. All the excitement of the day's events has left me drained and all I want to do now is just chill-out in peace. I pack-away all my shopping in their respective places, have a quick shower, just putting on my black mini-robe from LadySilk, and then do something for dinner. I'm having the steak I bought earlier along with chips, the broccoli, and some fried-onions. I down a bottle of pre-chilled lager as I prepare and cook my meal, leaving the steak to last as I want to have it extra-rare.

There's sod-all on the box to watch - so what's new? - so I raid my film collection and dig-out an erotic French thriller called *BAISE-MOI,* it being one of my favourites as it's fast-paced, violent, stylish, and has explicit sex scenes littered throughout that always lights my fire. The 2-main leading actresses have a great attitude and are immensely independent and strong - I love them.

I grab a couple more bottles of lager from the fridge and settle-down to watch the film and eat. I lose myself in the action before my eyes and I imagine shooting those fucking Slav fuckers that parked in my parking-space just like the 2-girls kill their victims in the movie.

***

I strip and fuck myself in my pussy doggy-style with my Lovehoney textured-glass dildo, pretending that it's the real cock of that guy Dave from the car dealership this morning that is fucking me. I shout at him to: "Fuck me harder you old bastard" and he responds immediately and I moan as his dick penetrates my hole with increased vigour. He pumps-away at me as I orgasm and cum myself and I shake like a mad bitch.

I pull my fake-cock out of my minge and roll-over onto my back and lick and suck the goo from it's bumpy surface, tasting my own love. I finger myself with 2-fingers and pretend that the 2-girls from the French film are both licking at my hole and that I love them with all my heart as I cum into their mouths.

***

I slept really well last night. I was totally bushed after the train journey, the driving, then shopping, all the drink and then masturbating myself to death!

It's now 9.40am, and as I gaze naked out of the living-room window, I notice that the crappy Slav van has fucked-off, never to be seen again. They've probably landed on some other poor unsuspecting soul to torture them with their shitty fucking Gypsy music and sub-human behaviour - bastards.

At least now I can move my orange bomber out of the visitors spot where I parked it last night and put it in my own space where it belongs. I just hope that this car brings me a bit more luck than the last one?

As I view my surroundings I spot a traffic warden - one of our black cousins - on the other side of the road just getting out of his crappy van. He's heading towards a black BMW 5-Series that's parked-up illegally half on the road and half on the pavement instead of being in a visitors parking bay. As he nears it the black guy who lives in the block of flats opposite mine suddenly appears from nowhere with yet another black guy in tow. The 3 of them stand around chatting for a short while before the warden turns and walks back to his van, smiling and giving a little wave back to his "brothers" as he does so. Typical isn't it? If the Beemer had been owned by a white person the warden would have nicked it for sure, but because its driver is a fellow coon it's happy fucking days all round and nothing is done - talk about "Blacks Unite"! And people say I'm racist!

7

Why?

I find it hard to believe how bad this year has been, so far anyway. It's been nothing but one fucking disaster after another. I try to dodge all the bullets aimed at me but some of them inevitably find their target, unfortunately not all of them are avoidable.

I sometimes have to wonder really just how strong I actually am? After all the knocks I've had throughout my life I think I've actually come through them pretty well. I know I've got my hang-ups - that goes without saying! - but they really have helped me get through life and move on, in a strange kinda way.

So why is it that I've survived? How have I survived? And why me? Why have I pulled through where other lesser mortals would have succumbed to similar immense pressure? There has to be a reason - doesn't there?

And so what has fate got in store for me next? I really do try to be a good girl. I know I can be a bit naughty sometimes, but life is for living, not for sitting on your arse vegetating like most people do. All this still doesn't answer my question though - why me? Why have I seemingly been singled-out for target practice? I know I'm being tested, but what is the point of it? And by who? What are they getting out of all this mess apart from a bloody-good laugh? There has to be a reason and an explanation and I'm determined to find it, whatever it costs.

My living nightmare continues.

***

Today I'm wearing a beautiful white buttoned blouse from Jabong that has a lace insert across the back and is both stylish and super-sexy, a leopard-print pencil-skirt and black belt from Polyvore, lime-green lace underwear from Nordstrom, and my pair of black suede open-toe ankle-boots from Polyvore. My hair is its usual impeccable self whilst my make-up is dark and moody, featuring heavy coal-black eyeshadow and blood-red lipstick. My perfume is *Poison* by Christian Dior.

I'm sitting here at work minding my own business, thinking about all the crap that I've just narrated to you, when my mobile phone suddenly starts to bleep. We've all been told that we're not allowed to use our mobiles during work hours or even make or take private calls on the company phones either as it's non-productive. Well, bollocks to that, I take my call regardless.

"Hello" I say inquisitively, not recognizing the number on the screen before me.

"Sarah, it's Mick. We've had a car accident. Kate's okay but Abigail's been hurt." Says Mick, Kate's stupid lazy boyfriend.

"What are you talking about?" I shout as I leap out of my chair, making my fellow co-workers stop and stare at me.

"We've had an accident, on the M25, it's Abigail."

"Is this one of your stupid fucking jokes? Are you pissed?" I shout back at him.

"No, Sarah, I'm serious. We're at the Hospital, St. Peter's in Chertsey."

"If you're bloody winding me up I'll fucking kill you." I warn him.

"Sarah, I'm not winding you up. We were hit from behind. Abigail was in the back, in her child-seat, she been hurt."

"OK, I'll be there as quick as I can. I'm warning you though, if this is one of your sick jokes then I'll fucking swing for you. Do you understand?"

I hang-up on him and sit back down in my chair with a thump. I really don't know whether to believe that lazy bastard or not? He sounded quite genuine so I guess I'll have to believe him. But only on face-value though, if this is a wind-up then I will actually kill him - idiot.

After tidying-up my desk, switching my computer off and then explaining the situation to my section-supervisor Paula, I head out the door and straight for the Hospital. In my car I exit Horsham and take a straight-line up the A24, through Dorking and Mickleham and the outskirts of Leatherhead, and then clockwise onto the M25. The turn-off for Chertsey isn't that far from this point, only a couple of junctions along, a distance of about 10-miles or so.

As I pass Junction-10, I notice the traffic on the other side of the road is snarled-up further ahead, along with the flashing blue lights of several Police cars, an ambulance and a couple of fire-engines.

My heart sinks to my stomach as I catch a brief glimpse of what looks like Mick's silver Ford Focus being winched onto the back of a flatbed recovery lorry. Surely that can't be it can it? There are so many of those cars around when you look for them so it could be anyone's, couldn't it? But was that actually Mick's car though? The fact that the rear-end was completely smashed-in and the roof had been removed by the fire-crew only underlines my fears - that he really was telling me the truth this time. People are such bastards these days that I can't tell the truth from the lies any more.

St. Peter's Hospital is easy to find, being right next door to the roundabout off of the A320. I really can't believe this is happening, it's just one bloody thing after another. And why does this have to happen now, on the eve of the anniversary of Mum's passing? This is just too cruel. I only hope that little baby Abigail is okay? If she isn't then I don't think I could cope with all the trauma. This is taking things too far.

After parking-up I get a vague direction from the woman on reception and make my way to the Accident and Emergency Department. There I find Mick sitting there on his own with a brace around his neck and with a face on him as white as a sheet.

"What's going on? Where's Kate and Abigail?" I question him.

"Kate's being looked at now by the Doctors. She's broken her collarbone. They've taken Abigail off somewhere but they're not telling us anything."

"What do you mean? Where have they taken her to?"

"She's in Intensive Care. They haven't told me anything else."

"Right, well, we'll soon see about that." I inform him bluntly.

I storm off to find a Doctor or at least someone with some sort-of intelligence, but when I round the corner I hear Kate call out to me from a room off to my left. She looks a right bloody mess, her neck also in a brace just like Mick has and with her left-arm in a sling. Her face just about says it all, it too as ashen as Mick's.

"Kate, what the Hell happened?" I ask her.

"Someone crashed into us. Abi's been hurt. They won't tell us anything." She says tearfully.

"Yes, I know, Mick just told me. What have the Doctors said?"

"Nothing" She says with tears in her eyes, making me start to well-up also.

At that moment we're joined in the room by Mick and a tall, skinny-gutted, female Doctor - obviously some kind of fucking Slav judging by the vacant look in her dead Polish eyes and her unmistakable guttural accent. She informs the 3 of us that Abigail is in Intensive Care and that they're doing everything they can for her, whatever that fucking means?

There's absolutely nothing we can do now except just sit here staring at each other and hope that she pulls through. If I had a God at this moment I would pray to him. Fate is in charge now though, not some fictitious entity.

Over an hour goes by without a word from anyone. I've drunk so much fake coffee that I think I'll be awake for the rest of the week. Finally though, after almost 2-hours, another

Doctor appears - an English one this time - who informs us that little Abigail is still critical but at least she's now stable - once again, whatever that means? Apparently a knock to her head in the accident has left her in a really sorry state, poor little kid. I'm just glad that Mum isn't here to witness all this as it would have simply been too much for her - I'm just about hanging-on myself as it is. All this waiting around for news is starting to drive me insane, I hate to think what Kate and Mick are feeling like? None of us feel like eating anything at the moment, I know I certainly don't, and even the bloody coffee has now run its course.

***

All this time waiting for any news clicks-away slowly. I've really had enough of all this by now and so I decide to go home, there's nothing I can do here anyway. The drive back home to the flat is a lonely one - in the car it's lonely, in the flat itself it's lonely, and I'm lonely myself in general. Not even my old friend Mr. Vodka can help me today, even though my little drinking habit has escalated back to the level it was before I hooked-up with Amanda, today it's useless and doesn't stop my pain.

I really am a lost soul and I don't know what to do. Even the thought of masturbating doesn't even enter my mind. I really must eat something though so I do myself a bowl of chips and have some cold chicken to go along with it, just enough to sustain me for the here and now.

I text Kate at least half-a-dozen times that evening but there's still no more news, good or bad.

***

I decide to bunk-off work the following day, even the very thought of going in there to see all those morons makes me shudder, so instead I head off back to the Hospital. I've just thrown on a t-shirt, a white v-neck one from AliExpress that exposes most of my voluptuous cleavage, my pair of pale-blue stonewash jeans from Boohoo, and my pair of white suede open-toe ankle-boots from Polyvore. My underwear is in black lace from Agent Provocateur. I do my make-up quickly and light. My perfume is *Luxe* by Avon.

The news and the look on both Kate and Mick's faces when I spot them are enough to make me weep. The Doctors have tried to get little Abi to breathe unaided but it was no use, she's just too weak to do it by herself so they had to put her back on life-support straight away. They say if she makes it through the nest 24-hours then there's a good chance she will pull through - poor little sod.

I spend the whole day with Kate and Mick, not talking about anything of any significance, just crap to pass the time, just to get from one end of the day to the other.

At 7.30pm I head back home once again. It's dark outside by now and there's a horrible chill in the air, like the Grim Reaper himself is breathing down the back of my neck.

***

My mobile rings and makes me jump out of my skin. Not that I was actually asleep, just dozing. It's 3.40am the following morning and it's Mick on the line, ringing from the Hospital.

It's little baby Abigail, my beautiful little niece who I love and adore like she is my one and only daughter - the daughter I will never have - died earlier this morning at 3.07am.

I cannot speak. I cannot move. I cannot comprehend the awful, miserable, sombre words that Mick has just told me. I am destroyed. Her demise has left me in a state of complete disillusionment. I am filled with overwhelming sorrow and I'm shattered beyond what any mere words can express. Things will never be the same again. I will never be the same again. Why does this shit have to happen? What is the reason for taking away the life of an innocent little child like this? Why? What is the fucking reason?

I have been left suspended in sorrow and pain and I don't think I'll ever come down. My soul is as black as death. My equilibrium has been shifted sideways. I don't believe in anything any more. My life is shattered.

I tell Mick that I'm on my way there to the Hospital. I know I can't bring little Abigail back to life but at least I can be with Kate and try to comfort her in her hour of need, poor girl. How the Hell am I going to comfort her? What the Hell do I say to her? Once again, why does this shit have to happen? I am so numb with shock that there are no tears, at least not yet.

I'm still dressed in yesterdays clothes, having fallen asleep on the sofa in them. Even so I still don't bother to change as I don't have time, just having a quick pee and tidy-up my face and hair. That's a fucking joke, me not having time. I have all the time in the World, unlike poor little Abigail, she doesn't have any more time at all - she's dead.

Back in the cold, empty Hospital, I'm guided along to the family bereavement room where I find both Kate and Mick sobbing in frozen time. The room is white, like a cloud, adorned with paintings of angels and other such imagery, all designed to sooth the pain of death. For me it doesn't work. I want to smash them all to Hell for the bullshit they portray. It's all meaningless, just like little Abigail's death. Why? What does any of it mean?

I hold Kate in my arms as she cries her flowing tears of loss on my shoulder. I try not to squeeze her too tightly due to her broken collarbone but her pain is 2-fold, being more emotional rather than psychical. As for myself, I have no tears, only anger at the bastard who did this to my family, my family of only 2-living souls now.

Mick looks at me also with tears in his eyes and I think he expects me to hug him as well but he's mistaken - I don't. I know it's the right and proper thing to do to console him also in the circumstances but I don't want to, I'm too bitter and too hard to comply. I have to wonder why Kate got back with him in the first place? If she haddn't then none of this shit wouldv'e happened would it? Why did little innocent Abigail have to die? Why couldn't it have been that fucking idiot Mick instead? Useless fat lazy tosser.

Kate asks me if I would like to go in and see Abigail, to see her lifeless little body. I really don't want to but I somehow feel compelled to go, at least to say "Goodbye" to her.

I'm on autopilot as I enter the stark mortuary room, guided by one of the Hospital staff, a young, tall, thin guy in his early-30's. A solitary table stands in the centre of the room, a white sheet draped over its entirety. The guy gently pulls-back the cover and there she is, laying there like a broken doll, my little baby Abigail. He leaves us alone together and I gaze at her white skin, its colour almost pearlescent in death. She looks so beautiful laying there all still, just like she's sleeping. Her tiny lips have turned pale and I want to kiss them with all my love but I just can't bring myself to do it, I'm frozen to the spot in fear of touching her. I cannot believe this has happened, that I'm here in a Hospital mortuary room with my dead niece. How has this happened? This is not real. I am in the middle of another fucking living nightmare.

Do I really have to go through all that shit again with another funeral so soon after the deaths of Lacey, Mum and Suzie? I dread even thinking about it.

I have to leave this place of horror and death so I say my muted "Farewells" to Kate and Mick and get the Hell out of here, back to my own little World where no-one can touch me.

***

I'm really dreading today, the day of little baby Abigail's funeral. It still hasn't sunk into my brain that she's actually gone and it was 3-weeks ago that the accident happened. Her death is still inconceivable.

I'm pretty sure you can all imagine the type of clothes I'm wearing today and how I've done my hair and make-up so there's no point in me explaining all that shit to you is there? You all know me well enough by now to have the image in your mind already as it's exactly the same outfit I wore at Mum's funeral ages ago.

I'm heading to the funeral under my own steam, it being held at the same crematorium as Mum's was, rather than going in the funeral-car with Kate and Mick. I think that would have been too much for me to bear today even though I know I should really be supporting my sister a little more throughout this horrible ordeal. Once again all the events of the past have a bearing on the events of now and the future.

For some reason I stupidly sent an Email to Amanda, firstly to tell her the awful news about Abigail, and secondly to ask her if she would come with me to the funeral to give me some support and a shoulder to cry on. Naturally - and not unsurprisingly - she replied telling me that she was obviously sorry to here of innocent little Abigail's sad death but "Fuck Off" to the second part. I can't blame her really.

I stand in the family section at the small church that adjoins the crematorium. I'm surrounded by people that I've no idea who they are, members of Mick's family

I'm guessing? There's only one of them I do actually recognize, a short fat girl in her mid-20's who I think is Mick's younger sister. I don't even know what her bloody name is?

Kate sits up the front on her own - it's what she wanted to do for some reason? - as the service begins. I try to overt my eyes to the proceedings but it's no good, and I watch in horror as Mick carries the small white coffin containing my beautiful Abigail down the isle in his arms with tears in his eyes. I become mesmerized by his courage, not believing he had any guts at all within him. There is no way I could have done such a thing. Even though I don't have a maternal bone in my body I'm mortified by the loss of "My" baby.

Beside me, Abigail's surviving Grandparents and her aunt weep-away as I just sit there motionless and numb as the sad music floats around the chapel like a vampire. The minister - a creepy old guy in his 60's who looks like some kind-of sick paedophile - starts spouting some sanctimonious preachings about God and all that shit. Oh really? So where was this fucking so-called "God" of yours when innocent little Abigail needed him? Arsehole.

The service passes by in only 20-minutes or so - although not quickly enough as far as I'm concerned - interspersed with a couple of hymns and a fake prayer, none of which I join in with, I'm not a fucking hypocrite. At service end, my darling love Abigail's little coffin unceremoniously disappears through a hole in the wall to our right and is gone - she is no more. I sit there dumbfounded by the ungraceful ending of her short life - and death - and can't help thinking that all this is one long sick joke, just as I said it was at the beginning.

Everyone rises and starts to make their way out of the building, most people in tears, all in shock. I stare at them all like I'm not actually a part of the event, like an outsider. Am I or not, I honestly don't know?

Outside, flowers from well-wishers cover a section of the paved courtyard. There's masses of them in a hundred different shapes, sizes and colours, all with condolence messages of *"Rest in Peace", My Angel"* and other similar words of heartbreaking sorrow. I don't read any of them as I can't, they're all way too painful and I know for sure that they would tip me over the edge of sanity.

Instead I go and grab a quick word with Kate before I leave. We kiss and hug and then chat briefly and quietly amongst ourselves about Abigail and how she must be here with us at this very moment, watching all the goings-on from the Spirit-World. Suddenly she lets slip that not only was Mick driving her car at the time of the accident, he was doing so without any insurance and had also been banned from driving 6-months beforehand for the same reason - WHAT THE FUCK!

I immediately sprint over to him as he stands there chatting with his parents, grabbing his shoulder and spinning him around to face me.

"YOU FUCKING IDIOT." I scream at him, simultaneously slapping him across the face with my right-hand.

"Why do you have to be such a fucking arsehole all the time?" I tell him.

"What did you do that for you stuck-up cow?" He bitches at me before he then tries to hit me back but thinks better of it and stops himself.

His Father steps-in between us and tries to restrain us both from fighting in front of everyone but the damage is done, he is a fucking arsehole of the highest order. I give Mick a look of pure hate as I turn on my heals and walk back over to Kate, she standing there like everyone else in a state of shock.

"I just don't believe you Kate, what the fuck do you see in him, are you fucking blind? He's a useless fucking moron and you're just as stupid as he is for going along with this charade." I stab at her but I get no reply.

I can't take any more of this shit so I turn and leave in disgust. And so it turns out that Kate told the Police that she was driving at the time of the crash to avoid the idiot being prosecuted! It's amazing isn't it, just what is wrong with these fucking people?

***

I stare at my naked body in my full-length mirror and wonder why I am who I am? Why do I look like this, so beautiful? Even today, with the death of a loved one, I am still beautiful in every way. What have I done to deserve such beauty?

I sate at my breasts, my legs, my vagina, my face and hair. I am perfect in every way. Anyone would want to fuck me. I look at my fingernails and even they too are gorgeous, flawless in every way. But why are they?

I watch the expression on my face as I insert 2-fingers on my right-hand into my hole and wank it. I try to force myself to cry but there are no tears. I force my whole hand into my vagina as I squat-down and spread my legs but it's still no use, I have no emotion. I pull my hand out of myself and punch myself in the face and then beat my fists on my breasts - why are they so perfect? - but still I don't react to any form of self-abuse.

I stand and gaze at my reflection once again and wonder if the person I see before me is really me? Maybe in reality I'm a big, fat, ugly bitch with rotten teeth and a fat saggy arse and that I only see what I want to see and not the actual truth?

I think about little Abigail. She will never grow up to experience life like I have. She will never discover the pleasures of sex, the thrill of being free, of being a woman. All that has been taken away from her by the incompetence and arrogance of others.

The mirror smashes into a million splinters as I hurl the metal soap-dish into it. I pick-up one of the sharp pointed shards and hold its piercing end against my right-breast. I have the power within me to alter my body right here and now if I want to, my body would never be the same ever again, no plastic-surgeon could ever rebuild it back into the condition that it's in now - an image that is beyond perfection.

My hand somehow begins to feel warm as I then notice the brilliant shade of red blood seeping from its wound. Dropping the glass in the basin with a clash, I scan the cuts to my hand, noting that they're actually not that deep after all, only superficial really. I run the scarlet mess over my face, neck and breasts like I'm performing some sort-of Paganistic ritual and it feels sticky and I both hate it and love it at once.

In the living-room I lean up against the back of the leather sofa with my bum stuck-up in the air. It doesn't have to wait long before I ease my thick chrome dildo - the one from Lovehoney - into her. The resistance is strong but the lubrication soon overcomes it and in it slides with pleasure. I fuck myself hard up the arse, pushing my fake cock into myself as far as it will go. It hurts me but still there are no tears, not of pleasure or pain.

I pull it out after a while and I fall onto the floor. Squatting over it I prop it up between the carpet and my vagina and then lower myself down. It goes in easier than in my bum-hole and I motion my body up and down and I moan as I grind-away on the phallus. I smack my tits as I cum but I don't stop, I want to punish myself for being born, for being alive, for this day.

I lay back on the carpet and open my legs as far as they will go, licking my cock free of my juice and muck and then ramming it into my mouth. I choke and cough as I insert it deeper into my gob and I can't breathe and splutter for air. I slap my pussy with the other hand harder and harder until it becomes red-raw and bruised but I am past caring.

I throw the dildo over to one side and get up and hit the vodka. I don't drink it though, I just stare at the bottle for an age and then pour its contents out over my head. It glugs-away as it empties, the liquid running down my face, my chin, neck and breasts, stinging my eyes and mixing itself with the drying blood from my hand.

I wish Amanda could see me now, as well as all my previous lovers, just so they could see all the damage that they and everyone else has been done to me, including the self-inflicted pain and the monumental suffering I have endure just by being alive.

I slug on the blue bottle of gin as I insert the end of the empty bottle of vodka into my fanny and wank it inside myself. I keep going for what seems like years until I can take no more alcohol or masturbation.

I collapse to my knees in tears, but still they don't come, I just sob without them over my plight. I think about Abigail's funeral this morning and the deaths of Lacey, Mum and Suzie. Fate is out of my hands an I am so angry that I don't have any control over it. If I could rule the World it would be such a better place that's for sure.

My poor gorgeous body is in a terrible sate, all battered, bruised and torn. I quickly clean-up all the mess around me and then myself, filling the bath with pipping-hot water and peach-scented bubble-bath. I lower myself into the loveliness and gently sooth my aches away as I settle myself down in the water. The thought of drowning myself enters my mind, and at least then I would be able to be with Mum, Abigail and the cats on the other side. I don't do it of course, knowing my appalling luck I'd be greeted at the Pearly Gates by the bastard that is the "Old Man"! Not only that, I also know I could never bring myself to actually do it, my freedom and independence mean far too much to me that to just throw it all away like that, no matter how much I suffer.

*****

I so desperately want to get to sleep but I can't. Every time I shut my eyes I see the terrifying visualisation of Abigail's dead body before me.

I am out of my head on vodka and Paracetamol's in an attempt to knock myself out but I'm still wide awake. I guess I'll have to resign myself to the fact that I won't be getting any sleep tonight.

In the end I decide to go for a little walk around the village and try to get some fresh air into my lungs, even though it's now almost 4am the following morning.

I throw on some clothes - jumper, jeans, boots, jacket - I don't care what colour they are, who made them or even if they match, I just want clothes - and exit my flat and the building.

The cool morning air chills my skin. Although I'm not naked I want to be, but I don't want to get caught wandering around starkers by some weirdo stranger, or worse, the fucking Police - I try to avoid those idiots at all costs.

I wander past the Red Lyon pub and think about all the recent events in my life, the state of the World and the state of my life and existence. This has been one of the saddest days of my life so far but how many more must I endure, this fucking year is only half-way so what else has life got in store for me? I know that we're all going to die eventually one day, but surely there must be more to our existence on this Planet than this?

My heart isn't completely made if ice, no-ones is. I also have feelings of loss but there are limits to what one can take and still remain relatively sane. We all have to find our own way in life, there is no-one to guide us apart from our unique and mischievous Guardian Angels, whoever they may be? The good times are emphasized by the bad and we must use this fact to keep pushing on with our lives, to do the very best we can. Appreciate what you have at this moment as you never know when it's all going to be taken away from you.

What did I say to you earlier about the bloody Police? Just as I'm making my way back home a sodding cop-car slowly glides past me. The 2-coppers inside - both female by the looks of them but I only just catch a glimpse of the driver so I could be wrong? - eyeball me as they pass and then disappear around the corner. No more than 5-seconds later I spot them again, heading back my way, heading straight for me - typical! This is all I bloody need, 2-smartarse coppers in my face after the fucking day I've just had.

They pull-up in front of me with the one in the passenger seat jumping out and standing right in front of me, blocking my intended path.

"Good morning Miss. Where are you going at this time of the morning?" She quizzes me, like I'm fucking 5-years old.

"I'm just off home. I've been out for a walk." I explain to her.

"At 4.30 in the morning?" She comes back at me, looking at her wristwatch.

"That's right. If I want to go for a walk at this time of the morning then that's what I'll do." I hit back at her, smug fucking cow.

"That seems a bit strange?"

"Not to me it doesn't."

"Can I have your name and address please Miss?"

"It's Sarah Knowles, with a "K", and my address is 13, Rickwood Close, Slinfold."

"That's just around the back here isn't it?" She says, pointing to behind her.

"That's right."

She turns and goes back to her colleague in the car, presumably to check-up on my details. I just don't believe this, I'm out for 5-bloody-minutes and I get hassle from the fucking Police straight away. I stand there trying to look as innocent as I possibly can when suddenly the copper returns back to me.

"Okay Sarah, if you would like to head-off straight back home. It's not really safe for a young woman to be wandering around at this time of the morning on her own, you understand?"

"Okay then, I will." I say, and just walk off back in the direction of my flat, leaving her standing there like the stupid fucking pig she is.

I cross the road and make my way home, detecting the cops following me in their patrol-car as their headlights light-up my figure from behind - fucking bitches. And how dare she call me Sarah, she doesn't fucking know me!

***

I try to draw a line under this horrible episode but it's impossible. There has to be a way of turning this terrible tragedy into something positive, there has to be, or I'll go completely fucking crazy.

Kate has Emailed me several times to keep me up to speed with events about poor Abigail's sad death. In one message she informs me about the autopsy report on her, carried out the day after she died, not that I really want to know about that, she's dead and that's all there is to it, nothing can bring her back. The report states that she had suffered heart failure, undoubtedly caused by all the trauma of the accident and the injuries she sustained to her body. The kid didn't stand a bloody chance.

And as for the bastard who hit them in the first place, have a guess at what fantastic sentence he received by our wonderful justice system for: *"Causing death whilst driving without due care and attention."* - 7-years!

Yes, you read that right, 7-fucking-years - unbelievable! He'll probably be out in 3 at the most - fucker. Well, if he thinks he's got off lightly then he can think again. I'll be fucking waiting for that cunt when he gets out and no mistake. I'll make that bastard suffer like he's never suffered before. I will be his worst fucking nightmare ever. He will not live to see another sunrise.

8

5 into 1

I've rejoined that stupid dating agency that I was with before about a year and a half ago, the one where I hooked-up with that guy Steve - remember him, the one with the fit body and the big dick?

The reason for rejoining is because I am completely fucking bored out of my skull and as pissed-off with life as I can possibly be. Plus of course I'm always frisky, my capricious appetite for love shows no sign of slowing down the older I get!

There is seemingly no end to the amount of shit that keeps getting thrown in my way. What is it all for? What is the fucking point of it all? I sob and laugh at the same time at my infliction, the pain of being me, of being beautiful, of being a crazy bitch. With the sadness of my niece Abigail's cruel death comes the self-destruction of my own life. Why do these horrendous things have to happen? Nothing can compensate for the loss of a child, just how my poor sister Kate is going to cope I just don't know? The devastation will forever be defined by this heartfelt event.

As for the job in hand, this time around as far as meeting guys is concerned, things are going to be a whole lot different. I'm after one thing specifically that will hopefully fulfil my needs for the here-and-now and then no more. This is purely a one-off event and then that's it, a hedonistic experiment if you like, to see if my mind and my body can take the punishment.

What I'm requesting is for several guys to screw and ravage me all at the same time, maybe 3 or 4 of them, guys with plenty of lead in their pencils! I've had 3-some's before of course, including with those 2-idiots I told you about in my first diary - Alan and Charlie. I know that you're probably thinking that I'm letting myself in for yet more shit and yes, you're right, once again, but life is for living and no-one is going to stop me. I can't even stop myself!

I'm not being spontaneous in my action, I've thought about this long and hard for some while and now it's time to act upon it. We all need love, in whatever shape or form it comes in, and I need these guys to exploit and abuse my body as I see fit. Once again, this is my want, although I'm not a piece of meat that everyone can just take a bite of whenever they feel like it! I don't care if you think I'm unladylike, it's okay, I probably am. I don't care if you think I'm some sort-of scrubber, maybe I'm that as well? That's only your opinion and not necessarily anyone else's, or even the right one for that matter. I can't help having a psychotic lust for love, even if sometimes it is sadistic and perverted. Even my thoughts are always salacious! At least no-one could ever accuse me of being vanilla!

Also trying to figure out how to word my online profile proved to be a little tricky, but in the end I'm putting one on nevertheless, that is after having racked my brains over it for almost an hour, so here it is:

> *"Tall, gorgeous, subservient slim blonde with fantastic figure, looking for 3-guys to take me all at the same time. Must be fit and clean with good attitude - respect is essential - I am not a whore, just a young woman who loves sex.*
>
> *Message me back if you fit the bill.*
>
> *All my love, Sarah."*

I light the blue touch-paper and send off my profile. I'm bound to receive some really dodgy replies but what else do you expect, that's the nature of the beast? So is this what I've turned into now, a sexual degenerate?

Once accepted, my profile becomes live and the messages come pouring in straight away, and as predicted, I get pretty-much the same kind-of response as I did previously. In under an hour I receive 49 replies, mostly from nutters and the like. Obviously there's a few nice ones mixed-in with the psychopaths, so I make a note of those to check-out their profiles later.

***

After 3-days of being on the site, I've received the grand total of 201 hits, the vast majority of those being misses! Of those, I soon whittle them down to only 16 and send each of them a reply. Some of the return messages are okay I guess, with statements like: "I really wanna fuck you", "Suck my cock bitch and eat my cum", "I'm going to fuck your mouth like a cunt", "Swallow my fuck you fucking whore bitch", "You can sit on my face anytime", and all that shit. I pass-by those and others, taking my score down to 9 possibles. They all seem like really nice guys but I still have to get the total down to my prerequisite number of 3 - one for each hole!

A few of the others are quite cheeky and I love it, I really hope they're as funny as that when we do actually meet and not fakers. In order to pick my 3-special guys, I've arranged to meet-up with all 9 of them on consecutive evenings just for a chat - there being no sex or anything else, not even letting any of them touch me in any way, no handshakes, kissing, hugging, nothing - in order to make my final decision. This should be an experience all in itself!

***

It's 7pm and I'm in my local pub, the Red Lyon, waiting with some anxiety it must be said, for my first victim. I'm wearing a white strapless criss-cross dress from BandageDressesOutlet that barely covers my essentials and that's it, no bra, no knickers, not even shoes, as it's a hot sticky evening and it's about to get stickier! My face I've done in full-on killer supermodel mode, featuring lashings of coal-black eyeshadow and orange lipstick. My beautiful blonde hair I leave as is in it's usual way. My perfume is *Poison* by Christian Dior. The only other item I have with me is a red plastic clutch-bag from Boticca containing my keys, mobile and cash.

I get the same old crap from all the other punters in the pub, all ogling my legs, my bum and especially my breasts as my nipples protrude through the thin fabric of my dress like the buttons on a Chesterfield! My drink is a pint of lager with a large neat vodka chaser, and I'm pretty-sure that I'm going to need several of those before the night is out, I just know it!

I'm meeting the first guy - Harry - a 24-year old builder from Croydon at 7.30pm, but things don't go well right from the start as he doesn't even bother to show up! I sit here on my own like a fucking lemon, being stared at by everyone until 8pm and then I fuck-off, I can't take any more of this and so I plod home a little dejected.

Once back indoors I strip naked and down several glasses of gin - 4 actually! - and then fuck myself with 2-fingers as I watch 2-naked gay guys sucking each others cocks in the woods on my laptop. Later that evening I fall asleep - still naked - on the sofa in front of the 10pm news, pissed, bored and tired.

* * *

It's the second evening of my interviews and I'm back in my local pub with seemingly the very same plebs all gorping at me as last night - it's 6.55pm.

Tonight I'm wearing my lime-green sleeveless bodycon dress from Wanelo that is super-tight. My underwear is in sexy white lace from Triumph - knickers only though as I'm not wearing a bra. My shoes are a pair of see-through plastic wedge-heals from Polyvore. My make-up I've done pretty-much as yesterdays but with a little more eyeshadow to emphasize my gorgeous blue eyes. My perfume is *Luxe* by Avon and my clutch-bag is some obscure black one I found lurking in my wardrobe, I've no-idea where its from or how I even come to have it?

Today's player is Stuart, a 27-year old supermarket section-leader from Crawley. He arrives 10-minutes early and we chat and talk the usual talk. He's really tall - he must be 6-foot-4 at least! - very good looking and is one of the guys I mentioned earlier. We really hit it off and we flirt with each other to the point of being disgusting and I love it and I want him to fuck me right here and now on the table right in front of all the other punters - he's defiantly in!

At the end of the evening we go our separate ways and I pull away from him when he tries to kiss my cheek. It's not what I want even though it really is as I'm saving myself for the "Big Event" and I don't want to get carried-away or get involved with any of his shit.

****

Evening number 3 and the bar staff try not to look at me but of course they can't resist it, standing there whispering amongst themselves as I sit my perfect bum down on a bench outside in the pub garden.

For tonight's meeting I'm wearing my white halter-neck top from Boohoo - with no bra once again! - along with my white leather skirt from French Connection.

My underwear - knickers only of course! - are a yellow lace pair from Figleaves. My hair, make-up and perfume are all as yesterday, even my clutch-bag is the same obscure one.

My full-breasts heave with anticipation from tonight's meeting, a guy called James, who sounded really posh and well educated on the phone earlier today, but it soon becomes obvious that he's not educated enough - he's yet another

fucking no-show! How fucking rude! That's the bloody second time in only 3-days! What the Hell is wrong with these guys?

A van with a couple of builder-types pull into the pub car-park and they both eye me up and down as they pass by me, sitting there on my Jack-Jones. I desperately want them to love me but nothing happens, I just sit there getting more and more pissed on lager until I eventually decide to call it a night, walking out and back home alone, passing the 2-builders who were obviously too scared to come and say "Hello" to my gorgeous intimidating self so they can both fuck-off.

Back at my flat I enjoy my own company, fucking myself anally with my glass 8-inch dildo from Lovehoney as I watch double-fisting lesbian porn on my computer.

***

I'm not in the best of moods as I sit at the bar on night-4 of my mission. I'm wearing my scarlet mini-bodycon dress from ASOS tonight which kind-of cheers me up as it really shows-off my perfect body to all the surrounding customers. My underwear is once again knickers only - a lace pair in red from Ultimo - as I couldn't be bothered with a bra, my breasts can look after themselves of that I've no-doubt! My shoes are my pair of red heels from Heels USA whilst my clutch-bag is the same red one from the other night. My hair and make-up I've done as per usual featuring bright-red gloss lipstick. My perfume is *Poison* by Christian Dior.

Jason is the next guy on my list of potentials, a 38-year old delivery driver from Ashington in West Sussex. He arrives 15-minutes late - it's 7.45pm - but I let this slide and don't pick him up on it. He has a really lovely smile and a super-fit body, although he does have one of those skinhead-type haircuts that I don't particularly like but I guess appearances can be deceptive of course.

Even so I generally quite like him and the following couple of hours goes well so I add him to my list as a "Yes" also.

***

The bar staff must be wondering why I'm in here yet again on my own, although obviously they don't and can't ask me "Why?" It's got fuck-all to do with them anyway and my black mood and expression must be subliminally telling them so.

My said mood is also reflected in this evenings attire. I'm wearing a little black mini-bodycon dress from The Xclusiv Boutique, this being my perfect choice. I haven't bothered with any underwear at all once again as there's no point is there? On my feet I'm wearing my pair of black suede open-toe platform court shoes from Polyvore. My clutch-bag is my Greta Deco Shell one from Vintage Styler. My hair and make-up are as yesterday but with black gloss lipstick to match the way I feel. My lips actually look like a couple of leaches are stuck to my face! My perfume is also as yesterday.

Tonight's guy is Kevin from Horsham, but once again my blackness is turned even blacker as he's yet another fucking no-show! I'm really fucking pissed-off with this now and I'm wondering why I'm even fucking bothering with this stupid venture at all? Why do I put myself through this shit? What is the fucking point?

I drink myself to death on lager, vodka and gin as my fellow drinkers and the bar-staff just stare at me all fucking evening like they've never seen a lonely, beautiful woman before in all their fucking small sad pathetic lives.

I stagger home totally pissed out of my skull, only just managing not to fall arse-over-tit into the road or someone's front garden. I smash myself beyond existence on more alcohol back at my flat before attempting to masturbate with 2-fingers in my vagina as I watch bisexual orgy porn on my laptop. The images of these 2-guys fucking and sucking each other as the sole female participant simultaneously has her twat and arsehole licked and fucked has no effect on me whatsoever and I fail to cum, the only liquid trickling from my body being tears of sadness down my face for being such a cunt.

***

The next chap on my list is Jon - with no "h"! - a 35-year old guy from Horsham - another one! He seems quite a smooth-talker in his messages so I'm giving him a go. For tonight's meet I'm wearing a white cotton sleeveless blouse from H&M - open to the max so everyone can see my tits, my leopard-print pencil-skirt from Polyvore, and on my feet my pair of white suede open-toe ankle-boots, also from Polyvore.

My underwear is once again knickers only, a super-sexy black pair in lace from ASOS. My clutch-bag is my white leather one from Swankyswans. I've done my hair and make-up similar to yesterday but less dramatic, featuring orange lipstick this time. My perfume is *Luxe* by Avon.

Although the meeting with Jon is supposed to be at 7.30pm, as were the others, it's now 8.05pm and there's still no fucking sign of him. I finish my vodka and go to leave but I'm suddenly stopped in my tracks by some old guy in his late-50's with a big unkempt bushy beard and hair, really scary eyes like Death himself and is wearing an awful old multi-coloured stripy jumper, dirty jeans - literally! - brown sandals and dirty socks all full of holes. He then leans down to me, staring at me with his dead fish-like eyes:

"Are you Sarah?" He quizzes me.

"Why? Who are you?"

"I'm Jon. Sorry I'm late, I've had some trouble with the car." Bleats Jon, my so-called "date"!

I rise to my feet and stand there in amazement at the sheer audacity of this old tosser, he doesn't look anything like the guy in his profile, not one bit, not even without the beard of a comb through his awful hair - unbelievable!

"You're Jon?" I say to him in shock.

"Yes, that's right. You're very beautiful Sarah, you have lovely breasts."

"Excuse me! Who the Hell are you? You don't look anything like the guy in your profile."

"Oh yes, I know. That's a photograph of my son Graham. I looked just like him when I was his age so I thought I'd use his picture."

"YOU'VE GOT TO BE FUCKING JOKING?" I scream at him.

"You really are a very gorgeous young lady Sarah."

"YOU CAN FUCK RIGHT OFF YOU OLD CUNT." I scream at him again, bringing my fellow drinkers to a halt as all eyes descend on me - again - as I storm out of the pub.

"Where are you going? Do you want another drink Sarah?" Bleats my "date".

He's too late of course as I'm already gone, the stupid old fucker. What the fuck are these people thinking? He had no fucking chance with me, a blind man could see that, so what was the fucking point? Why do I fucking bother?

The stupid things I do in the name of love!

For some strange reason I feel quite calm and collected as I sit myself down with a nice chilled glass of German white back at the flat, the image of beardy-weirdy

Jon banished from my mind - what a prick! That evening I have a quick masturbate to the images of gay orgy porn from the USA on my laptop, making doubly sure that none of the players have beards beforehand of course!

***

I'm sitting here with drink/s in hand - a pint of lager and a large neat vodka - wondering what the bar-staff and my surrounding drinkers are obviously thinking and talking about me. Like for instance:

"Why has she been in here on her own every evening meeting a different guy every time?"

"I bet she's a bloody prostitute. She dresses like one."

"Those breasts aren't real, no-one could be that perfect."

"Look at her, who does she think she is?"

This is what I get and other such jealous bitchiness, not that I give a fuck.

Anyway, tonight I'm wearing a white strapless criss-cross dress from BandageDressesOutlet that is to die for and really shows-off my superb perfect figure to the max. On my feet I'm again wearing my see-through plastic wedge-heals from Polyvore as they're fab, I love em. I'm not wearing any underwear tonight as I don't need to. My clutch-bag is my white leather one from Swankyswans. My hair and make-up is my usual style and my perfume is *Kenzo Flower* by Kenzo.

Tonight's guy is Martin, 32, who works for a car company in Worthing in their parts department. He turns up bang on time and although he's a little bit too chubby for my taste we get along like a house on fire, it's actually like we've known each other for years! I really do like him - especially his strange spiky hair! - although he's definitely not boyfriend material. As the evening wears-on he continually makes me laugh, so much so that my face begins to ache.

He also goes on my list as a "Yes" as well. We chin-wag until closing time and he offers me a lift home but my reply is a definite "No". I really like the guy but I don't want to lead him on - we have no future together.

Instead I stagger home a little pissed, strip naked, and spend the next half-an-hour searching for "Chubster Porn" on my laptop. Eventually I stumble across a film of some flabby guy giving a young gorgeous blonde honey - that I instantly fall for! - a really good portion of cock, fucking her mouth and up the bum as well, lucky bitch! I pleasure myself along to her screams of ecstasy until I cum myself and fall asleep naked, tired and hungry on the sofa until morning.

∗∗∗

I know I've interviewed 3-guys already for my mission but it wouldn't be fair not to see the other 2, then I can hopefully decide which 3 I want to love me. I'm back in the Red Lyon awaiting the next guy. Tonight I'm wearing my orange bodycon mini-dress from Polyvore and my pair of tan-coloured ankle-boots from AliExpress and nothing else. My clutch-bag, hair, make-up and perfume are all as last night.

I'm sitting here now with Andy, an electrician from Cranleigh in Surrey. He's the youngest of the lot at only 23, and like Jason he has one of those shaved-heads I don't particularly like. Each to their own I guess? Like most of the guys on the website they have photos of their dicks on their profile page and Andy is no exception, apart from the fact that he states his is 11-inches long! - or so he claims. Judging by his pictures his knob is also massive as well, a big fat purple helmet of a monster - wow! Height-wise, he's actually a couple of inches shorter than me, as well as being a tad overweight, but once again we both seem to hit it off okay. He has quite a lively personality and makes me laugh out loud during the entire meeting.

I find myself a bit stuck now and I don't know what to do? I've already got 3 nice guys that I need for my fun but I just can't get the image of Andy's massive cock out of my mind. What is a girl to do?

I'm actually not as pissed as last night and manage to find my way home without any probs. I just can't resist loving myself again back at the flat, I just have to. Of course my search just has to centre around giant dicks, it was a forgone conclusion really wasn't it? I find a video of some guy with a really humongous todger - 10-inches no less! - fucking some lucky dark-haired bitch in every hole. She screams the house down as his enormous weapon splits her bum in 2 as I fuck myself anally with my biggest dildo - the 12-inch realistic one from Bedroom Pleasures - and scream-along to her loving. Lucky fucking cow!

***

Finally, it's the last evening of meeting my potential love-makers. The last guy on my list is Roland from Dorking in Surrey. He's the same age as me and is an artist and amateur racing driver - a bit of an odd combination I know but what the Hell! Yet again he seems like another nice enough guy and the conversation somehow gets onto the subject of art and tattooing.

He has both his arms fully sleeved in a tribal-style and they look amazing. I tell him about mine and give him a quick tantalizing glimpse, nothing more, simultaneously catching him looking down my top at my breasts as I do so and I love it.

Tonight I'm wearing my black low-cut v-neck jumper from Bluefly, a red leather split-skirt from Farfetch, and my lovely pair of black suede ankle-boots from Miu Miu on my feet. Once again I'm underwear-free and I question myself as to why haven't I worn a bra all week? What is the reason? I wonder what it means? My clutch-bag is my red plastic one from Boticca. My hair and make-up is as per usual although featuring matt-black lipstick. My perfume is *Mademoiselle* by Coco Chanel and I look and smell as absolutely fucking gorgeous as I always do.

The subject of conversation then steers itself onto sex and bizarrely, just like my second interviewee Stuart, Roland is also bisexual. So what, a little bit of what you fancy does you good!

Once again, I sit here wondering what all the pub staff and the regulars are thinking about me with all these different guys night after night? If I was a guy and was meeting a different woman every evening they would probably think I was a bit of a player and that it was funny, but being a beautiful woman and doing the same thing is considered somehow disgusting and trashy - but what's the bloody difference? Do they think that I'm a whore? Am I a whore? I am a whore.

I don't give a fuck either way, that's the punk in me.

The chucking-out gong strikes and both Roland and myself head off in opposite directions - it's the story of my life. I don't bother to love myself once back at the flat as I couldn't be bothered tonight for whatever reason, the last 9-evenings have melted my brain and I am beyond tired.

***

I sit at work the following day pondering what to do? I find myself in a real dilemma, I went looking for 3-guys to love me and I end up with 5! I try to re-examine all their finer points verses the lesser ones and cut 2 out that way but its to no avail - I have no sense of proportion at all. Having 5-guys all fucking me at the same time is just pure madness and I'm not sure I could cope with it, 3 is pushing me hard but 5? This is as stupid as it is mad, what is the bloody point of it all? Why am I doing this? Should I just quit and say "No" to all of them?

***

I give myself plenty of time to get ready for the onslaught I'm about to receive to both my body and my mind. I'm pretty sure my body can take it, I know I'm physically strong enough, but its my mind that I'm worried about. I already have brain damage and I'm hoping this adventure doesn't tip me over the edge of my mental precipice. I'm on a knife-edge as it is and if I fall there will be no going back this time.

I spend about 45-minutes in the bath having a good scrub and a soak in almost boiling-hot water into which I've added orange-scented bubble-bath, all designed to make me smell and taste even better than I do naturally - if that's at all possible? As I lay there soaking-away I dream about nothing else except all those guys spunking over me at the same time and the more I think about it the hornier and dirtier I become.

I dry myself gently and slowly over my perfect body. It is probably in better shape now that it has ever been, even though I do abuse it, in more ways that one. I look so gorgeous that even I would fuck me!

By now it's early evening and I've decided not to have any dinner at all. I think it might make me sick as my stomach is already churning over with anticipation. I down a couple of large glasses of German white instead as I dance around the flat naked listening to one of my own home-made CD compilations featuring David Bowie's *Heroes* and *Moonage Daydream*, Velvet Underground *Venus in Furs*, The Damned *Smash it up*, Marc Bolan *21st Century Boy*, Blondie *Presence Dear, Atomic* and *Man Overboard*, The Moody Blues *Ride My See-Saw*, Siouxsie and the Banshees *Make up to Break up* and *Hong Kong Garden*, The Cramps *Naked Girl Falling Down the Stairs*, Joy Division *New Dawn Fades*, PJ Harvey *In the Dark Places*, The Rolling Stones *Gimme Shelter*, The Cult *Coming Down*, Alien Sex Fiend *Smells Like Shit*, The Fall *Deadbeat Descendants*, Japan *Quiet Life*, Marilyn Manson *Great Big White World*, and even some Bauhaus - the nasty, gloomy and murderous live version of *Dark Entries*, which fuels my couldn't-care-less attitude even more and plunges me to the depths of my subconscious mind.

* * *

The Churchill Hotel on the outskirts of Horsham is a really lovely place. It has a very up-market feel to it and so it should as the high-class suite I've booked for tonight has cost me the best part of £250, and that doesn't include the 3-bottles of Champagne that I've laid on for all of us either!

Tonight I'm wearing a super-tight Bandeau Bandage dress in white from Lipsy, and when I say super-tight then I really mean super-tight! My underwear is in sexy red lace from Ultimo. On my feet I have my favourite old pair of blue-suede Lola platform court-shoes on, hopefully to bring me some luck. My clutch-bag for this evening is my Greta Deco Shell one from Vintage Styler. I've really gone to town on my hair and make-up once again. My hair I have up - as is my usual want - and is tied-up with a white silk bow that I actually made myself using material I bought from a funny little sewing shop in Horsham. As for my face I've got on my full-on killer look tonight, featuring frosted silver-blue eye-shadow with black eye-liner, super-sharp cheekbones and cherry-red lipstick, all from Rimmel London, my favourite. My perfume is *Poison* by Christian Dior once again.

After checking-in at reception I sit myself down at a table in the bar on my own. A couple of guys have hit on me already and

I've only been sitting here a few bloody minutes! I had to give them short-shrift even though they were both pretty fit-looking. My drink of choice is a large neat vodka.

Roland is the first guy to arrive and he spots me easily. I'm not the only girl in the bar obviously but I'm by far the most gorgeous, light-years away even. He's dressed really smartly, with a crisp white cotton shirt, a white and silver patterned waistcoat, double-pleated black trousers and black patent shoes.

I order the first bottle of Champagne for the night - Bollinger, no shit! - and 6- glasses. Yes that's right, you heard me - 6. What's the point of being fucked by 3-guys when I could be fucked by 5? And yes, I know I'm putting myself in danger once again - I've heard it all before - but I'm going to do whatever I fucking want to do with my life before it's too late. I know I'm a masochist but that fucking car accident has changed me forever. I could have been killed right there and then and I wouldn't be sitting here now about to have one of the most exhilarating experiences of my life would I? Life is for living, not for wasting-away sitting on your arse watching mind-numbing depressing shit on the TV all fucking day long. Anyway, it's not like I'm going to marry with any of them is it?

Stuart is the next guy to join us. He's dressed casual in a black shirt and jeans but still looks nice though. Andy and Martin come over together, even though they don't know one another, closely followed by Jason. They too are dressed smart / casual and at least they've all made an effort to try and impress me.

They all seem okay, just average guys I suppose? As long as they're nice enough then what the Hell? They can fuck me in every hole and shoot their muck all over me, I really don't care any more. I want them to defile me.

The Champagne flows and we all sit there and chat and laugh about sex and other stuff. We recall tails about our previous conquests - fucking, shagging and any and every other type of coitus you can think of and more.

* * *

It's all the events of the past - not just the ones from this year - that has lead me to this point in my life. I don't even care if I have a reputation. Who are these people who've given me such a title anyway? My situation is neither good or bad, it's just the way it is. As I've already told you, after baby Abigail's death and everything else there are no limits any more. These are the things I do for love - like using my vagina as a weapon.

***

I'm upstairs in the Hotel room with a glass of Champagne in one hand and yet another bottle of "Bollie" in the other. I came up here on my own before all the guys as I though it might look highly suspicious if we all came up together. I don't want any hassle from the management, or anyone else for that matter.

My heart is pounding-away like a fucking Jack-Hammer at my impending fate as a wave of excitement floods my restless body. I am so incredibly nervous! I imagine all their naked torsos and being soaked by all their hot spunk shooting over my beautiful body and I want it all right now and more - I want one-hundred guys to drown me in their cum.

What the Hell have I let myself in for?

There's a knock at the door and it's them, my 5-lovers for tonight. I feel like an actress about to star in her very first film. But who is filming me? You all know the answer of course, it's no-one and everyone, I'm filming myself as well as directing the show. I almost pass-out as I go to answer the door, all the anticipation as well as the Champagne and the vodka have all conspired together to attack my senses and I am crazy for cock. I have used my superior artifice to trick them all, to lure them into my trap and I love it.

I let the guys in and more Champagne is consumed by one and all. With a look of pure innocence across my gorgeous face I kick-off my heals and watch them watching me as I do so. My dress falls to the floor and Stuart touches one of my breasts as Jason fingers my vagina through the thin material of my knickers. I start to pant heavily as all 5 of them touch, kiss and caress my body. They squeeze my bum and my tits and one of them penetrates my mouth with his tongue. It feels like I have a million-hands all over my flesh and I'm in love with them all - oh come on, FUCK ME!

I pull away and stand back from them and remove my bra and knickers. They all smirk and laugh at me as I then order them to: "Drown my throat in cum" and for them to "Kill me with their love." The power I exert over these feeble men makes me feel like the Goddess I am. I hold them all within my grasp to manipulate as I see fit. All 5 of them are obsequious to my desires and yet they are nothing to me at the same time.

I tell them all to undress and they need no second instruction. Watching the 5 of them all peel-off in front of me makes me LOL as some of them do so quickly and just chuck their clothes to one side without a care whilst others take more time and fold their garments neatly and precisely. Either way, in a matter of minutes all 6 of us stand there staring at each other stark bollock naked. They all desperately try not to look at Andy's massive appendage but that's exactly what they do, all in jealousy at its excessive length. In fairness it's difficult not to!

The sensation of being naked and alone with these men begins to drive me insane - it is insane. Is this a sausage-fest or what? They're like a pack of baying dogs on heat and I love each and every one of them - OH MY FUCKING GOD!

I insist on them all fucking me bareback as they all approach me together as one, surrounding me with cock and love. I give myself to them and I am completely servile to their want. They all wank themselves to get hard as they start to touch me all over - my fanny, bum, tits, face, arms, legs. I kiss them all as I grab 2-cocks and wank them gently although I can't do it for very long as my right-arm still pains me from the crash if I push it too hard.

Andy is true to his word as his cock is amazingly huge, with a long thick veiny shaft and a giant purple knob and I can't resist it. I sink down onto my haunches and lick him but trying to get his massive spongiosum into my mouth is difficult.

I just about manage to swallow him and I lose my mind as his cock completely fills my head. The sight of all this dick makes me cum on its own and I suck on all their cocks one by one like the nymphomaniac I am and then I have 2-cocks in my mouth and then I try 3 but they won't fit and one of the guys fucks my vagina as another fucks me up the arse and I have 4-cocks in my body and I want more - I want all 5 of them and I die.

The taste of them in my mouth overwhelms me as I them feel someone else slide in underneath me and it's Stuart, sucking on my lips. As he does so I let Andy slide out of my mouth and I wank him. As I do I turn my head to see Roland sucking on Stuarts cock as he wanks himself on the floor and I laugh out loud again at the sight of the guys sucking each other. Watching gay porn on my laptop is one thing but actually seeing it right here in front of me is another - I love it and fuck.

I suck on both Jason's and Martin's cocks as Andy wanks in my face. I cum my juice in Stuart's mouth as Andy spits his evil muck into my face and I lick it as I shudder out of control. I want them all to abuse me more, to slap my face, slap my tits and slap my arse as they fuck my mouth, vagina and bum as behind my beautiful face I start to cry inwardly.

I spin around on top of Stuart to 69 him and join Roland in sucking his cock. We kiss cock and each other and as we do so I suddenly feel the cold wet sensation of more lubrication on my bum, making me start. Jason fucks my arse and I cry with love and pain as Martin comes to join me and I suck on his love-lolly as Stuart and Roland lick at his testicles. Jason cums in my rectum and I surrender myself totally to them all. Martin then cums in my mouth and I don't want this night to ever end, all I want is fuck, cock and cum.

I scramble off of Stuart and sit on Roland's dick, his cock-ring keeping him as hard as rock, inserting the second dick into my rear-end. Alternatively I suck on Martins and Jasons cocks as

Stuart laps at my vagina and before long I cum again, quivering and vibrating with their love. He pulls Rolands cock from my arse and ATM's him, sucking on my juice and the taste of lube and brown, before reinserting it back into my awaiting anus.

Andy kneels-down before me and forcefully pushes his giant tool into my pussy, filling my box completely and I scream as I'm double-entered, their meat hitting my cervix and pelvic-bone as I am defiled. Stuart is behind me now, being sucked-off by Roland as he too cums up my bum. Martin cums in my face as Jason cums over my beautiful tits and I'm in love with them all as then Andy's massive cock squirts its grotesque muck deep into my vaginal tube - he's a real swordsman!

I am totally out of control as Jason pours the last of the expensive Champagne over my cum-face. It mixes with the seed - the bubbly grape and the gloopy man-milk - and I lick and swallow it all down like the cunt I am. Maybe I've just invented a new drink - CumBollie? - BollieCum?

I go to get up but fatigue hits me quickly and I end up rolling over onto my back. Andy lays beside me and turns me to one side. I think he's going to spoon me up the fanny but instead he forces his 11-inches straight into my rear. I scream and pant and cry as he repositions my body on top of him as he fucks my rectum with his huge tool, splitting me.

Roland and Stuart both enter my cunt together as they French-kiss each other and fondle and caress each others nipples and bums as another one of the guys takes me *coitus-in-axilla* and I love him forever.

Martin and Jason are either side of my face and I suck their cocks alternatively before they also enter me, pushing their members into my mouth as I now have all 5-cocks buried within my beautiful supple body, their wet smelly bodies writhing about over mine and I love them all. They fuck my cunt, arse and mouth as they slap and squeeze and hurt me and I am in my own private personal Heaven / Hell.

They cum on me and it splashes and spits over my skin and I rub it into myself - their cum is my cum now and I cum myself.

They all take turns to eat my vagina and I orgasm out of control as it literally feels like they really are eating me alive and I grit my teeth together so hard that I sense them cracking under the pressure. I shake violently and cum once more and I am totally wasted. They wipe their once hard cocks over my face and tits and pussy and bum and piss on me their nasty mixture of Champagne and seed and I drink them and swallow their shit as I piss myself on the carpet. I have no control over my vagina.

Stuart fucks Roland up the arse and we all laugh at his pain and joy. Roland then sucks on Andy's massive cock as Martin fucks my mouth and Jason fucks my cunt and we are all GONE TO HELL!

I am gone.

There is nothing left of me.

I am surrounded by cock and I take it in turn to suck on them all as hard as I can because that is what I want and I WANT MORE.

I lose my mind as I turn into one giant cocksucker and I imagine my life how it would be if this moment were stuck in time forever. I suck on each one of them until they shoot their respective loads into my mouth and down my throat, pumping me full of their pungent muck as I wank myself with the spout of the Bollinger bottle in and out of my pussy. Martin sticks his dick into my mouth and fucks it in and out hard as one of the other guys uses his fingers to penetrate my twat and I am useless.

"HARDER FUCK. HARDER FUCK" I shout at them all.

I have no-idea of where I am as another of them anal's me hard once again and I have 2-cocks in my mouth. The guy fingering my vagina rubs my clit vigorously with his thumb as yet another guy enters my hole while the fifth guy fondles my breasts and squeezes them with pain.

I want to puke, shit and cum at the same time but I have no control over myself so I just have to remain there on all fours as I am overpowered by sex. The 2-guys in my mouth spunk over my face and the mess squirts into my eyes, hair, nose and tongue and I begin to hate myself although I love myself at the same time as I love and hate what these 5-men are doing to my mind and body as the war upon me continues. They cum their mess over and into me as I lay there on the floor with my legs as wide apart as they will go, their cloudy-white seed spitting over my face, tits, belly, vagina, bumhole, hair, arms, legs, hands, feet and down my throat - I am covered in the stuff and as the end is near, they take it in turns, one by one, to unload their poisoned milk into my mouth as I lay there spluttering it out and over my face and tits.

I swallow a thick gelatinous, slug-like mass of their combined cum and I feel it slither down my gullet into my stomach and I feel terrible. I insert 3-fingers into my vagina and another 3 into my mouth and wank them both in a desperate attempt to fuck myself to death on an all-encompassing moment of glory.

All 5-guys laugh at me and one of them urinates in my face but I continue with my self-humiliation as another squats over me and shits on my tits and then rubs his scat into them, mingling his turd with the cum and piss and they all laugh at me even more so I insert my whole hand into my cunt and push it harder and harder and I have no more care left to care.

The laughter from the guys subsides into an eerie silence as they all just stand there naked watching this female "Thing" that I have become destroy itself as I continue to fist-fuck my mouth and vagina, moaning and groaning with pain and exertion and crying as my pleasure / dis-pleasuring becomes something else - this event has now turned into one of horror. I cannot stop smashing myself to pieces as the 5-guys continue to just stand there over me, motionless and perplexed at what to do next. My eyes are as wide as saucers but I'm not looking at anything, I am blind to my surroundings as I fuck.

I genuinely start to cry now as I plead:

"HELP ME. HELP ME PLEASE. WON'T ONE OF YOU PLEASE HELP ME?" I scream at them.

"FUCKING HELP ME YOU BASTARDS."

One of them - it doesn't matter who - grabs the Champagne bottle from behind me and positions my gorgeousness back on all fours and fucks me up the arse with it as I suck-off the other 4-cocks and lick their heavy, spunk-laden balls.

Cock has driven me insane and I live for no other reason, I just want more cock. I want to die from cock as my orgasm resonates within me and fractures my soul, making me scream insanely.

I shit myself into the Champagne bottle as my beautiful face becomes a sea of cum and it drips off of me, down onto my perfect breasts and then the stained carpet. I wipe the poo and cum into my bum and up my hole, wanking it with 3-fingers and then pushing my whole hand up my arse and I am beyond repair - I am as good as dead.

Another guy - I don't know which one and I don't fucking care - desperately tries to insert his cock into my cunt even though I have another cock inside it already. The first guy pulls out and they both cock me together as one but it's a fucking tight insufferable squeeze as my lips part and it hurts and I try to scream but I can't as I'm already choking on the 2-cocks in my mouth as then one of them cums his semen down my throat and I gag as I ingest the vile, repellent glop. Roland then cums up my arse and I feel his gruesome spunk spurt up into my rectum like ice, making me shudder. I've got parts of my body that ache that I didn't even know I had!

I feel like I'm loosing consciousness as I'm attacked by cock as then another guy spunks in my mouth and then another up my fanny but I can't cum - I've lost myself to them totally as someone else glops up me and they all pull out and I lick all their knobs free of spunk, vaginal juice and some red and brown.

I am no more.

I am no-longer human.

I am a piece of meat.

I am no-longer Sarah Knowles.

I am a shell that is female in form and fuck.

So what am I?

Am I a whore or a slag or a cunt?

I am all of these and worse and more.

I think I've really freaked 2 of the guys out as Jason and Martin dress and disappear out the door and my life. Andy then fucks my cunt as I suck on Roland's cock as he wanks Stuart's cock with his tongue and mouth. He fucks into me hard and deep in a rhythmic fluid motion and I feel myself bleed and become completely disempowered as Stuart cums into Roland's mouth. I wank Roland's cock with my mouth and he cums his jism on my tongue and tits and I lick it up as Andy shoots his fuck up my cunt.

I suck Stuart's cock as Roland fucks him up the arse and Andy vanishes and now we are down to just the 3 of us. Roland wears my beautiful dress and Stuart my underwear as I suck both of their dirty sordid cocks at the same time. I order them both to: "Scratch and slap my bum like a bitch" and it stings me as they do.

Stuart sits on the corner of the bed as Roland lowers himself down backwards onto his cock. I face both of them as I sit down on Roland's cock and it slides beautifully between my Mexican-saddlebags and into my awaiting vagina. The 3 of us bob up and down fucking until Roland cums his splodge into me with a squelch. I climb off and suck his spunky cock and lick his smooth shaved balls and he blows my mind as I blow his cock. I try to insert the little finger on my right-hand into his Japs-eye but with limited success. Even so he loves it and laughs and screams blue-murder - Ha!

Stuart starts to shake as he cums up Roland's arse and as I suck on his balls, his seed squirting out from Roland bum and down Stuart's cock onto my tongue. I eat his bull-milk as I suck on both their cocks and I am lost to fuck and I shit myself on the floor. I order them to: "Kiss each other and lick each others faces and eat cum" as they then shout back at me to: "Suck our cocks you dirty fucking whore bitch" and "Swallow our cum you fucking cunt." I call them a: "Couple of fucking queers" as

Roland retorts with; "Stick your tongue up my arsehole and eat my shit you fucking slag."

The 3 of us laugh at how the evening has gone as we play with each others bodies, with my tits and vagina and their 2-cocks. We clean ourselves up after Roland licks-out my cunt and Stuart sucks Roland's cock once more and I suck on Stuart's knob. We all kiss as we wank each other and then the evening is over.

The 3 of us redress and I walk down to the Hotel foyer with them and kiss them both "Goodbye" with lots of tongues and touching and I thank them for a wonderful evening and for fucking me. I give Roland my knickers and Stuart my bra as tokens to remember me by, not that I doubt at all that they will forget me in a hurry!

I kiss them both on the lips again and touch their cocks right in front of the late-night Hotel staff and a few fellow hoteliers and then I am left alone once more in this sad, beautiful, stupid World.

I don't want to actually spend the whole night in the Hotel on my own so I make my way back upstairs to my room to get the rest of my stuff before I crawl back home in shame. That was one Hell of a party and I know that I pushed it too far - as always! I'm really amazed at the durability of my body even though I feel like shit and my brain and my soul are burnt to a crisp, I can't even bloody see straight let-alone think straight!

I'm not going to tidy-up all this fucking mess either - the cum, the Champagne, the piss, the shit, the smell of sex, the empty tube of lubrication and other detritus - that's a job for the cleaners as it's what they're paid to do in the first place. And if they're stinking foreigners like Polish, Bulgarian, Romanian or some other type of Slav scum then that's even better; it's no more than they fucking deserve. They enjoy cleaning up shit as much as they enjoy living in it.

***

Little did I know when I rang the Medical Centre that Dr. Alexander, my dear old Doctor that I've had all my life, had retired some months ago. I feel quite sad in not having said "Goodbye" to her. As I've told before, she was like a second mother to me and I shall really miss her soothing and protective manner.

Her replacement is Dr. Green, a funny, smelly old guy in his 60's who whiffs of musty old furniture and has the look of a mad professor about him, although he seems nice enough. I had to go and see him a few weeks ago - only 2-weeks after my night of debauchery - as I hadn't been feeling well at all. I knew something was wrong, that I had obviously caught some kind of infection. There's no point in blaming any of the guys for this, there is only one person to blame for being so fucking reckless with my health and my life and that's me, as it was me that demanded no-one was to use a condom, and it is my licentious attitude that has lead me to this place in time, to this moment.

The upshot of all this crap is, after a couple of humiliating visits to said Doctor, is that I have contracted Chlamydia, a disgusting sexually transmitted infection that has increased in circulation alarmingly in the past few years mainly due to people like me and worse. It was only a matter of time before we found each other. It wasn't a question of "If", but of "When". It also doesn't matter which guy I caught it from, they're all the fucking same anyway.

My new Doctor has proscribed me a course of oral antibiotics called Azithromycin, for the duration of the next 7-days. These are supposed to clear everything up within that allotted time-zone, so hopefully I can then go back to square-one, to

having a clean bill of health. Although I do have to go back and see him for a retest in 2-weeks time, so hopefully I'll get the all-clear then.

I'm constantly amazed at how much punishment my poor body has taken over the years, and yet despite all the crap, I still look bloody fantastic!

As I mentioned before I met those guys, what is going on in my brain is a different story altogether. Each and every event takes its toll on me and it's only a matter of time before I reach the end of my rope, there will be no going back after that.

As far as my sexual gratification is concerned, I've had to knock that on the head for the time being, for obvious reasons, this being the second bloody time I've caught as STI in the last 18-months. When I think of the amount of spunk that I've had pumped into me, swallowed and digested over the years, it must be gallons of the stuff? Yuk / Gorgeous!

I've also cancelled my subscription to the website where I found the 5-guys the very next morning after our party. I've not heard a peep from any one of them, not that any of them have my personal contact details anyway. I never had any intention of meeting either one of them again - I've moved on.

Where I go from here I just don't know? The future will be whatever the future will be and that's the way it is. I have to survive regardless of whatever predicament or life-affirming situation I find myself in. That's what living in today's World is all about. Whatever choice one makes in life, you have to deal with whatever the outcome may be. And how you deal with that will also have its consequences, it's a viscous circle of never-ending crap.

9

Mark & Jane

At this present moment in time, the only really consistent thing in my life is work - how sad is that? Things here are pretty stable I guess, even though that obviously means I'm bored shitless! I do try to feign some sort-of interest but it just doesn't work. I come in here every working day, 5-days a week, do my job and do it well, but the reality is I'm just not fucking interested. I just don't care, I hate this job more and more each day, although I guess it won't be forever.

I'm certainly not going to prostitute myself for this company or any other for that matter, why the fuck should I? I'm like a fucking leper in this place - the World's most beautiful leper that is! Why I'm working in this hole in the first place I just don't know. I must want my fucking head tested!

Oh well, here we go again, another fucking day of shit. It's like a fucking pantomime in here with all these characters. Will this crap never end? At least it's Friday and we all get to go home early at 3.30pm - the long / short day that is Friday. I really can't wait to get out of this fucking hole, I hate these people.

Amazingly nothing of any significance has happened to me this week so I guess I can expect a double-dose of misfortune and unbelievable bad luck next week.

I'm really not in the mood for this shit today, or any other day for that matter. As per usual I spend most of the day yawning my bloody head off. I am so fucking bored I feel as though I'm about to implode. I should be on suicide-watch working here! Home-time cannot come around soon enough and then I'll be out of here as fast as a bullet.

Today I'm wearing the most gorgeous white Jersey dress from Designer Desirables that features black side-panels that make me look even curvier than I am naturally - it's to die for! My underwear is in yellow lace from Agent Provocateur whilst my shoes are my white Clarks Raffi Scent sandals. I've done my make-up featuring light-grey eyeshadow and matt-red lipstick. My perfume is *Luxe* by Avon. I also have a white and black plastic butterfly clip in my hair and I look beautiful and everyone fucking knows it.

As you've probably guessed I'm still working at the very same insurance company I told you about the last time around, the one in Horsham, West Sussex. I don't know what it is about this place, it's like a cross between a lunatic asylum, an old people's home and Steptoe's yard, with its ancient computers and office furniture. It really is shit, everything is literally held together with bits if sticky-tape and chewing-gum! I honestly don't know why I put up with it, I hate every fucking second. The one good thing about it is that it's only a couple of miles away from where I live in Slinfold Village, so it is handy for commuting I suppose, but that's about it.

Like I've said many times before, I absolutely hate working full-stop, not just here, but anywhere at all. I'm sick of wasting my precious time stuck here doing this meaningless shit with these pen-pushers every fucking day. Just think of all the things I could be doing if I wasn't chained to this bloody desk all day long working like a slave - having great sex (with either a guy or a girl - or both!), getting pissed, driving around in my car - the orange bomber - having fun, more sex, shopping, or even more sex yet again!

I've been thinking of leaving this job since the day I started, it's only transient after all. I had to lie through my back-teeth to land the job in the first place, giving them a bent CV and references. I make no excuses for that, everyone does it - it doesn't pay to be honest in this life. Like all companies, they don't give anything away so therefore I take. Even so, I'm not going to kill myself for them or any other company. I've learned my lessons the hard way with all my previous employers and I don't intend to make the same mistake again. I am sharper than a serpents tooth and I don't have to prove myself to anyone. My consciousness has elevated me to a higher plain than most people on this shitty, beautiful planet, and, like everything else in life these days, it's all become spurious in the extreme.

Isn't it strange when you join another company and get to know all the new people, your fellow co-workers, and all their funny little ways? Although they're completely different people in a completely different company, it's amazing just how similar everything is to the one before. My super-sharp perspicacity quickly sussed my co-workers out on day one. I have the ability to see right through things, to see right through people, just as if their skin was transparent.

These people know how to operate a phone but don't have a clue how to operate life, it's like *The Night of the Living Dead* in this place! I just can't get involved with these mentalists. After all those years of being mentally tortured by the "Old Man" and all his antics, I just can't deal with people like him or any of this lot - enough is enough.

Take the big boss for example, the owner of the company, or "Mr. Bill" as we all have to call him - don't ask my why, I don't know either? Why not just call him Bill, that's his fucking name after all? He's a short, fat, old guy in his 70's who spends most of his time doing dodgy-deals out on the bloody golf course - boring old git. I've been here for well over a year now and he still doesn't even know my name - which is typical - and nor does he want to or intend to. In the few times we actually have met, he kept calling me Susan for some bloody reason? Not that he was looking at my face anyway as he just stood there leering at my tits, dirty old bastard. I've seen him in his office a couple of times, during tea-break, supping his tea from a saucer. Why not use a cup like everyone else? I even caught him in the car-park once peeing up the side of his own car! What the Hell is all that about? Just like every other boss, he's not interested in us, the ordinary workers, and I'm certainly not bloody interested in him. All he wants is the rake-off generated by his minions so he can line his own pockets and fuck-off abroad for umpteen-times a year. Unfortunately this is the way it is in most companies. Don't these people realise that shit rolls down hill and we all get infected with the same couldn't-care-less attitude? Don't they ever learn? If I was a company owner I wouldn't treat my staff like shit. I'd want them to be happy at work, which in turn increases productivity amongst the inherent harmonious atmosphere. It's not fucking difficult. Fortunately, I'm largely ignored by the "men in suits" in this company. Their arrogance doesn't allow them to accept the fact that I even exist.

Once again, like every other company, this one also has its individual cliques of people, some talk to some, others talk to others - it's all so silly and pathetic. Personally, as ever, I try and keep myself to myself and not get involved in anyone else's shit. What's the point? Why should I run around after them, they don't fucking run around after me?

I don't know why it is I'm in a different category to everyone else, I just am I guess? Being a Scorpio by birth means that fortunately I'm always one step ahead of everyone else. I am on a completely different level than them, I know it and I feel it. I'm not telling you this to make myself sound big-headed, I'm telling you because it's a fact. I'm not like the rest of them, or you for that matter. So what if I'm a control junkie, what the fuck has it got to do with you anyway?

My immediate boss and the head of my section is Chris Johns, or CJ as he likes to be known - fuck knows why? He's a big, burly guy, somewhere in his mid-50's, and on the social side of things he is not a success. He doesn't have any kids of his own as he and his wife only married recently and she already had a couple of teenage daughters from a previous relationship. Anyway, that's neither here or there, the point is that it's no wonder this country's in such a fucking mess with tossers like him in charge. His shoddy management is just typical of most company bosses these days. He never seems to be on the section floor, he's always locked-away in his office either staring out of the window at the passing traffic and passers-by, reading his bloody newspaper or on his computer watching porn! The guy is totally fucking useless, and judging by the way he acts I'm pretty sure that he's a bloody Freemason as they're all cunts just like him. I've been to see him numerous times with one problem or another and he just doesn't want to know and dismisses me with a shrug and a sneer like the spineless moron he is. What is this country coming to with idiots like him in charge? As the old saying goes: "There's none so blind as those who don't want to see."

He's a big guy with a big mouth and a big attitude but when it comes down to it, he's just an empty shell - just like the fucking rest of them. I also wouldn't trust him as far as I could throw him. I got wind of him giving away company vouchers to his inherited daughters, vouchers that are meant for us workers as perks to keep us sweet and our mouths shut. Obviously this got right under my skin somewhat so I decided to do something about it, so early one morning, just before all the plebs arrived, I snuck into his office to help myself to some freebies. Unfortunately all his desk draws were locked so I had to try and pick them open with my trusty old Swiss Army knife to do so! With success on my side I gained entry and helped myself to a handful of said vouchers, there being at least fifty of them in a bunch from companies like Argos, John Lewis, Waitrose and others. With the proceeds (technically they wern't his anyway) I bought myself some nice goodies for the flat - a stainless-steel cutlery set, a DeLonghi 4-slice Scultara toaster in white, a Hoover Lithium-ion cordless handheld vacuum cleaner, a Tefal compact pressurised steam generator with an ultraglide soleplate, a DeLonghi Scultura kettle in white (to match the toaster) and a few other odds and sods. Why he thought he had the bloody right to keep the vouchers for himself in the first place is anyone's guess? It's just typical of the attitude of these so-called "Managers" who seem to think they can do just as they fucking like - they can't - and I won't let them get away with this sort of crap, I will do what I WANT, for myself.

He even got one of his "daughters" - Bella, the 17-year-old one - a temporary job in my office during the Easter school holidays, and a right little stuck-up bitch she turned out to be as well. Needles to say she got preferential treatment all the fucking time she was here from the weak management, being given all the easy jobs as well as extended break times and other perks. I bet you she was even earning more money than me as well. Nepotism rules OK in this fucking place.

On another subject, you should have seen CJ's face when I got myself my car - the orange bomber - he nearly crapped himself when he saw it! I've since worked out that most of the jealousy towards me stems not just because of my natural beauty but because of my car - how pathetic can people be? What do they expect me to drive around in, some crappy Nissan Micra for fucks sake?

Of course CJ has a company car - a boring BMW diesel estate - as have all the other managers. He's so fucking jealous it's unreal! I bet his crabby wife wouldn't allow him to have a beautiful car like mine anyway? What a meathead! If he resents me and my car so much then why doesn't he put his foot down and get himself a decent second car - talk about "under-the-thumb."

Talking of cars and how this company is run, I will give you all a good clear example of what I mean. Not long after I joined the firm - only about a couple of months or so - the "Big Cheese" decided to sell-off part of the company car-park to a developer for them to build a small block of flats on the land. Okay I here you say, so what? This of course obviously limited the amount of parking spaces for all the workers. So, how do you reckon he solved the problem? He decided to ban all staff - except the managers of course! - from parking in the remaining spaces, and rented part of a muddy field 2-miles away as staff parking, bought a mini-bus and took-on a full-time driver (at more expense) to ferry us to and fro from work at either ends of the bloody day - WTF! I've never heard anything so bloody stupid in all my days! How ridiculous is that? Needless to say, there was no bloody way I was going to comply with any of that shit, so I managed to seal an arrangement with a car-less elderly couple who live just around the corner to the workplace who have let me park on their driveway during the day for the grand sum of only £5 a week - result!

I know I've said this many times before, but this is just bloody typical of the crap I have to put up with in my life. Nothing is ever easy, I always have to fight for everything. The car-park thing is only one example, I could go on for evermore about this place and all the other shit companies and people I've had to deal with over the years.

Another continuing stupid episode here is with the recycling. We each have to sort out what is recyclable rubbish from the general rubbish - OK so far? That's fair enough of course, but when the bin-lorry arrives they just empty both loads of waste into the very same lorry, so what's the bloody point of us separating our rubbish in the first place then, what a complete waste of time and energy? When I pointed this fact out to Paula, my section supervisor, she went on to tell me that: "It is company policy that we continue to keep the recycling separate from the general waste in order to help the environment for future generations." What a load of fucking crap! Are these people fucking blind as well as fucking stupid? What the fuck is wrong with everyone?

Another case was with the staff bringing in water bottles. Just as the weather started to get warmer, the company banned them, stating that: "In case they split their contents onto the computers or phones." Needless to say, once again, I ignored their stupid ban and carried on using mine right up to this very day, I'm not sitting here on my arse all day in this weather dehydrating, they can fuck right off!

As you can probably tell, as is the norm in my life, I am totally and completely bemused by my co-workers apathy to life and their absolute lack of imagination. Can they all really be this boring, these killjoys? They're all completely oblivious as to what is happening in the World around them. Each and every one of them is a square peg in a round hole. None of them has any mettle, they're all snowflakes, all of them. I wonder what actually goes on in their infinitesimal brains - if anything at all? Not that I'm being cynical of course!

I don't trust any of them, they all give me the bloody creeps! I have absolutely no empathy towards any of them at all. I find it difficult - impossible even - to readjust my life to fit in with other people, other humans. We are simply not compatible, and I'm not going to sit here winding myself up by even thinking about them, they're just not worth it.

I do actually get along with a few of them, they're not all completely stupid! But the vast majority of them I steer well clear of. None of them are remotely interested in any way as to what I get up to or my life. They probably wouldn't believe me anyway, or would be horrified at my answer. I did in the early days of working here ask a few people about how their weekends had been but it was a one-sided conversation, I could never get a straight bloody answer anyway so what was the point? They were more than happy to tell me their tales but poo-pooed wanting to hear about mine. That's why I don't fucking bother any more, I'm not wasting my time on any of them, I don't have time to waste.

I suppose there must be almost 40-people on my floor, although they're not all in my section, with each section having its own supervisor and CJ being in charge

over the whole floor, which is a bloody joke as I've already mentioned as he's completely fucking useless!

Almost as useless is my supervisor - Paula. She's somewhere in her late-40's with greying hair and has a horrible pungent smokers breath on her. I don't know what her problem is, she's so distant and cold that the air literally freezes around her! The most amazing thing about her is the fact that she has 5-kids by 3-different men and wasn't married to any of them - classy! She's hardly ever here though, she's always off sick due to stress and problems either with her brats, money trouble, or having the Child Support Agency after her - something to do with access to the kids by their respective fathers, so I hear. Not that I really give a shit - stupid cow!

Of course there's also the usual foreign element mixed-in with everyone, and in my section alone there are the obligatory Poles - 4 of them in fact - and each one a fucking arrogant bastard, so I try to stay well clear of them at all costs.

There's also one obligatory Bud-Bud-Ding-Ding - Sabia I think her name is, or something like that? She's another nasty cow and I had to put her in her place on day one - typical arrogant bloody Paki.

There are more odd-balls in my department that you can shake a stick at. The oddest of the lot is Malcolm, the office dogsbody, general gofer and a complete retard. It's difficult to say how old he is - about 35 I suppose? - and he's definitely not playing with a full deck of cards! He keeps staring at me all the bloody time with his weird lecherous eyes and keeps showing me photos of his fucking Transit van on his phone. A typical conversation between us is like the one from a couple of weeks ago when he shoved his mobile phone right under my nose when I was busy trying to work:

"Transit van." He informs me yet again.

"Yes, I know. I don't want to see any more pictures of your van Malcolm. Just go away will you please, I'm working."

"Transit van."

"I know it's your Transit van, I just don't want to see any more photos of it okay?"

"It's white."

"Yes, I know that. Just piss-off will you please." Fucking perv. What a dipshit!

Another weirdo is Jack - or "Spam" as I've nicknamed him, as in "Spamhead". He's a sick, lecherous old git in his early-60's who always makes a beeline for me most mornings, putting his bloody arm around my shoulder and asking me:

"Have you been a good girl Sarah?" Stupid old bastard.

One of these days he's going to get a punch in the mouth! Unfortunately he sits not far from me, just across the isle, where

I have an almost full view of his pervy face. The worst thing is when he sits there yawning his bloody head off, as he has a set of false-teeth, and when he yawns the top set of dentures falls down exposing his gummy mouth - it's absolutely disgusting!

Then we have Stan - or as I call him, "Monster Breath" - a big fat bloke also around 60-ish who always slobbers from his mouth when he talks and has the foulest bad breath on this planet ever! I just can't stand being anywhere near him - he's vile.

And then there's Nora. A funny little woman in her early-60's with a hunched-back, although that doesn't seem to stop her thinking that she's some kind-of man-eating cougar, which she most definitely is not, in fact she's bloody horrible-looking! She can't even bloody walk in a straight line properly, more like a string-puppet, the result of some problem with her legs since childbirth. Apparently both her ankle-joints are fused together or some such crap - bloody raspberry! She's also got a gob on her like you wouldn't believe, a whining, squawking, nasal-toned voice that echo's around the whole department, spreading useless gossip around the office at every opportunity - there are more rumours flying around in this place than in Fleetwood Mac! - coming out with shit like:

"And she said this and she said that and she said this and she said that" and all that meaningless crap. She's got more rabbit than a bloody butchers shop! On top of all this bullshit we also get a running commentary on the state of the bloody weather, shouting out across the office an update on it every 30-fucking-seconds! She doesn't even stop for breath, it's just one long continuous sentence of shit:

"It's 24.5-degrees now, it's 25.6-degrees, had a spider in my bath this morning, colder towards the weekend, it's 25.7-degrees, it's going to be windy tomorrow, no it's not, it's going to be raining, I love my cooker, it's 25.8-degrees, my pussy was causing me problems again last night, it's sunny next week, no it isn't, it's going to be raining with possible hale, I bought a new rug on Saturday, it's 25.9-degrees, I keep stubbing me big toe, it's going to be fine tomorrow, I'm having sausages tonight, it's gone up to 26.0-degrees now with a chance of snow later, I'm having a pasty tomorrow, it's back down to 25.9-degrees again, I'll get me medical book out, it's 25.8-degrees, I put my bedroom light on this morning, it's still 25.8-degrees, no it's not, yes it is, it's 25.7-degrees, it's getting there slowly, that's all I know."

And on and on and on it fucking goes all fucking day long, she says more in the space of an hour than I do in a whole fucking week! Her biggest problem though is the fact that her mouth and her brain aren't connected. She just talks for the sake of talking as the words flow out of her mouth like a bloody waterfall. Also, every time someone walks past her desk, without fail she has to say something to them or make some sort-of comment, no matter how innocuous, and even if they walk-off uninterested in her crap she still carries-on yapping-away to herself - fucking nutcase! It's any excuse for a chin-wag and to waste more time, her mouth just doesn't fucking stop:

"I can't find my handcream, handcream, handcream, handcream."

Why doesn't she just shut the fuck up? On the ultra-rare occasions she does actually stop talking, all she does is sit there stuffing her big mouth with sweets or just sits there picking her nose - yuck! Anyway, I would have thought her pussy must have dried-up by now!

Another strange woman is Kat - with a "K" - who I've nicknamed "Miss World" due to the fact that she's so fucking ugly. In fact I don't think I've ever seen such an uglier woman in all my life, she looks like an extra from a *Planet of the Apes* film! She even claims to be younger than me - fuck-off is she, she must be 55 if she's a day! She also has this strange turquoise-coloured hair that looks like Italian ice-cream, and dresses like a bloody tramp in an awful dishevelled old duffel-coat that she wears all the time (even in Summer!) that is tied together around her waist with a piece of string! Believe me, you couldn't make this shit up! She also has some sort-of speech impediment which makes listening to her talking to customers on the phone an excruciating experience. What they must think I just don't know? She's yet another one that's full of useless shit, yapping-on all fucking day about bloody *Harry Potter* films and other such crap. How old is she - 12? She even claims that she was abandoned by her parents as a baby and left on Brighton beach - what a load of bullshit!

Someone else I can't make-out is Gerry, from Northern Ireland. I simply cannot understand a bloody word he's saying - it's impossible! Bumping into him is something I try to avoid at all times as his accent is a bloody nightmare.

There's also - strangely enough - another Irish guy in my section, also called Gerry, although he's from Southern Ireland and is far more intelligible. The downside to him though - which is a shame as he's quite an attractive guy and full of Irish charm - is the fact that he has some sort-of skin problem, psoriasis I think? - and bits of him keep falling off when we have the occasional chat together! He even asked me out on a date once, but I had to let him down gently, there was just no way I could put up with a guy with flaky skin - yuck!

In the centre section of our department there's a separate unit that deals with the administration of our work, to make sure that it's compliant with company policy and our governing body, for legal reasons obviously. This is made up of Carol, who I guess must have been a bit of a looker in her time. She must be in her late-50's but dresses even younger than I do! It just doesn't work - you get the picture, "mutton dressed as lamb" and all that? Sometimes you just have to face the fact that time moves on, you can't stay looking 21 for ever, even I know that.

Next to her sits Angie, a funny little Greek girl with a massive mop of curly springy dark hair and with an equally massive laugh. She seems like a really happy soul and always says "Hello" and chats whenever we bump into one another. I don't fancy her or anything like that - she's not in my league by a long way - it's just that out of all the people in this department she's probably the only one I actually have any rapport or can have a decent conversation with, even though she is a bit spaced-out - probably due to the effects of smoking too much pot! She's also had some problems in her short life, both privately and with this company. Not too long ago her elder brother died of a heart-attack, and of course naturally she was upset and distressed. When she phoned-in to tell our supervisor what had happened and that she needed some compassionate time off, Paula told her that she had to come into work because we were so busy! When she did actually scrape herself in she did nothing but sit at her desk crying her eyes out, so what was the fucking point of it all? In the end she got herself signed-off sick by her Doctor so she could grieve and to attend her brothers funeral. It's fucking unbelievable isn't it the way some companies treat their staff. As you well know, I've hated every company I've ever worked for but this was a new depth that surprised even me - bastards.

By her side sits Lilly, a horrible-looking little skank of a girl with no breasts. She's somewhere in her late-teens and just the sort of brat you would expect to find lurking around some Council estate sink-hole looking for another fix - she is rank. Her whole life seems to centre around her fucking mobile-phone, as is the norm with kids her age.

Another silly cow in this section is Linda - or "The Fat One" as I call her. How the Hell she managed to get this position I'll never know as she's as thick as 2-short planks! She probably only got the job by dropping down onto her fat knees! If we ever have a works Quiz Night I wouldn't want her on my team - she's as ignorant and as thick as shit! I mean, how can you take anyone serious who's favourite film is *Happy Feet* ? I think she's somewhere in her early-50's, unmarried, with no kids, and desperately trying to make herself look younger - and failing! - with her fake blonde bob haircut. She's actually not that bad-looking, except for one obvious thing, and that is the size of her enormous, fat arse - it's big enough to blot-out the Sun! Along with her saggy arse comes her saggy tits and her sagging 50-plus face. I take it all back, she's not that great-looking after all! We don't speak to each other any more now for several reasons - jealously because of my looks, my body, my car, my independence, all the usual old things - but mainly because of one stupid incident that occurred outside the company car-park one Monday morning when she cut right across in front of me, almost chopping the nose off the front of my car. Naturally I had a right old go at her once we got inside work, screaming in her face:

"CAN'T YOU SEE A BRIGHT ORANGE FUCKING CAR IN BROAD DAYLIGHT YOU STUPID FAT COW?"

Obviously she went and grassed me up immediately, crawling-off crying fake tears of "Boo Hoo Hoo Hoo Hoo" to Paula and then CJ.

I can't really believe how quickly she folded-up though, it was amazing! It just goes to show how fucking weak she is, stupid fat ignorant bitch. Of course I was soon called-up before the "beak" - CJ that is! - on that one, as well as a trip to see the stupid HR Manager woman, receiving a wrap across the knuckles for being a naughty girl. Yet another pathetic black-mark for *Moi,* not that I give a fuck. What was I supposed to do, just let her crash into me?

As far as her work is concerned, she doesn't seem to have anything to do all fucking day anyway except spy on people and then grass them up to CJ, especially about yours-truly, coming out with shit like:

"Sarah was talking to Angie."

"Sarah was late back from lunch."

"Sarah was on her mobile-phone."

"Sarah has a bottle of water on her desk."

"Sarah's clothes are too revealing."

"Sarah called me names."

"Sarah fucking this, Sarah fucking that." I just want to smack that fucking bitch in the mouth - fat cow. She has absolutely no personality whatsoever, nothing, she might as well not even exist.

There is also something weird going on between these 4 and Paula the supervisor. I've noticed them taking-over some of my work recently, I don't know what the Hell that's all about but no-doubt I'll find out eventually, not that I really give a fuck, I'm in the driving-seat of my own life.

Sitting to my right is JK (I've no-idea what his real name is - Jew Kike maybe?), or "Pinhead" as I call him due to the weird shape of his head. This odd shape is emphasized further by his strange haircut, with its shaved sides it looks just like a hedgehog has gone to sleep on top of his head - he looks a right twat! To go with this look he always wears a tracksuit to work every day, I guess because he's so short and fat, and tucks his tracksuit bottoms into his socks! What a great look that is! To make things worse he also has this fucking smartarse fucking attitude about him on every fucking subject under the Sun. Even though he's only a kid of 23, he has all the air about him of someone who's seen and done everything in life. This condescending attitude even extends towards the customers he deals with on the phone, but - once again - he's never pulled-up about it as our supervisor Paula is best friends with his bloody mother! How fucking fair is that?

Since my first day here he's never actually spoken one single fucking word to me, which suits me perfectly as I don't fucking want him to! If he died of a brain haemorrhage right here and now it wouldn't make a fucking difference to anything. I know he doesn't like me and I know why, as yet again it's more jealousy over my car - how sad! Maybe he should ask his mummy for a car like mine and get rid of that awful overrated Spik piece of crap he tears-around in. As far as his "work" is concerned, he spends most of his time pissing-about on his mobile phone, either texting his boyfriend or mumbling-away to himself as he sits there listening to his fucking black "music" on his headphones. Once again our supervisor seems to let this misdemeanour go just the same as the rest of them, probably once again due to the unfair Paula / mother connection - it makes my blood boil. Typical fucking arrogant Yid.

Next up we have Dennis and Caroline, a married couple who could not be more different if they tried. Dennis is a pasty-faced white guy of about 50 who would probably fall over in a slight breeze as he's so weedy! His wife is the exact polar opposite - a big, fat, black bitch that looks like a giant lump of chocolate! The very thought of them being together is disgusting and turns my stomach. How the Hell he could go down on that defies all logic.

Over in the far-corner there's Gary, the office smartarse and God's gift to all womankind. He's one of those cock-sure types who always dresses to impress, with his numerous expensive-looking power-suits, waistcoats and Italian pointed shoes. Well, he certainly doesn't impress me, even though he would no-doubt like to poke me, just they all would. We actually went to the same Senior School together many Moons ago, although I only vaguely remember him - he was a twat then and nothing has changed in the intervening years! - except the fact is that he's turned into a complete piss-head, even more so than I have! I watch him sometimes out of my office window, off to the pub around the corner to get bladdered one minute and then back the other way to the betting shop and then back to the pub again and so on and so on all fucking afternoon! You might very-well wonder how he gets away with all this shit? The answer is very simple, I actually caught him - during my very first week here to be exact - up in one of the upstairs offices after I had taken the wrong turn looking for CJ's office - when I saw him with his hand on the arse of one of the managers - a male manager that is - incredible! I guess he must have spotted me as he hasn't been anywhere near me since, not even to hit on me. The fact that he's married with 3-kids doesn't seem to have altered his attitude in any way. How his wife puts up with all his drinking, smoking and gambling I'll never know, especially with 3-kids in the mix, poor cow. Oh well, she married him after all.

By him sits Dave, a man who is literally a shadow of his former self. Apparently he used to be a really big fat guy who then shed loads of weight. The problem now though is that he's still wearing the very same clothes from when he was a lard-arse! To look at him is both comical and sad at the same time. He's also one of those nerdy, geeky types, one of those sad bastards that never leaves the house as he's chained to his computer playing silly little games all bloody night long with his stupid friends and then wonders why he's so fucking tired the following morning - maybe he should try getting a bloody life!

Next to Dave sits Jeremy, or "Lettuce" as I call him, on account of the fact that he's a complete non-entity of a man. He is so bloody boring I don't know why he exists at all? He has absolutely no redeeming qualities about him. Not only is he a dweeb, he's also a bloody Communist to boot! I don't think I've ever met anyone with such a Far-Left stance on life as him, it really is sick to listen to. I heard him talking shit the other week in the works tearoom during lunch-break, spouting his Left-Wing rhetoric to anyone who dared to listen when he suddenly declared:

"All I care about is the children of the World."

How very noble - bloody bed-wetter!

It makes me sick to think that people like him actually exist and are free to walk around amongst us. He should be put up against the wall and shot. Just lately though he has actually calmed down a bit, probably due to the fact that he got a bollocking from Paula for handing-out copies of *The Socialist Worker* to members of staff one lunchtime - what a twat! It's the stupid minority Left like him that is making life a misery for the rest of us - fucking Trotskyite idiot. These people haven't got a fucking clue. It's just typical of their uneducated liberal shit they dish out - and get away with. If I did the same thing and started preaching my Right-Wing views such as: "England for the English" and other such things, I would be sacked on the spot. Different rules for different people, that's the way things are in this place, and others also. There's nothing much I can do about it, except maybe shoot them all with a machine-gun!

Sitting adjacent to "Lettuce" is Mark. I've never really had much dealing with him as for some reason there seems to be some kind-of self-imposed distance between us, I don't know why, it's just one of those things I guess? He seems a nice enough guy though, attractive in his own way, and in his mid-40's I would say, although looks can be deceiving. I think we've only spoken a few times in all the time I've worked here, and that was only in the works canteen for a brief minute or 2. His wife also works for this company but in another department, although I can never remember her bloody name!

I've saved the best 2 - although I really mean the worst! - in the run-down of my fellow co-workers, to last, as they will both go in some way of proving to you what I have to put up with every time I walk into this fucking hole.

Penultimately on my list we have Mary Ellis, or "Mellis" as I call her due to how her name reads on her clocking-in card - M. Ellis. I absolutely detest everything about her - her body language, her mannerisms, her attitude, everything, even the hairs on her fat head. She is the dregs of a shit bucket. Everything that comes out of her mouth is poison. I think she may be even more of a cow than I am, and that's saying something! We've never got on right from day-1, it was daggers-drawn right from the very start. I don't know what it is between us, she just seems to yank my chain for some reason? Even though she's a bit younger than me - in her late-20's - she's no-way as good looking, even though she obviously thinks she is. She also has absolutely no sense of style, her dress sense is all over the fucking place with no co-ordination whatsoever. As the old saying goes: "You can't put lipstick on a pig." Her attitude is equally as bad, I have grown tired of her stupid asinine backchat, in fact that is probably why I can't fucking stand her, along with the fact that she's shacked-up with a black. She reminds me too much of the "Old Man", with her constant piss-taking and moaning about insignificant crap. If that's all she's got to complain about in life then she's got a nasty bloody shock coming. This bitch is a real pain in the arse - she's worse than haemorrhoids!

As always, I don't attack until someone attacks me, and on my very first day here she made some stupid quip to me about my chest hanging half-out. I soon put her in her bloody place of course, telling her to:

"Go to Hell" and "It's about time you grew some yourself."

Fortunately she didn't grass me up or I would have been out the door on my ear seeing as I was the newbie to the company. The following day I parked my car in her parking space on purpose just to piss her off. When she found out it was my car she still didn't complain, she must have realised that I was tougher competition than she had first thought - in more ways than one - and so backed-off. Since then she's had the occasional snipe at me but nothing I can't handle or counter. If I can survive all the shit from the "Old Man" then I can survive anyone, especially that stupid bitch. I hate her to the very core, she gives my arse a headache. I could quite easily hit that bitch over the head with an iron-bar and it wouldn't mean a fucking thing to me. One of these days I'm going to chop her fucking head off and laugh as I watch her walk around without it! She should have been smothered at birth.

I hope she gets cancer in her mouth.

Although Mellis is a sarcastic, nasty cow, she's nowhere near as bloody annoying as the final character in my department - John - known as "Captain Slow" in my World as he's only got 2-speeds - slow and stop! He's one of the most miserable and pathetic old gits I've ever had the misfortune to cross paths with in all my days. An aura of banality surrounds his very existence. He's definitely at the bottom-end of the evolutionary chain!

He's so incredibly lazy and boring I honestly don't know where to start describing him? Firstly, he's considerably nearer to death than I am - in his early-70's - with a sallow expression and a bald head which both make him look even older than he already is. In fact his head is exactly the same shape as Gollum! He also has these disgustingly-long wiry hairs sprouting from his nostrils - yuck! - and a horrible musty smell about him like an old bookshop or something! It's either that or the awful smell of TCP permeating the office. And why is he still bloody working at his age anyway? Not that I fucking care I don't!

Every fucking morning he swans-in at his regulation 3-minutes late without a care in the World, even though everyone around him are already working and the phones are ringing their bloody heads off, he doesn't seem to give a toss - pompous bastard. As he passes everyone on the way to his desk he has to call out to them in his own weird way of saying "Hello" just by shouting their names out as loud as he possibly can: "PAULA, MONIKA, KASHKIA, WIKTORIA, APOLONIUSZ, SABIA, MALCOLM, JACK, STAN, NORA, KAT, GERRY, GERRY, CAROL, ANGIE, LILLY, LINDA, JK, DENNIS, CAROLINE, GARY, DAVE, JEREMY, MARK, MARY." That's everyone except my name of course as we don't speak to each other. And that suits me fine, I don't fucking want him to speak to me - lazy arrogant old cunt.

In turn they all bleat back to him: "Good morning John" like the fucking pathetic hypocrites they are. They all make me fucking sick.

Apparently he goes and does his shopping every morning - that's EVERY morning! - at his local Tesco's store, and that's his so-called "excuse" for wandering in late, even though he's been sitting outside in his car for the last 15-minutes or more! Why he doesn't do just one shop per week like normal people is

beyond me - idiot! They must be sick of the fucking sight of him in there every bloody day. Someone told me that the reason he does this is because he doesn't possess either a fridge, freezer or even a microwave as he doesn't believe in them! What the fuck is all that about? Word has it that he was even banned from his local butchers shop for asking the owner too many questions! Who has ever heard of anyone being banned from their bloody butchers? Amazing, only this twat could manage something like that! What a fucking nutcase!

Next, he then proceeds to start spouting-off about all the so-called "bargains" that he's purchased at the supermarket that very morning:

"Oh yes, I bought a lovely bottle of Claret in Tesco's this morning."

Big fucking woo! So fucking what? He then starts moaning-on about all the traffic that he's encountered on the way to work, like he's the only person on the planet that it effects:

"Oh, terrible traffic coming through Billingshurst yes. BILLINGSHURST! BILLINGSHURST! He shouts.

And then we have to suffer the usual bloody ritual of him preparing himself for "work". This involves him firstly taking his woolly mittens off - who on Earth wears mittens these days, except if you're before the age of 5 that is? He's even got elastic in them that threads through the sleeves joining them together - yes really! He even came into work one day wearing a pair of those chunky grey gardening gloves, the ones with the stripes across the back of the hand, and continued to wear them all day long! Why? What's going on? And why didn't anyone quiz him about it? Doesn't anyone notice these things apart from me?

The ritual continues with him next removing his hat, sunglasses - he even wears sunglasses when it's dark outside! - rain-coat, coat, jacket, body-warmer and jumper. When it's been really pissing-down outside he actually comes in wearing one of those bright yellow Sou Wester hats - lunatic! And why is it that when old people get to a certain age they start wearing brown shoes? Is it some sort-of old people thing?

Then we have about 10-minutes of him rummaging around in his stupid fucking burgundy-coloured man-bag - for what I don't know, or care. The amount of time he wastes procrastinating over every detail of everything is a fucking joke.

What a bloody performance!

This is then followed by him re-adjusting the position of his office chair. Quite what this is about is anyone's guess as nobody has touched it since he did himself the previous day! He's even put little pin-markers in the office carpet to locate his chair accurately - nutter! Next comes at least 20-minutes of face-wiping with a kitchen-towel impregnated with methylated-spirit - I kid you not!

No-one should ever wipe that stuff on their face, everyone knows that, except him of course - R-Sole! Also for some bizarre reason he has 3-clocks on his desk. For someone who does't do anything all fucking day why is he so obsessed with time? I reckon he must have OCD or something like that, none of this shit is normal behaviour.

By now of course over half-an-hour has gone by and there's still no sign of any real action on his part.

Next we have his early-morning walkabout where he just wanders around talking inconsequential shit to all and sundry that could be bothered to listen to him - which surprisingly is no-one! He's a real fountain of information, 99% of which is fucking useless! He even had the bloody nerve one time to tell Nora that she talks too much - fucking cheek! And talk about "pick a subject and milk it", I've never heard such bollocks in all my life! We've had lectures on the War (and not just the Second World War either, I mean every bloody war since the dawn of time!), eggs, light bulbs, Brexit, the Euro, batteries, jam making, guns, different types of glue and their applications, paint brushes, chickens, art, aeroplanes, different types of wood, ship building, Byzantine churches, wine, Cyprus, synthetic oil, the Gregorian calender, breeds of dogs, Army boots, tropical island temperatures, lamps, window cleaning, pork, different types of biscuits, Scottish Law, tents, architecture, roundabouts, cheese, ice cube trays, metallurgy, English Imperialism at sea, World currency, photography, volcano's, cameras, nuts, politics, literature, cooking, Germany, teapots, cardboard manufacturing, golf, soil types, computers, fibre-optic cable polishing, tyres, picture framing, Zen gardens, grinding wheels, trees, crossword puzzles, oven chips, different types of fish, bicycles, structural engineering, crisps, American State Law, paint, First World War Dreadnoughts, past life regression, medicine, Chichester in the 1950's, marshmallow's, the human body, bricklaying, grades of sandpaper, model railways, the joys of the Surrey Hills, double-glazing, thermal dynamics, curry houses, bronze casting, bus and train timetables, mushroom growing, cricket, bananas, white goods, mustard, pens, door locks, bees, the current property market, soup, the different colours of postage stamps, teabags, electric generators, films, glass manufacturing, butter, how to make mayonnaise, solar energy, insurance, sofa design, the Gestapo, different types of cat food (even though he doesn't have a cat!), furniture, books, conversion tables, sprinkler systems, telephones, grades of pencils, map making, snow, fire alarms, beer, on-line shopping, soldering, decorating, rugs, different types of engine oil, pensions, carpentry, birds (the feathered type that is!), different types of rocks, carrier bags, departments of the Civil Service, ice cream making, earwax, the industrial revolution, blood types, the different varieties of potato (or "potarto" as he pronounces it!), brass rubbing, sandwiches, glass blowing, the game of darts, rice, angles of the Sun in relation to the Earth, pressure testing, frying pans, Gibraltar, helicopters, Kings and Queens of England, building regulations, tools, shipping lanes, batteries, the education system, different cuts of meat, shower units, tidal timetables, lama breeding, dry-ice, pastry, India, teeth, the weather - need I fucking go on?

All this is carried-out in his fake upper-class accent, a monotonous drone of a voice that resonates throughout the whole department in a never-ending barrage of superfluous hyperbole that rattles my brain and my nerves. Talk about "loving the sound of my own voice." And where did he get that bloody accent from in the first place, a joke shop? Saggy-arsed old git. Not even Prince Charles talks as plummy as him!

Why is it that there's always some bastard who thinks they know more than anyone else on any given subject at every company I've ever worked for? And how do these people get away with doing fuck-all all day long? If I did as little as he does I would either get a bollocking or the sack straight away, so how come he can get away with it?

I've had to have a pop at the old curmudgeon several times, with little success I must say. One time, a few months back, was at lunchtime in the works canteen. It was about his arrogant attitude towards everyone - including myself of course - when he suddenly came out with yet more crap:

"Oh yes. I remember in June 1958 purchasing my very first teapot yes." Is he for fucking real or what? Who fucking cares? With his superior attitude he continued on:

"Why I'm sitting here amongst you class of people I just don't know? I'm far too cultured and intelligent. I'm a Master Craftsman yes. This line of work is so beneath me."

Oh really? Conceited old fucker! Obviously there was no way I was going to let that sort of talk slide so I quickly bit back at him:

"Well, if you're so bloody clever then why are you sitting here doing this crap the same as the rest of us?" I snap.

"I'm not ignorant of the situation Sarah, at all." He whines back, like the aggravating old shit he is.

"Yes you are. You're ignorant to the fact that no-one is bloody interested in any of the crap that comes out of your mouth." Geriatric old bastard.

"Oh yes they are Sarah, oh yes they are."

"No they're not. No-one could give a toss about all the bullshit you spout."

"Oh yes they do Sarah, oh yes they do yes." Says the stupid old fuck.

"Why don't you do us all a favour and retire. Or go and hang yourself from the nearest tree."

"What are you talking about?" He plums.

"Because you're bloody useless that's why. You're nothing but a waste of space. You only come here to chat and sit on your arse all day doing nothing. Either that or sit there staring at my tits."

"How dare you talk to me like that young lady. I don't find this line of enquiry very funny at all no, yes. And stop slamming that door in my face."

"What door? What are you talking about?" I quiz him back.

"You know very well what I'm talking about Sarah."

"I haven't got the faintest idea; you're off your fucking head. And don't raise your voice at me like that you old git."

"I'm a gentleman."

"No you're not, you're an decrepit old tosser."

"Well, you're not very ladylike of that I'm sure yes." He returns.

"Bollocks-off." Fucking freak. What an arrogant old cunt!

With my last retort he just sat there gorping at me with a blank expression across his repulsive miserable face, completely oblivious to the fact that I was, of course, correct in my statement. Like most arrogant people, his bark is worse than his bite. Why do these old codgers have to be so ignorant as well as arrogant?

I have actually caught him staring at me on numerous occasions, especially if I'm wearing something short, low-cut, or tight - dirty old fucker. He usually stops and looks away when I stare him out or give him the finger. I wouldn't shag him if he was the last person on Earth. He's so repugnant I can't actually bare to look at him. Even though he does look at me in "that way", I have the awful feeling that he's a bit misogynistic, which is probably why he's never married, no woman would ever put up with his shit. He even had the fucking audacity one time to say that I "dressed like a tart"! Once again I had to put him straight:

"You should take a long hard look at yourself before you start criticizing me, particularly with the things you do, or rather the things you don't - like any bloody work for instance."

"I work harder than you do Sarah." He then bewilderingly claims.

"That's bullshit and you know it." I jab back at him.

"It isn't bullshit. No it isn't. No it isn't. No it isn't." And on and on and on and on it goes *ad nauseum*.

He pissed me off yet again the other week. It was a beautiful warm sunny day and so naturally I opened my office window and switched my fan on to keep myself cool. He obviously took some sort of affront to this as he then quickly put his big chunky coat back on and started bleating across the office at me like a demented parrot:

"I'm not having that. I'm not having that. I'm not having that. I'm not having that."

"What's your problem now?" I shout back over to him.

"It's far too draughty with that window open."

"What are you talking about? It's like a bloody oven in here so I'm opening my window. Anyway, the only draught around here is the one coming out of your gob." I stab back.

"Well I'm cold." He whines pathetically.

"Oh shut up you stupid old prick." I spit back at him.

Later that same day, when I came back from lunch, I found my window shut and my fan had been switched off! No surprises for guessing who had done that is there? In retaliation I obviously reopened my window (further than it was before this time!) and switched my fan back on full-blast just to fuck him off - ha! - destroyed!

He didn't say anything to me afterwards though, he just sat there huddled-up like he was suffering from hyperthermia - stupid old wanker!

Back in the earlier part of the year when it was really bloody freezing cold outside, I remember him ambling in at his usual snails-pace, bleating about the weather yet again:

"Oh dear, it's so cold. I had to scrape the ice orff the windscreen of my motorcar this morning. How incredibly tedious. What is one supposed to do? What? What? At all. Yes?" He whines like the fucking dickhead he is.

"Motorcar" he says! No-one ever calls their car that these days, apart from this arsehole, it's not 1920 any more! He's only got some horrible Jap piece of crap anyway - what a twat! Nobody bloody cares about any of that old shit, least of all me. I really wish he would shut his fucking mouth - or die!

I also remember him one day just sitting there spying on everyone - including myself - with a bloody pair of binoculars! What the fuck is going on? I'm pretty sure that there must be something mentally wrong with him, no company worth their salt would put up with his antics. Maybe it's company policy that they have to employ a certain number of people like him who have a screw-loose for some sort-of Government "Care in the Community" reason? No normal company would let him sit there doing nothing but stare into space all fucking day long or standing around with his hands on his hips like a fucking queer, or wander around aimlessly with them in his pockets sticking his bloody fat nose into other people's conversations and take them over or standing there laughing to himself like a nutter. I've even seen him sitting there at his desk popping bubble-wrap or tying all the office elastic-bands together or making cardboard cut-outs of household furniture and fittings - why? - or waving his arms around in the air like he's demented! - maybe he is? - or fiddle-arsing around on his desk doing shit-all or just sitting there reading his book on Greece or the local *Yellow Pages* or even using his iPad when he should be working. He could be looking up child porn for all anyone knows?

I've personally caught him doing other odd things - especially in the works canteen - several times when there's been no-one else around. One time he was staring at the light switch on the wall for at least half-an-hour, or studying the landscape pictures on the calendar with a magnifying glass, whilst another when he was reading the labels on the fire extinguishers - out loud that is! - or just sitting there talking to himself:

"You've got to wear sunglasses to stop the glare of all the chrome. Drop handlebars and Derailleur gears yes. Ha Ha Ha! How amusing yes, what?"

"What?" I say to him.

"I didn't say anything."

"Yes you did. You're off your bloody head you are."

"I'm going to put the front-wheel back on my motorbike this weekend yes."

"What the Hell are you talking about?" I say across to him but I receive no reply, he's in a fucking obfuscated World of his own.

And then there was another time when he went on a tour of the building and took all the Health & Safety notices down - fucking crazy! Another time I actually caught him talking to the fridge! And then once when I caught him caressing the walls in the hallway with his hands! Yet another was when I saw him carrying an electric fan around in the office above his head with it plugged-in to an extension-lead - with it switched on of course! I even caught him out in the works car park brushing a 2-metre square patch of the tarmac clean with a broom and then coming back in and laying down prone on the office floor in front of his desk! Why the fuck why? Once he took all morning cutting-up loads of pieces of linen-type material on his desk into little squares. When he had finished he then threw them all away in the bin! Why? None of this shit makes any sense? What was the fucking point of all that? Another time I sat there watching him take his works telephone completely to pieces (for what reason I know not?) and then fail in his attempt to put it back together again. After taking practically all fucking day at this he finally gave up and had to go to the Maintenance Department to ask them for a new phone! How the fuck does he get away with all this shit? It defies belief!

What does any of this mean? I've never known anything like this in all my working days. He literally doesn't do any fucking work all fucking day long. How can this be? Why is this shit in my life? He does all this shit and gets away with it because the so-called "management" are useless - Paula is never here and CJ isn't interested, that's the way it is. I've got no intention of putting-up with this shit for much longer, one day I will have my revenge on them, on everyone.

And then we have "Captain Slow's" constant sloping-off to the main rubbish bin in the corner of the office. This happens at least 25-times a day - I know, I've counted him! - all done at his usual snails-pace. Why, yet again? Why does he need to go to the fucking bin so many fucking times? As he does all this he wastes yet more time by staring out the office window at the trees and bushes surrounding the works car-park. Lets face it, it's the only bush he's ever likely to see again!

I watched him attempt to empty it once, trying to act smart in front of everyone, only for the contents to end up all over the bloody floor when the bag split - Ha-Fucking-Ha! In the end it took him 35-minutes to change just one bin! What the fuck can you do?

Another example of his attitude is this; the company runs an internal Lottery syndicate that most of us do every week - not that I've ever won a fucking bean in all my time here! We each have our own unique number - mine is 13 - and we all pay £1 to Paula every Monday as she's in control of proceedings.

Everyone dutifully pays-up on time most of the time, all except you-know-who of course - Mr. Bloody Arrogant Old Git John! Every bloody following day without fail Paula has to chase the old tosser for the money. It's only a fucking quid for fucks sake, how difficult can it be? And then of course we have the fucking performance of him trying to find the right amount of change:

"Oh, do you want the money now Paula?" He whinges every fucking time.

"Yes please John, if you don't mind?" She's then forced to say.

"Oh dear, I'm not sure I have enough change. I'll have to look." He whines.

Yeah, that's right. You fucking do that you fucking lazy bastard. Then the massive search commences as he starts rummaging through his sodding man-bag looking for his purse - and I really do men purse, a proper one like your old Granny used to have! All this takes at least another 15-minutes or more, anything to get out of doing any fucking work. Just who the fuck does he think he is? He goes from one fucking extreme to another.

Another ongoing source of irritation is his constant fiddling around with his crappy old transistor radio, trying to tune it in to Radio 4, the station for old farts who have nothing better to do in life except sit around on their bony arses waiting to die.

"Oh dear, I can't seem to get any reception for Radio 4 on my radio. How tedious yes." He bleats like the poor old soldier he is.

More like miserable old tosser. What a fucking shame? You can fuck Radio 4 you stupid old bastard and get on with doing some fucking work for a fucking change - cretin. Just to ram the message home he then proceeds to systematically turn the individual rows of office lights off and on again to check if it's them that's causing the interference - madness! I've even caught him sitting outside in his crappy car during work hours listening to the bloody radio for up to 20-minutes at a time - amazing!

The thing is though, no-one apparently seems to mind all this bullshit. They all seem to think that it's just a laugh and he's some kind-of eccentric old guy. It seriously makes me wonder whether if it's me that's the lunatic and that everyone else are the sane ones? In fact, one of the only few times I've ever seen him get a bollocking was last Christmas when Paula bent his ear for throwing away all his unopened Christmas cards from his co-workers in the bin - what a miserable bastard! Just what is his fucking problem? He replied to this with his typical bloody arrogance:

"I'm not really one for seasonal festivities no, yes." And that's it, conversation over as far as he's concerned, fucking old tosspot.

It obviously goes without saying that I didn't give him one (a card that is!). People only hand-out Christmas cards out of duty and sufferance anyway, it's something they feel they're obliged to HAVE to do rather than for any other reason, like celebrating the birth of the Jewish carpenter for instance!

Also last Christmas we all did a Secret Santa in the office where we all bought a little present for one other person in our department costing no more than £5 each. Once again we all purchased our gifts before the cut-off time, all of us except Mr. You-Know-Who that is. He waited right until the very last moment to get something, thus holding everyone up and ruining the whole show. What a fucking arsehole! Give him a fucking inch and he takes a fucking mile!

Incidentally, someone gave me a packet of biscuits as my present, which was all very well except that they were 3-years out of date! Do you see what I mean about these people - no imagination at all! I didn't really know what to expect in the first place, I mean, just look at them, they are the carcases of life! Obviously I won't be doing any more Secret Santa's ever again that's for sure. I fucking hate Christmas.

Up on the next floor the old bugger John has this so-called "friend" - Ronald - or "The Plank" as I call him as he's yet another miserable old git and has the personality of a plank of wood! He's also a bit of a weird-looking guy as apparently he had a nasty car accident donkey's-years ago and hit his head in his car stereo when he crashed as he wasn't wearing a seatbelt. He had to have a skin-graft to fix the wound and so now he's got a patch on his forehead in the shape of the stereo! I really shouldn't laugh but it does look bloody funny! To hear "Captain Slow" and "The Plank" together is a bloody nightmare, with both of them trying to out-bore one another with one inane subject after another:

"Ah, Ronald yes. There was a fabulous concert on Telly Vision last night yes. BBC 4 yes. Mahler. Did you see it at all?" Why he has to end virtually every sentence with "at all" I just don't know?

"No, I didn't no." Comes back boring old Ronald in his semi-comatose voice.

"Oh, you must have seen it, you really must have? I can't believe you didn't see it yes. Oh, is was wonderful yes. I do wish that I'd recorded it yes. It was superb yes. I was listening to it as I was having my Claret and cheese." He whines on and on and on. Claret and fucking cheese my arse!

And so this is how it goes on, an endless stream of bullshit from one day to another. And talking on TV's, apparently old misery John doesn't watch the commercial channels either, only the bloody BBC ones! Why, does he think he's going to catch some kind-of disease off them?

Another nauseating incident I had the misfortune to overhear was the "Spag-Bol" conversation between him and "The Plank":

"Ah, yes Ronald yes. Now I want to talk to you about the different variations of recipes regarding Spaghetti Bolognese in relation to their specific regions of Italy yes, at all. It really is a fascinating subject yes. I was looking it up on the internet this morning at 6am. Let me tell you all about it."

OH, FOR FUCKS SAKE! Spaghetti-bollock-fucking-nese my arse! Where do they get these bloody people from - "Mental Cases R Us?" That's it, I've really fucking had it this time.

"Is it raining at all Linda at all raining at all? Is it? Is it raining at all? Is it raining, at all, yes? Err, raining yes, at all? Shoulders back, chest out yes. What a jolly good wheeze this job is yes, What? What? What? I haven't done anything wrong no, yes.

Are you new here ? Are you new here? Are you new here? Discuss yes. Oh lets have

a conversation yes. Yes, lets do yes. I'll start yes. What is that noise? What is it, what? Orientation! Orientation yes! Arun Prospect! Arun Prospect! Sunglasses after dark yes. Oh cripes, oh cripes, oh cripes yes! Alan, Alan, Al. Love you Alan, love you yes. I want to have your babies Alan yes. You rang? Ho! Ho! Ho! Hello Dud. Dudley! Dudley! Lovely cuddly Dudley yes. LMG! LMG! What am I doing here? What am I doing here, what? I've started putting honey on my legs of an evening yes. Why has the sky gone black? Can you tell me? Can you tell me? Can you tell me, yes? What is one to do? What is one to do, yes? Dooooooooooooooo! Yessssssssssss!"

Drone, drone, drone, drone fucking drone. What a sad, sad, old bastard. If ever there was a case for euthanasia it's him. And if all this shit sounds somewhat familiar then you'd be right, as John is an almost exact replica of that old bitch Joan from the previous company I worked for, right down to a tea. As are the fucking rest of them, all amalgams of my previous fellow co-workers.

None of them have a fucking clue about anything, they're all as good as dead. If they want to make fools of themselves then that's their problem, even if they are all too fucking stupid to understand. I wonder if they think I'm as mad as I do them?

Do you see now what I have to put up with every fucking day, stuck in here with this motley crew? This whole scenario is so beyond absurd it's ridiculous. It's all a load of bollocks. If I wrote a book about all this shit no-one would ever believe me! I always try and do a good job for every one of my employers as I've told you all previously, and anyone who says otherwise loses my loyalty in an instant. So is it any wonder that I have a justifiable bitterness and resentment towards everyone and everything when I have to suffer this demoralizing shit every fucking day working here with these bunch of crazies? How can these people stoop so low in trying to ingratiate themselves with one another, especially with that idiot CJ? That is on the rare occasions when he decides to make an appearance in our department.

I sit here watching them all in amazement as they fawn and lick arse. I could never be like them, sacrificing my dignity and my principles. I will not compromise myself in any way to gain fake respect from anyone - this will never be. None of this bollocks is exactly job satisfaction is it? At least I try and do something with my life instead of stagnating like these bunch of cretins - the desperate and the lame.

I know I used to moan a lot about the previous company I worked for, but this one is on a completely different level entirely - its fucking mental! I could quite easily shoot each and every one of them between the eyes and it wouldn't mean anything to me.

And what is all that crap about "Capitan Slow" putting honey on his legs? What the fuck is all that about? The only thing he's going to attract are bees! The stupid old bugger should be put in a mental-home.

To cap off my day, at home-time Paula goes up to "Captain Slow" as he sits there staring into space and says to him:

"Thanks for all your hard work today John."

UN-FUCKING-BELIEVABLE!
I really do think I'm going insane.

***

It's 10.30am and time for this mornings tea-break and a biscuit or 2, and so I wander off down to the next floor to the works canteen. It's pretty much a self-service facility, although the company does provide all the milk, sugar, tea, coffee and other stuff free of charge, which is nice. You have to bring your own mug though, mine being a black one with the word *"BITCH"* written across it in big white letters!

As I pour the hot water into my mug I'm joined by another woman from a different department - Claims I think? - who I'm pretty sure her name is Jane. I would say that she's somewhere in her mid-40's, about 5-foot-3, with short mousy brown hair. She's quite attractive in her own way even though she is a little bit overweight. She's dressed smart / casual in a white blouse, blue jeans, and a rather nice pair of tan-coloured suede ankle-boots.

"It's Sarah isn't it?" She asks me in her small, mousy, quizzical way.

"That's right."

"Hi, I'm Jane, Marks wife. He's in your department."

"Oh yes." I say back, completely disinterested.

"I'm sorry to hear about you splitting up with your partner."

"Thanks, shit happens."

"I hope you don't mind me asking, but I understand you were married to another woman?"

"That's right. Why, is that a problem?" I snap back at her.

"No, no, I didn't mean any offence. It's just, well, I hope you don't mind me telling you this, but just between you and me, I've sometimes wondered what it would be like with another woman? I mean, it's always fascinated me in a curious way."

"Why don't you give it a try then?" I tell her.

"Maybe I will." She says with a small snigger.

I turn away and leave her alone to get her drink, walking off to find myself a seat away from everyone and hopefully grab a bit of peace and quiet. What the fuck was up with her? Was she suggesting what I think she was suggesting? Cheeky bloody cow!

No sooner as I sit my perfect arse down and take a sip of tea she's on me once again, taking the seat opposite mine. Is she for fucking real or what?

"Mark and I have been together for 15-years now." She starts to inform me, not that I want to know in the first bloody place!

"That's nice." I return, still disinterested.

"How long did you know your partner?"

"A couple of years or so."

"Is that all? Where did you meet her?"

"She was my cats vet."

"Oh really? How old is your cat?"

"She's dead. It was Amanda that put her down."

"Oh my God, I'm so sorry." So she claims.

"It's okay, it's a long story. I'd just split up with this guy and then Lacey got sick - that was my cat - and then Amanda came onto the scene."

"You used to go out with a guy?" She quizzes again.

"Yes, that's right. I'm not a todger-dodger you know."

"A what?"

"I'm not a lesbian. I like guys as well. I'm bisexual." Why am I telling her all this crap?

"Oh I see. That's a bit greedy isn't it?" She remarks.

I can't help but give a little laugh at her comment and now the ice is broken, we sit and chat some more about life, the universe, men, women, the company, and all the strange people we have in our respective departments. She actually seems to be quite genuine and we hit it off okay, although I don't want to get too close, not to her or anyone else for that matter.

* * *

At lunchtime, after yet another tedious morning in paradise, I need to go into town to get a few bits and pieces, food and stuff. Also the fresh-air might reinvigorate my brain a little so hopefully I won't feel as fucking bored this afternoon being stuck in this hole with this bunch of weirdo's.

I take the car and head down to the shops as I can't be bothered to walk there and back today. I park easily in the supermarket car-park, grab myself a small trolley and head in. There's a couple of young women in their early-20's yacking-away to each other by the entrance doors, both with kids. I sneer at them both when I spot the colour of their brats, as once again in my merry-go-round life, I notice that all of them are "Liquorice Allsorts" - yet more mixed-race mongrels bred by their nigger-loving mothers. Neither one of these bitches has any sense of national pride. I doubt even if they know what it means? As my old maternal Grandmother used to say: "The things you see when you haven't got your gun."

How on Earth did it all come to this?

I whiz around the store at my usual fast-pace, picking stuff from the shelves and putting them in my trolley - no more, no less. I notice other mothers of various ages, races and status all doing the same shit as me but desperately trying to juggle their brats at the same time. The Council-types are both the funniest and saddest as they usually have their unemployed waster boyfriends tagging-along behind them in their typical dejected and dishevelled states. They look like they have the whole World on their shoulders but in reality they are just lazy, useless non-entities of the human specimen. These people from poor areas are nothing but breeders of miniature versions of themselves. When these brats reach a certain age - usually around 15 or so - the whole situation repeats itself again with more unplanned offspring and off we all go once again on another era of wasters and scroungers and so the cycle goes on. They are all real living deadbeat descendants. Some of these kids they're breeding now are even too bloody weak and feeble to hold a pen! What has this World come to?

I have to fight for everything. Even going to the bloody supermarket is a fight.

I have to fight to get there and get back. I even have to fight for a bloody trolley, for space, for food, for the checkout. The whole situation is ridiculous and gets on my tits.

Out of the store I decide to wander further into town and have a look around the clothes shops. I take the shortcut through the alleyway that leads to the main High Street - West Street - but my exit is blocked by more visual detritus - bloody Gipsy scum this time. There is some horrid, dirty-looking bitch dressed in her Pikey rags standing before me, holding out her dirty paws, desperately trying to flog her mini bunches of heather to passers by. I wonder who's grave she stole those from? I can't even look at her, the image of this human-shit is too much for me to withstand. I hate her and everything she is with all of my being. I want to gas the fucking lot of them for destroying the local community with their anti-social behaviour, their dirt, and for shitting on the English taxpayer. They are nothing but filth.

I have a quick look around the clothes shops in Swan Walk but I can't find anything I like, I guess I'm not in the right mood? I emerge out into the open of the Carfax where I notice a bit of a kerfuffle in the near distance so I decide to be nosey and see what's going on. I soon realise I wish I hadn't bothered as before me on the Bandstand there's some fucking robed bastard standing there preaching his vile anti-Western bullshit whilst surrounded by his masked henchmen. His hateful antagonistic attitude and evil rhetoric starts to make me feel nauseous and I have to walk away, although I'd like to round the whole lot of them up and shot them all in the head one by one - fucking Jihadi scum.

There's no point in anyone calling the Police to arrest this piece of crap as the Cops are already here, not to keep him or his "Brothers" in check, but to protect him and his bearded cronies from the public! The World is upside-down. Just why are these bastards here? Apart from all the free handouts they receive from our weak, stupid, twisted Government, what do they want? I feel like a bloody foreigner in my own Country, like I'm the last English person alive. Please let there be someone out there who can save us all from this shit.

By now I've really had enough of the hate preacher as he continues to spew his obnoxious shit to those who want to here, and so I decide to head back to the car, retracing my path along the same route. Walking back through the tunnel that leads to the Forum, my immediate path is blocked once again, as this time I come up behind a horrible smelly black girl in my way. I hold my breath before I overtake her, I don't want to breath-in any of her disgusting black-tainted air and catch something.

As I make my way down the steps to the car-park there's an old guy standing at the bottom - at pavement level. He's about 70-ish, tall and thin, dressed all in black and with a Bible in hand. He's waffling-on to himself about God and damnation and that everyone is going to Hell if we all don't repent and denounce our sins. I feel in my case that I'm a little too late for any of that! I also think he's a bit nuts - just as are the rest of his fellow God-botherers - and that he's suffering from some kind-of paranoid delusion. Why do these people pretend that everything in the whole World is governed by this fictitious creation of theirs?

There is no need for a God, except if you're weak. Unfortunately the lunatics of every religious faith are all around us, it doesn't matter ecumenically which side of the fence these fanatics are from, they're all the fucking same - MAD - fucking hypocrites.

Back at my car I'm confronted by a big, fat woman standing behind the car that is parked next to mine. I think it's some sort-of Japanese rice-burner or some such crap. I open the tailgate of the ST by remote and place my single bag of shopping in the boot. As I go to close it, the fat woman - I guess she's about 30 or so, stone that is! - suddenly takes a swipe at my good-self:

"Excuse me, but you've parked your car far too close to mine. I can't get in that small gap." She bleats.

"Really? You do surprise me. Maybe if you wern't so bloody fat you wouldn't have a problem would you?"

"How dare you say that! I have a thyroid problem."

"No you don't, you have a pie problem. Maybe you should try keeping off them and get some bloody exercise you lazy fat cow!

"How dare you say that. I'm going to call the Police."

"Go ahead, I don't give a shit."

I get in my car, fire her up, exit the car-park and head back to work. I'm not going to let that fat old bitch rattle my cage, she doesn't even register in my memory.

By the time I get back to work I've gone some 20-minutes over the allocated lunch-break hour, not that I give a shit about that either. If that old tosser John and all my other co-workers can get away with it then so can I - fuck the lot of them.

***

It's the following day, and, unsurprisingly, I find myself in exactly the same position doing exactly the same thing I was doing at exactly the same time as yesterday - I am so fucking bored.

Today I'm wearing a royal-blue cross-over long-sleeved top from The 1015 Store that is both really stylish and shows-off my superb figure at the same time, a pair of grey stone-wash jeans from Forever 21 and my old pair of blue suede platform Lola court-shoes - love "em. My underwear is in sexy black lace from Victoria's Secret. My hair and make-up I've done pretty-much the same as yesterday but featuring light-blue eyeshadow. My perfume today is *Poison* by Christian Dior.

One of my fellow co-workers - Mark - sidles up to me, for the first time in ages actually, as I'm filling-out a customers insurance details on my computer.

"Hello Sarah. My wife Jane tells me that you and her had a little chat yesterday." He asks.

"Yeah, that's right. She seems nice."

"Yeah she is. So what were you both talking about?"

"Oh, just this and that, girl talk you know. Didn't she tell you?"

"Yes, she did actually, well, most of it I guess. The thing is, we were wondering if

you would like to go for a drink with us sometime, just the 3 of us? We have a little proposition for you." He questions me.

"What sort of proposition?" I question him back, as if I didn't bloody know where this is leading. Or have I got the wrong end of the stick - again?

"So, are you interested?"

"Yeah, okay. A drink can't hurt can it? It'll be fun."

"I hope so. I don't know who's more excited, me or Jane?" He enthuses.

"It's only a drink." I say back, shrugging my shoulders nonchalantly. What the Hell is up with him?

***

I'm wearing a scarlet mini-bodycon dress from ASOS that is so short and tight that is looks like my skin has actually been painted red! As for underwear, I'm not wearing a bra as I don't want to, although I am wearing a red thong just in case anyone catches a glimpse of my box! On my feet I'm wearing a pair of see-through plastic wedge-heals from Polyvore that look super-cool. My clutch-bag is a small heart-shaped one in red also from Polyvore. My perfume tonight is *Mademoiselle* by Coco Chanel. I've also got my full killer face on, featuring coal-black eye-shadow, super-sharp cheekbones and cherry-red lipstick.

I'm sitting on my own in the Red Lyon pub in Slinfold Village, just a stones-throw from where I live. I'm surrounded by what feels like a thousand eyes in the very same scenario as always, all boring into my beautiful body - the men and the women. There's nothing I can do about it or would even want to, so I just sit there looking pretty as I sip my extra-large gin, neat of course. I arrived here way too early - at 7pm - as I'm not due to meet Mark and Jane until 8pm. I just wanted to get plenty of alcohol down my throat before they arrive.

I sit here watching the people as they in turn watch me. What are they all thinking I wonder? I try to imagine all the thoughts that are going on in their strange little minds - the men desperately trying to keep control of their libidos, all that spunk churning-away inside them waiting to splat all over my hot naked body at any moment. And the women - envy and hate boiling-away in every fucking one of them. They all want to kill me right here and now but none of them have either the nerve or the inner-strength to do it - they are weak.

I WANT them all to kiss me.

I WANT them all to ravish me.

I WANT them all to love me.

I WANT Them all to fuck me.

At 7.51 Mark and Jane saunter in, say "Hello", order more drinks for the 3 of us and away we go on yet another adventure into the unknown. The conversation skirts it's way around the usual tired old cliches of work, relationships - I really do hate that bloody word! - a bit of general politics and then back to relationships once more. The chat ends up being steered onto the subject of me being bisexual and to which way I think I might go next - with a male or female lover?

"It's not as simple as that. My next partner may be male or female, I have no idea which gender it will be? Time will tell I guess?" I try to explain to them.

"Have you ever considered a couple? A man and woman. Like us for-instance, just for a bit of fun?" Says Mark with a grin across his face from ear to ear like a Cheshire cat, as has Jane.

"Excuse me? You're not serious? Are you suggesting a 3-some?" I say back in shock. What a bloody cheek!

They both answer me in the affirmative, although a blind man could have predicted this, I'm still a bit taken-aback and somewhat sickened by their proposal, as well as being turned-on at the same time.

"Well, I don't know. You've caught me a bit by surprise. I'll need some time to think about it. I'm not saying yes but I'm also not saying no."

"Of course Sarah. We don't want to pressurise you in any way. It's not something to enter into lightly." He says.

"You've got that right!" I say back to them, taking a large gulp of gin as I do.

"As I said to you the other day Sarah, I've always had a fantasy about what it would be like with another woman, for years even, but I've never had the courage to do anything about it. Well, not until now obviously." Says Jane, as she looks me straight in the eyes. I want to kiss her soft lips and touch her breasts right here and now but I don't, I just don't have the nerve.

Now, I know you think that I'm going to say "Yes" to their proposal straight away and go back to their place and fuck them both but there is more to me than you may realise. My life does not revolve around fucking everyone in sight, I do have some morals. They may not be the same as yours by a long-chalk but I do have them. I WANT and do what is right for me at any given moment regardless of what anyone says or thinks.

But as my dear old maternal Grandfather used to say:
"If it's free, take it."

***

I am in total ecstasy as Mark starts to lick and suck at my vagina. It twitches with his touch as he tongues me and I feel myself starting to shake with my own love. Jane alternately licks and caresses my tits and nipples and then she too demands a go at me, her first taste of another woman. She moves-in beside her husband and kneels before me as I lay back in the softness of their white leather sofa.

Tentatively she kisses my hole and then starts to lick me. Mark joins back in and I have 2-tongues flicking in and out of my quim and I begin to pant heavily as my breathing goes haywire. I can't control myself any longer and in a moment I orgasm and cum at them and I scream for them to tongue me harder and deeper.

We swap over and Jane and I take it in turns to suck, lick and swallow Mark's beautiful cock and balls. I kiss Jane's mouth and she mine and we touch and squeeze each others breasts and then suck on Mark's dick. I choke on it as I take his length fully to the back of my throat and I want it all inside me, to fill the entirety of my head with cock. We both wank and suck him until he starts to shake and then cums as I aim his Japs-eye towards Jane's open mouth, he shooting into her 4-thick spurts of his jism. I continue to wank him as I French-kiss Jane's spunk-laden mouth, swallowing his muck as I love her.

Jane squats-down cowgirl onto Mark's dirty cock as I use my right-hand to guide it into her wet vagina. I watch her internal muscles part to let him in and she starts to bob up and down on him rhythmically as he counters her motion. I lick cock and cunt as they mesh together and the sensation drives me wild. I wank myself with 2-fingers as I pull Mark's wet cock out of Jane's fanny and lick it like a lolly. I eat her pussy and gently suck her clit as I then reinsert his tool back into her box and take both his testicles into my mouth, rolling them around inside my gob with my tongue. He shouts and screams and cums another load of his milky glop into her, it oozing out under the pressure of fucking and I eat it as it dribbles out of her vagina into my awaiting mouth.

Jane is on all-fours on the living-room floor with Mark and myself behind her. He's laying on the floor licking at her heavy vulva as I ease myself down onto his bare cock. I take it easily and sit right down onto it, letting the full 6-inches of his meat slide inside me. As I fuck I lean forwards and lick and bite at Jane's bum-cheeks. I spit on her a toxic mixture of saliva, spunk and batter right onto her tight brown hole. I fuck it in with 1-finger at first, then 2 and then my tongue. She shudders at having her fanny and rectum licked simultaneously and almost collapses under the excitement, but both Mark and I just about manage to hold her upright with our hands as we nosh.

With Mark's batteries recharged - albeit not fully - Jane and I sit him back down on the sofa. Jane adds some lube to his cock and wanks him gently back to hard as I position myself squatting over him just as she did previously, although his time I lower myself down cowgirl-style onto his knob and press it firmly into my bumhole. It stings at first and then feels so beautiful inside me as I start to ride it slowly and I want him inside me forever.

Jane kneels down before us and starts to play with my vagina, firstly with her fingers and then with her mouth and tongue. I shoot into orbit with the electrifying sensation of being bum-fucked and tongue-fucked at the same time - I am in Heaven and Hell and I want it more and harder and I am out of my tiny mind and I cum and piss and shit as Mark ejaculates in my bum and I have no feelings for this beautiful, nasty World any more and I want everything to stop right now but I can't and don't want it to stop and I shout:

"FUCK ME HARDER" and "FUCK YOUR COCK INTO ME."

I love it when Jane calls me beautiful.

I love it when Mark's cock is inside me.

I have no brain as I suck his dirty cock. I lick it as Jane watches me with a slightly disgusted look on her face, she doesn't do anal and so naturally she doesn't do ATM either. I do even though I hate it as much as I love it.

***

I continued to see both Mark and Jane for sex for the next 3-months or so, fucking them 3 or 4-times a week. Sometimes I would stay over at their house in Southwater, West Sussex, for the night, but it wasn't really an ideal situation having 3-people trying to sleep in a bed only designed for 2.

Towards the end of our agreement though the scenario had gotten a bit out of hand. Mark's feelings towards me had changed from lust to love, whilst Jane's had turned from curiosity also into love.

During this time I started having sex with Mark behind Jane's back and visa-versa, as well as continuing to have sex with the both of them together. It all turned into a living nightmare and it started to do my head in even more so than it had already. Don't get me wrong though, I loved every second of the sex, but once the emotional side of things started to kick-in, it was game over.

My independence and state of mind mean more to me than fucking. Well, only just!

10
Work Shit

And so here I am yet again, at work, plugging-away on my computer inputting customers data like the fucking zombie I am. Every fucking day it's the same old thing over and over a-fucking-gain, with every working day blending into one long continuous bore. To say that it's mundane would be the fucking understatement of the century! I'd like to set fire to this fucking place with everyone still in it and watch them all burn to death. Or maybe even machine-gun them all and laugh as I watch their heads explode like little volcanos - Ha!

How can I carry on doing this shit? I keep thinking and hoping that everything will get better but it doesn't - everything I touch I contaminate to destruction and then it all falls apart on me. I simply cannot carry on like this, the line between what is real and pure fantasy is becoming more and more blurred as time passes by. Where will it all end? What is my end? What is my fate? Why am I even worrying myself over this shit? I am sick to the stomach of always being the harbinger of doom and gloom, why can't I have a nice life where everything runs smoothly? Why does my dream have to be so out of reach, my dream of peace and total freedom? We can all dream of course, but at the end of the day we must all face reality, something I'm finding increasingly harder to do.

The after-effects of all the shitty things that keep happening to me multiply in my brain, clogging up my thoughts and making me stumble. It's always the same old story, nothing ever changes, and with every shitty event the more I cut myself off from society - I just can't fucking win. I try to be good,

I really do, but it just doesn't work. I feel everything, every nuance of life pecks at my soul.

I desperately try to concentrate on the job in hand as I begin to feel eyes upon me, scrutinizing my very being. Why do they keep spying on me? Why won't everyone just fuck-off and leave me alone? What is their fucking problem?

***

Today I'm dressed all in black, as that's the mood I'm in. I'm wearing a low-cut v-neck jumper from Bluefly that is also nice and tight, emphasizing my bust and exposing my cleavage at the same time. I've also got on a really short mini-skirt from New Look that hugs my bum, coupled with tights from M&S that show off my legs to the max. My shoes are my pair of suede open-toe platform court-shoes from Polyvore and although they hurt my feet somewhat and I can't drive properly in them, they look fantastic, and that's all that matters. As it was pissing-down this morning I've got a black leather biker jacket on - a real one of course! - that I found on Ebay for the amazing price of only £30, and that included delivery - bargain or what! Seeing as its real leather it must have cost hundreds when new. I've modified it by adorning it with biker-patches and pin-badges that I also found on the internet, so now it looks even cooler than it did before. As it has loads of zip-up pockets all over it, there's also no need for me to carry any kind bag for all my crap. I've gone for a pale-look to my overall make-up today to contrast with all the black I'm wearing, whilst my perfume is *Poison* by Christian Dior. My hair-clip is also in black, in the shape of 2-skulls.

I really am so fucking bored, and pissed-off. I'm just like a fucking automaton, sitting here doing this mind-numbing shit all day every day. I try not to look at my fellow co-workers either, I am completely indifferent to them. Just one glimpse at this lot is enough to piss on anyone's bonfire!

My work-phone rings and I almost jump out of my beautiful smooth skin. It's Pam, the woman in charge of Human Resources, and a right stuck-up bitch she is as well:

"Is that Miss Knowles?" She plums.

"Sarah, yes." I return sarcastically.

"Ah, Miss Knowles. I wonder if you could pop upstairs to my office to see me. There seems to a problem with your holiday application form."

"Why? What's wrong with it?" I quiz her back.

"Well, if you come upstairs we can discuss it can't we?"

What is her fucking problem? Why does she have to be so up herself? Who the fuck does she think she is? And why can't she call me Sarah like everyone else, that is my fucking name after all!

I strut my stuff as I walk out of the department and into the outside corridor - making damn sure that everyone gets a good look at my bum and legs in the process - and then take the short flight of stairs up to the old bitch's office on the next floor. I don't bother to knock as I couldn't be bothered, and seeing as her office door is already open I just walk in unannounced.

"Ah, Miss Knowles." She bleats.

"It's Sarah, there's no need to be so formal." I vainly point out to her but my words fall on deaf ears, arrogant old cow. It makes me wonder if she acts like this on purpose or actually she really is a fucking snob?

I sit my pert arse down on the chair facing her desk, awaiting the obvious bullshit that is heading in my direction.

"You seem to be in some confusion about the amount of days off that the company has allocated to you?" She whines at me.

"There's no confusion. I'm allowed 22-days holiday per year right?" I point out to her.

"Yes, that's correct." She replies.

"OK, so what's the problem then?"

"You've booked another 3-days off when you only have 1-day left."

"No. I've got 4-days left. I've taken 15-days out of my 22 so far this year, plus the 3-days allocated for this coming Christmas, and that leaves me with 4-days still to take."

"No it doesn't, it leaves you only the 1." She claims.

"What are you talking about? You're saying that 22 minus 18 is 1?"

"Yes"

"You're off your fucking head." I fire at her directly.

"I beg your pardon?"

"You heard me. How can that be right?"

"I will not have language like that in my office thank you Miss Knowles. You've had a considerable amount of time off this year already and you only have 1-days holiday left, do you understand?"

"That's crap. It's not my fault I've had to have time off work with personal problems, I did have a car accident you know?"

"I am fully aware of your accident Miss Knowles, that is not the issue here. The issue is about all the other time off you've had. There have been numerous times that you've phoned-in sick but we haven't received a note from your Doctor, how do you explain that?"

"What's the point of going to the Doctor with PMS, what's he going to do about it?"

"I'm sure he could prescribe something to ease the problem."

"And how the Hell would you know? You're too old to have them any more." I fire back at her.

"Excuse me! How dare you say such things Miss Knowles. I shall report your insubordinate comments to your supervisor."

"Go ahead, that's if you can find him. He's probably in the toilet having a wank."

"I think you've said quite enough thank you Miss Knowles, now please leave my office."

"With pleasure. And it's Sarah, okay? And I'll be taking those 3-days off that I WANT, do you understand?" I say to her, pointing my finger in her stuck-up face.

I get to my feet, turn, and sashay out of her office with a big fat grin of deep satisfaction across my perfect face. Who the fuck do these people think they are talking to me like I'm nothing? This is yet another example of the pseudo middle-class for you, another band of twats pretending to be something they're not.

And I don't care either if the old bitch grasses me up to my idiot bloody supervisor, what's he going to do, sack me? I don't fucking care if he does anyway, I've still got plenty of money left over from the sale of Mum's house to fall back on so bring it on - wankers!

I sit myself down back at my desk and carry on with the mundane chore of filling-out customers details on my computer, once again amid a thousand stares from the plebs.

How do other people get through life, especially this lot? They seemingly just drift along through one day and into the next without a care in the World whilst I have to face shit all the fucking time no matter what I do? How is that possible? Why does this happen? Why does this happen to me? None of this crap makes any sense?

* * *

It's half-an-hour before lunchtime so I decide to go for a quick pee and a think, maybe that will break the monotony of being stuck in this shithole all day?

As I enter the toilet I'm confronted by the obnoxious vision of my nemesis - that stupid bitch Mellis - over at one of the basins washing her scrawny hands.

I can't believe how much I loath that fucking bitch. I completely ignore her as I don't want any more aggro today, although if she fucking starts on me then I'll fucking kill her right here and now.

"I hear that you've been fiddling your holiday forms again." The sarcastic cow quips at me as I head to a vacant cubicle.

"It's got fuck-all to do with you Mellis. If you don't get off my tail I'll sting you." I strike back at her.

"How's your wife?" She smirks back at me.

"She's fine thanks. How's your coon "Chicken George" these days?" I jab back at her, quickly wiping the smile off her face, but unfortunately not for long.

"So, what is it this week, pussy or cock? Or is it both?"

"Well, we can't all be Jigaboo-lovers like you can we?" I stab at her.

"What did you fucking say?" She whines back.

"You heard me bitch. I may be bisexual but at least I don't suck black cock. I do have some pride, unlike you. The pair of you should be gassed."

"You're nothing but a fucking whore."

"I'd rather be a whore than a fucking race-traitor."

"What's that supposed to mean? Errol's British, he has a British passport."

"A British passport doesn't make you British you stupid cow, it's only a piece of paper. And he'll certainly never be English either, he's not exactly Aryan is he?"

"British and English are the same thing." She suddenly bewilderingly claims.

"No they're fucking not you thick bitch."

"He was born in this Country so he must be British."

"You fucking idiot. So if a dog is born in a stable that makes it a horse then does it?" I question her.

"I don't understand?"

"No, you wouldn't would you. That's because you're ignorant, as well as fucking stupid. Fortunately not everyone is as pluralistic as you, Mellis."

"Don't keep calling me Mellis, you know what my name is."

"Yeah, nigger-loving whore, that's your name - Mellis."

Well, that was it wasn't it. That was the straw that broke the proverbial camel's back. And understandable really, this polemic encounter was never going to be pretty was it?

She lunges at me and tries to scratch-out my face but I'm way too quick for her and I give her a beautiful right-hook straight in the mouth, splitting her bottom-lip open so bad that it literally tears apart and spits out a long squirt of blood down her white blouse - quite a nice stylish one as well actually!

She stumbles backwards and I take my chance, grabbing her by the throat with both hands and pinning her up against the wall. I squeeze her as tightly as I dare without breaking anything - I'm not really going to kill her, just scare the fucking shit out of her - as I pressure her windpipe with both my thumbs.

"Now you fucking listen to me nigger. You don't mean Jack-Shit to me. Whatever you think of me I think less of you, do you understand? You are nothing. You are dead from this moment on."

I release her from my grip and she falls down onto the hard, tiled floor with a thud, spluttering and spitting blood out onto its shiny white surface.

"I'll have you for this." She bleats.

"Go ahead and do your worst, I dare you."

"I'll kill you."

"No you won't, you're too weak, just like all the others."

"I'll tell the boss. I'll tell CJ."

"Woo, big fucking threat. CJ isn't my boss. My boss is dead, but still alive."

I lean down to her and grab her by her hair, pulling her head right back with it so she faces me square-on.

"I have to inform you that I don't like threats, or bullshit for that matter, so you'll have to do better than that Mellis."

"Let go of me you fucking bitch." She splutters back.

"If you fucking grass me up, I'll fucking kill you, got it? You fucking keep away from me and keep that fat mouth of yours shut or you know what'll happen. One of these days you're going to have to face reality, and when that day comes, I'll be ready waiting for you with a knife to stab you in the back, got it?"

I let go of her and she sits down and back, pressuring her lip with both hands as the blood continues to flow steadily. I think I must have torn one of her veins or something as the red juice has now smeared her chin, run down her neck and soaked that lovely blouse of hers.

"You wait "till my husband hears about this."

"You mean Errol? That's a good old English name isn't it? Why, what's he going to do, put a voodoo on me? Sacrifice a chicken? If you're prepared to suffer the consequences Mellis then go ahead."

"You fucking whore." She repeats herself yet again.

"Yes Mellis whatever. Now clean yourself up, you look a right bloody mess. I'm off down the pub, see you later."

I wave her "Goodbye" as I exit the toilet, passing 3-eavesdroppers lurking there hovering outside the door earwigging at all the goings-on. They each step back as I emerge and walk past them as they then all hurry inside to see what has happened to poor little Mellis.

I make my way back to my desk to get my jacket. Although I'm perfectly calm and fluid, I desperately need a fucking drink or 2 - or 3! - so I'm going for a quick sojourn around the corner to The Black Jug, it's only a 2-minute walk away.

***

Once inside I find the pub reasonably busy for a lunchtime, and as per usual, just like I've mentioned a thousand-times before, I get plenty of looks from all the guys, and the jealous women. I wonder how other women actually perceive me, especially the not-so-great-looking ones? What really goes on in their minds when I appear in their vision? It can't be easy for them I guess, to be confronted by the beautiful image that is me. They must feel tremendous anger and resentment as to why it is that I'm so gorgeous and they're so mediocre, and / or ugly. There's nothing I can do about it of course, I was born this way just the same as they were born their's, the dice fortunately rolled in my favour - that's life. I dread to think what my life would be like if I looked like them, it doesn't bear thinking about.

I order myself a pint of lager with a large neat vodka chaser and sit myself down on a stool at the bar looking pretty and contemplate my fate. There's no-doubt that fucking nigger-loving bitch is going to grass me up, it's almost guaranteed.

I really fucking nailed her though didn't I? All that suppressed anger that has been boiling-away inside me for months, if not years, was suddenly realised and I felt a tremendous rush of energy fire through my body when I punched her in the mouth - that was some hit!

As I down my drinks, I hear plenty of gibber-jabber from a group of guys sitting near me, all obviously talking about me and all the lovely things they want to do to me. Don't they realise that I can hear what they're saying? Maybe they do? Idiots. I finish my lager quickly and gulp-down the large vodka in one go, go for the wee that I didn't have earlier, and then head back to the "Funny Farm" to face the music and certain death.

***

As I wander back into the office I'm suddenly hit by a piercing silence from the plebs and a cold wind of uncertainty whips itself around me. Placing the jacket over the back of my chair I quickly spot a large yellow *Post It* note stuck to my computer screen. It's from the hypocrite CJ, the "Mr-Fucking-Superior-Attitude" boss, inviting me to his office for an afternoon chat - how nice!

As I make my way out of the department, all the plebs stare at me with their stupid sideways glances, none of them actually wanting me to notice them doing so, but it's so bloody obvious what they're up to that their feeble attempts descend into a joke. Don't any of these fucking people have lives?

I head upstairs to see CJ on the next floor and find him sitting there in his office in his pale-pink shirt and blue and silver striped tie like the fucking twat he is, having a powwow with the stuck-up cow Pam. They make a right fucking pair these 2. I wonder what this could be about?

"You wanted to see me?" I say to CJ with all the innocence I possess - which admittedly isn't a lot!

Obviously I'm expecting a rocket up my arse here - and that won't be for the first time either! I know my bubble is about to burst but what can I do about it? I am what I am and that's all there is to it. I really don't fucking care anyway, I don't belong here any more, not that I ever really did in the first place.

"Ah, Sarah, yes. Shut the door behind you would you please and come and sit down." Says CJ in his condescending manner. The old bag Pam says nothing, although I can detect her laughing at me behind her stuck-up face - fucking bitch.

"I take it this is about my holiday application?" I say sweetly.

"No, this is about you allegedly causing psychical harm to another member of staff."

"You mean Mellis?"

"I'm talking about Mary Ellis. Did you hit her?"

"Yes. I punched her in the mouth. And a pretty good shot it was too."

"Sarah, I hope you realise what this means? We will not tolerate this inexcusable behaviour in the workplace. You leave me with no alternative but to give you instant dismissal."

"YOU'RE SACKING ME? BECAUSE OF THAT BITCH?" I scream.

"Yes, that's correct, that's the main reason anyway. But there are other issues to be taken into consideration - your timekeeping, your attendance record, as well as your attitude towards other members of staff, including the obnoxious way you spoke to Mrs. Hammerstein earlier today. Plus of course there's your secret little habit. We've known about the bottle of vodka that you keep hidden in your desk-draw for some time but we haven't done anything about it, until now, enough is enough."

"Right, well, if that's the way things are then you can stick your bloody job up your arse. If I've got an attitude problem it's because of other people's attitudes towards me. If they treat me like shit then I'll do exactly the same back to them, it's as simple as that."

"It's not as simple as that Sarah, your drinking is effecting your work. We've had to get other people to pick up the pieces from all the mistakes you've made."

"That's bullshit. So what if I like a drink, what's that got to do with you?"

"Sarah, if it effects your work then it effects everyone. The state of your customers records are abysmal. You've even been drinking this lunchtime haven't you? I can smell it from here."

"So what? It's got nothing to do with you what I do, you don't know my life. You don't like me because I have freedom and you don't."

"Sarah, I'm not going to argue with you, this is the end of the road okay? I mean, you've had so much time off work as well, we've just had enough. You're lucky Mary hasn't called the Police."

"Go ahead and call them then, I don't care." I return flippantly.

"That's not the point is it?"

"Look, it's not my fault I've had problems to deal with, I've been under a lot of pressure this year - my Father died (not that I give a fuck about that old cunt but it sounds like a good excuse under the present circumstances!), I had a car accident and broke my arm and lost my baby in the process. And I've had other problems as well - my niece was killed and I also split up with my partner you know?"

"Your "Wife" you mean?" He sneers at me sarcastically, sitting there with a smug expression across his stupid face.

"Why did you say it like that?" I question him back.

"Well, it's not exactly conventional is it?" He returns.

"What the fuck has it got to do with you? What the Hell do you know? You don't know anything about my life or what I've had to go through, you don't even know my fucking name."

"Is that a fact? So lets talk about your accident then shall we? You phoned-in sick that morning so how come you were out driving your car towards Chichester, answer me that one?"

"I can't remember." I lie. Of course I remember but I'm not telling either of them, they can eat my shit.

"Well, you're not exactly holier-than-thou are you? What about all those vouchers you've got stashed away in your desk-draw, the ones that are meant for the workers but you give to your family?" I attack him back.

"Those vouchers are for the staff."

"Really? So how come we never see them then? Because you line your own bloody pockets with them that's why."

"You're just being antagonistic."

"Maybe I am, but I wouldn't be antagonistic if I didn't have anything to be antagonistic about would I?"

"I see. If that's the way you want it you can have it. Do you want the corporate answer or do you want me to tell you straight Sarah?" He quizzes me.

"Meaning what exactly?" I stumble.

"We also know about your fun and games Sarah, rumours do get around you know? Like your little meetings with Mark and Jane for instance." He counter-attacks.

"That's got fuck-all to do with you either and you know it. What I do in my private life is just that - private. You're only jealous "cos you wern't invited. For all I know you're probably banging her." I say, pointing to the old cow, who so-far hasn't contributed anything to the conversation and just sits there with a look of objective destain on her face.

"MISS KNOWLES!" She shouts at me, suddenly bursting into life.

"It's Sarah, how many more fucking times have I got to say it?"

"Miss Knowles, I will have you know that I'm happily married." She bleats at me.

"Yeah, well so was I. And now that's gone tits-up as well, just like everything else."

"Have you ever seen death?" I aim back at CJ.

"What are you talking about now?"

"Have you ever seen a dead body, the body of someone you love?"

"What's that got to do will anything?"

"If you've never experienced death then how can you ever experience life. You've got no-idea what life is about have you? You people should try opening your eyes as to what is actually going on in this bloody company instead of sitting in your ivory-tower on your fat arses listening to gossip. Neither of you have got a fucking clue as to what's happening right under your very noses. The trouble with this place is that the management doesn't give a toss about the workers and the workers certainly don't give a toss about the management, the divide is too great.

It's up to you to do something about it before it's too late. And despite what you may think of me, I'm not fucking stupid, you should count yourself damn lucky that I'm here in the first place. I'm way better than any of you. I could run this place better and more efficiently than all of you lot put together. And how you can justify letting that lazy bastard John sit there and do nothing for the vast majority of the day just goes to show how incompetent you really are. You never say one fucking word to him about standing around talking shit all day and then you wonder why people are disenchanted and leave."

"John is one of our most valued workers." CJ suddenly claims.

"You're fucking joking arn't you? He's the laziest bastard on the planet ever."

"I will not have you talking about a well respected member of staff like that."

"What do you mean "Respected"? I've seen you on the shop floor when he's strolled-in late and you never said a fucking word to him about it."

"That never happened. You're exaggerating."

"I'm not exaggerating and you know it. You're systematic of the piss-poor fucking management in this Country that is driving it to its bitter end. And another thing, I'm bloody sick and tired of the double-standards in this place, there are different rules for different people and it's just not fair. You won't spend any more money on staff wages but you'll waste it on crap like a new fucking carpet for the office and other useless shit. Neither of you realise what is actually going on in this World do you?

CJ laughs at me like the arsehole he is, cackling a pathetic fake guffaw right in my face but I'm not having that, and so I rip back into him:

"And there you are." I say, pointing my finger in his face.

"That's what I'm talking about. That is just the typical arrogant attitude of people like you. You honestly think that because you've got a grandiose job title, earn more money than me, have a company car and a swish office you think you're somehow better than me. But you still don't get it do you? You're too stuck-up your own arses to be able to understand what I mean. You so-called "Managers" are all the fucking same, you're trapped by your own ego's and you can't get out. Just because you wear a suit and tie doesn't mean you're correct all the time, it means nothing, and because I'm free and have independence you don't like it do you? That's why you don't like me, because I can do what I WANT and you can't."

"You don't know what you're talking about, that's all rubbish." Exclaims the idiot that is CJ.

"The point is I do know what I'm talking about, but you're too fucking blinkered to see or even acknowledge it when someone like me points it out to you. You can't handle the fact that I'm right. You don't have a fucking clue, none of you. You're all lunatics. You're all fucking brain-dead. I wouldn't piss on either of you if you were on fire"

"THAT'S ENOUGH, I WANT YOU OUT OF HERE RIGHT NOW." He screams at me like a cunt.

"If sacking me is the worst thing you can do to me then that just goes to show how fucking pathetic you both are. There's nothing you can do or say to me that hasn't been done before so don't even fucking bother. I've had more bullshit in my life than you've had hot dinners so don't worry, I'm going. I don't wanna spend another second in this fucking hole anyway, I have my own agenda to stick to regardless of you or anyone else. You've both totally missed the point here haven't you?"

"Why? What do you mean?" Says CJ, like the dick he is.

"If you think you've won some kind-of victory over me then you're sadly mistaken, because I don't give a fucking shit."

And so, with all that done and dusted - it was inevitable really wasn't it? - I'm escorted back downstairs to clear out my desk, grabbing my silver-framed photo of Lacey, my leather jacket, my *BITCH* mug, my so-called "banned" water-bottle and mobile-phone, and the half-full bottle of vodka from my bottom-draw - what a naughty girl I am! Although it is slightly embarrassing to expose my little secret to the plebs, I handle the situation with my usual cool aplomb.

The plebs are obviously halted in their tracks by all the goings-on and it feels like I'm being stared at by one giant eyeball in the sky as they all gorp at me in unison. I don't say anything to any of them - not even funny little Angie - as none of them exist as far as I'm concerned.

Both the idiot CJ and stuck-up Pam virtually frog-march me downstairs to the main entrance and out the building, all done in total and complete silence. But I'm not having that, I'm not going quietly.

"If you don't fucking want me then I'll go with pleasure, you're nothing but……………………..."

"Just go Sarah, and don't come back." CJ cuts me off mid-sentence.

"I haven't finished with any of you. If you think this is the end of this then you're mistaken. You won't see me coming that's for sure, you fucking bastards."

I leave the company with my name besmirched with these idiots forever, not that I fucking care, the doors slamming behind me and then that's it - I'm out in the cold once again. I know that I've outstayed my welcome, not that I got much of a bloody welcome in the first place! From this moment on, this is the beginning of a new part of my life.

I take a swig from the bottle of vodka to take the edge off my foul mood, when suddenly the thought of lobbing the bottle through the glass front doors of the building flashes across my mind. I don't do it though, I'm not wasting good vodka on these arseholes. It's all the frustrations at work that has led me back onto the path of secret drinking in the first place, catalysed by that fucking lazy bastard John. I had to keep a bottle hidden in my desk-draw for emergency, just in case I needed to smash myself whenever the need arose, which over the last several months has become increasingly more and more. I'd also taken to stealing things from my stupid co-workers desks as some kind-of compensation / revenge for all the grief I was getting, just for a laugh and to see their stupid reactions as they search in vain for their missing items, just silly things - pens, note pads, *Post-It* notes and other crap. Occasionally I would steal more personal things and sometimes even money if it was left lying there waiting for me to pilfer, especially if it was off of bastards like Mellis and "Captain Slow". I know I was running the risk of getting caught and being sacked but I just couldn't help myself, the thrill of doing it and then getting away with it coupled with the satisfaction on my part was an overwhelming temptation I couldn't stop.

From my left a group of 6 or so office workers file past me as I take another swig from the bottle.

"HAVING A GOOD FUCKING LOOK?" I shout at them as they wander by. I'm pretty-sure they were the very same ones that were in The Black Jug earlier at lunchtime. They stare and whisper to each other as they pass but I don't fucking care, their looks and words are meaningless to me.

I make my way back down the road to my orange bomber and fire her up. There's no point in lingering around here any longer, it's all come to a bitter end.

* * *

Back at the flat I drink myself to oblivion - so what's new? - smashing myself on vodka and painkillers as images of my crazy life and hollow death flood my mind. Even though I've just got the sack - my first time ever believe it or not? - I somehow feel empowered by the fact that at least I stood-up for myself. I'm actually quite proud of way I conducted my defence. I'm not going to roll over for anyone or anything regardless of the fucking consequences. It may not have been the right thing to punch that bitch in the mouth, but it was in self-defence to be honest. There's no need for me to chastise myself for my action, I stand by what I've done 100%. I'm a stooge to no-one and proud of my recusant nature.

I don't understand why I'm in such a funny mood - that's funny peculiar, not funny Ha-Ha. Why is it that I suddenly feel so confident? Maybe it's the drink and the pills? As I've already told you, work has been the one consistent factor throughout this crappy year - and now even that has gone, as my so-called "career" with that company comes to its abrupt end. And yet I don't feel sad at all at its loss, in fact, I feel somehow quite pleased.

Why did that fucker sack me? What have I ever done wrong? How dare he question me over my private life. So what if I've fucked a lot of guys and married another girl, so what? It's got nothing to do with him or anyone else. There's a lot more to me than just a hole to be fucked!

Why did he sack me?

Why has everything turned around?

Why does no-one ever fucking listen to me?

With the half-bottle of vodka gone, I start on the gin. I strip naked and throw my clothes about to land wherever they may fall, and then pleasure myself with 2-fingers of my right-hand as I guzzle-away at the evil liquid. I laugh and cum and laugh as my brain turns to jelly. I orgasm myself and I am so happy.

Why does this day feel so strange? What does it mean for me? For some reason I suddenly feel invigorated about life and all the possibilities it holds for me. I can do anything I WANT. Maybe it's just the feeling of being free from that fucking place at long last?

I certainly don't want to be a miserable cow all my life. Those shitforbrains at work tried to tear me down but it simply didn't happen. I'd just like to know why is it that I'm always the bloody victim? I feel like that poor sod out of *The Book of Job* - being tested by his God all the bloody time to see just how strong he was.

I have become considerably more emotional and sentimental the older I've become. Just when I think I've got everything bolted down nice and tight, along comes yet another disaster to kick me in the bloody teeth. These feelings have led to greater disillusionment about life in general, not that I had much faith in anything in the first place.

But, as I say, today is different. I feel like I've turned a corner. But what have I turned into? What is it that faces me next?

I am so inebriated I cannot stand. I crash onto the sofa and fuck, inserting 2-fingers into my vagina and my thumb into my bumhole and I screw myself stupid.

I hit myself harder and harder, forcing my body to cum. It tries to resist but my will to self-abuse is too great and eventually I hit the sweet-spot and cum over the soft leather.

I can't take any more drink or masturbating, my head and my body are useless now. I try to think what the fuck am I going to do with the rest of my life but the future just seems so alien to me. It's not my fault I was born part of the Generation X. I know for one thing though, there is no fucking way that I'm going to sign-on at the dole, I just cannot face the humiliation of all that shit again. After the last bout on the dole I took-out Income Protection with my bank, not that I think I'll actually need it at the moment. I should be able to find something pretty soon job-wise, and, of course, I still have plenty of money left-over from Mum's house.

The remainder of this weird day is spent in a total stupor. I don't do anything and I don't know what I did. Everything and nothing all blends into one. I fall into a coma on the sofa, completely naked, somewhere around 8.30pm. I think?

I have seen things I shouldn't have.

I have done things I shouldn't have.

***

I'm jolted awake by a horrendous pain in my left-ear. It's a pain like no other and from the very depths of the Earth it stabs me. I crumble into dust with shrieking hurt as I'm gripped by Hell as the depression tears into my lonely soul.

I cry out loud for my Mum to help me but she doesn't come - she is dead. What the fuck is happening now? What is this evil pain in my head?

I don't know what to do. There is no-one to help me. Do I kill it with more alcohol or is it the drink that's caused it in the first place? Will some sort-of pain-relief help me or is it something more serious, something that I've inflicted upon myself during the night?

I look at my watch to check the time, it reads 1am - 13-o'clock - but that can't be right? I can see the black night sky has turned to a deep shade of blue so it must be later than that, it must be. I check the clock on the mantelpiece and that reads 5.15am. I look at my watch again - the lovely Russian one that Mum bought me for my 18th-birthday - and notice that that too is dead. Broken. Time has stopped.

My pain hasn't though, and it continues to stab me like a bastard. It literally feels like someone has driven a large knife right into the side of my brain. What have I done to deserve this? What the Hell can this be?

I find some Paracetamol's in the bathroom cabinet. It says on the packet to only take 2 at a time at the most but I ignore the advice and take 4, washed down with some chilled German white from the fridge. I continue drinking the alcohol in the desperate hope that it has some kind-of effect on me, for better or for worse.

It's now 5.50am and still I'm no better. In fact, I think I'm actually bloody worse. What the fuck is going on? What is happening to me? I'm being driven insane by the pain and the noise inside my head.

I can't carry on like this any more, so I decide to ring my Doctor, there being an emergency number on his card and so I give that a try. I cry down the phone to the woman on the other end of the line and she's so lovely and sympathetic that it makes me cry even more. She surmises that I have an ear infection and tells me to take some stronger pain-killers but I don't have anything else in the flat, only more Paracetamol's and I've had 4 of those already. She suggests I go straight to a 24-hour chemist and get something stronger, so I guess that's just what I'll have to do - Fucking Hell. This is madness.

By the time I've thrown some indiscriminate clothes on - t-shirt, jeans, boots - it's 6.25am. Just to add to my woes it's also pissing-down once again outside, but I don't bother with a jacket as I'm so out of my skull with the pain and the alcohol that I just don't fucking care. I grab my keys and some cash and go.

The drive to the chemist is about 3-miles away in Horsham but it might just as well be a thousand for what difference it makes, I'm so fucked I don't know where I am. I fire-up the car and head off into town, the traffic thankfully being virtually non-existent at this time of the morning. I park directly outside the chemist and head inside, there being not a soul in there, only me and the Asian assistant - a weedy little Paki guy with a moustache so thin it looks like he's drawn it on with an eyeliner-pencil! I try to explain my condition to him the best I can considering my pain, the effects of the booze, and his typical lack of grasp of the English language, and he sells me some extra-strong Codeine pain-killers. I throw him some money on the counter and then I'm away, they had better fucking work or I'll fucking come back and kill the bastard for sure. I take 2 of the pain-killers as soon as I get back in the car, swallowing them down without water as I don't have any with me.

Why has this shit happened now, the very next day after I get the sack? What is the fucking meaning of this? I scream at the top of my voice at the agony being inflicted upon me but there's no-one to hear me. I am being attacked by the fucking Devil.

I head back to Slinfold Village the best I can, if I fuck this up and crash the car then I'm really bloody for it. Once safely indoors I desperately try to calm myself down, making myself a big fat mug of milky coffee with loads of sugar and try to chill-out. I seriously don't think the pain is as bad now as it was before but I'm not taking any chances. Maybe there's some kind-of placebo-effect going on in my mind, who knows?

At 8am I ring the Doctors surgery once again and get an emergency appointment with my GP for 8.40am. I wind my way down there straight-away as there's no point in hanging around here suffering by myself, killing time.

Thankfully there's only a handful of people waiting at the surgery, mostly oldies, all looking like death. I can feel the pain starting to subside now as the drugs kick-in, although I'm still in a lot of discomfort. It's 8.50am when Dr. Jeffs pokes his head around the corner of his door and ushers me in. I actually changed over from old Dr. Green a while ago as I didn't like his old-fashioned ways and manner. This new guy seems much nicer and has a more spirited approach to his diagnosis and treatment, although unfortunately he's not my type at all as he's in his late-50's and ginger.

After a quick, painful examination, he confirms that it is an ear-infection - a particularly nasty one by all accounts - and proscribes me a course of antibiotics called Clarithromycin, to be taken 3-times a day for the next 2-weeks, although he instructs me to come off them after 3-days due to possible side-effects because of their high strength - apparently they contain an extract of Morphine! He also takes a swab from the inside of my ear to send away for analysis, it stinging me like fuck as he does so and I scream and swear at him for causing me more anguish.

I head back home to sanctuary after collecting my antibiotics from the in-house pharmacy and immediately down a couple of them with water and wait for them to take effect.

I simply cannot fucking believe how shit my life can be, honestly, what have I fucking done to deserve all this bollocks?

This is absolutely crazy.

***

It's 3-days later that I receive a call from one of the nurses at the GP surgery, asking me to come in as soon as possible. They've identified the problem and apparently I've caught some fucking horrendous bacterial infection called Pseudomonas, something which apparently can also effect the eyes as well as the ears. Along with the antibiotics I'm already taking, they're now giving me some anti-bacterial ear-drops called Gentamicin, so hopefully all this crap should kill off the problem.

Just my fucking luck it won't!

***

It's now over 4-weeks since I got the sack and had the ear infection and I don't know where I am - I am completely lost in my own little World.

The suffocating pain from the infection lasted over the 2-weeks of the antibiotics so I continued on using them, even though I should have come off them after 3-days as my Doctor specified. The result was yet more complications - headaches, nausea, dizziness and even diarrhoea. I was in such a fucking state that it has left me totally wrecked. To counter all this shit I fought it with alcohol, which, in turn, has led me to the position that I now find myself in - in a right fucking mess, just moping-about like a mindless, idle, lethargic shadow of my former self. Although being able to hear properly once again is a joy unto itself.

Obviously I haven't bothered looking for another job either in all the time off I've had since the sacking, I just haven't been in a fit state to do so. I'm reasonably okay for money still - I've easily enough left to last me for over a year if so need be. I can assure you that I'm in no rush to jump from one frying-pan straight into another! I'm not going to bother initiating my Income Protection from the bank either, I'll save that for later-on if I get desperate.

I did actually do a days work at a cat and dog boarding home on the edge of town but I hated every fucking second of it, it was basically just shovelling shit all fucking day long. And what a long bloody day it was too, the hours were terrible - 7am to 5.30pm with a 2-hour lunch-break, and that's 7-days a fucking week and no weekends to call my own! The pay was minimum wage also so there was no fucking way I was going to do that for the foreseeable future that's for sure. The guy that owned the place was someone that I actually went to Senior School with, or so he said. He seemed to remember me - who wouldn't? - but I had no recollection of him at all. I wonder how come he's ended up running his own business and has a wife and kids and I've ended up like this? Why has my life gone so wrong?

I also went for another job working at a local Gin Factory in their office but I had to turn it down when they told me the job was zero-hours contract. I'm not working 7-days a fucking week for anyone. The money there was shit anyway - £7.63 an hour is a fucking insult.

As you may recall, Mum's old watch that she gave me for my 18th, broke on the morning of the ear-infection. I took it to a specialist in town to be looked at only to be told that it's not repairable - apparently there are no more spare parts available for those old Russian watches any longer. And so yet another part of my life is halted in its tracks and comes to an ignominious end.

So what the Hell am I going to do with myself now? What path do I take? The past 4-weeks have been a fucking living nightmare, but now that the pain has gone and the infection has all but virtually cleared-up, what else is there left in my life - sorrow, contentment, anger, hate, emptiness?

As I've told you several times, I've turned to drink for solace - big time. My dear old friend Mr. Vodka and I have spent most of our days, and quite a few nights - as they are ruled by my insomnia - smashed out of my skull, just to get from one end of the day to the other.

Spending my time thinking about the past year or so only makes matters worse - the loss of Mum's old cat Suzie, Amanda, the cheating, the shit with the "Old Man", the car crash and losing my beautiful car and breaking my arm - not to mention the shock of the baby, Abigail's pointless death, fucking, men, women, money, work shit, the ear-infection, my precious watch breaking - need I go on? Where do I draw the fucking line?

Spiritually - mixed-in with a large portion of fate - I understand that all these horrible things that keep happening to me are supposed to keep me on the straight and narrow, but come on, really? I almost lost my bloody life this year! Is this the way it's always going to be for crying out loud, one long roller-coaster of pain and shit with the occasional shag thrown-in for good measure? It's all very well, but what can I really do about it? What can anyone do? And who gives a fucking toss anyway? There's not one person on this planet that fucking cares? As ever, I have to go my own way and do my own solitary thing, that is my *raison d'etre*.

No-one bangs my drum or pulls my strings.

I am a puppet to nobody.

＊＊＊

Look at my life. I should be happy. I'm still young, I'm beautiful, intelligent, independent, free-spirited and have my health - although I have to admit I do abuse it a bit too much.

I have the whole World at my feet.

And yet, despite all this, I am broken and alone.

11

Lush

I have become disillusioned with everything. My present situation is poisoning my entire body and I can see no way out. I am on the cusp of oblivion, which, in turn, has made me even more neurotic than I was before. Everything has gone to pieces. I just wanna leave this fucking planet and not come back.

I still haven't found myself another job, and even though my money-pot is still healthy I'm well aware that it won't last forever. At this very moment though, I simply don't give a shit.

Why has my life gone so wrong? How the fuck did I end up like this, in this position, wallowing in self-pity? Know I'm polymorphic but what can I do about it? My saturnine nature is part of my make-up and I can't change it. My brain swimming in negative thoughts. I know I've lost my way and I need to get back on track but it's just not that easy. My life is meaningless and hollow.

I have only just managed to keep sane all these years by believing in myself, along with the help and support of alcohol, music, and using my unyielding willpower of course - that goes without saying. I have absolute belief in my subconscious ability to win - at all costs - but is it enough?

As far as my drinking goes, I have always found solace in its ability to mask my problems. I know this is not the ultimate answer and it does have an adverse effect on my social life, and, more importantly, my health and all that shit, but what else do I have to comfort me? I have no lover - of either sex - so what else is there to ease the pain? I know it's the vodka that's causing my mood swings. I do try and stop myself drinking that shit but I always fail - I fail miserably every fucking time. My head is drowning in alcohol.

My only other real vice is my car as I simply love driving, it gives me so much power and freedom that it is both physically and spiritually part of my very being.

And then, yet again, I can't have it both ways as the alcohol and the driving are not compatible and I end up even more frustrated than I was before. Everything is one big viscous circle. I just can't fucking win.

This is the way my life is heading and there's nothing I can do about it, I just can't stop it. I'm like a meteorite flying through space, smashing everything in its path, causing destruction wherever I go.

***

There's a very fine line between trying to stay sane and losing your marbles. I seem to have one foot in both camps at all times. I am in the darkest place on Earth, from the very depths of despair. I am beyond rescue. I am set on self-destruction and no-one can stop me. My mind is nothing but a pitiful conflict of thoughts as they travel across a multitude of planes. I really must do something with my tawdry life or I will go even more fucking insane.

I am so fucking pissed-off I want to end it all, even though I know I can't and won't. I don't even want to think about suicide, that's not the answer to my on-going problems, although I honestly don't know what is? I do know that I have to keep pushing. I have to know where this story ends.

I fear I'm losing my grip on reality. My mood swings from extreme highs to extreme lows all within a matter of a split-second. The whole World is watching me and there is no escape from it. I am sick and tired of swimming against the tide of life all the bloody time. Is this what I've turned into, an embittered harpie?

I have no interest in anyone or anything. No-one even comes to my flat any more. No-one even knows that I'm here - or cares. I'm just sitting here on my own wallowing in self-pity like a neurotic couch-potato. Sitting here picking the fluff out of my belly-button - there wasn't any.

Having said that though, I did receive one little ray of light the other day. It was an Email from Angie, the funny little Greek girl with the big hair at the shithole company that was my last place of employment. She told me that CJ - my arsehole ex-boss - was caught nicking the long-service / retirement watches from the company secure-room and had been replacing them with inferior copies and then flogging the real ones off on Ebay! What is it with these people, they all seem to think that their shit doesn't smell and that they can get away with anything - bloody typical manager! He'd actually been with the company since he was 18 and only had 10-years to go until his retirement and had a nice big fat pension waiting for him so why couldn't the stupid bastard wait? Now he's gone and blown it all away and got the bloody sack - ha-bloody-ha! What a fucking twat!

I cherish my vision, my dreams and being alive. So why can't other people see that and just let me be me? Why can't I live my own life? I know I contradict myself all the time, but what can I do when everything always goes tits-up? I know that no-ones life is 100% rosy and that I have lived a bit of an adventurous life - for a multitude of reasons! - but come on, when is this shit going to stop?

✳✳✳

My binge-drinking has left me in a continuous stupor. I've had so much vodka - my happy-liquid - that it feels like I'm breathing fire out through my nostrils. My mouth is as dry as the bottom of a bird-cage and my blood has infused with the alcohol and gone bad. It's eating me alive.

But what can I do? The more I drink the more I descend into the abyss and the more sober I am the more that reality bites me. I haven't slept properly in months. I'm not stupid though, I do have self-awareness regarding my pitfalls. I also have the intuition and ability to survive anything that is flung my way. I am sick and tired of expending all my energy and not getting anywhere. Just what have I achieved? Where do I go from here?

I constantly feel physically sick but nothing ever happens, nothing comes up.

I just don't know what to do next. I may be supremely clever but I don't have the answers to everything.

I WANT my Lacey and I WANT my Mum.

***

It's 2.20am the following morning and I'm standing in front of Lacey's grave. I am completely pissed out of my head and in total grief and despair. I rip and tear at my clothes and discard the remnants around me in the car-park until I am as naked as the day I was born.

I am a crazy woman. I just don't fucking care any more. I drop to my knees in tears of pain. What is the fucking point of carrying on?

My Lacey.

I want to dig down to her dead body and cradle her in my arms as I used to but in reality I know that I can't. She isn't Lacey any more, she's just bones and dust. I place my hands on the earth above her to try at least to feel some of her energy transmit itself through to me but all I'm dealt is more emptiness and sorrow in return.

This defeat only strengthens my despair and I sob uncontrollably in the silent morning air. I'm going around in fucking circles once again with the images of *deja vu* as I've been in this position before when my poor old cat died of course. Nothing has changed - she is dead and I'm still alone.

I guzzle-down more of the vodka that I brought with me and I choke on it's vile taste. I've almost had the entire bottle by now and I am blinded by its poisonous effects. I feel like shit-on-Earth but I carry-on drinking, pouring the liquid down my throat and over my face and breasts.

I think I passed-out cold but I can't be certain, everything is black and nothing is real. That is except for the sound of an approaching car heading towards me from the right, the beam if its headlights catching my profile as I squat down on the road - it's the fucking Police. Some fucker has grassed me up in the middle of my moment of sorrow - the fucking bastards.

I remain rooted to the spot as the Patrol-car pulls-up and the 2-male officers get out and walk towards me, one of them calling-out to me in a concerned tone:

"Are you alright Miss?" He says, before I quickly spit back at them.

"DOES IT FUCKING LOOK LIKE I'M ALRIGHT? WHAT DO YOU FUCKING THINK?"

"It's okay Miss. We're here to assist you."

"Is that a fact? All you wanna do is fuck me. You're all the fucking same you men. Well go on then, fuck me pig, if that's what you want, go ahead."

In the wake of my outburst I roll over onto my back and open my legs wide apart for them to reveal my glistening oyster in all its naked glory. The 2-officers don't take my action very kindly and come at me, each grabbing one of my arms and lifting me up and walking me over to their car, propping me up against its side. One of them opens a rear-door and in I go head first, followed by the threads that once were my clothes. My footwear - whatever that was? - seemingly disappearing off the face of the Earth.

At the Police Station I think I'm breathalysed and then questioned but I don't really remember much else - only snippets.

I awaken some time later - I have no-idea how much time has past as I still haven't replaced my old broken watch - by a metallic clanking noise and the sight and sound of a Police officer shouting at me as he opens the door to the cell

I was unceremoniously stuffed into earlier this morning.

"COME ON MISS. TIME TO GO. ON YOUR FEET."

He hollers at me as I scrape my weary body off of what can only very loosely be described as a "bed", as I try to get to my feet. I seem to be wearing a horrible grey hooded sweat-shirt that has some blue writing on the front, a pair of black track-suit bottoms and a pair of crappy white trainers - all from the local Charity Shop by the looks of them.

He leads me into an interview room where I'm sat down on a chair facing one of the officers who picked me up earlier this morning - well, at least I think it's him? - and a female officer of about 25 and very attractive with nice sharp features, gorgeous green eyes and short blonde hair - I'd really love to sit on her face and have her lick me! I wonder if she's up for it?

After a brief lecture where they both try to intimidate me by telling me what a naughty girl I've been, the male officer gives me a slap on the wrist and a hollow caution for my naked indiscretion and for being pissed out of my head. Apparently the Cops have checked-up on me with my old company to get some history on me as obviously they don't have me on record for any other misdemeanours from my past, not even for the incident at the swimming-pool (alright then, Leisure Centre!) a few years back - remember all that shit?

I'm guessing they must have also spoken to either Amanda or my sister Kate or even that old bitch Pam - fucking old cow - in the HR Department and that one of them has filled them in with all what's happened to me over the past year or so.

I sit there like a dummy, nodding-along to his "Blah Blah Blah", but I'm not really listening, I have more important things whizzing about in my head than to pay any attention to this twat. I give them an empty promise that I won't do anything like this again and will get myself sorted out like a good girl. Yeah right - like fucking Hell I will!

With the grilling over and the Cops having taken everything into consideration, I'm free to leave without charge - so that's exactly what I do.

What has been the fucking point of all this then? The morning in a cell followed by 30-minutes of bullshit, all for nothing.

Mr. Smartarse copper warns me yet again not to drive home as I'm still severely hung-over from all the alcohol I've induced but do I take any notice - do I fuck?

I step out of the Police Station and into the fresh-air - if you can call it that! - of my old High Street in South London. There are bloody people everywhere, swarms of them, all milling-about like headless chickens. And then there's me - just standing there amongst the throng watching them as they dart around me. Don't they realise how stupid they are - and look?

I start walking back in the direction of where I left my car, it's only about half-a-mile from here so I should be able to make it, even though I still feel like shit. I just hope and prey that she's still there seeing as I must have left my keys in it, I certainly don't have them now, only a plastic carrier-bag containing the torn remains of my clothes and no keys. If some bastard has nicked my fucking car I'm going to go ape-shit.

This area has actually gotten worse and worse for crime since I've moved away, its turned into a right shithole, with fucking Polish, Romanian, Latvian, Bulgarian, Estonian and Lithuanian gangs fighting each other, all vying to be top dog - or should that be top Slav? It's not only them, you throw in the niggers, Paki's, Koreans, Muslims and now even the bloody Syrians joining the fray, and you've got one big melting-pot of scum. I tell you now, this multicultural fusion is not a success on any level.

I round the final corner and see a flash of orange before me as fortunately my car is still there - and in one piece! - what a bloody relief! I can't believe my eyes when I open the still unlocked drivers-door and find my car / flat keys on the footwell carpet-mat! I sit my bum down in the snug drivers bucket-seat and fire-up the engine. It bursts into life with a deep rumble and I fuck-off home. I'm dying for a fucking drink!

***

I gently ease my dildo - the 6-inch one from Nice-n-Naughty - in and out of my bumhole whilst on all-fours - or should that be all-threes? - as I watch porn on my laptop. I started off with UK gay-boy cock-sucking porn, followed by lesbian scat porn, lesbian fake-cock porn, and now I'm fucking myself to bisexual transgender porn from Brazil which I stumbled onto just by chance, so I thought I'd give that a go. There are a couple a trans-girls on screen, both gorgeous, one blonde and the other dark-haired. The dark one is fucking the blonde one up the arse as she strokes her own cock to climax and cums herself. The dark one is about to cum also and pulls out and squirts her seed over the blonde one's face and tits, much to my delight and I laugh. I pretend that they're both here with me now and they're penetrating my arse and vagina at the same time and I cum.

I drink myself stupid on Bombay Sapphire gin until I start to feel sick and dizzy. I am totally wasted I can only just about control my body with what remains of my brain.

I search the net for more extreme porn and I find some really nasty stuff featuring a girl - I think she my be drugged but I don't care, it's not my fucking problem! - and 2-creepy guys and a horse. The 2-weirdo's are holding the girl down on a table as the horse is fucking the poor girl with its huge cock - it must be at least half-a-metre long, thick, and black - it's fucking horrendous! I finger myself and wank as hard as I dare but I find it hard to connect with the terror before my eyes, as then the horse ejaculates a fountain of its equine spunk all over the screaming girl's naked body and I cum and cry - for the both of us.

I wash my mouth out with cold German white straight from the bottle that's in the fridge and it wakes me up a little. My breathing is so heavy I can barely control it at all and I wonder what is happening to me and where this is all going to lead?

Next I'm on the living-room floor on my back with my smooth anal dildo from Lovehoney up my bum, my clear-plastic ribbed dildo from Honour in my pussy and my multi-speed rubber vibrator from Bondara in my mouth. I've also covered my entire body, including my hair, with items from the kitchen - salad cream, garlic paste, a tin of Italian whole tomato's, runny-honey, a tin of baked beans and other stuff that I've spread all over myself. I slither about on the fluffy rug, totally ruining it in the process, as I shudder and shake like a mad-woman as I force the 3-cocks into my poor undeserving body. I choke and moan and grown as I cum and jump around on the floor like a fucking spastic.

I have completely gone.

Totally lost it.

Off my face.

Out of control.

On another planet.

And I cum.

***

I have no idea what time of day it is.

I have no idea what day it is.

I have no idea.

I've drunk so much shit over the last however many weeks that I think I've pickled myself. I really do feel like crap. My head is in a constant spin and I have a severe pain in my stomach, like my insides are on fire. I feel absolutely terrible. I think I've got brain damage.

I stumble around the flat wondering what the Hell is wrong with me this time? The pain is getting so bad I can barely move my legs - my beautiful long legs. I collapse to the floor in agony. Something serious has gone wrong and I am genuinely scared. There's no fucking around now, I'm really in trouble and I know it. What the fuck do I do?

I just about make it to the toilet for a pee and a poo but that's not what I purge - it's blood - and it's not menstrual blood either as the consistency and colour is all wrong, it's good old fashioned life-blood. My period isn't due for another 2-weeks yet anyway. I fear that this is not going to go my way this time.

I try to wipe up my mess the best I can and then stuff my bathroom towel between my legs just in case I start dripping blood all over the carpet. I wearily get to my feet and head back to the living-room to phone my Doctor, he must be able to help me, he must. It rings forever until it's picked-up by the receptionist - it's the young girl who I've seen a couple of times before, she's a bit green around the edges but nice enough. To my horror my Doctor isn't in today - fuck-it - but when I tell her of my nightmare she insists that I ring for the paramedics immediately. I hang-up on her and dial 999 and go through a repeat performance with the woman on the other end of the line.

I drop down onto the floor in terrible pain and try to crawl to the front-door, still with the towel wedged between my legs. I think I managed to unlock the door before I collapse back down to Earth once again, although by now I'm only semi-conscious and I don't really understand what the Hell is happening as my mind spins in a whirl.

I touch the outer rim of death and the Spirit World and it scares me.

* * *

I vaguely remember hands touching me and the colour green for some reason, and also the outlines of people around me and their muffled voices calling out my name. It is the journey towards death.

I recall a beautiful, long, peaceful sleep and a dream of a gorgeous white sandy beach with beautiful palm-trees and a sky of the finest blue, with me swimming naked in the clearest water that you've ever seen in your entire life, whilst over

the top of all this wonder plays the hypnotic music of Samuel Barber's beautiful *Adagio for Strings*. The whole scene is a work of genius. It is a lost paradise.

I emerge from the sea all shiny and glistening wet when I suddenly notice the figure of a tall man approaching me from the distance. I can't make out who it is at first as the heat blurs his image so I run to him. His features and demeanour become clearer the nearer I get and I begin to slow down my pace as I suddenly recognise the truly awful reality of who it is - it's the "Old Man."

I awake suddenly with a start and I jump into the air in shock and fear with my heart beating like crazy and sweat pouring from every pore. I'm in a bed in a room all by myself and I know immediately that once again I'm back in Hospital - for the second time this year. This is fucking unbelievable!

I feel so bloody tired but at least the horrendous pain in my stomach seems to have subsided, to a large degree anyway. I try to move but I'm almost pinned in position by several tubes sticking into my precious skin of my arms - my beautiful arms - not again.

There's a buzzer - or at least that's what I think it is? - by the side of me on a cord, so I press it several times but it makes no sound. I can't fucking believe this is happening, I really fucking scared myself this time. I've completely bloody knocked myself sideways, I cannot believe how much out of my head I was. I was near death and that is no exaggeration. Maybe it's only in death that I will find total freedom?

The door to my room suddenly opens and in-walks a Doctor - unsurprisingly another foreigner, some sort-of Asian - and a nurse - English and therefore white, who has a face on her like a smacked arse! She's going to be a barrel of laughs isn't she!

"How are you feeling?" Asks the Doc.

"Okay I guess. What Hospital am I in?"

"You're in East Surrey Hospital in Redhill. You were in quite a state when you brought in yesterday. We've run some tests and you have overloaded your liver quite badly. You have poisoned your blood with all the alcohol you have been drinking. We have had to give you intoxication treatment to clean you up, including pumping your stomach."

"I feel like crap. I could murder a cup of tea. When can I go home?"

"Not yet. You will have to spend a couple of days more in Hospital for

observation as well as having the intravenous drip in you arm to prevent dehydration. Also your cognitive functions are nowhere near where they should be. A lot of your symptoms you're experiencing are psychosomatic to the situation you're currently facing and is exasperating the problem. The more you are depressed the more you drink, and the more you drink the more depressed you become. It is a viscous circle." Preaches the Paki. I didn't realise I was in Hospital for a fucking lecture!

"How do you know all this stuff about me?"

"Your friend, she has been waiting a long time."

"What friend? Who is it?"

"You must rest. I will come and see you later to check."

Both the Paki and Miss Sourpuss bugger-off and leave me in peace at last. What a fucking cheek! What the fuck does he know about me? Come to think of it, what the fuck does he know about anything - except curry maybe?

I lay back and try to get some rest, just like the Asian says, but my peace is almost immediately interrupted by a knock at the door. It slowly opens and in-walks the beautiful vision that is Amanda - my love.

"Hello." I attempt saying to her cheerfully but I fail.

"Hi, how are you feeling?" She asks me in her beautiful Australian tone.

"Better now you're here. They've stuck tubes into me and given me a stomach pump."

"Yeah, well. The Hospital called me, they said you were in a bad way."

"Yeah, I guess so. Everything just got out of hand. I'm sick of it all."

"You can't keep beating yourself up Sarah, you're better and stronger than that."

"I know. Do you think there's still a chance we could get back together." I plead.

"No Sarah, there's no chance, be realistic. I've moved on. And you should too. It's all over between us, you know that. I can't carry-on any more with this relationship. I can't trust you."

"You're right I guess? I know I can't be trusted - I want more."

"Well there you are, that's just typical of you. That's you all over isn't it? More, more, more - that's all you ever want."

"What do you expect me to say - sorry? I am sorry, I really am. But at the same time I'm not, I'm glad I screwed Gary. It's what I wanted at the time. I can't help it."

"You're fucking unbelievable arn't you? I really thought we had something special going but no, you're not content with ruining our marriage so you thought you'd fuck-up your best friend's relationship at the same time. There's just no stopping you is there? Well, I've had enough Sarah. This is the end of the road for us and I want out. We'll split everything 50-50 and go our separate ways. There's no more to be said. There's already a letter in the post regarding the divorce."

"DIVORCE! You pick your moments don't you?"

"You're impossible Sarah. You'll never be happy."

"I'm not impossible. And it's other people that make me unhappy."

"And you knew that I wanted to have children but you're too selfish even for that."

"Yeah, well, I've never wanted kids. I told you that right at the beginning."

"It's all over Sarah, I've had enough."

I lay there staring at her for a while as I contemplate her reasoning. I call her a "Cat murderer" for killing Lacey and Suzie but I don't know why? Sometimes evil words just seem to spill out of my mouth for no real reason. I don't mean to be malicious on purpose, it's just that I have an underlying motivation to get what I want. And I want more - I always do.

I know that I've hurt Amanda badly and that in turn hurts me. In the end though she'll get over it and so will I. The trust we had between us has gone. All my relationships have ended in disaster. I have therefore consigned myself to the fact that I will never be happy as far as love with another person is concerned. Love saps my energy until there is nothing left to give or take.

Without another word from either of us, not even a "Goodbye" or "I still love you", Amanda turns and walks out the door and my life. I lay there open-mouthed at our final parting but I'm not really shocked, I'm the one that instigated the downfall after all. I'm not proud of it and at the end of the day Amanda is right - I do want more. I want it all right here and now. I want more sex - from men and women - more money, more love, more speed, more power, more drink, more of everything.

I want to fuck and be fucked all the fucking time.

***

I spend one more day in Hospital before I decide to discharge myself and go home. The Doctor's have run some more tests and have stuck all manner of things into me but I'm not interested in the results, I just want to get the Hell out of here - now - and continue my quest. I have to trust my instincts and believe in my ability to adapt and flourish in this harsh World of today.

My natural flair and ability to think outside of the box sets me apart from the majority of the population and no-one is going to stop me, regardless of the consequences.

I don't bother to sign any discharge forms or any of that crap as none of it means anything to me. I quickly put my clothes back on - the shit ones the stupid Police gave me - and fix my hair the best I can and then fuck off.

Once out into the fresh-air of the great outdoors, I breathe-in a lungful of life-giving oxygen and exhale all the stuffy, germ-ridden bad air from the past few days. It invigorates and rehabilitates me and makes me feel so alive. It really is good to be alive.

The problem now of course is how to get the fuck home? I don't have any money for a cab and my car is obviously back at the flat - I really hope that she's alright? - so I guess I'll have to wing-it and use my feminine charm!

I spot a couple of guys - builder types - about to get into their crappy van and leave so I ask them which way they're heading. They look at me just like they all do even though I don't have any make-up on or perfume and my hair is a right fucking mess, as are my dishevelled clothes. Unfortunately they're not going in my direction but deep down I know they want to take me - in more ways than one, that's men for you!

I spot another van, either delivering or picking something up from the Hospital so I collar the driver - a young guy in his early-20's, tall and slim and with a wedding-ring on his finger, not that that bloody means anything. I give him a sob-story about that I've just been visiting a relative on their last-legs and he caves-in almost immediately, agreeing to drop me off at his next stop at Broadbridge Heath, not too far from my village - only a couple of miles or so. He drives like a nutter as we head West and I start to feel a little sick at the fast pace we're going. He seems like a nice enough guy and I catch him several times looking at my breasts which in turn makes them heave even more as my breathing becomes over-exited. He drops me off at the big roundabout there and wishes my relative well and then he zooms off, never to be seen again. Oh well, you can't win them all!

The walk back to Slinfold Village is actually okay, it's really not that far, it being coterminous to Broadbridge Heath as that is itself to Horsham. The Sun is shining and I soak-up its rays and I actually feel pretty good despite all the trauma and sickness that I've experienced recently. It takes me bloody forever to walk back home though but I do make it - eventually!

As I enter the key-code into the pad on the main doors to my block, my lazy bastard of a next door neighbour - or "The

Retard" as I call him - is coming down the stairs, presumably heading off to sign-on. I don't think that he's ever done a days work in his entire fucking life. I've absolutely no idea what his name is either, nor do I care for that matter, although I think it says something like "Gummidge" on his entry-pad number. He stares at me as I walk right past him in silence, he was obviously expecting me to say something or maybe he's just wondering where I've been for the last few days. Like I say, I don't give a shit either way - fucking waster.

I step over a wad of about 10-letters, all sleeping on the door mat, as I enter my flat. Most of them are just crap - the electric bill, phone bill and such - except for a big brown A4-sized one that stands out from the rest and catches my eye, so I open that first. It's a letter from Amanda's solicitor and the *Decree Nisi* from the Court. Well, thank-you very bloody much, that was a nice welcome home!

I was going to chill-out with a nice big mug of milky, sugary coffee and read all my mail and watch shit on the TV, but seeing as the pint of milk in the fridge has turned to liquid mould and Amanda's bombshell solicitors letter has knocked me back, I have to resort to opening a new bottle of German white instead.

Do you see what I mean now about "I WANT", I don't want anything at all until I actually want it.

I sit back on the sofa and read through the document with a sense of apathy. Our so-called "marriage" was a sham right from the start really wasn't it? I mean, transgender witnesses, come on? I understand every relationship has its flaws, but ours was never going to last was it? Our love for each other kept us together but also drove us apart, not helped by my stupid infidelity it must be said.

Deep down I know it's all over and I don't want to prolong the agony of this crap any longer. If she wants out, then so be it. I sign the paper and it's all over, I'm not going to stand in the way of her future happiness. It's time to shit or get off the pot.

How do I find happiness and hang on to it?

I think I've actually lost the ability to love.

Love lives next door to hate.

***

It's 10.35am the following morning before I decide to scrape myself out of bed. What's the fucking point of getting up any earlier anyway? If yesterday was anything to go by there isn't any. I love my bed, to snuggle under the warm duvet and be embraced by its protection. Why can't my entire life be like that?

After a quick pee and a brush of teeth I head to the kitchen. As I click the kettle on the doorbell rings, making me jump out of my skin. I'm not expecting anyone so who the Hell can this be? I step on more bloody letters piled-up on the mat as I peer through the spyhole in the front-door. There's some bloody girl standing there with a collection-pot in hand. What the fuck does she want at this time of the morning? As I open the door we both stand there staring at each other in amazement. She looks like some sort-of Leftie judging by her clothes - frumpy, with big hobnail boots on and denim shorts with black tights, a big green woolly jumper and a French beret on her head. She's okay-looking I guess but nothing to write home about, and as I say, she definitely has a Left-Wing slant to her.

"Oh hi, I'm collecting for starving children in "?" - I can't actually remember the place she mentioned, but I think it was somewhere in Africa or some such Third World disease-ridden shithole.

"I'm not interested in that shit. As far as I'm concerned the only good nigger is a dead one." I bitch back at her like a bitch.

"Excuse me?" She bleats with a stunned expression across her stupid Leftie face as I then question her back.

"Hang on a second, how did you get in here, it's coded-entry only?"

"The front-doors are open. There's some workmen down there doing something to them." She replies.

I open the door fully and barge out the flat past her, my intention being to find out what the Hell is going on down stairs.

"Wait, where are you going?" She calls after me as I'm already half way down the first flight but I'm not interested.

"It's nothing to do with you." I snap back at her.

"But you haven't got any clothes on." She suddenly exclaims back.

Well, that certainly got my attention! I stop in my tracks as I suddenly realise that she's right - I'm still stark-bollock-naked - oh shit!

Now, I have 2-choices here, either admit defeat and turn around and go back indoors, or carry on downstairs and confront the alleged workmen in the nude. I decide I'm not going to be defeated and so I carry on. I turn on the bottom landing and amble down the last few steps to see 2-guys fiddling about with the entry key-pad. They immediately stop and stare at me, my breasts, legs and my beautiful shaved pussy in complete shock as I near them, the younger of the 2 giggling-away like a stupid girl.

"WHAT THE HELL ARE YOU DOING?" I scream at them.

"We're fixing the entry-pad gorgeous." Says the older one, a smartarse type with a big chip on his shoulder and a dirty grin across his face.

"Yeah well, we just can't have every Tom, Dick and Harry walk in here you know. GET IT FIXED AND LEAVE." I holler back.

"Nice rack." Quips the smartarse back at me.

"FUCK-OFF AND GET IT FUCKING FINISHED." I hiss back at him. Bastards.

I turn on my heals and scoot back upstairs as quickly as my unsupported breasts will allow me, all the while feeling the eyes of the 2-workmen burning into my legs and my bum.

Back at my front-door I notice that the little Leftie girl has vanished into thin air, presumably having hooked one of my race-traitor neighbours to part with their hard-earned cash - idiots. "Collecting for Africa" my arse, they can all fuck-off and die.

I slam the door shut hard behind me and scoop-up my mail, half-a-dozen letters in total this time. They're all the usual dreary old crap - circulars, scroungers, the odd bill, and my bank statement, which I always dread receiving. When I tear it open though my heart sinks when I read my balance as I appear to be some £800 lighter than I had already calculated. Looking down through my statement I notice the very same amount has been paid out to an online gaming company almost 3-weeks ago using my card details. Obviously there's no fucking way that I've done this myself of course so what the fuck is going on now?

There's no other way for it, I'm straight on the phone to my bank, demanding to them:

"WHAT THE HELL IS GOING ON?"

They then give me the phone number for their Fraud Department, so in turn I have to ring them and re-explain the situation once more. The girl on the other end of the line has a sweet, sexy voice that melts my heart and my mind begins to wander off the real reason for making the call in the first bloody place and onto images of me kissing her young breasts and sticking my tongue and fingers into her wet vagina - OH MY GOD!

She immediately cancels my card and issues me with a new one, telling me that I should receive it within the next few days at the most. For fucks sake, what a fucking nightmare!

Meanwhile of course, I now can't access my bloody bank account so I guess I'll have to get cash out from one of my Building Society accounts to tide myself over. What a fucking pain in the arse! I wonder who the fuck had got hold of my bloody card details in the first place? It's bound to be a sodding foreigner, I just know it. I bet it's one of those fucking Paki's at the Petrol Station up the road. If it is I'll fucking kill the bastards - fuckers.

This is all I need on top of all the other shit I've got to contend with. Why can't life be simpler? There's got to be more to life than this, hasn't there?

***

I spend the rest of the day stuck in front of the TV like a lazy moron, watching soporific-inducing crap and nothing else. I can't even be bothered to wash myself or to get pissed. Food wise, I just munch-away on toast, crisps and any other junk I fancy throughout the whole day and that's it - day over.

What a waste of fucking time.

12

Back Piece

Despite all the warnings and protestations from my Doctor and the quacks at the Hospital, I'm back on the drink once again, not that I ever really came off it completely of course. I've seriously fallen off the wagon this time though with a thud. I know deep down that I'm cutting my own throat but I intend to carry-on regardless. I need it, it's my drug and if I don't feed it I don't know what I'll do?

I'm pissed out of my skull - it's 10.05am - and I'm ringing John, my tattoo man, whilst laying on my bed naked and hot. I've not been in contact with him since my last inking, so that's well over a year ago now. But I need another fix, and this time it's gonna be a big one.

"Hi John, it's Sarah." I say somewhat muddled.

"Hello gorgeous, how's tricks?"

"Tricks are shit actually, if you must know."

"Why, what have you been up to now?"

"I got married, in Las Vegas."

"Well, congratulations! You never cease to surprise me."

"Yeah well, the biggest surprise is that I married another girl."

"Fuck-off! Are you serious?" He questions me.

"Would I lie to you? The trouble is though I cheated on her, with a guy, my best friend's husband actually, and got myself pregnant, and then I had a car accident and lost the baby, and then we split up, and then my niece was killed and now I've just got the sack from my crappy job."

"Bloody Hell Sarah, you don't half put yourself through it don't you? I didn't realise you batted for the other side though girl, I always thought you were as straight as a die."

"Well, I swing both ways actually."

"Well I am surprised. You've really shocked me this time girl."

"Yeah, well I think I've shocked myself, more than once! Anyway, how are you fixed for doing some more work on me?"

"You know me, I'll fit in you anytime!" He says cheekily.

"You mean fit me in?"

"I know what I mean girl."

"Now come on, how many more times do I have to say it? You're a married man. Seriously though, I've done some designs for my back so when can you do me? How about this coming Saturday?"

"Saturday is a no-go I'm afraid, I'm fully-booked all day. How about Sunday morning, about 10-ish?"

"Sunday? Yeah okay, this Sunday it is then." I confirm.

*** *** ***

Sunday turns out to be a really shitty day, weather-wise that is. In fact the whole weekend has been crap so far as it hasn't stopped pissing down at all. And as I never use an umbrella it looks as though I'm going to get a tad wet. Oh well!

I arrive at John's tattoo and piercing studio in good time - it's 9.45am - just as he turns up also - spooky!

"Morning." I say cheerfully.

"Hi Sarah, how the Devil are you?"

"Still alive." I quip back with my customary morbid line.

I'm wearing just a pair of old jeans and an old t-shirt today as there's no point in dressing-up just for this - I don't want to get my nice clothes spoilt with splashes of ink and blood. Having said that I do both my hair and make-up just as immaculate as always. My jeans are a pair of old tight-fitting blue stone-wash ones from New Look, whilst my t-shirt is a faded old BSA biker one in black from Grand Prix Legends. I don't actually wear it that often, only when I'm in the right mood, like when I'm feeling belligerent or when I'm pissed - or both! On my feet I've got on a pair of black hiking-boots that I found online - these ones coming from Blacks - that look and feel really great. I've also decided not to wear any underwear today, or socks, as I'm not in the mood. My perfume is *Poison* by Christian Dior. In my self-spiked bloodstream you will find vodka from Vladivar.

I do realise that you shouldn't drink alcohol before getting a tattoo - or drive for that bloody matter! - but this is the way things are and always will be for me so get over it.

We have a quick chat about shite, mainly all the fucking crap that I've gotten myself into, and then it's down to business discussing my new work. I'm having my entire back tattooed with the artwork being split into 2-separate parts down the centreline either side of my spine. On the left-hand half I'm having a *Hakenkrautz,* the ancient hooked-cross symbol of good-luck, peace and well-being - amongst other things! And on the other side I'm having a quote by the infamous mystic occultist Aleister Crowley, this being:

Do what thou wilt shall be the whole of the Law

done in old English lettering, all this of course whilst avoiding my precious tattoo of Lacey - my one and only love. I know you my think I'm crazy in doing this and that I must be off my rocker, but I've thought about doing this for ages - even before I married Amanda - so it's not a spur of the moment thing by any means.

I've self-prepared the complete stencil for John to use beforehand to save him some time - and me some money! - so we decide together to do the whole thing today in one big hit with no fucking around. Drawing out the initial sketches and the final artwork was a pure joy, I lost my mind to the images I was creating before me and buried myself within its formation. I adore art in all its forms. I was born with a pencil in my hand.

Rather than sit backwards in his special former dentist's chair, John suggests that we do the work on the floor on one one his green Japanese *Tatami* straw floor-mats, so that way he can position me better. When he unrolls one of them out on the studio floor it emits a lovely calming odour like freshly-cut grass that wafts its way around the room and fills me with such a tremendous sense of peace and tranquillity that it makes me melt. The effects of the vodka coupled with the smells of the studio - the ink, the disinfectant, my perfume, and now the floor mat, have sent me crazy already.

I strip-off all my clothes completely there and then and stand before John in all my super-smooth naked glory. He stares at the natural beauty of my body as he mixes-up the black ink for my tattoo. The sexual tension between us is so electric that I can physically see sparks before my very eyes jolting about the studio, ricocheting off the walls.

I stare back at him and take a gulp of air as I desperately try to contain myself.

I feel my breasts heaving as I do and I want him to fuck me right now, to take his cock right up inside me but no - that's not what I came here for, even though I crave the feeling of a real dick inside me once again.

John covers the straw mats with soft blue towels to make laying on them more comfortable and also to stop any of my blood and the ink dripping onto them - therefore ruining them completely. I lay myself down on the towels face-down and watch him as he approaches me with the stencil and ink in hand. He kneels down beside me and places the items next to the tattoo machine, the controller unit and his other tools of the trade. As he sprays the soft skin of my back with the smelly disinfectant, the sharp coldness if its effect almost makes me cum and I sigh loudly to him.

With the outline all prepped and primed he fires-up the tattoo machine, charges it with ink, and stabs me with the first of a thousand lines. I wince and moan at the pain but he ignores me and carries on drilling into my beautiful skin as my alcohol infused blood runs thinly out of my soul and is replaced forever by the thick blackness of the ink. I want the tattoo machine to hurt me, to take away the other pain, the pain of being alive, the pain of being me. This is my masochistic punishment for being who and what I am.

The sharp stinging subsides slowly though within the first half-an-hour, and for the duration of the session I drift away on another plane into the idyllic dream-world, the one where I can actually control my own life through the power of *ALTER* and *INITIATE,* instead of the reality where its controlled by mystical entities and the incompetence of all those around me.

I think of Mum and her words to me when I got my other tattoo - the portrait of Lacey on my shoulder - when she told me in no uncertain terms:

"I didn't give birth to you so you could cover yourself in tattoos."

Bless her, what was she like!

John and I suffer together for the total of almost 6-gruelling hours of pain, not even stopping for any lunch nor water or even the toilet. I enter into an altered state of consciousness and hallucinate as I lose myself in the pain, suffering for my art as I always do.

At 3.50pm it's all over and my back is scarred forever. The machine is switched-off and laid to rest by my side, my ears still ringing from the intense monotonous buzzing from its motor. John sprays my back with cleaning fluid and wipes-down my sore skin. I slowly try to stand and he has to help me, taking my arm as I struggle to my feet. He continues to wipe me, over my shoulders, down my spine, over my ribs, and then over my bum as the mixture of fluid, blood, ink and sweat has dribbled down to my cheeks and between. As I stand there in all my nakedness I feel his fingers part my rear to remove the last vestiges of the mess. I love it and my lungs lose all their breath at his touch.

I turn to look at him with a dizzy expression, just hoping that he can read my mind. Without hesitation I feel the touch of one of his fingers at the top of my smooth mound and I let him insert one of them into my vagina and pleasure me slowly but firmly. In seconds I scream and I cum for him and I almost collapse from the abuse on my body but I just about manage to hold myself together and stay standing, grabbing his shoulders to steady myself.

You cannot fucking believe how much I am so in love with myself and being alive right now but I can't and don't let him go any further, this has gone too far already. I pull away and start to rub one hand over my vulva and the other over my peaches as John starts to undo the belt to his jeans but I stop him - this not what I want. I do like him and I do want to fuck but I don't and can't, it's just not right, it's not fair on his wife and kids for one thing. I've screwed-up enough people already this year, including myself, and I don't need any more shit, I really don't.

I try and explain my situation to him politely but firmly as he continues to wipe my back free of more of the leaking mess. I turn my body away from him and admire his handy-work in the reflection of his floor-mounted mirror. It is simply stunning - and incredibly dark and mysterious - the sharp angular image of the cross mixed with the sinister undertones of the meaning of the text.

I thank him with all my love as he starts to apply a giant absorbing pad over my new ink, taping it over my shoulders and around my waist, so hopefully I don't start leaking blood and ink all over the place on my way back home.

I redress myself with some difficulty as I'm sore and stiff and hurt and we chat and laugh about nothing. I pay his bill of £700 - cheap for this amount of work - in cash, kiss him lightly on the cheek and then I'm gone, until next time.

***

I can't believe it's still fucking raining as I step back out into the open air, although the sky is much lighter now than it was this morning, not that that makes any fucking difference to anything! I ease myself gently into my car and my back feels very wet from all the goo, but once I'm settled back in my seat it's actually not too bad. The traffic is very light now, it being Sunday afternoon I guess, and I'm back home safe and sound in a trice.

I have a couple if big slugs of vodka straight from the bottle as soon as I walk through the front-door, then completely strip-off my clothes in the bathroom to try and sort myself out. Removing the enormous bandage proves to be a right bitch but after several tugs and some effing and blinding, it comes away in one piece. I try to flush the blood and ink-stained remains of it down the toilet but it jambs and backs-up with water when I pull the handle so I try to unblock it with the loo-brush and push it further along its path but I only end up compressing it into a solid mass of paper - bugger! In the end I have to stick my arm down the toilet and pull the bloody thing out manually and then dispose of it in the bin in the kitchen, it dripping a steady stream of water all the bloody way. Why doesn't anything ever go right?

I take another big gulp of vodka, bringing the bottle with me into the bathroom and having a couple more mouthfuls. I run the shower to clean off all the crap from my back, it now starting to feel a little tight. I try not to have the water too hot, just Luke-warm, as I have to be careful not to damage my new ink.

I stand directly under the shower-head and let the water cascade down my beautiful body, it hugging every curve. I love it so much it hurts and I touch myself all over with both hands. The effects of the vodka really start to kick in now and I feel so incredibly warm and cosy. I soap myself all over my gorgeous body and use its slipperiness to pleasure my vagina and I begin to pant erratically. The vodka pushes me over the edge of normality and I squat down on my haunches and insert the thick curved bar of *Dove* all the way into my pussy and I fall in love with my soap and I orgasm myself and shake and shudder and gasp uncontrollably and collapse in a drunken wet heap unconscious, just like the lush I have become.

I'm not out for very long, maybe only a couple of seconds, and I drag my carcass out of the shower and stumble as I try to stand. As I do so the heavy bar of soap suddenly plops itself out of my vagina and hits the floor with a dull thud and I laugh at both that and my reflection in the bathroom mirror. I gently pat myself dry with an old brown towel that I don't really like that much and rarely use as my back is still a bit leaky and I don't want to ruin one of my nice white Egyptian ones.

I then start to wrap some cling-film around my torso, hoping that will stop any further leaks throughout the rest of the day and in bed tonight.

I don't do much else for the rest of the day, just the usual old stuff - a light dinner, check my Emails, watch some internet porn featuring massive cock sucking and choking porn and another wank - this time anal using a peeled and sculptured cucumber - wine, TV, and then to bed early at 9.30pm with a lovely milky coffee with 2-sugars as I try to finish-off the last 2-chapters of the Aleister Crowley biography *A Magick Life* that I'm reading for the second time, the very book which sparked the idea for my back piece in the first place.

***

Monday morning dawns bright and early, in fact I'm lying, it's still raining, dull, and it's actually 11.05am.

I heard a thud ages ago - at least 3-hours - as I think it was the postman putting something in my slot. I attempt to rise from my lazy position and sure enough, just as I had predicted, my bandaged tattoo has leaked its nasty contents all over the fucking sheets in swirls of black ink and blood - what a mess!

I plod my way to the bathroom to remove the cling-film and it unfurls easily enough to reveal my new art. Its a breathtakingly wondrous vision of both abstract and mystical that is now a permanent part of my beautiful body. I love it as much as I love myself.

The scars on my back are there to give me protection in the future, just as the scars on my mind are there to remind me of my past - the good and the bad.

I wipe my body clean with toilet-paper, throw the soiled remains of the cling-film in the kitchen waste-bin, and go and fetch my mail from the front-door mat. There's only one envelope - another brown one - and when I tear it open and read its contents they have no effect on me whatsoever. Its the *Decree Absolute* from the Court. Amanda and I are now officially divorced.

I have no feeling. I have no emotion. Now the dichotomy is set I have the courage and tenacity to move forward in my life with the love of myself and my want.

***

I've made an appointment to see my Doctor at the Medical Centre in town at 6.30pm today. There's nothing wrong with me at all, I'm as fit as a fiddle, physically anyway, but I'm going to see him anyway as once again I'm being a bit of a naughty girl. I really can't help it, this is the way I am!

This evening I'm wearing a bright-yellow sleeveless blouse from AliExpress that I leave open dangerously-low so everyone can check-out my superb full cleavage, a pair of pale-blue tight jeans from Primark, underwear in white lace from Figleaves, and on my feet my dear old pair of blue-suede Lola heels - still going strong after all this time and all the things we've been through together. My hair and make-up I've done in my own classical style, featuring very pale-blue eyeshadow, lipstick and nail-varnish. My clutch-bag is my beautiful silver Art-Deco Shell one from Vintage Styler. My perfume is *Luxe* by Avon.

I sit there in the waiting room on my sweet bum minding my own business when Dr. Jeffs suddenly emerges from his consulting room and calls-out my name. We exchange the usual pleasantries as I enter the room as I then go to explain my slight "problem" to him. I tell him of the minor irritation in my vagina and ask him if he could check my out to see if there's anything wrong. He ushers me onto the high-standing bed over to one side of the room and asks me to remove my jeans and knickers as he puts-on a pair of white surgical latex gloves. I lay back and think of England as I open my legs to him.

Although he's not my type at all - he's in his 50's and ginger as I've already told you once before - I need and crave the touch of someone else on my pussy, touching myself just isn't the same. I give a little moan and a small shudder as he touches my lips and parts them. I feel the sensation of the speculum inside me and I want to scream and let go but I have to restrain myself or he will get suspicious and my cheap pleasuring trick will be terminated.

I dream that the probe is a human tongue and that I'm being eaten by some random hot girl with a hardbody or some fit guy with a cock of iron. I struggle to contain my composure as he touches my clit and my gorgeous legs start to quiver as I desperately try not to cum and squirt my love at him. Fortunately he backs-off just in time and my evil ruse comes to a sudden and abrupt end - Bloody Hell! Why do I do these things?

He informs me that there's nothing wrong - really! - and that I don't have anything to worry about, but if I continue to experience any further symptoms I have to come back asap.

Back in my car I rub myself through my clothes and I cum quickly. A few of my fellow humans walk past my side-window as I give a short piercing scream but I don't give a monkey's ring-piece about them. What I do is my fucking business, not their's.

* * *

I went back to see John again about 2-months later, not only to get some of my artwork retouched where some of the shading had missed-out, but also to have some more piercings done in my ears, these also being part of the "Grand Plan".

All the new stainless-steel jewellery for this work I pre-ordered beforehand ages ago from Wildcat in Brighton, East Sussex, the same company I sourced my previous items from.

This time around I've actually had some of the pieces custom-made by them for my own specific purposes, these including an industrial Trangus-Helix barbell (which is really annoying the fuck out of me at the moment, especially at night when I'm trying to sleep, but I have to and will stick with it), numerous rings and barbells around the Helix of both ears, rings through the Daith, Rook and Orbital of both ears, and a small Fleshtunnel featuring blue and white shark-fins inserted in my right ear-lobe, which over the coming months I will steadily increase the size of to reach the diameter of 5mm internally - it looks absolutely gorgeous, as do all the others, as do I.

13

We are Spirits

I need some direction in my life. I need and crave the answers to my future as to where I go from here? I can't carry on like this, my batteries are running low and I have to do something - but what?

It's 4.15 in the morning and I awake suddenly in tears of pain over my life and how things are right now. This is impossible, I can't lay here thinking about this shit any more and so I'm forced to get up. This sort-of thing has turned into being an almost daily occurrence these days and I can't seem to snap myself out of it. I wander around the flat in a semi-comatose daze, I literally do not know what to do next or where I'm going in life. I have all the tools I need to empower every aspect of my life, but what am I doing with them? Fuck-all that's what. I have completely lost my connection with my inner motivation, I simply don't have anything to do. Maybe I'll open my own cat sanctuary and spend the rest of my days looking after them in peace. I say it but I won't do it though.

I make myself a big mug of milky coffee and go back to bed - not to sleep - but to sit and think. And that's my problem, I think too much. And when I don't think I always seem to land myself in yet another scrape and so there you have it - I can't fucking win either way no matter what I do.

As per usual there's nothing but shit on the TV - channel after channel of telly-shopping, bloody American fitness adverts or stupid twats flogging super-mops and other such shit. Then there's always some crappy white sitcom on featuring a token black, or a crappy black sitcom featuring a token white - they all have to do this as it's the Law of the Left and their stupid multicultural ethos.

I click back onto the 24-hour news channel where there's a really fit-looking girl presenting. She's very pretty with dark curly hair and lovely breasts, and going on about that there's potentially another recession looming. I didn't realise that the last one had even ended! The rest of the news features nothing but an endless stream of doom and gloom - yet another group of terrorists blowing themselves up, more immigrants arriving by the fucking day, paedophiles, murderers, fat-cats on the fiddle, the twisted minds of the human-rights lobbyists, stupid bloody football players - it's nothing but endless fucking shit. TV has become the brain-washer of the World, with its controllers feeding us information that THEY want us to know instead of what is really happening, influencing the masses through mind-games and manipulation. What gives them the bloody right to tell me what's going on? Who do they think they are - God? Unfortunately people are so gullible these days that they'll gladly let themselves be sucked into whatever is presented before them on the screen. They want to look at shit, they love it and can't get enough of it.

I weep tears of sadness for my fellow humans. The whole fucking planet has gone completely crazy. Everything is a con. We're all being taken for a fucking ride.

I give up on all of this crap before it drives me insane, although not before I hit upon a moving spiritual program about the afterlife. I sit there transfixed and weepy-eyed at the people on the screen who are confronted by the voices of ghosts transmitted through the mouth of the medium hosting the show. Maybe I could find someone who could give me some spiritual guidance and point me in the right direction, some kind-of visualisation of my future?

I click my laptop on and search the surrounding area for help. I quickly find a strange mystical spirit shop in Henfield, West Sussex, called *The Magick Circle*, where they do quite an extensive list of services including a whole host of mind-boggling and crazy things, most of which I've never heard of - Tarot reading, Aura Balancing, Cupping, full body massage, Year Planning, Psychic reading, Rieki, Indian head massage, Hoppi ear candling, Past Life regression, Hypnosis, Hot Stone placement, Wicca, Feng Shui, Shamanic Journeying, Chakra Balancing, Angel reading, Yoga, Kinesiology, Tantra massage, Fairy workshops, Shiatsu, Aromatherapy, Cord Cutting, Clairvoyance, Rebirthing, Vortex Channelling, Crystal Healing, Astrology, Tantra Healing and Yoni Steaming!

I've no-idea what half these things are but even so, I decide to go and pay them a visit anyway, at least it will be something to do and get me out of the flat.

* * *

After a quick shower and breakfast of tea and cornflakes, I get ready for the day. Today I'm wearing my black low-cut v-neck jumper from Bluefly and a red leather split-skirt from Farfetch. I also have on a pair of black tights from Pretty Polly and a pair of red heels from Heels USA. My underwear is also in red, from Figleaves. My perfume is *Mademoiselle* by Coco Chanel. My make-up I do in my own classical style - to perfection of course! - and features orange lipstick to match my car. My clutch-bag is a small black leather one from Yves Saint Laurent.

Out on the road the bloody traffic is a real bitch as I make my way through Horsham and head South on the A281. I quite like this road as it twists and turns and I can usually give the car plenty of beans. But not today though, as I get stuck forever-more behind idiots doing 40 in a 50-zone when I can normally get the car over twice that speed on some stretches.

After half-an-hour or so I finally hit the little town of Henfield and instantly spot the little spirit shop over to my right. Parking in the High Street is really tight, not only because it's Saturday but because there are far too many cars on the road these days, each and every one of them getting in my bloody way. In the end though I find one remaining space in the small car-park up the hill behind the shops over to the left of the main road, it being free to park is an added bonus and a bit of a rarity these days.

I walk back down the hill and cross over the road, taking my life in my hands as I do so, and then down to the small shop. It's a weird-looking little place with a black facade and lots of strange objects in the window. The front-door opens to the sound of one of those old fashioned bells and inside it's jam-packed with stuff everywhere. There's also a horrible smell in the air, like something is burning, like incense or some other such crap that instantly gets right up my nose and makes me sneeze. I don't honestly know where to start looking first around the shop as there's so much stuff, so I just wander around nosing at things I have no-idea what the Hell they are - Dreamcatchers, Horse Tails (really?), a hundred different types of rock, minerals and gemstones in as many different colours, Skulls (some real, some not), loads of books and magazines on spiritualism and the occult, hundreds of figurines depicting angels and cherubs and all that stuff, scented candles, Runes, spiritual paintings and cards, jewellery, Ouija boards, love potions (not that I need any of that I don't!), Talismans, singing bowls, Smudge Sticks, flower essences, crystal balls, pendulums, oils, herbal medicine, incense, handmade soaps, ambient music, Native American Shamanic drums, wind-chimes, bewitching tools and Fair Trade clothing.

The woman who I naturally presume is the shop owner suddenly appears out of the blue and from nowhere, although it's actually from behind a tall shelving unit full of spiritual books and other paraphernalia to my right. She's in her early-50's by the looks of her, with a pretty face but is several stone overweight and has these bloody awful red streaks in her hair and is dressed in one of those giant tent-like hippy outfits from the late-60's that she's obviously wearing to hide all the rolls of fat - how very stylish!

"Hello, may I help you?" She says to me cheerfully.

"Yes, I hope so. Do you do psychic reading?"

"Yes we do. I don't actually do it myself, I have someone who comes in by appointment only. She's very good."

"Okay then, I'd like to make an appointment then please if you could. Do you know if she's available sometime during this coming week?" I question her.

After checking her appointment book over on the front counter, she confirms that this coming Monday is completely free. We mutually agree on a time of 11am, that giving me enough time in the morning for a little lay-in and also to tart myself up and then get my arse over here.

While I'm here I also purchase one of her figurines - one of 2-lovers entwined in each others bodies, a man and a woman - made from some sort-of smooth milky white stone that sets me back the grand sum of £29.99. I don't care about the price, I want it so I buy it.

***

I really don't know what to expect from today, even though subconsciously in the back of my mind I know exactly which way this day is going to go - one of yet more pain and tears no doubt, of that I can be sure.

I'm not going stupid on today's outfit either, just keeping it simple with a nice top and jeans. My top is a white lace batwing blouse from AliExpress which looks absolutely gorgeous on me - as does everything else! - with my jeans being my pair of pale-blue stonewash ones from BooHoo that really hug and show off my perfect figure. On my feet I'm wearing my pair of tan-coloured ankle-boots from AliExpress. My underwear is in white lace from Agent Provocateur. My make-up and hair is in its usual immaculate condition, featuring waterproof mascara just in case I do start to blubber! My perfume today is *Poison* by Christian Dior.

My clutch-bag is another metal one, this being a Reiss Anish swirl-metal one from Polyvore and is ultra-stylish.

I've crammed it full of tissues, once again if there are any waterworks on my part!

As is the norm, there's not one fucking parking space to be had on any road surrounding the vicinity of the spirit shop, even though today is a Monday. Once again I decide to park in the town car-park on the hill behind the High Street and walk back. This parking shit is totally out of control.

I still make it to the shop in good time though for my appointment - I did leave the flat earlier than I should have just to give myself some leeway - so there's no harm done in the end.

The same woman I saw before - the big hippy one - greets me by the front counter sorting out some stuff, business cards and flyers and such by the looks of it. We exchange the usual pleasantries as one does as she then leads me to the rear of the shop, through a couple of doors and then to a small room on the left. It's dark and gloomy inside and there's also a strange smell, not like the horrible incense candles in the main shop, this is something else and I begin to wonder what the Hell I've got myself into this bloody time? As I enter the room an icy chill grabs hold of me and immediately gives me the creeps - what the fuck is all this about now? Suddenly another woman appears from behind us and introduces herself to me, a short woman of about 60 with attractive features and short blonde hair, dressed very smartly although casual.

"Hello, you must be Sarah? I'm Susan Ford, I'm going to be your guide for today's session." She says to me in the most soothing, mellow, hypnotic voice that I've ever heard in my life - it's a voice of an angel. We shake hands and I feel my body freeze as we look into each others eyes.

"Oh hi, pleased to meet you." I say diffidently.

"You're a pretty girl aren't you? But then you know that don't you Sarah?" She quizzes me, making me feel a little strange at her questioning.

"Thank you." I reply as I shudder once more.

"Have we met somewhere before?" She then asks me.

"No, no, I don't think so. I'm sure I would have remembered." I stumble my reply as her aura overwhelms me and I start to feel a bit light-headed.

The large shop-owner woman departs silently and leaves the 2 of us alone together. We sit ourselves down next to each other on a lovely black leather sofa, facing each other but at a slight angle. No-sooner do I park my bum down though she completely floors me with one sentence - like a bullet straight to my heart:

"I have your uncle Alf here Sarah, he's standing right behind you."

In a split second I collapse within myself in tears of overwhelming shock and love. How can she know about him, Mum's younger brother who died of cancer years ago at far too young an age - my Guardian Angel?

"You know who I mean don't you Sarah?" She pushes me further.

"Yes, yes I do." I splutter. His metaphysical presence is so real it becomes almost tangible and I want to reach out and touch him but I know it's impossible.

"You've known all along about him haven't you, your Guardian Angel?"

"Yes, I know. I know there's someone there. I can feel it. There always seems to be something operating behind the scenes that's protecting me."

"He's watching over you at all times. You are never alone Sarah, even when you believe you are."

"I know." I blubber back.

"He says not to be so hard on him. All the things that happen to you in your life are for a reason and are out of his control. It's your own negative thoughts that are influencing your life."

"I don't understand. How the Hell am I supposed to not have negative thoughts when all this shit keeps happening to me? It's impossible."

I break down and sob my heart out uncontrollably. I have given up all hope. At least I thought I had, until she stabs me once more through the heart with another of her emotional one-liners.

"Lacey is here for you now. In the arms of your Guardian Angel. Isn't she a beautiful cat?"

"OH FOR FUCKS SAKE!" I exclaim.

It's with this revelation that I completely lose it big-time. I want to destroy everything in this fucking shitty World, including myself. Why am I putting myself through this torture? How does she know about my life? She only knows my first name so how is this possible? I want to get out of here but the pull of knowing my future, the possibility of some kind-of direction in my life, procures me to stay and take more pain. I have to know, regardless of how I get there and the final outcome.

I gently wipe away my tears with a few of the tissues from my bag but the rivulets just keeps flowing down my perfect face. After all the fucking shit I've had to contend with recently, the build-up of emotion has finally burst its banks and refuses to stop. The bloody bitch, what is she trying to do to me as she takes yet another pop:

"Your Guardian Angel can only help you so much Sarah. Your relationship with Amanda wasn't meant to be long-term, it was only a stepping-stone to your future."

"How do you know about her, about Amanda? How do you know all these things about me?" I fire at her as she continues to freak me out.

"I know your complete life Sarah. Fate is unstoppable. Whatever you do in your life is meant to be, even your car accident was part of your pre-ordained destiny in your total life span."

"What? Are you telling me my car crash was on purpose?"

"No, not on purpose, it wasn't serendipity. It was just meant to be."

"But why? How can that be? I lost my baby in that crash. What is the point of it all? Where do I go from here?"

"Everything will become clear. The only real tangible thing I can relate to you is that you must learn by your mistakes Sarah. But only you can decide what your mistakes actually are."

"That sounds like a cop-out to me. So where was my Guardian Angel when all this was happening? What's the fucking point of having a Guardian Angel that doesn't guard? Instead of punishing me with interfering in my everyday life, why doesn't he fucking help me instead? How about something good happening in my life for a change?"

"You must wake up to the truth Sarah. Recognise your value and retain your dignity. Get things in perspective. Nothing changes if you don't change yourself. The path you're heading along is one that only you can lead. You must have faith in yourself to succeed. You are part of the fabric of the Universe and the white light of that Universe will guide you through your troubles. The sequence for future events has now been set in motion. You are ready now to move on in your life. All the events of the past have lead to this moment and with the death of your Father you can now begin to heal your childhood wounds. We all have a part to play in death as well as in life. There is nothing anyone can do to stop it, it is already written in the books of the future.

You have been tested by your spirits, and indeed by yourself, over the past few years Sarah. You have learned and adapted yourself to these changes and that is good. It will hold you in good stead for the next part of your mortal existence. It has been a year of personal revelation, discovery and teaching and it will give you the knowledge for your journey into the unknown.

I know you're finding it hard to believe me, but I know deep down that you do. You have the power Sarah, the power to take control of your life. Your new love will reveal himself to you soon, it won't be long now. In fact you've already met him, albeit only briefly." She tells me as she holds both my hands with hers.

"I have? Who is this guy? What's his name?" I question her back.

"You must have patience Sarah. You will be released through the death of circumstance, opening the door to a new start in your life, a change of lifestyle involving travels abroad. Your new love will make you financially secure for the rest of your life."

"You mean he's rich?"

"The revelation will be your awakening and will bring you all the power, freedom, peace and karma for your next adventure. The transition is almost complete. You will find your salvation. You must have the courage, the commitment and the faith. Your path forward is more defined from now on. Your dreams will become reality."

"Really? I can assure you I have some pretty weird dreams." I joke back to her.

"Your transformation period is reaching its climax. Your perseverance will pay dividends Sarah. You will get what you deserve. You will get what you want."

"Bloody Hell! But I want so much, all the time. So when is all this going to happen?"

"You cannot force fate Sarah. Everything is in place. But please tread carefully, you must look after your health. And you know what I mean by that don't you?"

"My drinking."

"Yes. Your spirits from the past are here to guide your future but they cannot dictate. You cannot go on destroying yourself. But you will find peace. Your new love will take care of your future, it is already written.

There, I think we should leave it now Sarah. I think we're both pretty exhausted after all that aren't we?"

"I'm absolutely bloody knackered! How do you know all that stuff?"

"I've had the gift since the day I was born. I've always been able to see the spirits. My Mother always said I was a witch!"

"I really don't know what to say. I feel completely drained."

"It will take you quite a while for you to come to terms with what I've revealed, but you will. You also have some level of psychic power yourself Sarah, but then you already know that don't you?"

"Yes I know I do. I do have something. I feel different somehow." I reveal to her.

"That's because you look at life differently to other people Sarah. You have the vision, and you have tremendous will."

"Can you tell me more about this guy I'm supposed to meet? Who is he? What's his name?"

"I know everything about him but I cannot tell you. He will make you happy beyond your dreams but you must be patient. He's coming to you now."

"And what about Lacey, is she happy?"

"She has found comfort and peace in the arms of your uncle Alf in the Spirit World."

I suddenly feel myself start to well-up with tears once again as I think about Lacey - my best friend - but I just about maintain my composure. We both make our way back into the confines of the shop where she reaches out to me with both hands to hug me tightly - a little too tightly and for too long for comfort - and it makes me feel uneasy but at the same time I can also feel her energy seeping into my soul as an icy chill shoots its way down my spine, almost freaking me out, and I have to forcibly break away from her hold, telling her:

"Right, well, goodbye then. And thanks for everything."

"You're very welcome Sarah. Please take care for me."

"I will. And I apologise for my foul language back there." I tell her.

"That's quite alright. Emotions can run a little high during a these things."

"Yeah, I guess so. Bye then." I say, giving her a small wave as I head towards the front of the shop.

"Love and light Sarah. Love and light." She calls out to me and I turn my head back to face her but there's no-one there, she's disappeared like a phantom, back to her World of spirits and ghosts.

I pay my fee to the shop-owner woman at the front counter - £120 in cash - and then make my exit out of the shop and back into fresh air and freedom. But is it freedom? If my life is already mapped-out then am I truly free? Or is it all complete bullshit? I actually think I'm even more confused and dejected now than I was before. I feel like my life is impersonating my art. It's almost like I'm trapped inside a giant karaoke machine and there's no escape, I'm locked-in forever. The similarity between my art and reality get ever narrower as events keep jumping right off the page and smacking me in the mouth at any given moment.

I take a slow, weary plod back to the car-park. I'm not in a rush and I'm not in the right frame of mind anyway, not for anything, I am completely drained. As I near to where I parked my car, I notice someone lurking around it, none other than a bloody traffic-warden, a Joe-Daki one at that, writing out a ticket - just my fucking luck!

"Oi! WHAT DO YOU THINK YOU'RE DOING? GET AWAY FROM MY CAR, I DON'T WANT YOUR DIRTY PAWS ALL OVER IT." I holler at him - bloody Paki.

"You are not allowed to park here and shop somewhere else. There is a sign." He bleats at me.

"YOU CAN FUCK YOUR SIGN." I scream back at him as I peel-off the parking -ticket that he'd just that very second stuck to my windscreen. I screw it up and throw it at his shit-brown face, hitting him squire-on - good shot!

I completely ignore his protestations as I climb into my orange bomber, fire her up, and leave him standing there like the fucking waste of space he is as I roar away. What an arsehole!

✳ ✳ ✳

Back at the flat I don't know which way to turn, I am haunted by myself. Once again I've confused my brain with my own actions in the search for the truth about my life and my future. I know the psychic woman warned me about my drinking, and she's right of course, but even so I pour myself a large glass of German white from the bottle that's been nestling-away in the fridge, just hiding there with my name on it, waiting for the right moment. As soon as I take my first sip I immediately have a strange sensation of being watched, but by whom? I already know of course but the reality part of my brain won't let me fully believe it.

An image of my Guardian Angel - my uncle Alf - holding Lacey in his arms, comes into vision before my very eyes and I can't block it out, it's etched into my eyeballs like a tattoo.

Watching my life.

Watching my dreams.

Watching my death.

I try to turn away from it but it follows me about like a living nightmare. I swallow my wine in one huge gulp and then have another and the image is gone. I am exhausted beyond exhaustion. I think I'm going insane.

I'm not really in the mood for food so lunch is out. Instead I pour myself another big fat glass of wine. I'm also not in the mood for pleasuring myself either, even though I really want to. The thought of my uncle's spirit watching over me as I masturbate turns me off completely. I don't think I'll ever be able to have sex again knowing that he's here with me by my side all the bloody time.

What am I saying? How can any of this crap be real? What is real? What is not? Am I real? Maybe I'm the spirit and everything around me is the reality? I don't know what the fuck I'm saying or doing.

So what about this guy in my future, my future love? Who the Hell is he? And have we really met already? And if so, when was it? I try my hardest to think who it could possibly be but I just end up confusing myself even more. I start on the vodka next but that doesn't help either and I end up crying at the sadness of my life and FUCK IT ALL TO HELL.

***

Do not try to make me into an image of thy self, for it will not be. If you try and manipulate me into doing something I don't want to do then I will kill myself and kill you - again.

***

Now you fucking listen to me Mr. Guarding Angel. I want you to fucking leave me alone and let me get on with my life and stop tripping me up at every fucking opportunity, do you understand me? I am sick and fucking tired of all these stupid fucking games you keep playing on me - it stops today - here and now. If you fuck with my life once more I will cut you off completely and put the rest of my life on the road to destruction. If you take one more thing away from me - my beautiful car or my flat or anything else - I'll fucking end it all and meet you on the other side and then we'll fucking sort it out face to face.

So come on then, so-called Guardian Angel or whatever you are. You've taken my cat, my Mother, my car, my baby, my lover, my niece and my job, so what's next? Why not me? Why not take my life if that's what you want? Or are you saving me for something so terrible that I can't even imagine it?

COME ON THEN, DO YOUR FUCKING WORST YOU FUCKING BASTARD.

14

Andy

I'm in my living-room sitting on my perfect bum watching crap on the TV with a glass of chilled German white in one hand and the remote in the other. Suddenly my mobile-phone bursts into life, almost making me spill my wine down my cleavage just as I go to take a sip.

"Hello?" I say, trying to speak and swallow my wine at the same time.

"Oh hello. May I speak to Sarah Knowles please." Says the voice on the other end of the line.

"Yes, speaking."

"Oh hi Sarah, this is Andrew. I don't know if you remember me but I was the first person on the scene when you had your car accident on the A27, months back."

"Oh right. Er no, I'm sorry, I don't really remember much about it to be honest."

"Oh I see. Well, I was in the car right behind the one that hit you. After I'd put the small fire out with my extinguisher I tried to open your door but it was jammed."

"Well, as I say, I don't remember much about it at all really." I reiterate.

"Okay. Well, it's taken me quite a while to trace your number. I was basically just ringing to see how you're doing?"

"I'm okay I guess. How did you get my number?" I question him back.

"Oh, I pulled a few strings here and there. I tried to get hold of you through your registration number but that was a dead-end."

"Yeah, my car was a write-off. Apparently my insurance company sold it for spare parts."

"Oh really? That's a shame. So how are you? You were pretty-much out of it with shock when I got to you."

"Really? Yeah, I guess I was. I broke my arm in the crash but otherwise I was okay.

I've had other problems since then though, I won't bore you with the details."

"No, it's okay, go on, a trouble shared is a trouble halved as they say."

"Well, I've just got a divorce and I lost my job, as well as other things."

"Oh Hell! All this as well as the accident?"

"Welcome to my life." I underline to him.

"Didn't your sister tell you that I came to see you in hospital?"

"No she didn't. Are you sure it was my sister? Can you remember her name?"

"No, I'm afraid I can't. I only met her for a brief moment."

"Was it Kate or Amanda?" I enquire.

"Amanda, that was it. The blonde girl with the accent."

"Ah right. She's not my sister, she's my wife, or ex-wife as she is now."

"Your wife! Oh I see, I didn't realise."

"There was no way you could have known that I was married to another woman."

"Well no, I guess not."

"Does it make a difference?"

"Uh no, I don't think so? It's just that I've never met anyone like you before, someone married to someone of the same sex I mean."

"Well you have now. I do like guys as well you know? In fact I was seeing a guy before I met Amanda but that went tits-up as well."

"Oh right, I see." He says with a mysterious caution in his voice.

"So, are you married?" I enquire, although I don't know why?

"No, I never seem to meet the right girl. I'm always busy with work."

"Really? What do you do for a living?"

"Well, I suppose you could say that I'm in the car trade."

"That sounds a bit dodgy?"

"No, not at all. It's just that I've made my money the hard way and now I use my time spending it."

"Good for you. If you need any help with the spending then I'm you're girl!" I say cheekily.

"I might just take you up on that." He laughs back.

"So where about's do you live?" I ask.

"I live in Foxhill, near Petworth. Do you know it?"

"No, I've never heard of it. I know Petworth a little bit but not the other one. I live in Slinfold, near Horsham."

"Yes I know, I've got your address." He suddenly claims.

"You've got my address as well? You're not a stalker are you?" I question him back.

"No, I'm not a stalker! I was genuinely worried about you so I got hold of your details. Honestly, it's nothing untoward."

"Yeah, I believe you, thousands wouldn't!" I laugh back.

"So would you be interested in meeting up then Sarah, for a drink I mean?"

"Wow! You don't hang about do you?"

"I didn't get where I am today by hanging about. And anyway, it's not like we haven't met before is it?"

His last few words resonate inside my brain - "We've met before." That was what Susan Ford, the psychic woman told me, that I would meet "The One" and that we had already met. Is this for real? Could this guy Andrew really be him? I can't honestly believe any of this crap, it's bullshit, it has to be? How can this be possible?

But what if it is? What will happen if I turn this chance down? What will happen if I do accept his offer to meet - again? This is crazy. What the fuck is happening to my life? Why does this shit keep happening to me? How many times do I have to keep saying that?

"Sarah, are you still there?"

"Yes, I'm still here. Sorry, my mind went off on a tangent there for a minute. Yes, okay then. If you want to meet up that's fine." I commit myself.

What the Hell am I doing? I've gone and done it again haven't I ? What the fuck is wrong with me? Why did I say "Yes" to him? I don't know this guy from Adam and here I am agreeing to meet up with him after just 10-minutes on the bloody phone! I must be fucking mad?

I look around me and wonder what it is that I've actually got to lose? My sanity deserted me years ago so it won't be that. I guess that's why I've gotten myself into so many scrapes?

And so here we go again, on yet another adventure into the unknown. This is ridiculous.

***

I'm meeting-up with Andrew tonight at 8pm for a drink - nothing more. I don't even know what the guy looks like for a start, I simply don't remember, so I'm a little bit suspicious as to what I'm entering into. Not that it's ever stopped me in the past, but that's not the point.

We've arranged to meet at the Blacksmith's Arms in Adversane, West Sussex, as it's roughly equidistant to where we both live. I've been past the pub a hundred times but never once ventured inside, so at least it'll be another watering-hole I can tick off my list if tonight does go tits-up!

For some reason it's been a real dilemma deciding what to wear for tonight. I can't make up my mind whether to go for a more casual approach or go for the jugular with my full-on supermodel look. In the end I go for the latter as that's what I want and that's who I am - the ultimate femme fatale. I've got it so I'm going to flaunt it!

My dress is an extremely short sleeveless mini-bodycon dress in orange - bought specifically to match my car of course! - from Polyvore that really shows-off my embonpoint, bum and legs to the max. As for underwear I'm wearing a super-sexy lace number in red from Ultimo. My shoes are my pair of tan-suede platform court shoes from Polyvore that really accentuate my long toned legs even further. My black leather clutch-bag is from Yves Saint Laurent. There's no need harping-on about my hair and make-up as you should all know by now what my style is so there's no reason for me to explain it all again. The only thing I have to tell you is that my lipstick and nails are also in orange - get it? My perfume tonight is *Poison* by Christian Dior. As it's a little chilly out tonight - it is early-October after all - I'm putting my white leather biker jacket on just to take the edge off the night air.

I pull-up in the car-park to the Blacksmith's Arms in good time - it's 7.40pm - and park the ST next to a beautiful green Ford Focus RS. I'd really love one of those but the prices are way out of my league, even for a second-hand one.

As per usual the whole World stops and stares at me as I walk through the entrance door and I feel a million-pairs of eyes gaze upon my body as I make my way over to the bar. A guy sitting there with drink in hand turns to me and smiles. Could this be him? A sudden flashback to the crash bursts into my mind as I do actually recognize his face and yes, I do remember him now, it's the guy that spoke to me and held my arm.

"Hi Sarah, how are you? You look amazing. I'm so glad you could make it tonight." He beams as he stands and holds out his right-hand for me to shake - how very polite and formal!

My reply stumbles out of my mouth like rocks crashing down a mountain as I search for the gravity of where this meeting could potentially end up - and I don't necessarily mean in bed!

"Oh hi, nice to meet you too." I bleat as we shake and he kisses me softly on my right-cheek - he smells really lovely as his pheromones give me a warm peaceful glow throughout my entire body. I actually start to blush and I feel somewhat overawed by his presence - what the Hell is happening now, I've never felt like this before! I desperately try to clear my mind and come back down to Earth as I continue to break the ice:

"I do remember you now, you held my hand when I was trapped in my car."

"That's right, you were pretty shaken up though, it was a nasty accident. I've never seen anything like it."

"Well, it's not something I want to repeat anytime soon."

"No, I guess not. So, what would you like to drink?"

"Oh, I'll have a large vodka please, neat, no ice."

He orders the same for himself also and we grab our drinks and go and settle ourselves down in the corner out the way of the prying eyes all gorping at my gorgeous tight body. Andrew comes across as a really nice guy, although way older than my usual conquests, somewhere in his late-40's I would guess? He seems warm and friendly and is dressed nicely in what looks like expensive clothes - especially his shoes. He also has a certain air about himself, of someone who is very confident and knows what he wants in life and how to get it.

We chat endlessly for the next couple of hours or so about life, work, my failed marriage to Amanda - he's not and has never been married, or so he says - my escapade with the drinking and ending up in hospital, politics and the state of the country, holidays, and a whole myriad of subjects. He tells me about his house in Foxhill, his cars and his life - although I get a strange gut-feeling that he's pulling my leg a bit - and that he's always made his own money his own way, not that I'm after him for that, although obviously it helps!

He seems to have a similar cynical view to life as I do, as well as a dark sense of humour, and we laugh and joke and everything is peachy. He tells me that it took him ages to try and track me down, and as I'm not on Facebook or Twitter or any of that social media shit I can probably understand why.

I don't mention to him my encounter with the psychic woman though or any of that stuff, I don't want him to think that I'm some sort-of crank!

The evening eventually begins to draw to a close and we carry on chatting until way after the pub bell has chimed. We exchange Email addresses, drink up, and make our way out to the car-park. As we head for our respective cars we both suddenly realise that we're both going in the very same direction, me towards my orange ST and Andrew towards his green RS. We stop and look at each other and laugh - how spooky is it that we should both have sister cars and have parked them right next to each another? We say our "Goodbyes" and he kisses me once more on the cheek, softly and tenderly. He lets me drive away first and I smile a big beaming smile and give a little wave to him as I exit, turn left, and head back home on the A29.

I think about him, and us, all the way home and later back at the flat. I still can't get my head around what the psychic woman said to me, her prediction just can't be real, can it? Am I just expected to give my body and soul over to this guy, nice enough as he seems to be? I simply find all this very hard to believe. It's all too good to be true.

***

I'm up early the following morning - it's 8.05am - as I didn't get much in the way of sleep last night. Naturally I kept thinking about Andrew and that bloody psychic woman and all that shit. I can't seem to get either of them out of my head.

I make breakfast of tea and toast with lashings of marmalade and sit my perfect arse down in front of breakfast TV and I sit there like a bloody zombie, being force-fed an endless stream of crap. It's Saturday, well, at least I think it is, as not going to work any more these days has totally fucked-up my knowledge of which day it is!

An hour and a half later my mobile-phone starts to bleep as a text message is beamed through, snapping me out of my TV coma. It's from Andrew, thanking me for meeting up with him last night along with other pleasantries and all that stuff. He asks me: "What are you doing tomorrow morning?" and:

"Would you like to go to breakfast with me at a car club I belong to?"

I honestly can't find any reason within me to say "No", it'll be something different to do after all, so I text him back telling him that: "I would love to." What the Hell, I've got sod-all else to do!

I spend the rest of the day doing not very much at all, a bit of cleaning around the flat and some light cooking - nothing fancy as I couldn't be bothered - depilating, soaking in the bath, and a vodka or 6. I also masturbate 3-times whilst watching porn on the internet - firstly to bisexual orgy porn, followed by extreme orgasm porn, and then the last one to scat porn, featuring shit-in-pussy action which I find both repellent and addictive at the same time.

Then it's off to bed with a big fat mug of hot milk as Andrew is picking me up early tomorrow morning at 7am and I want to look my best, which isn't difficult to do is it?

***

I'm up like a lark again this morning. I'm really looking forward to today's events as I've never been to anything like this before. I just hope that it's not full of geeky, nerdy types with their hot-hatches and booming bloody sound systems blasting out black shit from their massive speakers - I can't bloody stand any of that crap and I'll scream if I hear it.

The air is quite crisp outside this morning so I'm dressing accordingly, it's not the sort of do that you would wear a mini-dress or anything like that anyway, but even so I still want to look my gorgeous best. I'm wearing my black low-cut v-neck jumper from Bluefly, a figure-hugging black knee-length split-skirt from M&S that really shows off the curves of my bum, black wool tights from ASOS, and my black suede open-toe court-shoes from Polyvore. My underwear is from Ultimo in sexy black lace. I'm not going out wearing a coat or jacket this morning even though it's cold outside, so I'm going to brave it by just wearing a black cashmere poncho from Peter Hahn and take the risk. My clutch-bag today is my old vintage chrome one from Vintage Styler because as ever, I don't want to lug around some ginormous bloody great bag all day long! Unusually, on my right-hand I'm wearing a Gothic-styled hand jewellery in black lace that I bought online from BornPrettyStore.

It's 6.59am when I hear a ferocious roar of an engine outside but I don't bother to look out my window to see who it is as I'm still putting the finishing touches to my hair. 1-minute later the entry-phone rings and its Andrew, bang on time, and I release the front-door and usher him upstairs to my flat.

"Morning Sarah, you all set?" He says somewhat over-cheerfully for this time of the day as we kiss cheek to cheek.

"As ready as I'll ever be." I say back as I feel my stomach turning over, partly in anticipation of the day ahead, partly due to nerves, and partly due to the fact I haven't had any breakfast - yet.

"So, how do I look?" I question him.

"You look beautiful." He affirms back.

"Why thank you kind sir." I come back with a cheeky grin across my my chops.

"You smell lovely as well, your perfume."

"Yes I know, it's *Poison* by Christian Dior." I tell him and he gives me a little chuckle back at my self-confident reply.

"You know your own mind Sarah don't you?" He suddenly says.

"You have to in life, it's the one thing that has kept me going." I state.

We make our way downstairs and outside into the fresh morning air, Andy leading me across the road by my hand and I love it. He guides me across the road to his car and I cannot believe what I'm seeing in the road before me, sitting their looking like an evil monster waiting to pounce.

"Is this yours?" I say in amazement.

"Do you like it? I haven't had it very long."

"It's fantastic. It's the most incredible car I think I've ever seen."

"Most women don't like it. They seem to think it's either some sort-of posers car or for guys with small dicks, or both!"

"No, that's bullshit. I think it's gorgeous. What sort of Lamborghini is it?"

"It's an Aventador LP700-4."

"Wow! How fast does she go?"

"It's good for nearly 220mph." He confirms.

"Bloody Hell! It's absolutely beautiful. What a crazy car! Is it really yours?" I enquire, still not believing what I'm seeing.

"Yes, of course it is."

"Are you rich?" I question him further.

"Yes." He says, a little smugly.

"Really?" I return, still not convinced.

"Yes, really."

He opens the passenger door for me - as a gentleman should - itself already unlocked and disarmed by remote-control, and it swings upwards like the wing of a bird, not out to the side like a normal car and he takes my left-hand to steady me as I attempt to enter this beautiful beast. It's so bloody low to the ground that getting in is not easy, especially in my skirt and shoes! And I have to slide my bum over the corner of the seat first and then put my long legs in after. I settle down in the tight, hugging bucket-seat and Andrew closes my door with a solid thud. Being in this car is like being back in the womb as it tightly encompasses and embraces my whole body. Andrew gets in the other side and fires-up the engine to this big white monster, not by using a key but by pushing a big red fighter-plane style starter-button mounted on the centre-console - how cool is that? The engine bursts into life with a deep-throated roar and with a click of the steering-wheel mounted paddle-shift, we zoom-off through the narrow roads of the village with the car spitting fire from its exhausts.

We turn-left out onto the A29 and Andrew opens the car up and I'm instantly pushed back into my seat as we hurtle along, I don't know what speed we're doing but he's definitely not hanging around that's for sure! The car handles like a dream, it gripping the road like shit to a blanket, as we power on past Five Oaks and then Billingshurst. We head right for Petworth on the A272 and I take a quick glance across to see the speed on the dashboard reading 140mph - Bloody Hell!

The few people that are up and about at this time of the morning in the town all stop and stare at us as the noise from the tail-pipes resonates off the walls of the tight confines of the village and we both laugh. This thing is more like an alien spaceship on wheels than a car!

Our destination is Goodwood, again another place I've never been to, as Andrew is a member of the Goodwood Breakfast Club, whatever that is? After several high-speed blasts along the tight and twisty bends and straights of the A285 we're soon there, and the place is already pretty packed with all manner of different cars in all shapes and sizes lined-up on the race track itself. I have to say that it's not quite what I was expecting, I honestly thought it was going to be a muddy field in the middle of nowhere with a single solitary burger-van and a load of snotty-nosed brats with their caps on back to front all in their crappy Euroboxes! I could not have been more wrong, it's all actually very well organized and there is a certain upper-class ambience about the place.

We park-up next to a gleaming red Ferrari and we get more stares from other people, especially I do, when I open my door and attempt to extract myself from my cocoon. Some guy immediately comes up to Andrew and shakes his hand, obviously someone he hasn't seen in a while judging by their banter, who then introduces me to him with a handshake and a friendly "Hello".

After a while we wander off in the opposite direction to do what we came here for in the first place - to have breakfast of course, as the glorious smell of fried onions and other odours waft over me.

"Who's that guy?" I quiz Andy nosily.

"Oh, he bought a few cars off me a while ago. I don't really know him that well."

"Are you a Freemason?" I suddenly hit him with.

"No, what makes you say that?"

"It's just that I noticed the funny handshake."

"Really? You're sharp aren't you? I'm not a Freemason I can assure you. He might well be but I'm certainly not. I can't really say that I'm interested in that sort of thing."

"I can't stand them either. Bunch of fucking weirdo's pretending they own the Country and manipulating justice." I fire at him.

He laughs at my statement and then quizzes me back:

"Is there anyone you do actually like Sarah?"

"I like you." I coyly reply with one of my wicked knowing expressions spread across my beautiful face.

"Well, I like you too Sarah." He says with his inherent super-confidence as he grips my hand tighter, making me respond with the same gesture.

The food wagons themselves are not your average ones either, being very posh and smart, as are the prices of the food and drinks which are all a bit on the expensive side. It's a good job Andrew's paying as there's no way I can really afford to in my current situation - I have to watch the pennies you know. You would not believe how much the wedding / honeymoon trip to Las Vegas cost me, it ran into thousands and has put a massive dent in my bank balance.

We have a bacon-roll and a mug of coffee each and plod around looking at all the cars as we munch-away. There's some amazing cars here - other Lamborghini's, Ferrari's, Aston Martin's, Bentley's, Porsche's, Lotus's, Rolls-Royce's, and plenty of big American cars to - Mustang's, Pontiac's, Cadillac's, along with other more run-of-the-mill cars and motorbikes all mixed-in together.

We chat about all the cars, bikes, life and other things as we stroll around looking at all the fantastic machinery for the rest of the morning. The bacon roll slides down lovely, so much so that we both have another, plus more coffee, as by now, we've been here nearly 2 1/5-hours already. The whole event is very

English, with not a single Wog, Paki or fucking Slav piece of scum in sight - just the way it fucking should be.

Suddenly, out of the blue, Andrew asks me if I would like to come back to his place - just like that! What a bloody cheek! Even so, seeing as it's not too far from here anyway, of course I say "Yes" without even giving it time for thought, and so we both clamber back into the Lamborghini - with naturally yet more staring eyes and much gorping - we burble our way out of Goodwood circuit and blast back up the road. We head back on the A285 for several exhilarating miles, then blast through Petworth town once again and then back onto the A272. Suddenly he turns a sharp right into a leafy gated driveway, the ornate white-painted gates opening automatically to our presence as we sprint through them at unabated speed.

"What's this place?" I enquire with concern, wondering what I've got myself into for the hundredth time?

"It's where I live. You'll see in a minute." He returns with a big grin across his face.

The driveway sure enough ends and opens-out into the mid-day Sun to reveal a large circular paved courtyard featuring a massive fountain at its centre with 2-naked bronze women bursting out of the water, directing its vertical flow with their beautiful smooth bodies - a sculpture by artist David Goode. We drive around the fountain to the left where I'm confronted by the sight of the house itself - a massive, white classically-styled villa with 4-columns of white stone guarding its entrance, double white-painted front doors, some kind of creeping vine to the left of the building and a pair of white electrically-operated automatic roller-doors to the right. He really must be rich to afford a place like this. This is the power of money. What a flash bastard!

"Is this really your house?" I quiz him yet again, not quite believing what I'm seeing.

"Of course it is. Nice isn't it? I designed it myself a few years ago."

"It's amazing, just like the car. And you live in this place all on your own?"

"Yes, I'm afraid so. Sad isn't it?"

"No, its not sad at all. If I had the chance to live in a place like this I would jump at it."

"Really? Come on then, I'll show you around."

He guides me by hand to the main entrance, opening one of the leaves of the double front-doors - the right-hand one - to reveal a beautiful, brilliant white-painted square entrance hall with a floor of black and white marble squares set diagonally and rimmed with a contrasting pattern of black hooked-crosses. Directly in front of me an ornate staircase rises up and splits into 2-opposing directions, both connecting to the upper-floor. Everything is so clean and crisp and with beautiful lines, all finished to the highest quality. Another smaller set of stairs to the left, goes down and right, but as yet I don't know where to? It later transpires that it leads down to the gymnasium, utilities room and the control room for the solar-powered heating and lighting for the entire house as well as for the swimming pool - how very posh!

Andrew removes his jacket and hangs it up in one of the cupboards to our left. As I remove my poncho I catch a quick glimpse of him eyeballing my breasts and I laugh inwardly at his attention - I love it and it makes me feel wanted.

To the right of the hall, in the corner, there's an ancient-looking sideboard - more of a chest really - all in black with heavy, deep carvings depicting deer and other animals and strange runic characters and symbols dotted around them. When I quiz him about it he seems reluctant to explain its origin and meaning and instead leads me into a room next to the piece. A wave of blue colour hits me as I enter what is obviously the dining-room, with blue-painted walls and an expensive blue carpet that my feet sink into deeply. The walls themselves are hung with paintings of racing cars and boats, and 2-large cabinets flank each other on opposing sides of the room, they filled with beautiful models of the same and more. The rectangular dining-table and high-backed chairs fill the centre of the room, the tabletop polished to a mirror finish that reflects the blue of the walls.

Back across the other side of the hall, Andrew guides me through a pair of double-doors into the main open-plan living-room and dining area. Everything is in pure white - the walls, the deep carpet, the large L-shaped leather sofa and the cabinets and shelves. The room stretches right from the front of the house to the rear where a more informal glass-topped circular dining table and chairs reside. The nearside wall features a bar - not a tacky 1970's-styled creation but one more contemporary and tasteful - featuring a giant antique (and rusty!) Coca Cola sign as a backdrop. The wall facing me features a giant Bang & Olufsen curved-screen TV that must have cost a bomb, hundreds of films on Blue-Ray, DVD and Video, a 1950's-style Wurlitzer jukebox in red, orange, yellow and chrome, a really weird-looking round glass coffee table made out of an old aeroplane engine - not as crazy as it sounds, its actually quite cool - and in the far corner a massive sliding-glass door that leads to where? Beautifully framed posters line the white walls - David Bowie, Marc Bolan, and even one of my favourites: Jackson Pollock and one of his drip paintings, what great taste! There's even a beautiful wall-mounted chrome-plated guitar that is to die for - I love it.

To the rear of the room, another similar door leads out onto a vast patio area paved with pale-stone and roofed by a wooden pergola. The walls are flanked with massive Greek-style pots and urns with an enormous circular glass-topped table with parasol and lounge chairs at its heart.

To say that I'm a little awestruck by all this extravagance is an understatement. The echo of the psychic woman's message about finding "The One" that continues to rattle-around in my brain doesn't help either.

Andrew leads me through the sliding glass-door in the far-left-hand corner of the room and into what I can now see is a beautiful indoor swimming pool. Once again the room is in pure white, with more white marble as in the main entrance hall. Huge paintings of brilliantly-coloured flowers adorn all 4-walls, whilst at the far end - the deep end no doubt - a medium-height diving-board awaits its next user.

We walk hand-in-hand down past the pool to the far end and to another door. A flick of the light-switch reveals a games-room, painted not in white this time but in a deep terracotta-red, almost the same colour as bricks. A full-sized professional snooker table sits in centre stage, whilst down at the far end sits a strange machine with a car racing seat, steering wheel and a wrap-around screen. Andrew explains that it's a motor-racing game-station that he had custom designed for himself and that naturally it was very expensive. I gaze around at the walls, noticing that they're all adorned with literally hundreds of framed photographs. Looking closer I see they are all of famous actors, actresses, singers, racing drivers and other famous people - I spot Laurel & Hardy, David Bowie, Anthony Hopkins, Joan Collins, Laurence Olivier, Debbie Harry, The Beatles, The Rolling Stones, Peter O'Toole, Bridget Bardot, Tony Curtis, Audrey Hepburn, Richard Burton, Lauren Bacall, Marlon Brando, Clint Eastwood, Steve McQueen, John Hurt, Ingrid Bergman, Bela Lugosi, Marlene Dietrich, Christopher Lee and tones more, the list is endless and very impressive, if somewhat overawing.

"Come on, I want to show you something special." He says.

"Oh yes! That's a bit cheeky isn't it?" I smirk back.

"Not that! Come on, we have to go through the kitchen, this way."

We head back past the pool, through the long living-room / dining area, and then back across the entrance hall to the right-hand side of the stairs. Another door to the right reveals the kitchen, another pure white room with shining surfaces and appliances of the highest quality German engineering. I'm not really into cooking much but with a kitchen like this at my disposal I'd give it a bloody good try!

There are 2-small doors at the far end, the barn-style split door on the left obviously leading out onto the patio area at the rear of the house, whilst the other, directly in front of me, is yet another mystery. Andrew opens the door outwards and steps through and I follow behind where we emerge into an enormous garage, once again bedecked in white, with white polished tiles on the floor, white-painted walls and a white ceiling reinforced with red-painted castellated steel beams. The massive floor-space is jambed-full with a collection of bikes and cars that could have easily beaten anything we saw earlier at Goodwood - I am literally blown away.

"I take it all these are yours?" I ask him in amazement, as if I hadn't already worked it out for myself!

"They certainly are. They're my pride and joy."

"I don't know what to say. I'm actually speechless for the first time in my life!"

We laugh together as he points out his collection, explaining each bike and car to me as he guides me along - some of the names of which I've never heard of - a BSA Gold Star, a Vincent Black Shadow and a Norton Manx, all bikes from the 1950's. A red and silver MV Augusta and a beautiful black Harley-Davidson custom trike that is pure crazy! A Norton Rotary from the late-1980's and a lovely 1930's Brough-Superior that must be worth a mint on its own, a 1928 Morgan Super Aero in white, a silver 2009 Morgan Aeromax, a 1966 Ford GT40 MK1 - a real one that is, not a crappy plastic repro - also in white with a blue stripe down the middle, a yellow and green 1993 Lister Storm V12 that looks as mean as Hell, a gorgeous silver 2012 Aston Martin Vantage V12, a beautiful blue 1970 Ford Mustang Shelby GT500 Fastback that I would die for, an early 1980's Lotus Formula One car with beautiful curvaceous black bodywork and in full running order, a brand new Bentley Continental GT in green, a beautiful 1971 Jaguar E-Type V12 Coupé in pale blue, an outrageous 1959 Cadillac convertible in white that has these 2-crazy fins sticking up at the rear, a stunning red Ferrari 438 Itallia that's also brand new, a 1932 Ford Model B Coupe Hot Rod in black with flames of white, yellow, orange and red painted over the front end, a strange 1950's-style bubble-top Hot Rod in metalflake green that is completely mad, the lovely green Ford Focus RS that he used for our meeting the other night, a crazy 1941 Willys Coupé

Gasser in flat-yellow with a number 13 painted on both doors, a funny little BMW Isetta 300 bubble-car from the late-1950's in blue over white, an early-1920's Napier racing car with an enormous engine spilling out of the front of it and wild exhaust-pipes everywhere, a 1969 Dodge Challenger R/T also in white, a little white Mini Clubman - again a real one, not one of those bloody BMW things! - with big fat wheels on it, a new white Lotus Evora and a beautiful 1984 DeTomaso Pantera GT5 in blue that are both to die for. And that's about the lot - I don't think I've left one out but I can't be sure! I don't know which way to turn as I'm in love with them all. Even the garage itself is impressive, with painting, drawings, old signs, old number plates and other motoring paraphernalia crowding the walls, the ceiling and the floor. There's even an old Penny Farthing bicycle hanging on one wall.

After Andrew quickly retrieves our outdoor clothes from the hall, we exit the garage through another door and straight out onto the massive patio area outside. I quickly notice fixed to the patio walls on either side are images of the Green Man, each one of them staring at yours-truly with their mischievous eyes that follow my every move. What are they thinking I wonder? Are they trying to tell me something? Is it a warning?

Andy then starts to lead me by hand into and around the landscaped garden. Now let me tell you this, if there's one thing I can't bloody stand it's gardening, it really gets on my tits! I have absolutely no time for it at all. Having said that though, the garden, like the rest of the house, really blows me away - "30-acres of it" - Andy tells me, although obviously we don't walk around all of it, we'd be there all bloody day otherwise! A path of pale-yellow bricks winds its way left from the edge of the patio to around the side of the house, where amongst all the bushes, shrubs and trees hide statues and other works of art of all descriptions - abstract, naked bodies (both male and female), animals, body parts cast in bronze, and also industrial pieces, all scattered about as we tour around. The path leads us further and deeper into the garden - just how much land has this guy really got? - until we come upon a small clearing and a beautiful pine summer house in pale-yellow with a decked veranda. Past this, we wind our way around the back of the garden, through the many various species of trees - I've no idea what make they are, I've never really had an interest in them before, but they are lovely - and then a sea of Winter flowers and out into the sunlight once more.

More statues await us, these being more of a saucy nature - giant penises, legs, breasts, vaginas and other sexual and phallic symbols. We pass through an open tunnel of metal and wood as we reach the back of the house once again. Behind the garage hides a medium-sized vegetable patch, all laid-out in super-organized rows of potatoes, onions, runner beans, carrots, cucumbers, courgettes and other veg.

The middle of the garden though contains my favourite feature, a beautiful kidney-shaped mini-lake overshadowed at the rear by several willow-trees that dangle their branches over and down into the water with their inherent grace. In the middle of the lake sits a gorgeous oriental-style hexagonal gazebo - also painted in white - accessed by an arched oriental bridge from the edge of the path.

The whole image is as idyllic as it is beautiful and I have a strange sense of well-being come over me, of somehow being "HOME."

***

He takes me by both hands and gently pulls me closer to him. We kiss. It's soft and warm and tender and I feel a heady glow begin to smoulder within me, my whole body and soul succumbing to him as my defences melt away to nothing and we give ourselves to each other.

Back in the house Andrew guides me up the elegant staircase to the upper floor. The landing is lit by sunlight from a strange runic-shaped window - one of happiness and peace - and features just a single solitary piece of furniture, an elegantly beautiful white-painted chaise-long with a lime-green buttoned covering of pure silk.

And then to the bedrooms. For such a large house there are only 5 of them, although all are huge and en-suite, with the biggest one - located above the garage - being the master, Andy's room. We enter through its double-doors and hold each other firmly and kiss. Once again the white theme continues in the bedroom, even the massive 4-poster bed in the centre of the room is white. The walls are hung with numerous pictures and paintings of erotic art, from ones featuring naked tattooed Japanese women to Aubrey Beardsley illustrations from the book *Lysistrata* by Aristophanes, depicting men with massive penises and giant over-the-top wigs and women farting! There's also a beautiful Otto Dix print of the German dancer Anita Berber in red that I fall in love with at first sight and what look like original framed erotic photographs of American pin-up girl Betty Page from the 1950's. Sculptures in various shapes and sizes are dotted around the room, small ivory Japanese ones of couples copulating placed alongside enormous ceramic phalluses.

Andrew removes his jacket, as do I my poncho, and we hug and kiss and touch. He undresses me, caresses me, and I offer no resistance to his seduction as we bare ourselves to each other for the first time. We run our hands over each others bodies, touching bare skin, arms, hands, fingers, necks, breasts, bums, stomachs, backs, cock, vagina. We collapse together onto the bed naked amidst heat, passion and exploration as we lose ourselves in adventure.

We don't fuck or shag or hump or screw or anything with a horrible and sleazy nomenclature like that - we make love. He treats me like a woman, not like a piece of meat as all the others have. He seduces me and I fall into his strong arms and take it all without hesitation as he wraps me in his love. I lay there in rapture as he covers me in soft kisses all over my naked body as the essence of pure love beats within my heart.

"You're mine." He whispers to me as he penetrates me and I both smile and grimace as he loves me.

"Take me." I whisper back as we are one.

I want him and need him as much and more as he wants and needs me. From this moment on I am lost to him, he has literally swept me off my feet, this man who I had no memory of only a few simple days ago.

***

It's Monday morning and the whole wide World and everything in it smells of roses. Even though I'm still out of work and this has been one of the - if not THE - worst years of my life so far, nothing can hurt me today. Not now.

I stayed over at Andy's last night - you know you would have done as well lets face it! - and we had the most beautiful and sensual time ever. We made love twice more yesterday, nothing else was needed or required, and it was perfect. There's nowhere I'd rather be than here right now with my love.

As Andy is his own boss - in fact in reality he doesn't actually work as he's made his own money and only dabbles in the car trade every now and then - we're again spending the whole day together. We might go out or we might stay in, who knows?

He brings me breakfast in bed on an antique silver tray - real solid silver that is, no plated shit! - with grapefruit, toast with lashings of marmalade just how I like it (How does he know that?), freshly squeezed orange juice and not crap from a carton, and a big mug of breakfast tea. In bed and over breakfast we talk about life and things and I tell him more of my life and troubles. I don't pour my heart out to him completely as I don't want to scare him off with horror stories from my past. I also don't want him to feel sorry for me, at the end of the day I will always stand on my own 2-feet no matter whatever shit comes my way.

Like me, Andy doesn't have much of a family either, with both his parents having passed-away he only has a younger sister left and he doesn't have much contact with her - echoes of my own situation.

We shower together in his en-suite wet-room and dry each other off with lots of touching and kissing. I need a change of clothes so we decide to go back to my place and then on to somewhere else afterwards. It must be a bit weird having a fleet of cars at your disposal, I know I would find it so, as he decides to take the silver Aston out today as we head off to mine.

We reach my flat in super-quick time, it now being almost mid-day. I show him around but there isn't much really to see compared to his place, and it only takes an embarrassing couple if minutes to see it all! He watches me under full control as I strip completely naked and redress, he resisting the obviously overwhelming urge to jump on my bones as I do so, whereas most guys - or girls! - would have made a play for me and either grabbed my tits or slapped my bum! He's so different to all my previous lovers that I'm feeling out of my depth to a certain degree. I'm actually a little bit in awe of him.

I put on some new underwear - a sexy black lacy bra and knickers from Victoria's Secret, a pair of black jeans from GAP that really emphasize my long legs and pert bum, a white silk blouse from Reiss that cost me a mint, my pair of black-suede ankle-boots from Miu Miu, and my white studded leather jacket again that "what's-his-face" bought me a couple of Christmas's ago. After tidying-up my hair and make-up and adding a few squirts of *Luxe* by Avon, I grab my clutch-bag and off we go.

Andy knows of some place we can go for lunch just the other side of Dorking and so we head off North. The A24 winds its own way as we speed along the twisty single-lane section from Warnham to Rusper, the Aston gripping the road like a leach. I really hate this section of road, it's like playing bloody Russian Roulette with other drivers every time I use it. Once out onto the duel-carriageway, Andy opens the car up and we tear along at well over a hundred. The roar from the engine is fantastic and we both look at each other and laugh at the sound of our mutual passion - it's gorgeous.

At Dorking we turn right at the roundabout with the big silver chicken on top and continue East along the A25 to Betchworth, The Arkle Manor being just up here on the right-hand side. I've never been to this place either, it's always seemed a bit out of my league for some reason, I don't know why?

We order ourselves a couple of drinks - a very large neat vodka for myself and just a Coke for Andy as he doesn't want to risk drinking even the one proper drink with driving the Aston. I bet that car is an absolute magnet for the local fuzz, especially the way he drives!

We grab a table in the corner and laugh at ourselves for being us and finding each other the way we have, I don't think either of us truly believe that this is actually happening? We eat a lovely lunch of slow-cooked pork-belly with seared scallops, black pudding, mashed potato and green beans with a lovely apple and vanilla sauce, followed by more drinks of vodka for me and another Coke for him, although I don't want to go too over-the-top with the drinking and end up all piddly and embarrass myself!

Andy asks me about Amanda but I only give him a basic outline of our love and how it all went tits-up when I cheated on her, something with hindsight I now don't regret at all. He looks at me like I'm from outer space, I still don't think he believes that I was actually married to another woman? Maybe he will never believe me, there's nothing I can do about it, that's his problem at the end of the day.

The day is still young and so we decide to head back to Dorking itself and have a mooch around the shops there, you never know, he might buy me something nice! We park easily enough in the car-park behind the shops off of Wathen Road but no-sooner do we get out of the Aston we're pounced upon by some big burly fucking Slav bastard with the all too familiar tone of:

"Car washer, car washer."

Before Andy even has time to answer "Yes" or "No", I quickly jump in with a firm "No", shutting the bastard up immediately. I'm guessing that he's a fucking Bulgarian by the looks of him, also judging by his foreign number-plated and no-doubt uninsured shitty car parked next to his massive water container - fucking cunts.

Andy looks at me a little bemused. I don't know why, I've explained to him my political beliefs and he seemed okay with it at the time - a crack appearing between us already maybe?

After putting a couple of hours in the meter we head through the narrow alleyway that leads out onto the High Street. Unfortunately my life never seems to be that simple as I immediately spot some dirty-looking bearded middle-Eastern fucker wearing some sort-of long nightshirt, trousers and sandals, sitting on one of the tubular bike-racks talking foreign shit into his mobile-phone. My blood starts to boil over and I get the sudden overwhelming urge to knife the bastard in the throat right here and now and watch him bleed to death at my feet. There is no hope for my England now.

Andy and I stroll arm-in-arm up the High Street window-shopping at nothing much in particular. I avoid my gaze from looking at the wedding dresses in one shop and walk on past it without saying a word about them. Looking at them only brings back all the memories of Amanda and Las Vegas and I don't want those images in my head today, or any other day for that matter.

Dorking is a very traditional type of old town, you either like that sort of thing or not. Personally I quite like it, it's slow-paced and peaceful and quite chilled-out. We wander down St. Martin's Walk to the small supermarket there as I need to get some food shopping for later. We're not staying together tonight as he has an early start tomorrow - "car business" so he says, so I only need a few things for myself. I quickly grab the items I want from the shelves and head towards the tills, the express checkout being far too crowded for my liking so I aim us both to one of the normal tills and unload my basket of items - 6 in total - onto the conveyor and place the "Next Customer" divider behind my stuff. Another couple move in behind us - both in their late-60's by the looks of them - and do the same, although they have a trolley and more shopping than I have. I stand there holding Andy's hand, minding my own business awaiting my turn when all of a sudden the old guy behind me launches into an unprovoked attack on my good-self:

"The express checkouts are over there." He bleats at me as he points over to the left of us.

"Yes, I know they are." I bite back at him sharply as I stare at him with daggers in my eyes.

"Why don't you go over there then?" He answers me back.

"Because I'm standing here that's why."

"But those checkouts are for customers with limited items."

"Yeah, and? What's it got to do with you?"

"You've only got a few items. You should be over there." He continues.

"I'LL STAND WHERE I FUCKING-WELL LIKE. AND IF YOU DON'T LIKE IT YOU CAN GO AND FUCK YOURSELF." I snap at him.

The whole shop grinds to a halt at my loud defensive tone. How fucking dare this twat tell me what to fucking do - what an arsehole! Andy then goes to poke his nose in but I back him off with a wave from my hand, I can fight my own bloody battles without the intervention of anyone else thank you.

A semblance of normality suddenly sweeps back over the shop and everyone starts to reanimate once more and go about their own business.

Un-fucking-believable!

Back out in the High Street we wander hand-in-hand along to West Street where all the antique shops are gathered. We window-shop them all except one, a big double-fronted shop in white that invites us both inside. The whole shop is jamb-packed with stuff - antique furniture, jewellery and tons of other quality items and nicknack's in cabinets, all secreted away in one room after another. It takes us ages to amble around the entire shop, taking-in all the weird and wonderful things on display. Andy spots something and guides me over to a cabinet of antique silver jewellery and asks me what I think of them? I'm not actually into jewellery much, I don't really like things dangling off my ears or around my neck or even rings on my fingers. I know I have my piercings in my ears and my belly but that's different - they're actually physically part of my body.

"What do you think of that necklace Sarah?" He says, pointing to an absolutely gorgeous solid silver crescent-shaped antique piece that really is something else, as is the price at £875!

"It's beautiful. Way out of my price range though." I admit to him.

"I want to buy it for you."

"What? Are you mad? I can't accept that. We've only known each other for 5-minutes!" I underline to him.

"I don't care. I want you to have it. Consider it an early birthday present. It will be something for you to keep for always, to remember me by."

"But it's so expensive."

"It's yours Sarah, for ever and ever. I want to buy it for you."

I have to give in gracefully. He's obviously determined to get it. It is a beautiful piece and I will treasure it until my dying day. The framework of all my previous lovers has been stripped-away and recovered with a new skin - made from Andy's love. Even my once super-strong love for Amanda has melted away due to his loving tenderness towards me.

We make our way back down the main High Street, this time on the opposite side of the road. Again we just window-shop quickly as the car-park ticket only has 10-minutes to go before it expires.

There's no sign of the dirty rag-head as we enter back into the car-park, he must have fucked-off for another prayer to his non-existent God - it won't save him or his dirty brothers, they're all heading straight to Hell anyway. The stinking Slav car-cleaner is still around though, lurking about waiting for his next victim. He stares at me like I'm just a piece of meat so I discretely give him the finger, out of eye-shot of Andy of course as I don't want him involved in my private battle. He continues to stare at me as we head for the Aston, he's far too fucking stupid to understand my gesticulation anyway. He's too stupid to understand what it's like to be English either - fucking scum. They'd sell their own Mothers for a fiver if they could.

***

We roar our way back through the centre of town amid plenty of gorping from the shoppers at the sound and beauty of the Aston, and we're back at my place in under 20-minutes.

Once safely indoors I drop to my knees and suck Andy's cock in the living-room. I strip completely naked as I continue to swallow his meat and he moans in ecstasy at my love. I stop to put on the beautiful silver necklace he bought for me and then take him into my mouth once more and within 5-minutes I detect his hips starting to shake as suddenly he cums down my throat and I swallow his evil muck.

All spent, I let him plop out of me and wank him gently to try and get every last drop of seed from his shaft. His spunk dribbles from my mouth and I laugh as it rolls down my chin and onto the silver necklace and then my perfect tits and I lick it off all 3.

We both go and clean ourselves up in the bathroom and as I wash Andy's cock I suck him once more as I simultaneously finger my vagina and we cum.

***

It's 7.45pm in the evening. With Andy long gone and my dinner of sausages, French beans, pasta and sauce now eaten, I'm on all-fours on my bed with an 8-inch white plastic dildo from

Bondara up my bum and with Andy's silver necklace still around my neck as I try to force my whole hand into my mouth. I haven't bothered to dress since I sucked Andy's cock earlier, not even when I cooked and ate my dinner as there was no point.

Yet again I'm pissed as a fuck as I've sunk 3-bottles of lager, several vodkas and several more gins. Yes, I know what you're thinking and what the fucking quacks told me but fuck off, I want a fucking drink and no-one is going to fucking stop me.

I imagine that Andy is fucking me up the arse and that Amanda is flicking her tongue in and out of my cunt and that guy Steve has his thick cock in my mouth and they all cum on me and I fuck them and then they all shit and piss on me and I cum and then I cry myself to sleep because I don't know what I'm doing or where I'm going as I AM COMPLETELY LOST.

***

Andy and I are going out to lunch again today and I'm actually going to experience something a little bit different, something that I've never done before.

He's taking me out on one of his motorbikes, the Italian beauty that is the MV Augusta. I have to say that I'm actually a little nervous, bikes are dangerous things at the best of times and knowing Andy and the way he drives he's bound to ride it like he stole it!

We're off out to a little pub the other side of Henfield in West Sussex called The Ginger Fox, in Hassocks, another pub I've been past a hundred times but never ventured into. Today I'm wearing a white long-sleeved cotton blouse from Hawes & Curtis, a pair of grey skinny jeans from River Island, and my old pair of black-suede knee-length boots from Farfetch that are super-sexy. My gorgeous underwear is in black lace from Ultimo whilst my perfume is *Luxe* by Avon. As for a jacket I'm wearing the white leather biker one that was a present from Steve moons-ago, with my gloves being my old pair of pearl

Izumi cycling gloves. I'm not taking a clutch-bag out today as Andy is paying - just as a gentleman should! Any essentials such as keys and things I've secreted in my jacket pockets anyway. This being my first time out on a motorbike I obviously don't have a crash helmet so I'm using one of Andy's spares, a beautifully stylish Simpson Speedway RX one in white with an iridium-tinted visor - it's super-cool - just like me! Because of having to wear a helmet, I've therefore had to modify my usual high-mounted ponytail in my hair, positioning it lower than I normally have it as otherwise I wouldn't be able to put my helmet on - it's no real bother, I still look hot to fuck either way! I've also had to keep my make-up lighter than usual as I don't want it rubbing off on the inside of the helmet - oh the things I do for love!

All ready to go, Andy fires-up the red and silver beast with a deep throaty roar and she sounds beautiful. Because it's a sports bike I'm actually sitting up quite high up on it behind Andy and have to lean forwards at an awkward angle to hold onto him, although I quickly get the hang of it. We pull out of Andy's driveway and onto the A272, turning right with Andy giving the bike some beans and we take-off like a bloody rocket - it's really fucking quick and really scary and I have to hang-on to my love for dear life!

We power along the back-roads of Billingshurst to the A24 and head South-East, turning left back onto the A272 at the Buckbarn Crossroads. It's a beautiful sunny day and we pick-off cars with ease along the A281 at every opportunity as the MV lights-up the road. It's absolutely glorious, the power and the freedom the bike exudes is electrifying and I've fallen in love with her already.

We trundle through Henfield town at a steady safe pace, that is until some stupid bitch in a black Audi Q7 pulls out on us from a side turning from our left without even looking. What is it with these fucking Audi drivers? In fact what is it with people who drive 4x4's, are they all fucking blind as well as stupid? Andy speeds up and pulls alongside the dozy bitch - a woman of about my age, good-looking and blonde with 2-kids in the rear of her car. Andy bashes her car door with his fist and I stick 2-fingers up to her as we speed on by. Does she say "Sorry" for pulling out on us? Does she even recognise that she's done anything wrong? Can blacks walk properly in shoes?

"NO" is the answer to all 3.

At the silly mini-roundabout at the other end of town we take a left-turn and stay on the A281 and tear-along heading for our destination, the pub situated ahead of us at a nasty right-hand bend in the road. We pull-up and park in the pubs car-park with plenty of stares and mutterings from the lunchtime punters as well as a couple of the staff. After disrobing our biker-gear and helmets we settle ourselves down at a vacant table in the small secluded garden there. The pub itself a beautiful old thatched building from way-back-when in what was once no-doubt a more pleasant era in time.

Our waitress is a young girl probably in her late-teens, attractive, very slim and with long dark hair and surprisingly not a bloody Slav. She's dressed all in black with a black apron, as are all the other waiters and waitresses, and is as efficient as can be as she smiles as she takes our orders. For our drinks Andy orders an orange juice for himself as he's driving (riding?) whilst I have a pint of lager with a large vodka chaser as per usual. We both have the same for lunch - Roast Sirloin of Redlands Farm beef with Yorkshire pudding with mashed potato and spinach in red wine gravy - and it is glorious, beautifully cooked and presented and just melts in our mouths and tastes like Heaven. We sit and eat and drink and talk and laugh and hold hands and kiss like lovers do and everything is perfect.

And yet behind all this joy, behind this life of mine that is a lie, I am destroyed within. I see nothing around me but death and misery and I want to add to it even though I don't and won't. Why can't I truly be happy? Why can't this big beautiful beaming smile across my face be real? Why?

With our meals finished Andy orders us more drinks, a coffee for himself and another lager for the perfect / imperfect me.

Whilst we wait I make my excuses and head-off to the toilet. In the cubicle I desperately want to cry and rip my heart out but I have no tears to shed, I just sit there having a pee whilst my mind destroys itself.

I head back to Andy behind the facade that is my beautiful exterior. We kiss and laugh as I touch his face with tenderness - my darling love - and with our drinks consumed we collect ourselves together to leave. Andy goes to pay the bill as I head across the car-park to the bike on my own, once again being followed by a thousand-eyes burning into me. I just wish they would all die right here and now and leave me alone.

Andy soon joins me at my side and fires-up the Italian piece of automotive art, it bursting into life like a startled monster. He puts his arm around my waist and squeezes me to him and I really do love him, at least I think I do? A pool of tears begin to form in the corners of my eyes so I close the visor of my helmet to stop him seeing my inner turmoil. We mount-up and roar out of the car-park, much to the dismay of my spies - all obviously anti-bike and all anti-fun.

We speed back to Foxhill surprisingly without much drama, the traffic somehow being considerably lighter now. I fix us both a couple of drinks, a large neat vodka for myself and a small whisky on the rocks for my man.

He takes me to Heaven on the soft white leather sofa, touching, holding, kissing, licking, and loving me like a real man does. I pant breathlessly as he gives me oral pleasure and I want to die at the very moment I peak with his love so I don't have to come back down to Earth and face the reality that is me, whatever reality is?

Whatever I really am?

***

I'd like to believe that in some way that I've turned a corner in my life by being with Andy, but I just know that subconsciously, cruel fate is waiting for me yet again to fuck me over.

15

Berlin

Where do I start with this one? I guess the major news is that Andy and I are now living together, at his beautiful house in Foxhill.

I know I haven't known him for very long - it's a matter of weeks rather than months - but you know what I'm like, in for a penny, in for a pound! I know what side my bread is buttered on - both sides! Obviously it's been a bit of a whirlwind romance - I never thought I'd ever seriously use that word! - but with Andy by my side I'm looking upon my life with a renewed sense of optimism. I don't know what it is but ever since I've been seeing Andy everything has gone perfectly with my life. There has not even been a little disaster let alone a major one. Why? What has caused this to happen? Has there been a shift in my timeline? Or am I being spared for something really nasty next time around?

I'm also fully aware of the fact that he's a little bit too old for me really, there is a 15-years age gap to take into consideration after all. But, as ever, what the Hell?

My old flat in Slinfold Village has obviously now gone. Amanda wanted her share of it so that's all done and dusted now, she was entitled after all. She's with another girl now anyway - a fellow vet - so good-luck to her, if that's what she wants then go for it. I mean her no harm.

It's not just Andy and myself who live here though, there is in fact the 3 of us now in total. In complete surprise, for my 35th birthday in November, Andy bought me another cat - a beautiful female Seal-point Siamese - with the most gorgeous face you've ever seen in your life, with a black / brown face and ears and the loveliest pair of blue-eyes next to my own. She's great, she just doesn't stop talking! I love her to bits. She's totally crazy - I think she's possibly from outer a space! I've called her Eva, named after the wife of "The Great One."

I really can't believe that I'm 35 now, and in only 5-years time I'm going to be 40! What the Hell is going to happen to me then? I don't want to lose my looks or my figure or I'll go completely insane. I did actually spend my birthday here on my own - although obviously Eva was here to comfort me - as Andy had to go away on business for a couple of days. I just spent the whole day chilling-out doing my own thing, which was not a lot! A bit of drinking, sexing myself, more drinking - you know how it goes!

I didn't even get a birthday card from my sister Kate, the miserable cow. I didn't really expect one to be fair so, whatever? I wasn't expecting one from Rachael either and none was received. I can't really blame her of course, it was me that pushed her guy into poking me after all. I did get one from Amanda though which was a bit of a surprise, along with a short note as to how she's doing, which is OK. She also begged me not to fuck-up this relationship as well so I really must take note. I will have to Email her back to thank her for the card and to wish her and her girlfriend all the best and my love. I don't regret the way things have turned-out between us, although I could have done without the problems that I know I caused.

Anyway, enough of all that crap. It's 9.20am and Andy and I are both still in bed - both naked - just laying here talking about stuff that lovers do, while the underfloor heating and the duvet keeps the mid-December chill firmly at bay. There is simply nothing better in life than to snuggle under the duvet and get nice and warm and cosy, especially with a lover in the dead of winter. It really is a great time to be alive.

"How would you like to go Berlin for Christmas?" Andy suddenly asks me out of the blue.

"Berlin! In Germany?" I quiz him.

"Yes, I believe that's where it is. Not unless they've moved it!"

"Are you taking the piss?" I say laughingly.

"Well? Do you fancy it? The Germans go crazy for Christmas, I guarantee you'll love it."

"Okay then, lets go." I agree without hesitation.

"Good, because I've already booked the hotel and the flights, ages ago."

"What? How bloody sneaky are you?" I come back at him.

"Very." He laughs.

"The Christmas markets there are something else, there's so much to see and do, we'll have a great time, I promise." We kiss and cuddle and touch. I want to tell him that I love him, I really do, but it's way too soon, I'm afraid that I'll scare him off and that's the last thing I want to do right now.

We shower together in the en-suite wet-room and I suck him until he cums in my face and then he wanks me with 2-fingers and I orgasm and flail about like stupid.

Our afternoon is spent in Chichester shopping, shopping for things for me to wear for our Christmas trip to Germany. Today though I'm wearing my black low-cut v-neck jumper from Bluefly, my white figure-hugging jeans from River Island, my tan-suede ankle-boots from AliExpress, and underwear from Figleaves in sexy red and black lace. As it's bloody freezing outside today, I'm wearing a lovely black bomber-type jacket that Andy bought for me from Jacketvests, its warm and comfortable without being too restrictive and also has internal pockets for my money, cards and keys and other crap so there's no need for a bag of any kind. My hair and make-up is done in its same old usual style but I've emphasized my face a little more today with sharper cheekbones and dark eyeshadow as I want everyone to notice me - and they will. My perfume is *Mademoiselle* by Coco Chanel.

We're taking the Bentley out today, travelling in style as well as speed, and we hit Chichester in only 20-minutes or so, the car whooshing us along like a we're speeding on a giant cloud. We park fairly easily considering the enormous size of the car, and then take a mooch around the shops, first down East Street, looking at this and that. I buy more shoes and tops and nicknack's and yet more shoes, as is my want. Andy pays for everything I want so I get more stuff, being the shameless greedy fucking bitch I am.

We get a couple of large Cornish pasties in North Street and go and eat them in the old Market Squire building in the middle of the Cross, they're pipping-hot and taste of pure gorgeousness. I take the piss out of some of the passers-by as we sit and eat - the scum, the Paki's and the stinking Slavs - and we both laugh.

"Why do you hate foreigners so much?" Andy suddenly quips.

"I don't hate foreigners. Amanda was Australian and I loved her with all my heart. It's the blacks and the Paki's I can't fucking stand, and especially the Slavs, they're like a fucking plague, destroying everything everywhere they go. They're the scum of the Earth."

"That's not strictly true Sarah is it?"

"Oh yes it is. I've seen it and lived through it. My home town in South London has been taken-over by them - they're bloody everywhere."

The conversation immediately dies on its knees, and the cold chill of the December air freezes the next 10-minutes of our lunchtime. I'm not going to apologize or make any excuses for my words. I know I'm right and that's all there is to it, multiculturalism is out of control and there is no going back now. I've felt this way since the age of about 9 or 10 when I woke up to the truth and saw the World for what it is, a World of liars and cheats where nothing is real. If Andy or anyone else can't see what's happening right in front of them then there is no hope for this country. All the changes in the World today are stripping-away peoples freedom and security, their jobs, money, homes, relationships, and now even their national identities. If you don't agree with what I'm saying then you're ignoring the truth.

I begin to wonder if Germany has as many Slavs as we do? I bet they don't. Even so, I know they've got their own problems with the fucking stinking Turks, they're just as fucking bad. Europe has become a cesspit for human waste.

I'm not British, and I'm definitely not European. I am English and bloody proud of it.

***

The first-class Lufthansa flight from Gatwick to Berlin's Tegal Airport was fairly hassle-free and didn't actually take that long, amazingly under 2-hours. As you would expect from being only 2-days before Christmas, the Tegal Airport is bursting at the seams with people, although we actually check-out pretty quickly. We're staying in Berlin for the best part of the next 6-days, at the beautiful 5-star Hotel Adlon Berlin on Unter den Linden, right opposite the magnificent Brandenburg Gate. It goes without saying that Andy has paid for everything, and why shouldn't he? He loves me as much as I adore him.

What did I say a couple of weeks ago about foreigners in Germany? Sure enough, when Andy hails us a cab - fortunately he can speak fluent German - lo-and-behold, the bloody taxi driver turns-out to be a stinking Turk - what a fucking surprise! The Hotel is only about 15-kilometres away - or about 9-miles in old money - but it still takes us 30-minutes to get there because of the heavy Christmas traffic.

I send my sister Kate a quick text message to say that we've arrived in Germany okay. She's staying at the house over Christmas to look after Eva for me.

Obviously we're back on speaking terms once again, just as it should be. We are the only family that we've got after all now. Also at long bloody last she's finally got rid of that useless idiot Mick, with Abigail gone there was no reason to stick around I guess? Why it's taken her so long to see the light I'll never know? Andy did have to put his foot down with her though, as for some reason she's taken up smoking again. Quite naturally neither of us want to come home to a stinking house or a burnt-out shell do we? At the end of the day though, if she wants to kill herself by sucking on cancer-sticks then there's nothing I can say or do to stop her - stupid girl.

Today I'm wearing a black cotton long-sleeved wrap-top from ASOS, sexy black leather trousers from AliExpress, my black suede open-toed ankle-boots from Polyvore and my black leather biker-jacket that I got off Ebay. My underwear is also in sexy black lace from Victoria's Secret. My hair is as per usual whilst my make-up features coal-black eyeshadow and deep-red lipstick. My perfume is *Kenzo Flower* by Kenzo.

We pull-up outside the Hotel Adlon and it is beautiful - simply stunning - built in typical Teutonic style and perfection, big, bold and square. A couple of Hotel porters suddenly appear as if from nowhere and come and take our luggage into the lobby as Andy goes to check us in at the reception desk. The entrance lobby is as beautiful as it is opulent, with it's curved ceiling and white marble floor - it's all very German, just as one would expect.

Our room - or suite to be exact - is on the top floor, and once again it is perfect and incredibly romantic. Apparently the hotel boasts over 300-rooms spread over 7-floors, 4-restaurants including the Quarre Restaurant and the 2-star Lorenz Adlon dining-room which serves classic German cuisine. There are also 5-bars, a boutique, and it even has its own swimming pool - amazing! I'll definitely be having some of that!

The 2-porters piss-off after Andy tips them and then we're alone at last - alone to play. I strip naked before my man, throwing my clothes off willy-nilly, and lay back on the bed with my arms stretched-out above me and my gorgeous legs spread as wide apart as they will go. I tell him to "Take me" and "Love me" and I wince loudly as I sense the touch of Andy's tongue flicking at my vagina and I start to shake uncontrollably. I orgasm and cum in under a minute and I scream for more. He fingers me deeply and I lose control completely, my legs kicking-out at nothing but air and I spit at him as I cum once more.

I gasp for breath as I tear Andy's clothes off. He touches my heaving breasts, my bum, my neck, my swollen and wet vagina, and then he to is bare and mine to take. I push him backwards hard onto the bed and take his hard cock into my mouth. I suck him with all my power as I pull gently on his balls, making him groan in both pleasure and pain. I gag and cough as I take him to the back of my throat and he can resist me no more, ejaculating his jism within me, down my throat, over my tongue and over my teeth. I swallow the contents of my mouth and then release him, kissing his knob and we both laugh at our love.

I do love him. I really do.

We shower together to wash-away our sins and the cum and then unpack our bags and redress. I'm wearing my white cotton sleeveless-blouse from H&M, my short tight mini-skirt in black from New Look, my black tights from Pretty Polly, and my black suede open-toe platform court-shoes from Polyvore. My underwear is in white lace from Agent Provocateur and my perfume is *Poison* by Christian Dior. I'm putting my leather biker-jacket back on as we're both going out for a quick stroll around the city, not too far as we want to be back in time to redress for dinner.

As the day has gone on - it's actually dark outside now - the temperature has also dropped quite significantly. We cuddle each other as we wander along past the British Embassy and down to the Behrenstrasse and I am so happy. I think to myself that if that stupid bitch hadn't crashed into me months ago, Andy wouldn't have stopped to help and I wouldn't be here in Germany with him now. Isn't fate odd? We window-shop as we walk along, gazing at all the things that are now within my evil grasp. Andy has already lavished gift upon gift on me in the short time I've been seeing him and I'll take advantage of my good-fortune - to a certain degree anyway, I'm not a complete piss-taker! Or am I ?

There's tons of seasonal things for sale, some of which are quite tacky but most do have a certain charm about them, in a typical German way.

An hour-and-a-half later we're back in our suite. As Andy changes I strip naked and touch my breasts. I take a couple of large swigs of vodka from the bottle I secretly secreted-away in one of my luggage bags. Even though I'm more contented now than I have been for ages, I still need the nasty liquid inside me to calm myself down or I will go completely mad. Andy comes-up behind me and kisses my neck and cups my breasts and fondles them, rubbing them together and pulling them apart. I insert one of my index fingers into my pussy and flick and rub my clit as Andy squeezes my tits and pinches my nipples playfully. I remove my finger and suck my own juice, its sweet taste mixing with the vodka on my tongue and numbing my mind.

I don't bother with any underwear for this evening as they're not necessary, so the only item of clothing I'm wearing is my beautiful white strapless criss-cross dress from BandageDressesOutlet that really hugs my perfect figure and shows-off my breasts, bum and my beautiful legs to the max. On my feet I'm wearing a pair of white suede open-toe ankle-boots from Polyvore, whilst in my hair I have a white cotton bow that I've tied around my ponytail. I'm also wearing the gorgeous silver necklace that Andy bought me in our very first week together, it really complements my whole look. I've redone my make-up for a sharper look and overall I look absolutely stunning. No-one can resist me, not even myself! My perfume is as before, but more of it naturally.

All eyes are upon us as we take our seats in the beautiful, sumptuous Hotel dining-room. I know I'm fucking gorgeous and now so does everyone else. I'm also stronger than them, and scary too! Andy orders each course for the both of us - in German - as well as the excellent wine. No surprises for guessing what that is! For starters we have a spinach salad each which tastes divine, followed by our main of Paderborn chicken breast with potatoes, green beans and carrots and then lemon sorbet for dessert. The food is absolutely glorious and is served by the highly-efficient and courteous staff. The whole experience could not be more perfect.

We sit and chat and talk about things that every other couple in the World talks about. He tells me that he has some business to take care of first-thing tomorrow morning - Christmas Eve - and that he won't be out very long. When I quiz him he just says that it's: "A surprise" and: "Not to worry."

But I do worry. I have a horrible feeling that he's not telling me everything about what he gets up to. I have to confess though that the same could be said of myself. Only time will tell I guess?

My beautiful dress falls to the bedroom floor and we kiss and touch each others bodies passionately. He kneads my breast with one-hand and runs the other between the cheeks of my bum as I wank his cock and balls. He bends me over and I lean on the bed with my arse stuck-up in the air. I still have my ankle-boots on and they remain so for the next hour. I feel his cock enter my body from behind and I exhale loudly under its pressure. He fucks me slowly but firmly and my legs turn to jelly as he bangs-away at my vagina. We moan and groan together as then we cum as one, my internal juices mixing with the gloopy muck of his spunk. He continues to poke me until he is no more and falls out. I turn around to lick and suck at his messy shaft, playing with his testicles as I eat our blended mess. I order him onto his hands and knees as I then start to lick at his balls from behind. I suck them both into my mouth and gently play with them with my tongue and he cries and screams at me, calling me a "Fucking dirty bitch" and I love it and order him to say more and worse as it really turns me on.

Releasing him, I then stick my dirty tongue into his bumhole, flicking it at him. I finger him, pushing my digit all the way into his rectum as I wank his cock back to hard with my other hand. He moans loudly as it takes him a good 5-minutes before he's ready to unload again. I squeeze his nuts and wank his cock into my awaiting mouth and he cums into me, not as much as the first time but enough to make me choke momentarily. I swallow every trace of his seed I find, squeezing his penis as hard as I can to extract every last drop onto my tongue.

"You're a very naughty girl Sarah." He sighs to me.

"Yes, I know. Now lick my pussy. Lick me" I beg him.

***

I awake Christmas Eve morning to find myself alone in bed. There's no sign of Andy in the bedroom, the en-suite bathroom or even in the rest of the suite - he's seemingly vanished into thin air. I gaze naked out through the frosty glass of the balcony doors at the snow-covered vista that is Berlin. What a beautiful city she is. I actually think to myself that I could one day give-up my precious England to come and live here permanently.

No I couldn't.

Seeing as Andy has buggered-off out, I decide to make good use of the Hotel's swimming pool before I have breakfast and get sorted for the day. I'm wearing a short, white pure silk robe from LilySilk that Andy bought for me over my white cut-out plunge swimsuit from ASOS. It's so gorgeous and fits my beautiful figure perfectly, showing-off my full-breasts and tight bum. Unsurprisingly there's no-one about at this time of the morning - or year for that matter - as I discard my robe poolside and jump in, the pool itself actually being nowhere near as big as our one back home in England. The warm water is so invigorating and I swim almost the entire length below the surface before I emerge for air. I muck-around by myself for the next half-an-hour or so, doing backstrokes, breaststrokes and generally sodding-about without a single fucking care in the World. This is what it feels like to be free.

Back in our suite I strip naked and shower, then order myself room-service - continental-style - and then dress for the day, even though I have no-idea where I'm going or what time Andy will be back. Today I'm wearing my white v-neck t-shirt from AliExpress, my black low-cut jumper from Bluefly, my pair of pale-blue stone-wash jeans from BooHoo and my old pair of knee-length black suede boots that I bought ages ago from Farfetch. My underwear is in yellow from Nordstrom whilst today's perfume is *Luxe* by Avon. As it's bloody freezing outside I'm going to wear my black bomber-jacket from Jacketvests once again.

My mobile-phone suddenly begins to chime and it's a text from Andy, asking me to meet him at the WeihnachtsZauber Market on Alexanderplatz, and that he'll only be a short while. I get directions and a map from a sweet young blonde girl at the Hotel's reception desk and head out into the cold. The location of the Market is a brisk walk away, made somewhat longer by the throngs of Christmas shoppers out and about. Anyhow I stride-along at my usual busy pace and I arrive there in some 25-minutes or so. The Market itself is something else, with seemingly hundreds of stalls selling all manner of stuff - handicrafts, pretzels, traditional German art, mulled wines, cakes, seasonal delicacies, beer, German sausages, chocolates, clothes, stocking-fillers - the list goes on and on.

My mobile rings once more and it's Andy, instructing me to meet him over by the massive Christmas tree. No-one can miss it and I find him easily, standing there waiting for me.

"Where have you been? I was worried." I question him and we kiss like lovers.

"I told you, it's a surprise. You'll have to wait until tomorrow." He beams back with a smile.

"I thought we'd grab some lunch here and then have a look around an art museum on the way back to the Hotel, if that's alright with you?"

"Okay, that sounds fine to me." I tell him and we kiss again.

We walk on arm-in-arm, quickly finding a stall selling all manner of German sausages - Bockwurst, Bratwurst, Frankenfurter Wurstchen, Weggla, Knackwurst, Landjager - all cooked on an enormous circular hotplate that must be at least 2-metres in diameter. Andy orders once again as he knows more about the local cuisine than I do, and anyway, he speaks the language as I've said. We have an enormous Bockwurst sausage each in a bread-roll, topped with a heap of sauerkraut and covered in tomato sauce and a weird German mustard called

Senf that tastes a bit strange at first, not strong and powerful like English mustard does, but I soon get used to it and start to really enjoy it. Next door to us is a beer stall, so Andy orders us a massive great stein of lager each to help wash-down the giant banger. We sit ourselves down on one of the bench-seats and munch-away and drink and talk. The sausage and the lager are both glorious with the beer being especially strong, making me a little light-headed. We finish-up and walk off arm-in-arm once again, heading to our next destination - the art gallery.

The Martin-Gropius-Bau itself is back in the direction of our Hotel, on the Niederkirchner Strasse, and we're soon there after a short walk. The gallery is another magnificent German building, not dissimilar to our Hotel in design - on the outside anyway - and once inside we wander around like lovers at our own pace looking at all the beautiful works of art on display. We see works by Piet Mondrian, David Hockney and sculptures by Anthony Caro. They're all so beautiful and serine and they give me a tremendous feeling of inner peace and tranquillity, like I'm floating on a cloud of the purest air.

After an hour or so we decide to head back to our Hotel as it's now late-afternoon. I'm so knackered from all the walking I've done today, not to mention the giant sausage and the lager - I am absolutely stuffed!

I lay on the corner of the bed completely naked in an almost fetal position. I've pushed plenty of lubrication in to ease the pain and extract the pleasure. I feel my man behind me and then sense his approach. The touch of his cock on my body sends my breathing haywire as he then pushes into me and I gasp and wince as I grit my teeth together hard as I let him fuck me anally. He slides in without too much trouble and then starts to poke me in a steady rhythmic motion. I moan and curse him with abuse such as: "You bastard", "Cunt" and "Fucking shit", and he laughs at me as he carries-on screwing. He rams me up the arse for nearly 5-minutes and then pulls out with a pronounced squelching-noise and I turn over to watch him spunk me over my face and my tits as I sit there breathless and a little sore.

We shower together and then both dress for dinner, the time is now 7.20pm. I'm wearing my white buttoned blouse with a lace insert from Polyvore that is super-stylish and chic, my black short mini-skirt from New Look with my black wool tights from ASOS and my black suede ankle-boots from Miu Miu. My underwear is also in sexy black lace from Ultimo and makes me look and feel really hot. I refresh my make-up - nothing fancy - and then add perfume, *Kenzo Flower* by Kenzo.

For dinner Andy orders us Mackerel in a green Gazpacho of Bell Pepper with caviar of pineapple, white bread, walnut oil and mint - it's delish! This is then followed by Crème Brulee for dessert, cognac, coffee, and then to bed to sleep but no sex at 11.35pm.

***

It's Christmas morning and Andy is already awake when I open my eyes to the day, sitting here in bed beside me reading some obscure German car magazine called *Auto Bild*.

"Morning." I say wearily.

"Hello you. Merry Christmas Sarah." He says as he leans down to me and kisses me on my shoulder.

"And to you." I say, kissing him back with all my love.

"Did you sleep well?"

"Yeah, I was out like a light."

"So did I. Here, this is for you, with all my love." He says, kissing me again, this time my mouth.

Did you notice he said "Love" ?

He hands me a small squire box wrapped in red paper with gold Christmas trees emblazoned upon it, secured by a lace bow, also in gold. Inside is a black presentation box - unmarked - and when I open it, there before me is the most beautiful wristwatch in the whole World - a Breitling Colt Orange - one of those fuck-off expensive ones.

"Oh Andy, it's gorgeous, thank you." I exude.

"I remembered you telling me about the watch your Mother gave you had packed-up, so it was the obvious thing to get."

I kiss him on the cheek and hug and hold him but it's no use, the sinister overtones of all my past Christmas's overwhelms me and I can't contain all the turmoil that has built-up within my mind any longer. I start to sob my heart out for all the World to see as my annual Seasonal Affective Disorder kicks me in the teeth once more.

Andy tries to console me in every way possible but he's too late - I'm gone and I weep endless tears of loss - plus a few of happiness - at my life, at all the shit that I've had to endure and all the shit yet still to come - loosing Lacey, Mum, Amanda, Abigail, my car, my sanity, my job, my Country, the baby. There is no point in going on, you all know the fucking score.

"Oh Sarah, come on, what is it? What's the matter? Have I done something wrong?" He says in a concerned tone.

"No, it's not you, it's me and everything else. I want to thank you for rescuing me. For saving me from oblivion."

"What do you mean Sarah? Please tell me."

"Promise me you'll never leave me." I beg of him.

"Sarah, I can't promise you that, no-one can. What's brought all this on?"

"I hate this time of year. I've never had a proper Christmas. The last 2 were pretty good, first with Mum, my sister Kate and baby Abigail, and then last year with Amanda, and now this year with you. But way before all that, when I was a kid, living at home with the "Old Man", it was all just a fucking nightmare. Birthday's were the fucking same as well. Guess what he bought me for my 18th birthday present?"

"I've no idea, your first car maybe?"

"You've got to be joking? He bought me a fucking tyre-pressure gauge, and it didn't even fucking work!"

"Are you serious? I don't believe it, a tyre-pressure gauge! Why?"

"Because he was a total and complete arsehole. Every day and night was like living on a knife-edge. He was like a time-bomb, we never knew when he was going to explode or which direction the blast would be aimed at. Usually it was me for some reason? I could never understand why other families weren't the same as us. I thought it was normal for Fathers to be bastards like him. Even when I was at school and I would go around girlfriends houses after school or at weekends and their Fathers would talk to them nicely and they would do the same back. I used to wonder:

"What the fuck is going on here?"

"Why are they being nice to one another?"

"Why aren't they shouting?"

"Where are all the tears?"

I thought they where the odd ones and my so-called "Family" was the norm. When I finally discovered that what I was faced with wasn't actually normal, I first turned to music to escape, and then alcohol. And that started me on the slippery-slope of addiction. I vaguely remember looking in my diary one day only to discover to my horror that I'd actually "lost" 3-months of my life due to drinking. They were completely missing. This was in my teens when I was still living at home of course. I knew I had to get out of there or either he would have killed me or I would have killed him, it really got that bad. And so here I am. What you see before you now is the end result of all that bewildering mess from the first 20-years or so of my life. I honestly don't know how I survived it all. This is why I can't stand people pissing me around, it brings back all the horrible memories of that old bastard."

"But your Father's not around any more, he's dead."

"That's not the point is it? He damaged me. I will always be scarred. No-one can fix it."

"So why do you have that "thing" tattooed on your back? Is that because of the way your Father treated you as well?"

"No, that's different, that's because of the way England is going, and Europe and the rest of the World. You either have to accept that or go your own way."

My last statement is met with another expanse of strained silence. I don't mean to sound harsh to him, even though I do care about Andy I have to stand on my own firm moral ground regarding my political beliefs. No-one is ever going to take that away from me.

I get up and go for a quick pee and to tidy-up my face from all my tears as Andy orders us room-service - with Champagne of course! I return to him in bed and hand over my Christmas present to him as I still continue to sniffle. I've bought him a lovely scale model of speed ace Donald Campbell's Bluebird land speed record car that I found online back in England. What do you buy for a man who has everything he desires - and that includes me?

He loves it.

And I love him.

I really do.

Some 10-minutes later and breakfast is served. I sink a couple of glasses of Champagne before eating, just to help me get over my earlier tears and try to move on with the rest of the day. I really wish I had more control over my thoughts, they drive me fucking insane all the fucking time.

It's gone mid-day before we extract ourselves from bed. Andy licks my vagina and fingers me and I cum. I suck his cock and he squirts his glue into my face and I swallow it, washing it down with the remains of the Champagne.

We're just going out for a walk around Berlin this afternoon, nothing much else. It's snowed some more overnight so we probably won't get very far anyway. I'm wearing the same clothes as I did from the other day, the white t-shirt, black jumper, blue jeans and black suede boots, as I'm guessing we won't be out long. Today's underwear is in deep-red silk from Figleaves and my perfume is *Poison* by Christian Dior. I only have light make-up on, nothing fancy. My jacket is also the same black one from the other day.

We exit the Hotel and turn to our left. In front of us is the amazing structure that is the towering Brandenburg Gate - as I mentioned earlier - with the magnificent bronze horses, chariot and the figure of Victoria, the Roman goddess of victory mounted on top. I take a few shots of it with my camera as we then cross

Unter den Linden to admire its splendour up close. Andy asks a young couple there if they would take a shot of us both together as we cuddle in the freezing air. Its a photo that I will treasure always.

From there we decide to go for a walk around the block where the Hotel is situated, down Wilhelmstrasse and then right along Behrenstrasse and right again past the American Embassy to the Pariser Platz and then back to the Hotel itself. I hope I can make it, it's so bloody cold outside I think my ears and nose are about to drop off!

Back inside the warmth of the Hotel we head to one of the many bars it features, with Andy ordering a large brandy for himself and a large neat vodka for yours-truly. We sit at the bar and talk about life and all that shit and the conversation somehow steers itself back onto the same fucking subject that I suffered this morning - that of the "Old Man." I really don't want to talk about that old fucker again and so I manage to segue the conversation onto the subject of cars by using my superior female persuasive powers.

"Are you happy Sarah, with me I mean?" He suddenly quizzes me.

"Yes of course I'm happy. What makes you say that?"

"I just needed to know that's all."

But am I really happy? What does that word actually mean? I don't think I know any more.

Back up in our suite I pleasure Andy's cock as he lays there naked on our bed with his legs wide apart. I climb on top of him and sit on it, letting my weight gently ease down onto its firmness and then I have him. I fuck up and down as I steady myself on his chest. He plays with my breasts and my bum as I ride his shaft and the passion and the vodka and even the very thought of being here in this Hotel in Berlin - in Germany even - heightens my emotions. We cum almost together - he slightly before I do - and I scream as his seed floods my internal passage and spills out. I climb off and lick his dirty cock and I just don't care about anything else - just his penis in my mouth and that's all, I have lost my mind to it completely.

We shower together and wash each others bodies. We kiss and touch and he fingers my vagina as I pull-back the skin on his dick as hard as I dare, making his knob swell to explode and I suck it.

The evening is upon us quickly and it's almost 8pm before we sit ourselves down for dinner. I'm wearing a black mini-bodycon dress from AliExpress that Andy bought for me and a pair of black Christian Laboutin shoes that are to die for - also another gift from my man - that must have cost him an arm and a leg, but that's not my problem. If he wants to throw expensive gifts at me then bring it on, I won't resist!

I'm not wearing any underwear as I don't fucking want to. My make-up is done to its usual perfection, with my look this evening edging towards the dark side of my mind as that's been my mood all day - it's not my fault, that's the way it works. We sink our second bottle of Champagne of the day - Moet - no shit - as we are treated like royalty by the fantastically efficient and friendly staff. We have prawns in chicken liver to start, followed by the main of Pork Shoulder and potatoes. I just love eating meat, it's a necessary evil that I enjoy. For desert we have an amazing carrot cake with dill ice-cream and rosemary cotton candy - it is wow!

I have no idea what the time is when we finally enter our suite, it might even be tomorrow - Boxing Day - for all I know are care. My dress and shoes are removed from my beautiful body in a matter of seconds and I lay back completely naked on the bed. I raise my legs up and hold them there with both hands as my love gently pushes his rigid weapon into my primed rectum. He fucks me with all the confidence he possesses as he knows that I love to fuck anal. He fingers my vagina and clit as he bangs-away at my bumhole, making me wet and reducing me to a quivering wreck almost instantly. About to cum he pulls out and shoots himself over my torso, my tits, face and pussy and I want to drown and die in his white horror.

***

Boxing Day dawns lovely and bright with no sign of any more snow. We're off out today to see one of Andy's clients on the outskirts of the city - Hans and his wife Hedwig - a couple of fellow car collectors apparently.

After a beautiful breakfast of two Weisswurst floating in a sea of minced chives, we hire a taxi for the relatively short drive of about 35-minutes to their villa on the shore of the graceful Lake Wannsee.

As soon as we approach the location I get a sense of the type of people I'm about to spend the day with - stinking rich! Their gravel-driveway is at least a quarter of a mile long and beautifully lined with trees and manicured lawns, bushes and shrubs. The house itself is something else again, more like a mansion really, all in white with towering columns guarding its entranceway. In essence its a little like Andy's (our!) place but is of considerably more grandeur.

I grip Andy's hand for reassurance as we make our way to the front-door, treading our way through the remains of the previous few days of snow. I've really pulled-out all the stops today regarding my look, I'm not going to be outdone by another woman, I don't care what her age or her so-called "status" is. I'm wearing a white knee-length bodycon floral dress from Lipsy that sticks to my gorgeous curves like glue, along with my pair of white suede open-toe ankle-boots from Polyvore that are killer - in more ways than one! My underwear is in white lace from Victoria's Secret, whilst in my hair I have a white cotton bow fixing my ponytail. My make-up is full-on, featuring dark-grey eye-shadow, plenty of blusher to accentuate my cheekbones and pale-red lipstick. My perfume is *Poison* by Christian Dior. I've had to wear my big black winter jacket as it was the only one really appropriate considering the cold.

We're greeted at the front-door by our hosts Hans and Hedwig who are both considerably older than I imagined them to be for whatever reason, they must be in their mid to late-70's at least. Once inside, all my fears and speculations about them being arrogant snobs go straight out the window as soon as the introductions are dealt with - you could not find 2-nicer people if you tried, although their German accents are thick and quite hard to understand at first but I soon get the hang of it.

Inside the villa it's all very typical of its type, with white-painted walls and a beautiful white marble hall floor and an ornate spiralling staircase over to our right. We're ushered into the lounge where our outer garments are taken by Hedwig. I notice her looking at my body as she then makes a comment to Andy:

"Andrew, you did not tell us how beautiful your girlfriend was, that was very naughty of you!" She jokes as she then questions to me:

"I do hope that he is treating you well Sarah?"

"I don't have any complaints so far!" I joke back to her.

I warm to her instantly and even more so as the day goes on, she's like a Mother-figure to me already rather than someone that I've only just met - weird!

I notice that the furniture in the lounge is that horrible crappy old brown shit that I just cannot stand but obviously I don't tell them that. I know it suits the style of the house and even the owners but it doesn't suit me, it's awful. We sit and chat about things as Hedwig serves us lovely hot chocolate in giant oversized cups. She enquires about my life back in England and I open-up to her - just a little anyway, not mentioning that I'm bisexual or about my little drinking habit, why would I ? - just telling her about my car accident and loosing my Mum and niece.

She seems quite horrified as I say all this to her and touches my arm in compassion at my loss and I'm a little-bit overawed by her kindness, making me cry on the inside.

With our drinks finished we all wrap-up warm to go outside to have a look at their car collection. It's actually housed in what looks like a glorified shed built adjacent to one side at the rear of the villa, but on closer inspection it's actually more like a barn. My breath is taken-away as we all venture inside - I was wrong, it's more like a museum in here! There are cars and motoring memorabilia everywhere, even more so than in Andy's garage (our garage!). There must be at least 50 cars, maybe more. All down one side sits a line of gleaming red Ferrari's, from a beautiful 1964 250 GTO that is to die for, right up to a brand new LaFerrari that is pure crazy! Other exotic cars include a 1969 Lamborghini Muira in lime-green, a silver 1994 McLaren F1, a 2014 Bugatti Veyron in black and orange, a yellow 1929 Isotta-Fraschini 8A Convertible Sedan and a beautiful blue 1931 Hispano-Suiza Type 68 V12, this being one of the cars that Andy had sourced for them over the years. Another row features all American cars - Cadillac, Lincoln, Ford, Pontiac, a couple of Corvette Stingrays, a blue 1948 Tucker Torpedo, a yellow 1951 Munze Jet Convertible, a white 1955 Kaiser Darrin Roadster and a line of earlier rare cars - a 1933 Pierce-Arrow Silver Arrow, a 1938 Packard Super 8, a 1934 Stutz Blackhawk, a 1936 Cord Roadster, a 1937 Duesenberg SJ and the most gorgeous 1937 Auburn Speedster in pale-yellow.

Behind all these is a group of German cars - a couple of Porsche racecars, a 935 and a 911 GT1, a bright-red 1980 BMW M1 and a beautiful silver 1955 Mercedes 300 SL Gullwing. Another row of German cars include a 1932 Horch 670 Cabriolet, a 1938 Maybach Tourer and a Bitter SC Convertible - a strange German car from the late-1980's.

I could go on all bloody day about the rest of the collection as there's actually another 2-more barns further down the garden, one full of motorcycles and the other containing a rare Nazi aeroplane from the war and other stuff - mad!

We make our way back to the house for a late-lunch, it now having gone 2pm. Hedwig has pre-prepared a big tray of sandwiches for us all, featuring a strange-smelling and looking German sausage that actually tastes really lovely - especially with the fiery German mustard that she's made herself and served in an elegant little China pot with its own elegant little China spoon! She's so nice and friendly and I'm so glad that we've hit it off like this, it makes a lovely change to have a proper chat with another woman again - particularly one of her age and intelligence. She begins to tell me about her life as a dancer in the late-1950's and how she came to meet Hans at a theatre she was performing at in Berlin at the time and then falling in love, getting married and having their daughter Magda who herself is married to an American guy and lives over in the States with their 3-children, they all being American born.

As the darkness of the Winter sky descends, it's time to say our "Farewells" and to thank them for the day and I've really had a wonderful time, they've both been so lovely. Hedwig and I hug and kiss each other cheek-to-cheek with mutual warmth and respect as she whispers to me:

"Please take care of yourself Sarah my love." And I tell her: "I will."

But I don't know if I ever can, I will always be damaged beyond repair.

Andy and I catch another cab back to the Hotel and the meeting with the old German couple, especially Hedwig, has left me in a strange melancholy frame of mind. I don't want sex tonight, I just want Andy to hold me in his arms and to tell me that he loves me but he doesn't do the latter, I'm just left hanging from a rope once again.

I hit the vodka as we change for dinner, pissing myself out of control. This evening I'm wearing my black bodycon mini-dress from AliExpress, my pair of black-suede ankle-boots from Miu Miu and sexy black-lace underwear from Ultimo. My make-up I only touch-up. My perfume is *Poison* by Christian Dior. I'm also wearing my gorgeous silver necklace again.

I only have a light dinner of Red Mullet in a curry sauce followed by a dessert of coconut and passion fruit due to our quite filling lunch earlier. Even so, we still manage to sink 2-bottles of wine between us - German obviously! - on top of all the food.

That night we still don't make love, we just lay there in bed next to each other in the warm and talk. I ask him if he thinks that he and I will end up like Hans and Hedwig in the future when we're their age but I don't get an answer from him, just silence.

***

It's our last full-day in Berlin already and I can't believe how bloody quickly the time has gone. I'm in a slightly better frame of mind this morning, I really don't understand how meeting Hedwig yesterday affected me so much?

I play with Andy's dick and balls and he fondles and squeezes my right-breast. I wank him and he moans with pleasure. He kisses and tongues at my nipples and then pushes me flat onto my back. Spreading my legs wide apart I accept him into my body as his cock slides beautifully and gracefully into my vagina. He starts to fuck me hard as that's how I demand it from him. He plays with my tits as he pokes me and kisses my neck and within a matter of only minutes I feel him cum his jism into my hole, the nasty muck splashing around up inside my box.

I flip over onto my hands and knees and order my love to take me in the rear with my dildo, the 8-inch realistic one from Lovehoney. I use his cum from the bukkake oozing from my fanny, along with some of my split and gob, as lube on my bumhole. I feel the fake knob pushing against me, my orifice resisting at first, as then it parts and burns as it penetrates my love. Andy fucks me slow and deep with it and I almost pass-out as it hits the other side of my womb. He fingers my dirty twat at the same time with his other hand and it's not long before I start to shudder all over and I scream and cum again. The mess from my fanny spits-out over my legs onto the sheets below and I use my right-hand to scoop whatever I can of the detritus up and onto my tongue, swallowing it all completely.

I am out of my mind.

I collapse onto the bed and Andy pulls the dildo out of my bum. I push it back into myself, into my vagina, as I suck and nibble on Andy's stiff cock. I have totally lost control of myself as I wank and eat him. I orgasm before he does and I push the plastic cock further into my body as then he cums at me, squirting his milk down my throat and I love him as much as he loves me.

We're going on a sightseeing tour around Berlin today. I'm wearing a black t-shirt from River Island and the same jeans, jumper, boots and jacket that I had on the other day. My underwear is also in black, a lace set from Figleaves. My make-up is light but at the same time stunning. My perfume is *Kenzo Flower* by Kenzo.

After a late buffet breakfast in the Hotel we catch a taxi - driven by yet another smelly bloody Turk! - over to the tour starting point at Tauentzienstrasse. There's already about 20 or so people waiting here for the trip, mainly fellow English actually, along with some Americans, a few Japanese, French and one German couple. I honestly can't remember the last time I went on a bus, but it must have been at least 20-years ago!

We all climb onboard and sit our arses down to the introduction by the tour-guide. She's as sweet as sweet can be, about 25, blonde, really pretty, and with a nice tight body primed for me to lick and fuck. Her accent makes me melt and I imagine having her naked on my bed with my fingers in her tight German vagina as she cums her love into my face.

She chats-away as we drive around for the next 2-hours, taking-in the sites of beautiful Berlin in Winter - the magnificent Scloss Charlottenburg, the Reichtag with its imposing columns, the lovely and peaceful Tiergarten including the beautiful Englisher Garten, along the edge and over the River Spree, the cold grey and graffitied remains of the old Berlin Wall at Potsdamer Platz, Checkpoint Charlie and other popular tourist traps.

At journey's end the tour guide girl gives me a big beaming smile as we all file past her to exit. She sets my heart on fire and I get an overpowering urge to kiss her full-on the lips right in front of Andy and all the other passengers but I don't of course, I can't. I'm crazy but not that stupid.

My love and I decide to go for a walk around the shops - Andy that is, not the German honey! - just window-shopping. That is until we find a huge department store called the Kaufhaus des Westens that is full of this, that and everything - I'm like a kid in a candy-store! Andy buys me a gorgeous pair of Jimmy Choo Hector 100 peep-toe ankle-boots in black leopard-print that cost's him nearly 900-Euros - madness! The money and power I now have at my disposal is truly amazing, the whole World is my oyster. I go mad in Lacoste, Estee Lauda, Burberry, Dior and all the other super-expensive shops, buying shit that I don't really need or even want but I take it all anyway.

With arms fully-loaded we get another taxi back to the Hotel. The cab driver is a big, fat German guy with no neck who keeps staring at me in the rear-view mirror, obviously obsessed with my stunning beauty - it's not my fault I'm so gorgeous!

Back in our Hotel suite I drown myself in shit from the mini-bar - vodka, gin, whisky (which I hate but drink it anyway), peach schnapps, brandy, cognac and others, as Andy makes a couple of phone-calls in the other room. I strip naked and look out the window over Berlin and the people down below me, they are the very same people that I used to see from my own balcony back home in England. It's the same shit the whole World over.

I go and sit on the sofa and wait for his return. My legs are wide open and I finger and pull on my lips and the look on Andy's face when he sees me makes me giggle like a big soppy girl. There are no words between us as he drops to his knees and starts to lick me and I try to imagine that it's the German tour-guide honey from earlier that's sucking my vagina.

I slap my breasts hard as Andy sticks his tongue and fingers into my minge and I want the pain, I want to hurt myself, I want him to bite my labia and make me bleed, I want him to write the word "CUNT" across my breasts in my own blood.

PLEASE HELP ME.

***

Last night for dinner I had the most gorgeous piece of steak I've ever had in all my days - rare, lightly seasoned, juicy and tasty - with chips, chestnut mushrooms, a side-salad, and German white - beautiful.

Seeing as it was our last evening in Berlin I wore my sexy white strapless criss-cross dress from BandageDressesOutlet and my white suede open-toe ankle-boots from Polyvore. I didn't bother with any underwear either. My perfume was *Mademoiselle* by Coco Chanel. I also wore my lovely silver necklace to finish-off my look.

As our flight back to England isn't until 7pm this evening, we're off to Winterwelt at the Potsdamer Platz until about lunchtime, which should give us plenty of time to get to the airport to check-in later.

Today I'm wearing my black low-cut v-neck jumper from Bluefly, my pail-blue stonewash jeans from BooHoo, and my black suede ankle-boots from Miu Miu. My underwear is in white lace from Figleaves. My make-up is super-sharp featuring coal-black eyeshadow for a nasty look along with light-purple lipstick. My perfume is *Poison* by Christian Dior. As it's obviously still bloody freezing outside, I'm wearing my black bomber jacket from Jacketvests as well.

We catch one of the yellow trams for the short run down to Market Squire and it's just like stepping back in time being on one of these things as it rattles and shakes its way along the tracked road! The Potsdamer Platz Market is something else again with an amazing array of stalls, carol-singers, and a really funny Bavarian Oompah-band that has me in stitches as it features these big fat guys in traditional German dress with massive moustaches all in different shapes, sizes and colours. Unbelievably, the market also features a toboggan run, supposedly the largest mobile run in the whole of Europe! There's also a curling rink and an open-air ice rink that I beg Andy to take me on. I hug and kiss him as we swap our footwear for the skating-boots and venture out onto its slippery surface, although no-sooner do I put my foot on the ice I fall arse-over-tit straight away, landing on my bum with a thud - shit! We laugh as my man helps me back onto my blades, even though that really did fucking hurt. We join the throng of the other skaters and slide-along together hand-in-hand as we wizz around in circuit.

For lunch we find another sausage stall similar to the one from the other day and have a huge Bratwurst banger in a roll each with fried onions, sauerkraut, that funny mustard again and tomato sauce. We grab a coffee each and then go and watch and laugh at the people on the snow-tube scare themselves stupid.

"Thank you for this Andy." I whisper to him - my love.

"That's okay, they're lovely aren't they?" He says back.

"No, I don't mean the sausages, I mean for everything, for bringing me here and for all the gifts and introducing me to Hans and Hedwig and everything."

"There's no need to thank me Sarah, I wanted you to come because I love you."

Did you hear that? Did you hear what he just said to me? It's hardly surprising really is it, I mean, who in their right mind wouldn't love me?

I go to him and kiss his mouth and tell him:

"I love you to." Even though I have a mouthful of German sausage in my gob and saucy lips!

We take a slow wander around the market stalls, they selling everything from baked apples with chocolate icing, sweets galore, wicker baskets, clay pots and candlesticks and all manner of things. We eyeball all the weird and wonderful things around us as the band and the singers provide our background entertainment. I buy a little model figurine of the Brandenburg Gate, a really nasty cheap tacky one, as something to always remember our Christmas in Berlin together.

Andy hails us a taxi for the ride over to another museum on Klingelhoferstrasse, the ultra-modern Bauhaus-Archiv. It's a typical German contemporary building in design, all clean and crisp with pure white lines and I could quite easily imagine living in a building like this myself - it is heaven. On display inside is an array of beautiful artefacts straight out of the Bauhaus history books - futuristic chrome chairs, lamps and teapots from the 1920's and "30's, as well as period photographs from their glory days. In the museum shop I treat myself to a set of chrome Bauhaus salt and pepper shakers and a bold and striking reproduction poster by Joost Schmidt for the 1923 Bauhaus exhibition that I just know is going to look fantastic framed and hung up against the pure white background in the hallway. I fall deeply in love with it at first glance.

From there we take a tram back to the Hotel and we laugh with each other as it rattles-along on its tracks. It's been such a perfect day and I couldn't wish for anything more.

In the warmth of our bedroom I position my naked self leaning over onto the firm mattress. Andy is behind me and I feel the touch of his knob upon my labia and I pant with anticipation of him entering my body. He suddenly pushes into me and I feel my vagina parting to accept his length and I squeal with pleasure and pain as he starts to bang-away at me. I order him to: "Fuck me harder" as my tits start to wobble and sway to themselves below me and my breathing becomes disjointed. He groans as he cums into me and I scream as I orgasm to meet him in Heaven.

As he removes himself from me I turn and drop to my knees and take his cock into my mouth. I tongue at the remains of his seed, it turning to string as it mixes with my saliva and I swallow it down my throat. I wank him empty as I lick his testicles and he groans and moans and calls me a "Little bitch" and a "Fucking dirty cow" and a "Bloody whore" and I egg him on to give me more verbal abuse and I love it and I wank myself.

We shower together and kiss and wash-away our sex and then redress in readiness for the flight back home to England. I'm wearing a black Boyfriend shirt from ASOS, my black short miniskirt from New Look along with black tights from Pretty Poly and my black suede open-toe platform court-shoes from

Polyvore. My underwear is also in black, a lace set including suspender-belt from Figleaves. My make-up and hair are both done as per its usual self and features dark-grey eyeshadow and pale-red lipstick. My perfume is *Poison* by Christian Dior. Just for the outside I'm also wearing my black leather jacket, the second-hand biker-chick one with all the patches and badges on.

Our packing only takes the both of us less than half-an-hour and is collected by the typically super-efficient and friendly German staff and is taken out to our awaiting taxi.

We both say "Goodbye" to our lovely suite and I'm really sad at having to leave it. Whatever it takes I will be back here again one day, no matter what happens. We thank all the Hotel staff for looking after us so well, and it's not without a few tears of sadness that we exit the Hotel Adlon and head off to the airport. Our taxi-driver is another bloody stinking Turk.

* * *

We don't get back home to Foxhill until gone 10pm that night. There was some sort-of dispute at Gatwick that caused the delay - probably bloody union related shit? - but at least we're now back through the front-door.

We're greeted in the hallway by Kate and Eva, it's so lovely to see them both, especially my beautiful little girl and I hug and kiss her with all my heart as she purrs-away, I've missed her so much it hurts.

Andy and I both ate on the plane over but even so I'm still a little bit peckish. I go and make us all a sandwich each and a good old-fashioned cup of tea, as only us English can make. Foreigners never seem to do it right somehow?

The 4 of us chill-out in the lounge with Eva curling-up on my lap with a thousand purrs. We tell Kate of our wonderful trip - the glorious Hotel, the food, the beer, the sausages, Hans and Hedwig, the snow, all the beautiful places and buildings we've seen, the markets, the Oompar-band, the bruise on my bum, the art gallery, the River Spree, the Wall, the gorgeous watch that Andy bought me, the shoes, the funny trams and everything.

We leave the unpacking to tomorrow as we're both too bloody tired to do it now, personally I'm absolutely knackered!

***

I lay in bed until 10.25am the following morning. We didn't make love last night, just straight to bed to sleep and dream. I nodded-off to the memories of Hans and Hedwig and how her persona flooded my brain with a wave of calm serenity.

After a very late breakfast, Andy and I kiss and hug and say our "Goodbyes" and "Thank you's" to Kate for looking after the house and my beautiful Eva. I'm so glad that we've made-up and sorted out our differences - to a large degree anyway. Hopefully a new chapter will begin now in both our lives, whatever that may be?

I have to keep pushing.

Why should I stop?

16

This is the end

You will never guess in a million-years as to where or what I'm doing right now?

Go on, have a guess?

No, I'm not in Heaven, or Hell for that matter, or in jail as some of you are probably thinking? Or in Hospital again either - shame on you for even thinking such things!

I'm actually in Nice, in the South of France, at Andy's private villa. Yes, that's right, you heard me, and I'm sunning myself whilst completely naked and without a fucking care in the whole rotten World that it is.

I'm laying sanguine on one of the sun-loungers on the stone terrace by the swimming pool, supping on ice-cold Champagne of the finest quality that money can buy - Krug Grande Cuvee - no crap with this girl, not any more! I'm taking the rest of my life off!

So there you are, didn't see that one coming did you?

We've actually been out here for nearly a week now and we're staying for the next 2-months or so. Plus Andy has some business to attend to in town, that of course leaving me free to do whatever I fucking want - which is not a lot!

And so here I am, crazy, psychotic, Sarah Knowles from South London, in paradise. This time I really am a queen. This time I really have made it. Everything has come up (cum up!) Sarah.

I guess I should also tell you that Andy and I have got married! - 2-weeks ago in fact - in a small and quiet private registry-office in Chichester, so we're treating this break away as our honeymoon. I have devoted my heart and soul to him. Andy proposed to me on New Years day, not long after we returned from our Christmas break away in Berlin. It's hard to believe that was over 3-months ago now. The older I get the faster time seems to fly!

Andy bought me the most beautiful ring on Planet Earth, a bloody-great rock of a diamond - from Tiffany's in London no less. No crap with him either! I wear it all the time of course as its so gorgeous, right next to the one that Amanda gave me for our wedding in Vegas. I don't see why I shouldn't wear both, the fact that I've been married twice - once to another woman and now Andy - has got fuck-all to do with anyone so there!

It's completely mad how things have turned around, this time last year I had been to Las Vegas to get married to my girlfriend and was also trying hold down my job at that shithole insurance company in Horsham. I don't miss working at all, I'd always hated it right from day-1 anyway and I'm glad I'll never have to do it ever again. Fortunately that crap doesn't apply to me any more so why should I degrade myself with any of that bollocks? I find any notions of working ever again completely untenable, they're just not in my mind any more. I'd rather drown in shit than go back to all that again. So now look at me, I'm having the time of my life and I've never felt so at peace. I literally do not have a fucking care in the World. Although I do worry about leaving Eva at home alone, I miss her so much. Our neighbour - dear old Mrs. DeAngelis - has agreed to pop around and feed her and give her cuddles, bless her. I must remember to get her something nice as a "Thank you."

As I've already said, we're out here for the next couple of months or so and then we have to get back to England in order to prepare for a big car show at Goodwood, just down the road from where we live - I think Andy said it was called the "Festival of Speed" or something like that? - in June as Andy is showing 3-cars there, the Lotus F1 car, the Ford

GT40, and the Willys Coupé Gasser. I'll also be there of course, it will be something different to do and hopefully it should be a bit of a laugh. Andy says that it's a pretty big do so bring it on!

I also should tell you that my sister Kate and I are not on speaking terms once again. Would you believe that stupid bitch has got herself involved with a bloody Indian guy! Not only that, he's nearly twice her age, divorced and with 3-kids for fucks sake! I know it's her own life and all that crap but come on, that's taking the fucking piss.

The blazing rays from the Sun beat down on my beautiful skin. I rub myself all over - and I mean "all over!" - with some more high-factor sunblock to protect myself. Obviously I'd like a nice all-over tan but I also don't want to be burnt to a bloody crisp either!

It's in stark contrast to the weather we left behind in England, it was terrible, it had been pissing-down for days on end. Anyway, I don't want to depress myself by thinking about that old crap, I'm going to bloody enjoy myself come what may.

I'm so happy I'm like a dog with 2-tails!

I take a couple more sips of the chilled Champagne and head down to the far-end of the swimming pool. One graceful spring off the diving-board and in I go with a resounding splash. It wasn't often that I had much of a chance to swim naked - especially in public places, rules being rules such as they are - and the water feels fantastically sensual as I glide through and across its fluidity, it touching and penetrating every crevice of my beautiful naked body. I float on its gently waving surface with the Sun warming me as I lay there bobbing-about whilst dreaming of money and power and freedom and sex.

After a good half-an-hour of lazing I step out and start to dry myself off in the heat. I rub my perfect body gently all over and I'm so in love with myself I cannot explain it to you fully. I drop down onto my hands and knees and fondle my breasts and then my vagina, masturbating it with 2-fingers. Using my thumb on my clit I fuck myself on the patio and bring myself to my sexual crescendo as I scream and pant as I cum and continue to wank. I am done.

After wiping-up the mess with the towel I down a couple more mouthfuls of Champagne straight from the bottle and then go inside to change. Andy's villa - our villa - is so beautiful, I just love it to bits. It's a lot smaller than our house back home in England of course, there being only 4-bedrooms, and the layout is totally different. The house is built in a typically French-style but with a modern twist, the redesign being done by Andy himself when he bought it some 5-years ago. Everything is in white, the smooth plastered walls, the marble floors, the patio area, the swimming pool, everything. There's also a big double-garage to one side, set away and not joined to the house. Of course, to cope with the typical South of France heat, the villa is fully air-conditioned.

The gardens that surround the property are truly magnificent - featuring palm trees, big spiky bushes and exotic flowers, all set in almost 6-acres of land - it is totally gorgeous. Naturally Andy has to engage a local company to maintain the upkeep of the garden as his time out here is limited by his car dealings and other commitments - like me now for instance!

Inside the villa is also furnished in typical French-style, again though with Andy's twist, with all the sofas, chaise lounge and chairs all covered in buttoned white leather. The kitchen is very modern - just like the one in our house back in Foxhill - with expensive super-efficient German equipment and clean straight lines.

I make my way to our bedroom - itself, another example of pure French elegance - to get dressed, as I'm going out for lunch with myself today. I put on

a gorgeous white bodycon dress that Andy bought for me from Christian Lacroix, and my pair of open-toe white ankle-boots from Polyvore. My underwear is in sexy-white lace from Figleaves and my perfume is No.5 by Chanel. My leather clutch-bag is also in white from Gucci. My hair and make-up I do to my usual high standard, featuring a white butterfly-clip my hair along with deep-purple eyeshadow and pale-pink lipstick on the beautiful canvas that is my face.

Andy has used his French-based car for his trip out of town, a fantastic French-registered left-hand drive Jaguar F-Type V8 S Roadster in red that goes as good as it sounds. This of course means I get to use the Aston for my short blast into down-town Nice. I fire her up and tear-off down the road like a scalded cat, hitting the centre of town after only 20-minutes at the most.

It's pretty busy here already - even for this time of the year - but I still manage to park easily enough outside one of the many expensive small restaurants dotted around Nice, parking between a yellow Ferrari and a white Rolls. I get the usual stares from all the stuck-up rich bitches as they munch-away on their lettuces and sip their mineral waters but I pay no real attention to them. Anyone can spot them a mile off, they're all in their 50's and 60's and all desperately trying to look 25 again - and failing! - with their fake tans (why they all have fake tans with this weather I'll never understand?), fake teeth, rigid Botox faces and plastic breasts and all calling each other "Darling" and all that shit. I will never be like them, I may be rich now but I'll never be stuck-up.

Even though I'm probably already over the limit from the Champagne this morning, I still order myself a lager with a neat vodka chaser, much to the disgust of the snobby old bags all around me but I laugh in their faces - you can take the girl out of South London but you can't take South London out of the girl! - to go along with my lunch of salmon, pasta, green beans, tomatoes and the ubiquitous lettuce. The food is beautiful though and it slides down lovely.

I finish off my vodka whilst I sit there listening to all the useless crap coming out of my fellow diners gobs, all bitching about their useless husbands and so-called "friends" and who said what to whom and blah blah blah blah fucking blah - get a fucking life why don't they? I'd hate to end up like these stuck-up cows.

I am not, and never will be, a trophy-wife to anyone. I didn't even take Andy's surname - it's Clark by the way! - when we got married. I have to retain a certain amount if independence or I will cease to exist, and that is unimaginable.

***

"Are you okay? You don't seem quite yourself today?" I question him.

"Yeah, I'm okay. I'm just tired that's all." He says.

"Do you wanna get pissed and fool around?"

Andy sniggers at my question and kisses me on the cheek but we don't drink or have sex, we just cuddle and talk about our day ahead. We decide to just go into Nice for lunch - again - and take it from there, nothing strenuous.

I'm wearing a red sleeveless cotton blouse from Hugo Boss, a white leather above-the-knee skirt from French Connection and my white suede open-toe ankle-boots again from Polyvore. I'm not wearing any underwear at all. I have a nasty-look to my make-up today with coal-black eyeshadow, heavy blusher to accentuate my cheekbones and deep-red lipstick as that's the way it is. I've done my hair as per usual and I look killer. My clutch-bag is in red leather from Prada - another prezzie from my man.

We take the Jag out today and blast-off with the top down - naturally - and head into town. It's another gloriously beautiful sunny day and the wind as we rush-along billows in my face and hair.

We park along the main Promenade des Anglais beach-front road and head off to the shops. We walk along hand-in-hand as we window-shop at all the beautiful things that I want and deserve. I buy more shoes - what a surprise! - clothes and yet another clutch-bag, a white-grain leather one from Burberry that costs Andy over one-thousand fucking Euros - WHAT! We have lunch at a posh eatery full of yet more snobs, none of whom have ever done an honest days work in their sad fucking insulated lives. We both order courgette flowers stuffed with veal that tastes like pure heaven and I could have easily have eaten Andy's lunch as well as my own as its so glorious! I down 3-large neat vodka's with my food while Andy only has water. I've noticed he doesn't seem to drink much alcohol recently for some reason and when I question him about it he just pooh-pooh's me. We natter and laugh about crap and our fellow dinners and then take another short stroll along the beach-front in the sun before we head for home.

After half-an-hour or so of walking along, kicking sand and mucking about by the waters edge and having fun, we sprint back to the villa at unabated speed. Inside we kiss and I run my hand between Andy's legs and touch his cock but once again I get nowhere. He tells me that he needs to go and lay down and rest and that he has to make an important phone-call to one of his business clients in Switzerland and so I reluctantly have to let him go.

I strip naked before him in the bedroom - it seemingly having no effect on him - and then head back outside to the pool. I take a run and jump into the water, plunging almost down to the bottom. The following couple of hours go quickly as I spend the time just sodding-about by myself, doing my own thing. I sink a couple of bottles of lager on the patio as I lounge-around naked on one of the Sun-chairs and think of my life and how its changed completely in just a short time. Thinking back, its all been pretty shit really, interspersed with flashes of pleasure, and they've been all to few and far between. I think of all the stupid idiots that I've had to put up with over the years, particularly all that lot at my previous company. Fortunately I've not had any contact with any of them - not even little Greek Angie - and why should I, they're nothing to me and they can all go to Hell.

So much has happened I don't know how I've coped with it, even though I do really, and so do you. I go and grab another lager from the fridge in the kitchen.

Andy and I spend a quiet evening together watching an old film on the TV as I lay there, wrapped in the arms of my man.

An hour or so later I notice him actually falling asleep on me before the film has even ended. When it does eventually finish, I have extract myself from his embrace, turn the TV off, go and lock up the house, and then head off to bed - alone. I need an early night anyway as it looks as though tomorrow is going to be a long day as we're off to Monte Carlo so we're going to make a reasonably early start.

In bed I touch my vagina and my breasts, although for some peculiar reason I back-off and don't push myself to climax. I want Andy to do that but he's not with me, he's downstairs asleep on the sofa instead of being here with me in our bed together, like the husband and wife we are - or dare I say it, should be?

***

We have tea and toast for breakfast at poolside, with lashings of marmalade and freshly squeezed orange juice. It's another gorgeous morning as we sit out on the patio, a perfect day for our trip to Monaco, the playground of the super-rich.

I'm wearing a beautiful red cotton mini-dress from DHGate along with my tan-coloured suede ankle-boots from AliExpress. As the dress is so tight and firm I'm not going to wear a bra today, my only underwear being red-lace knickers from Ultimo. My make-up is real killer, featuring super-sharp cheekbones and coal-black and silver-grey eyeshadow along with cherry-red lipstick. My hair is done to its usual high-standard with a red bow as a tie. My perfume is *Poison* by Christian Dior whilst my clutch-bag is my Prada red-leather one.

We're taking the Jag today and I'm driving - so that should be a laugh! I fire-up the engine and she bursts into life with a throaty roar from the exhausts and off we go. We take the coastal road that leads East from Nice along the Avenue Raymond Poincare, passing through the beautiful Villefranche-sur-Mer, Beaulieu-sur-Mer and Cap-d'Ail and then directly into Monaco. I power the car around the twisty narrow road that leads into the

Principality and we laugh and joke as I push the Jag to its limit and beyond, although the actual streets around the town itself are tight and crowded and we have to creep-along at snails-pace. The harbour is equally packed with yachts, all ranging in size from medium to bloody enormous, some of them being ships really, mainly belonging to stinking uber-rich Arabs and of course the obligatory fucking Russian scum. Andy has been here loads of times before and so knows several little places to park the car out of the way, slightly further inland, so that's what we do.

Once settled into our spot, we wander around the super-expensive and exclusive shops, mingling with all the other beautiful people as we window-shop.

Along by the harbour we gaze in wonder at the vast array of boats and their occupants, all sitting there in the heady Sun supping on the finest Champagne. The men, most of them being old and unattractive - like the saying goes: "There's no such thing as an ugly millionaire" - all undress me with their eyes as we walk by, whilst the women - mainly young things a good 5 to 10-years younger than I am - gorp at me and my natural beauty. I have no jealousy towards them, they don't have anything I want. They're all mostly fake anyway, in fact I don't think I've yet seen a real pair of tits in all the time we've been out here! I do spot one particular little honey though, laying there topless on the deck of one of the larger medium-sized yachts. She's in her early-20's with short blonde hair, a gorgeous face and a really tight slim body. My heartbeat starts to race as I get the sudden urge to climb aboard and 69 her right here and now, to stick my fingers and my tongue into her sweet little pussy and drink her love. I long for the taste of another woman again but I can't cheat on Andy, not after everything he's given and done for me, I just can't, even though I desperately want to.

We stop for lunch at a little cafe-bar, Andy ordering us a latte" each - in perfect French of course! - and we while-away the time talking about life, love, cars, the surrounding boats and the future.

Into the afternoon we carry-on wandering around the shops and take-in some more of the harbour. Andy buys me an absolutely beautiful Hermes Jige clutch-bag in orange - to match my car of course! - from another exclusive shop, although it costs him a whopping 2,300-Euros - bloody Hell!

He also wants to have a wander around a small car museum located at Terrasses de Fontvielle so that's where we head to next. I don't really mind of course, being a bit of a petrol-head myself it doesn't bother me like it would most other women. The museum itself is beautifully laid-out and features road-cars as well as racing stuff. There's nearly 100-cars in total on display and each one is restored to fantastic condition - Formula 1 cars, prototypes, beautiful classic road-cars from the 1920's and 30's, sportscars and others - it's a car-lovers dream and I'm in love with them all and I cry at their beauty.

Further in town we have lunch at a classy eatery, with Andy ordering us fried vegetable ravioli that tastes simply divine, and a bottle of chilled Champagne to wash it down with. The restaurant is full of yet more idle-rich snobby bitches. I really can't fucking stand them, they make the hairs on the back of my neck stand to attention with rage. I'd like to sentence the whole bloody lot of them to 6-months hard-labour breaking rocks, they wouldn't be so bloody smug after that!

I have to say that by now I'm getting a little bored with my surroundings. It's all very high-class and sophisticated and all that, but I feel like a fish out of water. I'm a working-class girl as I've said before and that will never change, and neither do I want it to, regardless of all Andy's money. I certainly look the part though - in fact I haven't seen one girl here that could beat me in the beauty stakes - but this place is just not my thing. It's all fake. None of it is real. Who are these people? What do they do? They have no life. They're not even alive, not one of them.

We wander back to the car to find a couple of guys - Latin-types, probably Italian or something like that, and both in their late-20's I would guess - standing there admiring the Jag. They don't say anything to us and just stand and stare - at me mainly! - and jabber-away to each other in their fast-talking language. I throw them a quick smile and a knowing flash with my eyes, wetting my appetite for carnal love, and they suddenly burst into yet more feverish yacking.

Men, aren't they funny creatures? We can control them totally just by using our expressions and our body language. They're just like puppets.

The journey back to the villa is considerably easier and quicker, for some reason there being less traffic now in early-evening. I nail the Jag along a fast straight stretch of road and the supercharged 5.0-litre V8 growls deeply as we accelerate.

By the time we get home it's gone 6pm and I guess all in all it's been a lovely day,

even though being surrounded by all those idle rich bitches made me feel like puking.

I take Andy's hand and lead him out the back of the villa to the patio area. We've both removed each others clothes in the house and we stand by the pool and kiss passionately and embrace.

I am so lucky. How many other women are in a similar position to me right now? I have love, money, no need to work ever again, 2-beautiful houses, a garage full of cars at my disposal, my gorgeous cat Eva, all the clothes and shoes any girl could want, and above all I still retain most of my precious freedom. I am as rare as hens-teeth! Fate has dealt me a good hand this time around and I'm not going to let go easily.

I take all the apples from the tree.

I take all the honey from the pot.

I lay back on the sun-lounger and spread my legs as wide apart as they will go. I feel Andy's breath on my vagina as he closes in on me and the anticipation of his oral pleasuring makes my blood pump to overload and my head start to spin. I dream of the semi-naked blonde girl laying on the deck of that yacht earlier and that it's her that's going down on me. The first lick sends me into orbit and I spaz and twist and fling my arms around in reaction. I shudder as I feel fingers pulling my lips apart and then more tongue, playing with my clit. I pant and moan and the scream as I cum and I can feel my juice squirting out from within my body and I love it. I love my cum.

The punishment continues as Andy pushes his rigid cock within me and I wince as it fills my love-tube. He pokes-away at me as we both moan in unison at our love. He starts to speed-up as he reaches his crescendo and moans loudly as he ejaculates his milk inside me.

We both laugh and kiss and hug one-another. I say to him: "I love you" and he echoes my declaration. Hand on heart I do love him but I fear that's it's not enough - I WANT MORE - I want the little blonde girl and the 2-Italian guys from today to all fuck me at the same time right here and now and push me over the edge but my commitment to my husband forbids me. It's gnawing-away inside of me and I hate it. I hate not being totally 100% free. The fear of having my independence completely annihilated haunts me like death itself.

***

I've been stuck at the villa on my own for the past 3-days now as Andy had to fly off to Switzerland on business or something, so I've been kicking my heals for the duration - it's yet another lost weekend. At least he's due back late tonight so hopefully we can then resume our honeymoon.

I've decided I'm not spending another day bored out of my bloody skull so I'm going to take the Jag out for a spin somewhere, I don't know where, I'll just see wherever it takes me.

The sky is completely cloudless and the air is really hot and humid as I pull out of the drive and floor the gas. Today I'm wearing a blue sequin burlesque corset from CorsetCity, my white leather skirt from French Connection and nothing else - no underwear at all as I don't fucking feel like it or need to. On my feet are my pair of white suede open-toe ankle-boots from

Polyvore, whilst my perfume is *Luxe* by Avon. My hair and make-up are as per usual, featuring silver-blue eyeshadow once again as this has become the norm recently for some obscure reason.

I'm heading North from Nice along the twisty M19, not for any particular purpose, it's just because I have nowhere else to go. No sooner do I get going quickly I have one of those big fat Rolls-Royce's in front of me - one of those enormous ones that's built like a tank that takes up the whole bloody road - doing about 50. I drop the Jag down a gear and nail the fat Roller going into a hairpin bend on the wrong side of the road. The driver - some old tosser of about 95 - and his misses, both stare at me in disgust as I pass them but I just laugh in their faces - bloody snobs.

I power the car through Saint-Andre-de-la-Roche, Falicon and La Clue and then turn off several klicks later where I find myself in a sleepy little village in the middle of nowhere, so I decide to stop here and have a nose around. It's an amazing little village, there is literally nothing here. But that's what I want, after all the fake glamour of Nice and Monaco this is a welcome relief. All the locals seem as ancient as the buildings, all old and crusty and dishevelled and in desperate need of repair! But that's the way it is and should be, these places need to exist in order for outsiders like myself to be able to experience and appreciate the other side of life, to get back to reality.

There only seems to be one shop in the whole town, a kind-of grocery / store / coffee shop. I sit my bum down at one of the crappy old rusty metal tables outside and try to order a coffee and a croissant in my best pidgin-French from the little old lady serving - she must be 104-years old if she's a day! She's small and round with the sweetest little round wrinkled face on Earth - I love her to bits!

There's also a line of really old guys sitting on a broken wall by the side of the shop, at least half-a-dozen or so of them, all obviously talking about me and the car as I sip my drink and munch-away. I don't mind of course, they're all harmless old codgers just living out the rest of their days in peace with one another, and "good-luck" to them. If they want to look at my breasts and my bum and my beautiful long legs then I'm not going to stop them.

Some 30-minutes later and with my light lunch finished, I stroll pass the old guys and bit them "Au Revoir", giving them a little girlie wave and making sure they all get a good look at my body as I do so. I fire-up the Jag and head back to the villa, I don't want to be late as Andy is due back tonight and I don't want any crap in my way between now and then spoiling my day.

I play and have fun with the car as I head home, burning-off anyone who gets in my fucking way with the beautiful power of the Jag - snobs, arseholes, vans and crap.

It's just gone 4pm when I drive through the electric gates of the villa. Once inside I go for a quick pee and then strip naked in the coolness of the air-conditioned bedroom, flinging my clothes wherever. Back in the living-room I down a couple of neat gins and a large vodka and then head outside into the heat for a dip in the pool. The water feels so lovely against my naked body and I swim a couple of lengths in pure pleasure of its touch. The alcohol soon takes a grip of me in the Sun and I begin to lose focus, not in an unconscious way, but just enough to take the edge off of my inherent sharp attitude. I go and collect one of the dildo's I brought with me - the ribbed glass one from Lovehoney - as I never go anywhere without one, along with some lube and my vibrating love-egg - also from Lovehoney, and then return to poolside. I suck on the dildo lengthways as I finger my vagina and I quickly and easily begin to love myself. I lube my anus with 2-fingers and then slowly push the phallus into my rear, it stinging and biting me at first but once it's in about 10-centimetres or so it feels so fucking good. I wank it in and out of my bum as I simultaneously insert 3-fingers into my pussy. My eyes start to roll back into my head as I fuck myself harder and harder. I try to push my whole hand into myself but for some reason it just won't go in, not even when I really force it, my hole just won't open up fully to let myself in.

Super-annoyed, I click-on my love-egg and push that into myself, it buzzing and vibrating-away in my vagina but the frustration builds within me at my failure and so I smash myself with more vodka and then throw myself down onto the floor with a thud. I reinsert the dildo into my bum whilst on all fours and push it in further than before, more than I've ever done. It hurts like fucking Hell and I slap and pull at my pussy-lips hard. I cum as I wank my clit with my whole hand and the dildo pops out of my bum with a funny squelchy-sound as my internal muscles contract themselves. I squeeze out my egg and it drops to the floor, it still whirring-away to itself and I kick it away, silencing the little fucker.

My self-pleasuring has been a complete failure and back in the villa I down a large swig of gin straight from the bottle to compensate but I fail yet again. I collapse onto the sofa semi-conscious and I hate myself. I want to die and never return. I want to fuck and fuck-off and shit cum on myself for being a cunt and a slag and a fucking whore and this is the end of everything.

***

It's 10pm when Andy finally walks through the door. He sent me a text from Geneva airport saying that he would get a taxi home rather have me come and pick him up from the Airport Nice Cote d'Azur - why?

Obviously I've cleaned all my mess up from earlier, as well as myself, and I greet him at the door wearing just my black pure-silk mini-robe from LilySilk covering my perfect body. We hug and kiss but he seems somehow distant from me, like he's here but not really here?

Terrible thoughts race through my mind at 200-miles-an-hour that maybe he has another girl and is cheating on me with her. If it's true I will kill them both and then myself.

What is wrong? I can tell that there's something up but when I quiz him he just dismisses me with a wave of his hand. Why can't he tell me? What has gone wrong? What have I done? Am I too demanding?

In the bedroom I don't even attempt to initiate sex. We hug and kiss as we lay next to each other naked but that's it, nothing more - again.

***

Unfortunately - and very untypically for this time of the year - it's a bit cloudy and dull outside today. Even so we're sill going out, to the art museum in town, the Le Musee" D'Art Moderne et D'Art Contemporain at Place Yves Klein. Andy has never been there himself either so this will be a first for the both of us.

Today I'm wearing a beautiful pale-blue wrap-around mini-dress from Krisztina Williams and my old pair of blue suede Lola platform court-shoes that are knocking-on a bit now - nearly 2-years old, maybe more! I can't get rid of them, we've been through too much together - poor old shoes. My underwear is in white lace from Agent Provocateur and my perfume is *Poison* by Christian Dior. My clutch-bag is a gorgeous pure-white leather one from Prada, another prezzie from Andy that cost him an arm-and-a-leg - oh well!

Because of the uncertainty of the weather, I'm also wearing a white woollen tasselled poncho from Peter Hahn. We're also taking the Aston today for the same reason.

The Nice art museum is a weird looking place, although a very contemporary building, and almost monolithic in its appearance, consisting of 2-square towers flaking a glass central section where the entrance is located. Thankfully there's not too many people here as I really hate crowds, although the main cause of concern is a large group of French students all jabbering-away talking shit and fiddling with their bloody mobile-phones instead of looking at the beautiful art on display. Every one of them is a pain in the arse.

Andy and I wander around hand-in-hand at our leisure, taking-in all the different types of work, mainly all contemporary modern pieces. The main feature artist is the works of Yves Klein himself and I get won-over by his crazy but beautiful blue paintings. Another artist I'm also taken by is the German sculptor Joseph Beuys, even though some of his work is a bit over my head to say the least! The only ones that really grab me though are the works by American artists Roy Lichtenstein and Andy Warhol with their "Pop Art" paintings. As an aesthete, I lose myself in the many varied visions before me and I start to hallucinate from all the bright colours and images penetrating my brain. I begin to feel so chilled that my heart seemingly slows to only one beat per-minute as time and everything around me winds-down to slow motion. What can be happening? What does my Guardian Angel want from me now? Is it a warning from the other side? Or is it just the effects of the several large vodkas I've already consumed this morning before we left the villa? I don't know and I don't fucking care a cunt.

We take lunch at another local restaurant, nothing fancy and only light - Salmon en Croute which tastes like pure Heaven, along with a latte" each - and we sit and chat about art, the meaning of life and other stuff. Andy once again seems a little distant and his conversation somewhat evasive.

I want to get pissed and fuck him right here and now in front of our fellow diners but this doesn't happen of course, I just sit here like a fucking lemon as my mind destroys itself. I think of Eva and I want to go home. I miss her so much, she is my whole World at the moment. I know it won't be long now before I see her again, our 2-months in Nice is nearly up and we only have just over a week to go before the long drive back to England.

Neither of us say one single solitary word to one another during the trip back to the villa and the silence is deafening.

It's only the roar from the Aston's exhausts that is keeping me from putting my hands around Andy's neck and strangulating any kind of answer from him. What the fuck am I going to do? This debacle is driving me mad.

***

It's only 4-days to go now before we head back to England. We have to get back then as the 3-cars Andy's exhibiting at Goodwood need to be prepped and primed for the show, although the Lotus Formula 1 car has already been sorted by a friend of his and is therefore ready to go. Andy isn't driving the car at the event though - something to do with insurance reasons so he tells me - so someone else is taking the wheel. I can't wait to see and here it go, it must sound amazing? The GT40 and the Willys are only on static display so there's no real problem with them, again to be handled by another of Andy's car friends.

It's late - gone midnight - and we're in our bedroom fucking. I'm sitting on the floor wanking my vagina with one-hand and squeezing my tits with the other as Andy is fucking my mouth. I gag and choke as he slides his cock in and out of my face and it's only a matter of a couple of minutes before he moans and cums and shoots his sperm down my throat. I splutter as his jelly trickles down my pipe and I use my tongue and teeth on his shaft to empty him.

I reposition myself on the bed on all fours and tell him to: "Lick my pussy." His tongue on my vagina feels wonderful and I sigh and moan and shudder as I cum my honey on him. He pants breathlessly as I do - more so than usual I notice - but continues to lick-away at me nevertheless. We both collapse onto the bed and hold one another tightly and laugh and kiss. I can taste the sweetness of my pussy on his lips and I kiss him harder as I want to sense my own love.

I play with his cock and balls, desperately trying to pump it back to hard but he cries enough and grabs my hand to stop me.

"What's wrong?" I question him.

"Nothing. I'm just tired that's all."

"You're always tired these days. Why won't you let me pleasure you?"

"Sarah, I'm tired. Just leave it will you, please."

He gets up and goes into the en-suite bathroom to pee and wash himself. I follow him and do the same and I take his cock into my hand as he lathers himself up, in some sort-of attempt to resurrect his meat. He allows me to wash him but nothing else happens - there is no wood.

We fall asleep in silence once again and I dream of Amanda and how I let her down so badly and how bloody stupid I've been. Why was I so stupid?

For some reason I then start to think of all those idiots I used to work with, not just the ones at the last place in Horsham but all of them, right from my very first job onwards.

Eventually I nod-off and then I'm gone, away with the fairies and yet more dreams of love, hate, sex, shit and death.

***

I'm woken at 2.30am by Andy getting out of bed and going to the bathroom. He's in there for ages but I don't call out to him or get out of bed or anything, I just lay there half-asleep, listening to his every move. Eventually he climbs back into bed with me, slowly, and I drift-away and dream of my life and wonder where the fuck it's going to go next?

***

The Sun shines in through the bedroom windows and wakes me with a start and I'm sure I can hear a woman's voice calling out to me. It's Mum's voice, as clear as day, calling my name but it can't be, that's bloody stupid, as well as impossible. I check my watch on the bedside table and it's only 7.10am. I turn over and put my right-arm over Andy's waist but he doesn't respond.

He feels a little cold so I rub his body to try to get some sort-of reaction from him but there is none. There is nothing. I sit up and shake his shoulder but still I get no response. What the fuck is happening now? I shout at him to wake up and I hit him on the arm and shake him harder but still there is nothing - there is no response at all. I roll him over to face me and I scream at the expression on his face - he is dead.

I get a sudden flash of the images of both Mum and baby Abigail laying on the slab before me and their death-masks burning into me and here I am once again - faced with yet more of the same horror and I am lost and found in a different state of being.

I want to touch him, to make him come alive. I want to touch his dick and make him hard for me but none of this is ever going to happen ever again. Slowly I climb off the bed backwards and stand there staring at him in shock laying there peacefully in bed. The whole room - even that of myself - is frozen in time. Nothing moves and how can it?

Why is he dead?

Was it our sex yesterday that has done this?

Did I kill him with my love?

Did I kill him with my fuck?

I have to do something. I can't stand here stark-naked and rooted to the spot forever. I don't even know the number for the emergency services so I can't ring them. Even if I did I can't bloody speak French so how will they know what I'm on about? They probably do all speak English anyway but that's academic without knowing the fucking number.

The neighbours, that's the answer, the French couple next door. They can help me can't they, they must be able to? I have no choice, everything is like a dream and this cannot be real. Of course it can, this is me we're taking about - I always seem to be halfway between myself and the next disaster.

I suddenly snap-to and put on my robe - nothing else - and then run down-stares. I unbolt the front-door and sprint up the front drive to the metal security gate with the hardness of the driveway tearing at the soles of my bare feet in the process. I press the release-button and then run next-door to the neighbours house - a French couple in their late-60's who I've only met briefly. I just hope and prey that they're at home, or at least one of them is. I press the intercom button on their front-gate and the wife answers my call, thankfully. I plead with her to help me and within seconds both her and her husband come running out of their villa and over to me. I try to explain to them the best I can what has happened and we all head back into ours. I wait downstairs in the living-room with the wife - I think her name is Marion? - while the husband makes his way upstairs. She puts her arm around me to try to comfort me as we sit there on the sofa. She talks to me but I'm not listening and just sit there in numb shock staring into space. Before long, the husband returns and says something to his wife in their native language and then gets on the house phone, presumably to call the Police or for an ambulance. He then pours me a brandy but I can only take one sip, I'm too numb and bewildered even for alcohol.

We sit and wait and talk about Andy, England and some of my troubles I've had with life in the past. I know they're only trying to help but talking about my shit just makes things worse and I freeze. Some 20-minutes later the front-gate buzzer sounds and the husband - Claude - answers it. It's both the French Police and an ambulance and within a matter of seconds I'm caught-up in a whirlpool of questions, all fired at me repeatedly without end. I don't know which way to turn and I just sit there and stare at everyone, totally dejected and bemused - why don't they all just fuck-off and leave me in peace?

"PLEASE LEAVE ME ALONE."

As has become a bit of a normality these past few years when I've been faced with one tragedy after another, there are no tears on my part - nothing. Of course I'm sad and crestfallen beyond belief, but once again there is no sign of any waterworks. Maybe there is nothing left inside me to give?

***

The rest of that days events fly by in a speedy blur. Interviews with the Police, a Doctor, offers of help from Marion and Claude - bless them both - and general chaos and bullshit. Unbelievably an official from the British Embassy in Paris has already contacted me regarding flying Andy's body back home to England in due course. Fortunately they're going to make all the arrangements, which is just as well as I haven't got a bloody clue about such things.

It's gone 6pm in the evening before everyone leaves me in peace at last. And that's the fucking problem - I am now back on my fucking own once again, stuck in a foreign country far from home without a shoulder to cry on - even though I still haven't - apart from Marion and Claude of course, but there is a limit as to what they can do.

I wander around the villa aimlessly, peering into every room but I have no idea as to why? In our bedroom the duvet, pillows and the bed itself are a viscous reminder of mine and Andy's time together - having fun, making love, talking, holding, kissing, cuddling, sleeping together. Now it is all just memories, some of it is already forgotten and not even one single day has yet passed. There's also no way I could ever sleep in that bed ever again, not now, so I guess it's the spare room for me tonight, not that I feel much like sleeping at all.

I haven't even had anything to eat all day, despite Marion's insistence that I should. I just don't want to. I don't want anything, except to get back home to England as soon as possible, back to the house to see my little girl Eva. I so wish that she was here with me now, I feel so lost without her.

The long drive back home is going to be lonely that's for sure. And what do I do with all of Andy's clothes and things? What about his passport? I'll have to get back in touch with the guy from the British Embassy again. I don't know whether I'm coming or going.

I turn the TV on to try and escape this nightmare but it's so full of shit that I don't understand and I just can't watch any of that crap, not today. I go and sit out by the pool for the remainder of the evening, forcing myself into serenity, with a bottle of chilled German white as I contemplate my fate. I desperately want to go home.

What have I done to deserve this?

What?

***

It's almost 2-weeks now since Andy's funeral, and nearly 4-weeks since the long drive back from the South of France on my own. Needless to say, it was somewhat of a sad and lonely return journey, although thankfully without incident, even if I did naturally make a few wrong turns here and there.

Andy's funeral was a small, quiet affair held locally, and once again there were still no tears on my part. In fact the only time I've cried was when I stepped through the front-door after my return drive and held Eva in my arms. I really let go then, although I think it was more tears of joy at seeing her and being back home in England than tears of sadness at Andy's loss. I don't know, maybe it was a combination of all three?

As I say, the funeral was short and sweet. The attendee's were mostly made-up of Andy's car friends, a most of whom I'd actually met before. Obviously the 3-cars that we were due to take to Goodwood never made it there, and neither did I. It never even crossed my mind as I had more important things to worry about. Unfortunately neither Hans or Hedwig could make it over from Germany as she wasn't well herself. I do hope that she's going to be okay as I'd hate to lose her on top of everything else.

As far as Andy's family is concerned, he only has his estranged younger - by 4-years - sister Angela left. She turned out to be a right hard-nosed cow and didn't like me at all from the start. The feeling is mutual. I had to put her in her place at the very first moment we met after she unexpectedly quipped at me:

"You were too young for him anyway." She stabbed at me.

What the fuck has it got to do with her? Stupid old bitch. She even tried to worm her way into staying at the house after the funeral so I had to put a stop to that straight away:

"I thought I'd stay here for a couple of days." She curtly informed me.

"Usually it's normal to be invited first, rather than just invite yourself." I quickly stab back at her without hesitation.

"Well, I don't see what the problem is seeing as the house and everything is going to be all mine anyway. I have the right to stay." She bitches on.

"Oh yes? And how did you come to that conclusion?"

"Because Andy was my brother, that's how."

"He was also my husband and that counts for more in my book."

"You only knew him for 5-minutes you gold-digger."

"FUCK YOU! GET OUT OF MY HOUSE NOW YOU FUCKING OLD BITCH!" I scream at her, ending our one and only conversation up to this point.

Do you see what I mean? What a cow! They hadn't even seen one another for nearly 7-years and now she thinks she can just take over everything. It is NOT going to happen.

So what has become of me I here you ask? Well, not much it has to be said. I find myself in a state of limbo. I'm trying to be philosophical about life and everything but it just doesn't work. Maybe the hippies and the crusties were right after all and we should all just lead a pastoral existence and just chill-out all the time and smoke dope and not give a fuck about anything? Hopefully things will be clearer after the reading of Andy's Will next week and that might give me some sort-of direction but I'm not betting on it.

The coroners report into Andy's death stated that the cause of death was due to a "Congenital Heart Defect." And according to a letter I received from his solicitor Mr. Simpson, Andy had apparently known all about his condition for years. That was what his sudden trip to Switzerland was all about, not to see a customer about a car deal or to see another girl but to see a consultant specialist in Geneva about his condition. If he knew something was wrong with his heart all along why didn't he tell me about it? He knew I would have supported him no matter what.

I always had the underlying feeling, ever since our very first date that something somewhere was wrong. Why didn't he tell me? Why didn't I pressure him more for an answer? How could I have been so naive?

I guess all this just goes to prove how fragile life really is. Life is so short and we mustn't waste a second of it. And as far as relationships and marriage are concerned, all this also goes to show that no-one really knows another person 100%, how can they? It's physically and mentally impossible. I haven't even told you, my dear reader, half of what my life has been like. I am part of my own secret society.

At the end of the day, when the chips are down, I mean more to myself than anything else on this shitty planet.

***

It's the big day of the reading of Andy's Will at his solicitor and confident Mr. Simpson's chambers in Chichester, West Sussex.

I'm not going to be outdone by that nasty bitch sister-in-law of mine Angela today either - or anyone else for that matter! - so I'm going for my full-on killer-look. I'm wearing my white Bandeau Bandage dress from Lipsy, and on my feet my pair of white suede open-toe ankle-boots from Polyvore. My underwear is in sexy pink from Victoria's Secret whilst my perfume is *Poison* by Christian Dior. As I've said, my make-up is full-on killer today, featuring coal-black and pale-orange eyeshadow with pale-orange lipstick and extra-sharp blusher to accentuate my sharp cheekbones. My clutch-bag is the beautiful orange Hermes one Andy bought for me in Nice. I'm also going to wear the solid-silver necklace Andy gave me, actually for the first time since he died, but when I open its case I find a yellow *Post It* note stuck to it that says "P.T.O." in Andy's handwriting. When I remove the necklace and turn it over, my breath is taken away by the inscription Andy has had secretly engraved upon it:

> *"Do what thou wilt shall be the whole of the Law"*

> *All my love, Andy*

The quote is of course the very same Aleister Crowley one I had tattooed on my back last year by John. I stand there staring at it completely dumbstruck, I just can't believe it. What a lovely, sweet thing to do. I start to well-up with tears but I just about hold myself together. I don't want to let go, not today.

Even though I have to drive to the solicitors office I still down a large stiff one - vodka that is - just to steady my nerves and sharpen myself up. I've decided to take the Lamborghini for my short journey to Chichester, which despite its size and difficulty to park due to its limited rearward visibility, its like nothing on Earth that I've ever driven before - its fucking crazy! Its so bloody fast it is literally unbelievable, and the handling is something else again, it's like its actually attached to the road. It is my favourite car ever.

I set off in good time as ideally I'd like to get there before that bitch does and it's amazing how many looks I get in the Lambo as I tear-along the length of the A29, way more than I do in my orange ST even and that's a lot! I'm not sure if it's jealously or in admiration though, probably a mixture of both? The power of the car is fantastic as I click my way through its 7-speed paddle-shift gearbox, and when some twat in a blue Subaru Impreza tries to have a go at me on the A27, the Lambo just pisses over it like it was standing still - what an idiot! Why do they fucking bother?

Fortunately the car-park in Chichester is relatively clear and I park-up easily. An elderly couple and a girl in her early-20's all give me eyeballs as I try to exit myself from the car gracefully - without much success! - as I unfortunately give everyone a quick flash of my underwear - oh well! I guess I'll have to keep practising exiting the car a few times to avoid further embarrassments, not that I really give a shit about showing any flange!

I soon discover that the old cow Angela is already here at the chambers - damn it! - supping on a cup of tea and laughing and joking with Mr. Simpson. How fucking cosy! I introduce myself to the solicitor and say a curt "Hello" to the old bag although she doesn't answer me and just looks me up and down with yet more jealousy. I decline Mr. Simpson's offer of a drink and the reading commences, there being just the 3 of us in the dusty old office.

The result of Andy's Will is fairly straightforward - his nasty bitch of a sister gets the villa in Nice - and the Jag - and I get everything else - the house in Foxhill, all the cars and bikes and all the money - all 216-million quid of it!

Naturally, none of this goes down too well with you-know-who, as she suddenly goes mental at the solicitor and myself as I just sit there in stunned silence as to what has just landed on my lap.

"THAT'S NOT FAIR, EVERYTHING SHOULD BE MINE, NOT THAT GOLD-DIGGING WHORE!" She wails.

"EXCUSE ME! WHAT DO YOU MEAN EVERYTHING SHOULD BE YOURS? ANDY WAS MARRIED TO ME NOT YOU, YOU STUPID BITCH." I holler back at her.

"YOU WERE ONLY MARRIED TO HIM FOR 5-MINUTES, I SHOULD GET ALL THE MONEY AND THE HOUSE." She bleats back.

"NOW YOU FUCKING LISTEN TO ME BITCH. WE'VE ALREADY HAD THIS BLOODY CONVERSATION ONCE. WHATEVER IS IN ANDY'S WILL IS FINAL SO IF YOU DON'T LIKE IT YOU CAN FUCK-OFF, YOU STUPID OLD COW.!

"Ladies please." Interjects the solicitor meekly but he's quickly cut-off by the bitch with yet more whining.

"It's not fair." She bleats again.

"Life isn't fair so get over it. I should know, I was widowed on my honeymoon. And don't fucking call me a gold-digging whore, I met Andy literally by accident as well you know."

"Well, you look like a whore dressed like that."

"How I fucking dress is my business. It's not my fault you're a frumpy old bitch."

The meeting crumbles into dissension and bitterness and there's no turning back now. Mr. Simpson tries in vain to pacify the us both but the die has already been set - it's game over. The old bitch flings one final shot at me as I shake Mr. Simpson's hand in thanks, pathetically warning me:

"YOU HAVEN'T HEARD THE LAST OF THIS YOU BITCH."

"FUCK-OFF." I say back to her as I turn to leave. I don't have time to stand here listening to her bollocks, I have a life to live.

I wander back down East Street in a complete daze. I'm not actually looking at or listening to anything, all I can think of is the crazy amount of money that Andy has left me - £216-million! What the fuck am I going to do with all that? This is mental! Is this for fucking real or am I dreaming?

I slide back into the Lamborghini and I don't know whether to laugh or cry? I can't stop thinking about my previous life and all that shit. And here I am, I'm now a multi-millionairess - WHAT THE FUCK! I just can't take it in, talk about rags to riches! This is absolutely pure madness. I have truly arrived at a new beginning.

I fire-up the engine and head out of town and back home, my mind in utter turmoil as I pick-off every car that gets in my fucking way.

Back in the garage - my garage! - I step out of the Lambo and gaze around at all the other cars - all my cars now. What the Hell am I going to do with them? I can't keep them all and I don't want them all.

Eva comes to greet me as I enter the kitchen, I would be completely lost without her. I pick her up and cuddle and kiss her in my arms as she back-chats me in her own unique Siamese way. In the living-room I kick-off my boots and swig a couple of large mouthfuls of vodka straight from the bottle. A wave of mellow calmness soon filters throughout my body as the evil spirit mixes with my blood. Eva looks at me like I'm possessed and I smile back at her as I take another complete mouthful.

Before me, the silver-framed photo on the mantelpiece tries to stare me out. It's the picture Andy and I had taken in Berlin at Christmas by the Brandenburg Gate. I cast a smile at us, 2-lovers seemingly without a care in the World. And yet there's something hidden in the photo, hidden behind the eyes of one of them - the man is keeping the truth from the woman. He has a death-sentence hanging over him and hasn't told his love, his future wife.

I swallow another mouthful of vodka and head next door to the pool. I strip naked, vodka, and then jump in head-first. The alcohol and the water and the events of the day all infuse throughout my soul and I feel so alive and free, probably the most free I've ever felt in my entire life so far.

As I emerge from the water, Eva chirps one of her funny noises at me as she sits there watching my every move and I can't help but laugh. If only I was another cat and we could play and communicate properly with one another, or if I was a male cat and we were lovers in this big beautiful house of ours together. Think of all the fun we could have?

I stay in the pool for another 20-minutes or so and then take a wander out to the patio without bothering to dry myself or to redress. I follow the path around to the Summer House where I use the long neck of the vodka bottle to fuck myself. The heat from the English Sun on my beautiful wet body and the sensation of the bottle entering my vagina instantly makes me start to pant in ecstasy. I fuck it in and out of my hole and in a moment I feel myself tighten as I orgasm my love. I pull the bottle out and lick and drink down the vodka-infused cum and laugh at myself for being a fucker - a filthy rich fucker!

***

A multiplicity of conflicting thoughts dart throughout my mind. Things couldn't actually be better than they are right now. And that's the problem, now that I've got it good, now that I've got it all, the only way is down and I don't want to go back there again. Now I find myself in a position of immense power and freedom, I'm faced with the dilemma of what to do next? I don't want to end up a poisoned, spoilt bitch bored out of my tree. Although at the same time, no-one could ever accuse me of having parsimony!

This is the paradox of my life, my very existence. For instance, what am I going to do with the house? It's far too big just for me to rattle-around in on my own, although it is beautiful and I love it. And as I've said before, what about all the cars and bikes? I definitely can't keep all of those - about half-a-dozen or so maybe?

I have cast-off the shackles of my previous life. Andrew saved me from oblivion with his love and now he's been taken from me. Why fucking why do I have to keep enduring this shit all the time? What is the meaning to life, to my life? Has it all been real? Did any of this crap really happen or has it all just been a nasty dream?

I have so many dreams and this is the problem, the burden of being me, I don't know which way to turn next. If I turn left, someone doesn't like it. If I turn right, someone else doesn't like that either. It doesn't matter either bloody way so I just do my own thing - as per usual.

I don't care about anything any more. My life is over.

I am possessed with the images of life and death.

I only exist in the twilight World of my own imagination.

I don't believe in luck or any of that crap any more, although I think we all create our own luck to a certain degree anyway. Why make more fucking problems for yourself than is necessary? Just look at my life for the answer to that one!

My window of hope for the future is now closed. Today is an extension of yesterday. My future lifespan is a chain-reaction of my self-absorbed nature - my dark, impulsive nature. My only touchstone I can rely on is my will to survive this life of mine, my life of loss and longing. I have passed through so many iterations and yet here I am - still alive and kicking!

You may think that what I've been telling you my dear reader is a load of bullshit, but you never know what is waiting for you in life just around the corner.

I understand that the universe won't collapse without me, but even so, I must prepare for the worst and hope for the best, I can't do any more than that.

I need to compartmentalize my life and concentrate on moving forward now. I can't help the fact that I'm misanthropic, that's also in my nature. I've been punched in the heart too many times now to care. Therefore I must continue with my polyamorous adventure and find new and further enlightenment, powered by my superior wealth and fuelled by my superior mind and my want.

***

The events and trials and tribulations of the last couple of months have all come and gone. I have evolved and moved-on to a new level. I have the ability to see the World from a different perspective to everyone else. I have more control over my brain-power and a higher perception of life than the average person - and that includes you my beautiful reader! Nobody made me like this, I just am.

I am one of a dying breed. I will dominate the World with my new power. I'm not going to be controlled by outside influences any longer.

My life is the embodiment of today's modern-day society and all its hang-ups. These are changing times for all of us and we must all change with them. If we don't there will be no future for any of us.

Throughout the course of history, mankind has come a long way. So why on Earth do we keep inflicting more pain on one another? Life is a precious miracle, so why do we have to fuck it up all the time? Open your eyes to the World and try to look at life as I do. You won't like what you will find even though it is the truth.

Self-realization of who and what we are is a major key to surviving whatever fate is undoubtedly going to throw at us. Use it to understand yourself and feed it.

***

My time and days are now spent being mostly idle. Although one thing I have recently discovered about myself is that I've become quite green-fingered, tending to the vegetable patch and the garden. I've actually surprised myself - me, a gardener!

I did even think about getting some chickens and a pig but decided against it in the end, they're far too much responsibility and I'm just not responsible enough.

I've also made a monumental decision in order to relieve my boredom - and that is that I'm going to attempt to write my autobiography. I have actually started it, using my extensive back-collection of diaries and incorporating as many of my exploits - and sexploits! - as possible. I have so much to tell, so much to say, although I doubt if anyone would actually believe me? I don't really care if they do or not, that's not my bloody problem.

I've titled the book *I WANT,* as that seems to be my *raison d'etra* - I always want more of everything! I also intend to get the book published, although I know from my research that this is a supremely difficult thing to do but it's not going to stop me. As per usual in life, if you're a Z-list so-called "celebrity" and / or an arsehole, getting a book published isn't a problem - publishers will swarm around you like flies around shit wanting to sign you up. But if you're an ordinary person like me (me, ordinary?) then you have to fight tooth and nail for a bloody chance - typical.

Of course I wouldn't be where I am today if it wasn't for Andy. I owe him everything, even my life. He undoubtedly saved me in the crash and now he's gone, gone and left me to my own devises to once again face the World and all its beauty and horror. It just goes to show that money isn't everything. If you haven't got your health then no amount of money will save you.

With the money I inherited from Andy's Will I felt I had to make a couple of donations, one to the Hospital I was taken to after my accident for all their hard work, and another to the rescue service for saving me. My donation of £500,000 to each was gratefully received with much thanks on all sides. Everyone's days are numbered, that's a given fact. Everything is quantifiable and I will stand until I fall. Our futures - mine and yours - will be whatever they will be, and that's why I felt I had to do something for them as thanks and to help others like me. Linked to all this, I've also given up reading my horoscope in the paper. It's nothing but pure hokum and has tried to fool me for far too long. My accident was just that and nothing more.

Also at some point in the not too distant future though I'd like to meet another partner - either a man or a woman. I want to fall in love again and be loved, regardless of their gender, it makes no difference either way to me. There's no point in being blinkered about these things, I know what I WANT as well as you do. I can do anything I fucking want now with my life by imposing my will to succeed. I will continue to walk my lonely path of pure existentialism. Having shit-loads of money has been a truly liberating experience and I intend to liberate to the extreme.

And as far as the house and money is concerned, they're going to have to prize it out of my dead fingers!

***

It's a fantastically beautiful sunny day out today and I've just finished washing the Lamborghini outside the front of the house - completely naked of course! It's super-hot, well into the early-30's even though it's only 11.30am.

I decide to have a wander around in the garden, still without a stitch on, as Eva follows along behind me. A strange thing is happening to the both of us, I'm becoming more like her and she more like me as each day passes. It's like we're slowly morphing into one single being - weird!

The Sun almost blinds me as I take a swig of German white straight from the bottle that I've brought outside with me. The chilled liquid feels so good as it cascades down my throat and nullifies my mind of any bad thoughts from the past.

The birds twitter in the beautiful trees around me, probably warning each other that I'm approaching, as well as wondering what I'm about to do next. I walk mid-way over the oriental bridge that connects to the gazebo in the centre of the mini-lake and gaze down into the still liquid below. There's no fish in there at all but I do spot a big fat slimy toad sitting on the bottom, minding his own business. I wander across to the other end of the bridge and sit myself down on the seat that encircles the inside of the wooden structure and take another swig of poison. With my gorgeous long legs spread wide apart I rub the cold glass of the bottle against my smooth shaved vagina, the chill making me wince at first as then I begin to love it. I swallow another mouthful of wine and then insert the neck of the bottle into myself but it's not enough, I need something thicker.

I return to the gazebo after fetching a couple of dildo's from the house, my glass ribbed one and the weird-looking hand-shaped one, both from Lovehoney, as well as a tube of lube. I fuck myself in the pussy with the rubbery hand-shaped dildo whilst up-side-down on the seat and it feels so glorious as I wank it in and out of my slot.

I reposition myself on the wooden floor and slowly push the greasy glass phallus into my bumhole. It resists and fights me and I almost fail but I force it through my tight internal muscles until it finally gives way to overwhelming pressure. The sensation is so beautiful and I pretend that it's Amanda's tongue that's inside my ass and I squeal with pleasure and the inherent discomfort. I suck and lick on the other dildo and then push it firmly into my cunt. My heartbeat goes berserk and an image of Andy dying of his broken heart flashes across my vision for a split-second but I continue to fuck - I WANT MORE FUCK.

The sweat pours out of my perfectly smooth skin in all the heat as I cum and scream with pleasure. I lick my juice from the hand-shaped dildo and wash it down with another glug of wine, loving it as I love myself. I finger my clit as I remove the other dildo from my bum and it slides out quickly with the retraction of my internal muscles.

I collapse back onto the seat with a sigh and in total exhaustion, the heady mix of heat and sex sapping my energy, although I still continue to gently play with my button and my lips.

Eva looks at me like I'm from outer space - maybe I am? Maybe that's why I'm always treated differently by everyone? There is something about me that makes me different from the rest, but what is it? I readily admit to being self-righteous but so what? Having visions of the future gives me this advantage over everyone - including you.

I grab my toys and the remains of the wine and head back over the bridge with Eva in tow. We both settle ourselves down on the Sun-scorched grass by the edge of the water and play and talk and laugh about life and tell each other of our thoughts, dreams and wishes:

What will it be like when I die?

Will it be in peace or will it be in pain?

Will anyone grieve for me at my secular send-off?

Will I even have a funeral?

Will anyone care?

I wonder how I have survived all my trauma intact and reached this moment in life? I honestly have no idea.

Isn't the human body an amazing thing? Mine is more than just a vision of beauty, it has inner strength way beyond what most people could endure or even understand.

This is the start of something new for the both of us, it's time to move on with our lives.

I think I'm ready to unload.

I tell Eva that I'm going to get that fucking bitch Mellis for what she did to me - getting me the sack and all that shit. Reprisal and revenge are both within my grasp, my power and wealth will see to that.

Although this is the end of this part of my life, I'm not finished yet. You all know me well enough by now to know that I WANT MORE.